VAGABONDS

VAGABONDS

HAO JINGFANG

TRANSLATED BY KEN LIU

An Ad Astra Book

This is an Ad Astra Book, first published in the UK in 2020
by Head of Zeus Ltd
This paperback edition first published in the UK in 2021
by Head of Zeus Ltd

9 7 5 3 1 2 4 6 8

A catalogue record for this book is available from
the British Library.

ISBN (PB): 9781786696526
ISBN (E): 9781786696496

Typeset by Adrian McLaughlin

Printed and bound in Great Britain by
CPI Group (UK) Ltd, Croydon CR0 4YY

MIX
Paper from
responsible sources
FSC® C020471

Head of Zeus Ltd
First Floor East
5–8 Hardwick Street
London EC1R 4RG

WWW.HEADOFZEUS.COM

VAGABONDS

PART ONE

STAR DANCE

PROLOGUE

Once, a group of children was born on one world and grew up on another.

The world they were born into was a tower of rigid rules; the world they grew up on was a garden of rambling disorder. One was a magnificent, austere blueprint; the other was a wild bacchanalia. The two worlds shaped the children's lives one after the other, without seeking their consent, without consideration for their feelings, like two links in the chain of fate, sweeping them up in cold, irresistible tides.

What had been put together in the tower was smashed to bits in the garden; what had been forgotten in drunken revelry was still memorialized in the blueprint. Those who lived only in the tower never suffered the loss of faith; those who lived only for the pursuit of pleasure had no vision to strive for. Only those who had wandered through both worlds could experience that particular stormy night in which distant mirages faded away and countless strange flowers blossomed in the wasteland.

As a result of their experience, they suffered in silence and became the target of every criticism.

Who these children were and how they came to live such lives are questions that could be fully answered only with the help of two hundred years of complicated history. Even the children themselves couldn't offer a lucid explanation.

They were perhaps among the youngest in the millennia-long history of the exiled. Before they even understood what fate was, they had been tossed into its vortex; while still ignorant of the existence of other worlds, another world had snatched them away. Their exile began at home, and they had no vote in history's direction.

Our story begins at the moment when the children were returning home. The body's journey was coming to an end, but the heart's exile was only about to begin.

This is the tale of the fall of the last utopia.

THE SHIP

The ship was about to dock. Time to turn out the lights.

The ship swayed in space like a drop of water gently flowing into the arc-shaped port. The ship was very old and glowed dimly like a badge that had been polished by time until the sharp angles and edges had worn away. Against the darkness of space, the ship seemed minuscule, and the vacuum accentuated its loneliness. The ship, the sun, and Mars formed a straight line, with the sun at the far end, Mars close at hand, and in the middle, the ship whose course was straight as a sword, its edge fading into obscurity.

Surrounded by darkness, the silvery drop of water approached the shore, very much alone.

This was *Maearth*, the only link between Earth and Mars.

The ship was unaware that, a hundred years before its birth, this port had been filled with transports shuttling back and forth like barges along a busy river. It was the second half of the twenty-first century, when humanity had finally broken through the triple barriers of gravity, the atmosphere, and psychology, and, full of anxiety and excitement, they sent cargo of every description to the distant red planet of their dreams. Competition extended from low Earth orbit all the way to the surface of Mars as men and women serving different governments in different uniforms speaking different languages, completed different missions pursuant to different development plans. The transports back then had been clumsy, like metal elephants wrapped in thick gray-green steel skin, stepping across the gulf of space, slow and steady, thumping into the dusty surface of Mars, yawning open their cargo bay doors to disgorge heavy machinery, boxes of food, and eager minds full of passion.

The ship was also unaware that, seventy years before its birth, government transports were gradually replaced by private commercial development vessels. For thirty years Martian bases were all the rage, and the sensitive feelers of merchants, like magic beanstalks, rose inch by inch into the sky, and Jacks climbed up with bills of lading and lines of credit, ready to explore this wonderland of sandstorms. Initially businesses focused on physical goods, and an alliance between big business and big government connected the two worlds with a web woven from land easements, sourcing licenses, and space product development rights, all gilded with stirring lines of poetry. Eventually attention shifted to knowledge itself, following the same path traced by the historical development of economies on Earth, except that a process that had taken two centuries in the past was compressed into twenty years. Intangible assets dominated business deals, and those who loved money plucked the brains of scientists like ripe fruits until virtual fences rose up between Martian bases. Back then the ships that plied the dark sea of space had carried spinning restaurants filled with cocktail parties and talk of contracts, an attempt to replicate the hubbub on Earth.

The ship was also unaware that, forty years before its birth, warships appeared along its current route. Once the war for Martian independence erupted—there were many causes—the adventurers and engineers of the various Martian bases united

6

to resist their Earth-based overseers. With astronautics and prospecting technology, they sought to overcome money and political power. Warships linked together like Themistocles's wooden wall to repel the invaders, a force as magnificent as the swelling tide, and which retreated just as quickly. Nimble, speedy warplanes then rushed in, propelled across the gulf of space by the rage of betrayal, at once wild and dispassionate, dropped their bombs so that bloody flowers bloomed silently in the dust.

The ship knew none of these things, because by the time it was born, a cease-fire had been in place for ten years. The night sky was once again silent, and the once-busy shipping route deserted. It was born in all-consuming darkness. Assembled from metallic fragments drifting in space, it faced the starry sea alone, shuttling back and forth between two planets, plying an ancient trade route that had witnessed both the glory of commerce and the devastation of war.

The ship sailed noiselessly across empty space, a single silvery drop traversing distance, traversing vacuum, traversing invisible ramparts, traversing a history deliberately forgotten.

Thirty years had passed since the ship's birth, and time's lasting tracks adorned its worn shell.

The inside of the ship was a maze. Except for the captain, no one understood its true layout.

It was a huge ship. Stairways connected multiple decks filled with twisting passages and honeycombed cabins. Large storage compartments scattered around the ship resembled palaces fallen into ruin, their spacious interiors piled with goods and equipment, their dusty corners confessing to an absence of visitors. Narrow passageways connected these palaces with bedrooms and dining halls, and the knotty structure resembled the plot of some particularly complicated novel.

Passengers walked on the inside of the cylindrical hull, held there by centrifugal force as the hull spun. The thick central axis was the sky. The ship was full of outdated decorative elements: columns with relief carvings, tiled floors, old-fashioned mirrors hanging on walls, ceilings covered by murals. This was how the ship paid respect to time, commemorated the fact that there had once been a time when humanity was not divided from itself.

On this particular journey the ship carried three separate groups of passengers: one was a fifty-member delegation from Earth, the second a fifty-member delegation from Mars, and the last twenty students from Mars who had been studying on Earth.

The two official delegations were putting on two world's fairs on two planets. After the successful conclusion of the Martian world's fair on Earth, the first ever Terran world's fair was about to open on Mars. The two delegations brought all kinds of interesting goods to show Earth the wonders of Mars, and vice versa, so that each side could be reminded of the presence of the other. After a long period of mutual isolation, this was how they would get to know each other again.

The students, all aged eighteen, were called the Mercury Group. Having spent the last five years living on Earth, they were now on their way home. Mercury was the messenger of the gods and also a planet outside the dyad of Earth and Mars; it represented the desire to communicate.

The war had concluded forty years earlier, and the ship had been the only link between Earth and Mars for thirty.

The ship had witnessed multiple rounds of negotiations, concluded deals, signed treaties, and table-pounding, chair-scraping, door-slamming conflicts. But other than these, it spent most of its time in idleness. The spacious holds were without cargo, the cabins passengers, the dining rooms food and music, and the pilots duties.

The pilots consisted of the captain and the co-captain, who was also the captain's wife. Both of them had wrinkled faces and silvery hair. They had worked on the ship for thirty years and grown old in its maze. The ship was their home, their life, their world.

A pretty girl stood outside the captains' quarters.

"Have you never gone down to the surface, then?" she asked.

"We did go down a few times early on," the co-captain replied with a smile. Silvery curls piled atop her head, and two crescent-shaped creases radiated from the corners of her mouth. Her pose was graceful, like a tree in winter. "But then we got old and stopped."

"Why?"

"Frequent changes in gravity can be tough on old bones."

"Then why didn't you retire?"

"Garcia doesn't want to. He'd like to die on the ship."

"Are there many people on the ship?"

"When there's a mission, we have a crew of about twenty. Most of the time it's just the two of us."

"How often do you get missions?"

"It's a bit unpredictable. Sometimes the gap between flights is only four months, but it can be as long as more than a year."

"Don't you get lonely then?"

"Not at all. We're used to it."

The girl was quiet for a while. Her long lashes drooped and then lifted again.

"My grandfather mentions you often. He misses you."

"We think of him often as well. On Garcia's desk there's a photograph of the four of them, and he looks at it every day. When you get back, bring him our good wishes."

The girl smiled, warm but with a trace of sorrow.

"I'll come back and visit you again, Granny Ellie," she said. Her smile was warm because she liked the old woman. It was sad because she didn't think she would return, at least not for a long time.

"I look forward to it," the co-captain said, also smiling. She reached out and gently brushed the hair off the girl's shoulders. "You look as beautiful as your mother."

The captains' quarters were at the bow of the ship, right next to the cockpit and the weightless gym. The door to the set of cabins was located at the intersection of two hallways, and it was easy to walk past it without noticing. A blue spherical lamp hung above the door, illuminating the old woman and the youth as gently as the moon. The lamp was identical to the lamps found in front of homes on Mars, and each time a Martian passed by, the blue glow reminded them of home. The door itself was frosted glass, blending into the white walls on each side, and only the small decorative sculpture hanging on the door like a knocker showed that this panel was different from the others. The sculpture was a small, silvery space-ship, nose tilted up, with a string of silver bells hanging from the tail fins. Below was a line in flowery script: *Ellie, Garcia, and* Maearth.

The door usually stayed closed, and the two hallways, both empty, extended into the distance until the ends were lost to sight.

Garcia, the captain, was a lifelong friend of the girl's grand-father, Hans. In their youth the two had been pilots in the same squadron and had fought and flown side by side for more than a decade. After the war they both became pillars of the newborn Martian Republic. While Hans stayed on the planet, Garcia moved into the sky.

For a long period after the end of the war, the Martians had to endure unprecedented hardships. The poor soil, the thin air, the perpetual lack of water, the dangerous level of radiation—each one could have been fatal, and all were obstacles in the way of bare survival. Before the war, all development on Mars had been sustained by supplies from Earth, and most of the food had to be shipped in. Mars was like an unborn child, still tethered to the mother world by an umbilical cord. Independence was like the pain of labor, and the baby, with its cord cut, had to learn to breathe and eat on its own. There were things that could not be obtained except from Earth, things that even brilliant minds could not create out of nothing, things like animals, beneficial microbes, macromolecules derived from petroleum. Without these, life could barely sustain itself, let alone thrive.

That was when Garcia decided to come aboard *Maearth*.

It was the tenth year after the end of the war, and most Martians were still opposed to begging from Earth. But Garcia persisted. His was the first attempt at diplomacy by Mars, and he fought doggedly and alone at the border of Earth. More than anyone else, he had a clear understanding of prevailing attitudes on Earth: the shame of defeat turning into the pleasure of seeing the rebels suffer, of vengeance. But he refused to back down. To retreat was to accept that his newborn home would be forever stunted in its growth.

The second half of Garcia's life thus became entwined with the ship. He lived on the ship, sending message after message to Earth. He pleaded, insisted, threatened, enticed. He offered technologies invented on Mars for the necessities of life. For thirty years he did not return to the surface of his home planet. He was the entirety of the Martian diplomatic corps. He was responsible for the first deal between the two worlds, the first interchange delegations, the first world's fairs, the first interplanetary students. "Garcia" and "the Captain" became synonyms. His name and his position could no longer be distinguished, like flesh and blood.

Ellie, Garcia, and Maearth.

After saying their goodbyes, the girl turned away and was about to head off, when Ellie called to her.

"Oh, I almost forgot. Garcia would like you to bring a message to your grandfather." The girl waited.

"'Sometimes the fight over the treasure is more important than the treasure itself.'"

The girl pondered the cryptic message. Her lips parted, as though she wanted to ask a question, but she stopped herself. She knew that the captain's message had to do with diplomacy, but she wasn't likely to understand the meaning behind such sensitive political matters. She nodded, assured Ellie that she would pass the message on, and left. She kept her legs straight, the tips of her toes pointing slightly outward, and glided away, as light and graceful as a striding crane, a dragonfly dipping over a pond, or a dustless breeze.

Ellie watched until the girl had disappeared before entering her quarters and shutting the door, the tinkling of the bells on the door lingering in the empty corridors.

She looked around the dark cabin and sighed. Garcia was already asleep. He was growing more frail with each passing day, and he had been so exhausted from the earlier conversation that he had to climb into bed right after. She didn't know how many more days he would last at his post, nor, for that matter, how many more days she herself would last. She knew only that at the long-ago moment when the two of them had set foot on this ship, she had already foreseen this day. The two of them had always been prepared to grow old here and die here. As long as they breathed, they would ply the space between Earth and Mars.

The girl who had just left was called Luoying. She was a member of the Mercury Group, and her specialty was dance.

———

"Maearth" was cobbled together from the names of the ship's two ports and indicative of its mission. The name showed the yearning to communicate and the spirit of compromise, but it was also a classic instance of pragmatism in action, lacking euphony.

The ship's technology wasn't sophisticated. Both the structure and the engines were based on traditional designs dating back to the prewar era. Solar panels generated electricity, and the spinning hull simulated gravity. The design was strong, time-tested, but it was also clumsy and slow. Both Earth and Mars had experienced leaps in technology driven by the needs of war and could now produce far more advanced ships capable of completing the interplanetary trip in much less time. Still, after thirty years, no other ship had taken *Maearth*'s place. Its clumsiness and bulk also meant that it presented no threat, a perfect platform on which to compromise and achieve balance. Its ungainly appearance was better than sleek outlines; its lethargic pace better than nimbleness; its ineptitude better than capability. In a cold vacuum still suffused with suspicion and fear, it was like a giant whale that slowly carved out its own trail. Better than anyone, it understood that, for old foes, the hardest hurdle to cross wasn't physical distance. The most antiquated choice was also sometimes the most suitable.

The interior of the cylindrical hull was radially divided into four sections. The four quarters were interconnected, but the passageways were so complicated and far apart that few ever bothered to visit the other quarters. The crew took up one of the quarters, and the Terran delegation, the Martian delegation, and the Mercury Group each took up another. Although the four groups had been traveling together for almost a hundred days, there were few cross-group visits. Plenty of all-hands parties were held, to be sure, but the conversation was always strained and formal.

A different mood prevailed among each of the three delegations. The Martian delegates had completed their mission and were relaxed and joyful as they approached home. They no longer bothered with formal dress, and their conversation with one another was dominated by children, good food, their strange and silly experiences on Earth, the anxieties of middle age, and similar topics. In the dining hall of their quarter, they held daily gatherings, where homestyle cooking was salted with wit and laughter.

The Mercury Group, on the other hand, seemed to be holding a months-long postgraduation party. The twenty students had been away from Mars since they were thirteen years of age, and for the last five years, they had grown closer than blood siblings. During their time on Earth, they were scattered to every corner of the globe, and so this trip represented for them a rare reunion. They enjoyed and celebrated their youth: drinking, joking, flirting, singing, playing ball in the spherical weightless gym at the bow of the ship.

The Terran delegation presented yet another sight. The delegates were from different countries, and they didn't know each other well. Other than business dinners, they spoke to each other only cautiously in bars. In a sense, the delegates were too similar to each other—prominent politicians, famous scientists, tycoons of industry, and big media stars—used to being the center of attention, and thus unable to be close to anyone. They dressed simply, with tasteful accents of luxury. They spoke warmly and casually but rarely disclosed anything personal. They tried to look humble but made sure that the effort was noticed.

In a small bar in the Terran quarter, delegates often gathered in small clusters of two or three, whispering among themselves. The bar was decorated after the fashion of Earth: dim lamps, stools around small tables, ice clinking in tumblers as the light refracted through the amber whiskey.

"What do you think of the tension between Antonov and Wang?"

"Really? I haven't noticed."

"Observe. You need to observe."

The speakers were a middle-aged, balding man and a young man with brown hair. The middle-aged man, a charming grin on his face, had asked the first question. His chin glowed blue from a close shave, and his gray eyes twinkled like the sea in summer. The younger man didn't say much, often answering a query with nothing more than a smile. Brown curls spilled over his brow, and his dark eyes were deeply set, so that in the dim light of the bar it was difficult to tell his expression. The middle-aged man was Thomas Theon, CEO of the Thales Media Group and heir to the vast Thales fortune. The younger man was Eko Lu, a filmmaker and one of the Thales Group's featured artists, there to document the delegation's visit to Mars.

Antonov and Wang were the delegates from Russia and China, respectively. Due to the long-lasting border dispute between their two countries, they gave each other the cold shoulder. The Terran delegates came from countries with complicated mutual animosities, and though everyone tried to remain polite in public, there was much jostling and score keeping beneath the surface.

Theon, on the other hand, was a man without a nation. He held passports from four countries, maintained residences in five, appreciated the cuisines of six, and dealt with jet lag in seven. When nationalistic passions flared, he preferred to observe from the sidelines, popcorn in hand. His attitude was typical of the elites of the second half of the twenty-second century: nation-states were not things to be taken seriously, and the historical problems left unresolved by the era of globalization should be mocked rather than understood.

Eko understood what Theon was getting at, but he preferred not to engage. The delegation was full of people with conflicting desires and goals, and this was as it should be. Everyone came to Mars in search of something, including Eko.

"May I suggest a subject for your documentary?" asked Theon, still wearing that charming smile.

"Please."

"A girl."

"A girl?"

"A girl from the Mercury Group. Her name is Luoying."

"Luoying... Which one is she again?"

"She has black hair—the one with the longest hair. Fair-skinned. A dancer."

"I think I know who you're talking about. Why her?"

"She's going to give a solo recital once she gets back to Mars. It ought to be good. The market will eat up the footage."

"Tell me more."

"More...? What do you mean?"

"Your real reason for asking me to film her."

"You are much too paranoid," said Theon with a laugh. "All right, I can tell you that her grandfather is Hans Sloan, the current consul of Mars. She's the only granddaughter of the great dictator. I just found out myself."

"Does that mean I need to obtain the consul's permission first?"

"No. Don't let anyone know about your plans. Less trouble that way."

"Aren't you worried this will cause us trouble back home?"

"Let's worry about that when we get back."

Eko said nothing. He made no sign that he was accepting the suggestion, and he made no sign that he was rejecting it. Theon also didn't ask him to clarify. Mutual silence where there was no apparent consensus of any sort was best. Eko wasn't bound by any promise, and Theon couldn't be blamed for inciting anything. Gently, Eko shook the ice in his glass. Kindly, Theon continued to watch him.

A veteran of more film releases than he cared to count, Theon knew very well how to target different audiences with exactly the right pitch. He was skilled at courting controversy for profit while evading responsibility. Eko was still too young to be free of the idealistic air of the academy. He was a thoughtful young man who disliked following trends. But Theon trusted in the power of time. He had seen far too many young artists, each believing themselves too creative to follow mere formula; he had also seen far too many artists experience the epiphany that only products that sold had any value. The market was merciless with youthful pride.

The bar played Nu Jazz, and the lilting melody provided good cover for the private discussions and whispered secrets at the separate tables. The room was warm; ties were loosened and collars unbuttoned. There was no bartender, and everyone mixed their own drinks from the glass case along the wall. Glass domes hung down from the ceiling over each table, illuminating the apparently friendly faces that masked the churning thoughts behind them. Once in a while peals of laughter burst from a table. The patrons were wrapping up their final conversations before docking.

Although the delegates from Earth each had their own goal, the overall thrust of their desire was for technology. Technology equaled wealth. For the whole of the twenty-second century, technology and know-how formed the foundation for every component of society all over the globe and became the new currency of the financial system. International economy relied on technology the same way old national economies had once depended on the gold standard. Control of technical know-how became the only way to maintain a difficult balance in an increasingly complex and fragile world.

Commerce in knowledge thus played a most pivotal role. It was thirst for technology that broke through the barriers created by memories of the war and built this new Silk Road that reached Mars. Terrans realized that Mars was like a farm whose most important crop was skilled engineers. Knowledge had allowed Mars to become independent, and it also meant that there was profit to be found on the red planet.

The music continued to play; the lights continued to glow; the smiling faces continued to nod and turn; the calculations behind them grew ever more intricate.

In the dim light of the bar, no one paid attention to the photographs hanging on the walls. These new patrons didn't understand that the photographs disguised traces of the past. Behind one of the photos was a bullet hole from twenty years earlier, and behind another was concealed a crack left when something slammed against the wall ten years ago. Once, an old man had roared here like a golden-maned lion, and another old man with silvery hair and beard had uncovered a deceitful scheme. Their names were Galiman and Ronen, and they were the other two men in the photograph on the captain's desk.

All conflicts had subsided, and all the unpleasantness of the past had been recorded in the official histories as misunderstandings. The scars of the past were covered up. The bar remained a comfortable, pleasant drinking hole, and the photographs rested in their dark brown frames, neatly in a grid.

Maearth was going to dock in another few hours. The parties would soon end, and passionate laughter would soon subside into silence. The dance floor would be disassembled, and the fancy napkins and centerpieces would be put away. Pillows and sleeping bags were about to be collected. Screens were about to dim. The floor would be swept. The palatial storerooms would be emptied.

The only thing left behind would be the smooth floors and glass furniture, the naked body of the ship itself.

The ship had many experiences of being filled and being stripped. Every table had been covered by tablecloths from successive eras, and every rug had borne witness to changing conflicts of the passing years. The ship was used to going from full to empty, from colorless canvas to rainbow painting back to colorless canvas again.

Photographs filled the ship's winding passageways: everything from the earliest black-and-white images dating back to a time when humanity had not yet dreamed of going to the stars to the holographic displays showing the pride and joy of two peoples going their separate ways after the war. As one walked along one of these curving corridors, one hand caressing the wall, or climbed up and down the stairs, it was possible to travel through time, to view a montage of sliced-up history. There was no end or beginning to this journey, for the photographs were not arranged chronologically. Postwar photos might directly precede prewar ones, and 2096 might come right after 1905. To ignore sequencing in time was also a way to ignore disagreements. On these walls at least, Mars and Earth coexisted side by side in peace, and by taking a different course through the passageways one could reconstruct a different cycle of history.

Each time when the ship docked, decorations throughout the vessel were packed up and put away—except these photographs. No one knew that, during the days when the ship lay idle, the captain walked through every corridor, gently wiping off the dust from each frame.

The party reached its climax just before docking.

Luoying had never figured out the mazelike layout of the ship, but she thought of the weightless gym as a polestar of sorts. The weightless gym was the largest compartment on *Maearth*, spherical in shape, and it did not spin along with the rest of the hull. Outside the gym was an annular observation platform, where she liked to go to relax. Wide viewports around the observation platform gave one the illusion of floating in space.

Coming from the captains' quarters, she rushed through the empty observation platform, surrounded by the stars. A loud cheer from inside the gym told her that the game was nearly at an end. Hurrying to the door, she pulled it open.

Waves of chaotic colors and sounds washed over her as

though the spherical compartment were filled with exploding fireworks.

"Who's winning?" Luoying asked the person floating nearest to her.

Before she got an answer, someone had pulled her into an embrace. She looked up and saw that it was Leon.

"Our last match," mumbled Leon.

He let go of Luoying and opened his arms to Kingsley. They embraced and then slapped each other on the shoulders. Anka pushed his way through the crowd to face Luoying, but before he could say anything, Sorin had grabbed him by the shoulders from behind. Chania drifted by the group, and Luoying saw tears at the corners of her eyes.

Mira opened a couple of bottles of Martian Gio, and together the students poured the wine into the center of the spherical hall. Innumerable golden droplets glistened in the air. Everyone kicked off the wall and drifted into the middle. As they twirled and tumbled through the air, they opened their mouths and caught the globules of alcohol.

"To victory!" called out Anka. Everyone cheered.

"To a safe landing," Anka whispered right after. Only Luoying, who was close by, heard him.

She closed her eyes, tilted back her head, and let herself drift.

Invisible hands lifted her into the embrace of the stars.

This was the last night that would belong only to them.

At six in the morning Mars time, *Maearth* approached the still-asleep planet along with the rising sun. The ship aimed for the port in aerostationary orbit. The port was a giant ring in space: the inside was the berth for *Maearth*, and the outside was for the fifteen shuttles that would bring the passengers to the surface.

The docking procedure would take three hours, leaving the passengers plenty of time to snooze. As the ship gently glided into the center of the ring, those looking out the front viewports saw the gate to a magnificent temple, and the ship was like a dove gliding toward the altar, holy and completely at ease. Sunlight glistened off the port's metallic curve, and the shuttles lining up with their left wings touching the ring and right wings pointing at the dusty soil of Mars resembled temple guards silently standing at attention.

Out of the ship's one hundred and twenty passengers, thirty-five were awake. Sitting or standing, in their own cabins or in some obscure corner, they watched as the ship slowly settled into its perch. As the ship came to a complete stop, the observers returned to their own beds without anyone noticing. The ship was completely at peace.

Half an hour later, everyone woke up to soft music, rubbed the sleep out of their eyes, and greeted one another. The disembarkation process was orderly and quick, and the passengers politely said their goodbyes, boarded separate shuttles, and headed for the surface.

It was the year 2190 on Earth, the year 40 on Mars.

THE HOTEL

Eko stood next to the window and looked outside. The empty surface of Mars evoked for him the music of bagpipes.

The room was extremely bright. Floor-to-ceiling glass walls allowed his view to extend unimpeded from his feet to the horizon. The red desert stretched flat like an endless scroll recording an epic—wild, vast, uninhibited.

Is this where you wanted to be buried? Eko thought.

Though he had never been to Mars, the scenery before him wasn't unfamiliar. The first time he had visited his teacher, when he was fifteen, this same eternal red view was projected on his teacher's wall.

He had stood at the door to the study, gazing at the desert of another world, not daring to go in. His teacher was sitting in a high-backed chair facing the wall, back to the door, his blond hair spilling from the edges of the chair back. Bagpipe music played over the sound system, and it seemed to be coming from every direction. Although at first the desert on the wall appeared as a still photograph, closer examination revealed movement. The footage was shot from a low-flying aircraft that wasn't flying very fast, though the rocks on the ground hurtled through the view, too quick for the eyes to focus on any one. The star-studded sky loomed in the distance.

He stood, mesmerized, until a deep canyon suddenly swept

into view. He cried in surprise and knocked over a wooden statue by the door. By the time he managed to lift up the statue, his teacher was standing next to him.

He put a hand on the boy's shoulder.

Eko, is it? Please come in.

He looked up, and the desert was gone. The bagpipe music lingered in the empty air. He was disappointed.

Eko had never told anyone of that encounter, and during the ten years he had studied with his teacher, they rarely spoke of it. It was a secret between the two of them, a secret concerning two worlds. His teacher did not speak of Mars. No matter how much film theory and technique he taught Eko, he never showed him any films about Mars.

Ten years later, Eko was finally face-to-face with the real Mars. The bagpipes played in his mind as he stared at the landscape etched into his memory from long ago.

———

After a hot shower, Eko sank into a soft chair and stretched his legs. The hotel was very comfortable, and he felt relaxed.

He liked being alone. Though he could get along with just about anyone, though he was charming at film openings and cocktail parties, though he was required to deal with all kinds of people for his movies, he still preferred to be by himself. When with others, he could never be completely at ease. Always he held his breath and kept his senses sharpened. Only when he was shut in his room was he able to sigh with relief and let the tension in his body fall away, to fully luxuriate in his own existence.

He leaned back and gazed up at the ceiling. Everything on this planet aroused his curiosity. Before arriving, he had imagined all kinds of fantastic scenarios on Mars, but the reality was nothing like his visions. He couldn't say whether reality was better or worse, but he was sure that the real Mars deviated from his imagination in unexpected ways. He had been dreaming about this place since he was fifteen, wondering how Mars could have kept his teacher away from home for eight years.

In his mind he had pictured the planet as the last utopia of humankind, a place where crude commercial interests yielded to pure intellect. He knew that this was not how the consensus on Earth portrayed the red planet, but he didn't care.

Looking around, he thought his room wasn't too different from his cabin on *Maearth*: transparent desk, transparent dresser, transparent bedposts. It was a transparent shade of blue, though lighter in some places and darker in others. Even the chair he sat in was transparent, as though made from inflated glass fabric that changed shape as his body shifted. The walls facing outside were also transparent, and from his chair he could see all the way to the horizon. Only the wall next to the hallway was an opaque white that gave him privacy from the other guests. The whole room reminded him of a crystal box—even the ceiling was translucent, like an azure sheet of frosted glass. Through it he could see the blurred sun, like a white lamp.

What does all this transparency mean? The word "transparent" was politically significant. A room that should be one's own made transparent suggested surveillance. When all the rooms were transparent, it suggested mass surveillance. He could take this as a symbol of the conquest of individual privacy by the collective and turn it into a bit of political commentary, a critique.

That sort of approach would be exactly what mainstream Earth opinion expected. His documentary would naturally be well received. The proponents of individualism on Earth had been waiting for just this kind of evidence, incontrovertible proof of the accusations leveled against the "hell in heaven." It would also provide the hawks with yet more support for an attack against Mars.

But Eko didn't want to go down that route—at least, he wasn't willing to abandon himself to received wisdom so easily. He refused to believe that a place so spiritually oppressive could be where his teacher had willingly devoted eight years of his life.

He never told anyone his real purpose for agreeing to come to Mars. Maybe someone could guess it; he wasn't sure.

It wasn't a secret that he had studied filmmaking with Arthur Davosky. Ostensibly the award he had won a year earlier was why he had been chosen as a member of the Terran delegation, but he knew that Theon had recommended him in large measure because of his friendship with Arthur. He accepted the offer to join the delegation without probing deeply into the reasons, and Theon never offered an explanation. At Arthur's funeral, he had seen Theon's bald head and sunglasses, bowed from start to finish.

Gently, he retrieved the chip nestled in his shirt pocket and admired it in his palm. His teacher's memories from near the end of his life were stored on it—supposedly in the form of neural activity converted into ones and zeros. Rationally he didn't believe in the practicality of this technology, but emotionally he wanted to believe. After a man died, if his memories could be kept alive—if he could still decide where the memories would find eternal rest—then the dissolution of death represented no absolute victory.

———

Feeling his stomach growl, Eko got up and walked to the wall to activate the room-service menu. Most of the dishes were unfamiliar, so he picked a few items at random. It took but a few minutes for the delivery light to come on, and a tray rose up from within a tunnel behind the glass wall like a dumbwaiter. The tray stopped, and the glass door slid open.

He picked up the tray and examined the food with interest: his first encounter with authentic Martian cuisine. On *Maearth*, the Terran delegation's supplies had all come from Earth, and for the duration of the trip they had no opportunity to sample Martian food. He had heard rumors about what the Martians ate, stories tinged with the bloodthirsty imagination of pirate tales. Some said that Martians ate worms grown in sand dunes, and others claimed that they ate plastic and metal debris. It was always the habit of people who had never gone anywhere to invent outrageous stories about faraway places, to gain the self-satisfaction of an imaginary civilized person through manufactured fantasies of barbarism.

Staring at the tray in his hand, Eko wasn't sure if he should film some aesthetically pleasing scenes of Martian haute cuisine. Such footage would add a hint of romance and, when spread through the fashion media channels, would convert fancied barbarity into fancy for the exotic. He knew that process was easy to initiate and had occurred countless times.

The dying words of Arthur Davosky came unbidden to his mind: *To be interesting, rely on your head; to be faithful, rely on your heart and eyes.* He didn't know what he was supposed to have faith in. But the image of his teacher floated before his eyes: thinning hair, curled up in the high-backed armchair like a shriveled shrimp.

By then, speaking was a struggle for Arthur Davosky, and so he sketched out what he meant with his trembling hands in the air as he whispered.

To be interesting—he pointed to his head—*to be faithful*—he pointed to his eyes and heart.

Eko wasn't concentrating on listening; instead, he was staring at the old man's slender fingers as though looking at the vanes of a windmill that had stopped turning. *Fifty isn't so old*, he thought, *but he looks like a starving child, wrapped up in that thick blanket.* Realizing that a lifetime's worth of courage had been reduced to such helplessness emptied his heart of all feeling.

Language is the mirror of the Light, his teacher said slowly.

Eko nodded, uncertain what was meant.

Don't forget the Light by focusing on the mirror.

"I understand."

Listen. Don't be in a rush.

"What am I listening for?"

Instead of answering, his teacher stared at the air, as though lost in thought. His eyes glazed over. Eko was just about to panic at the thought that Davosky had died, when the old man's fingers moved again in the dying sunlight like the jagged fringe of an iceberg.

If you ever get to go to Mars, take this with you.

Eko looked where he was pointing and saw the button-like chip on the desk. An icy dagger plunged into his heart as he understood that his teacher was trying to dispose of his remains after death. He was pointing at his true self, saying goodbye to his memories with his decaying flesh. His words were muddled but calm, and that made Eko's eyes swell with hot tears.

That night Davosky sank into a coma, and he died two days later. During those last two days he recovered consciousness only once, at which point he tried to write to Eko on a notepad. The only mark he managed to make before he fell back into his coma was the letter *B*. Eko waited by his bedside until he was declared dead.

Silently, Eko ate his breakfast, so absorbed in the past that he forgot to taste the food. By the time he had returned from reminiscence to the present, most of the tray was empty, save for two small biscuits and a side dish that resembled mashed potatoes. He picked up one of the biscuits and bit into it, but it was as though he had lost his sense of taste. He couldn't say whether it was delicious or bland.

He tried to focus on the documentary he was supposed to make to shake off the feeling of helplessness. Perhaps he should make it into a visual feast, a baroque dance. After all, everything here was already so baroque, so fluid. He caressed the table, and the table caressed him back. Some details that had seemed insignificant at first became, upon closer examination, fresh and interesting. The edge of the glass table, for instance, was decorated with the curves of a spraying fountain. The frame of the mirror mounted on the wall resembled rising flames, and the borders of the breakfast tray were filled with carved flowers. The decorations weren't too ostentatious, but together they endowed the room with a baroque-style sense of motion: a fluidity in the edges and a transcendence in the details. Most of the furniture was connected to the walls, so that the desk, bed, and dresser were like turns taken by a surging stream through the mountains, forming a coherent whole in which the curve of the desk was like the crest of a furled wave. Eko found the aesthetic interesting. He had always thought that on Mars a precise, clean mechanical aesthetic would

29

reign supreme, but the reality turned out to be humane and natural, as though he had walked into a distant vale far from urban bustle.

He took out his camera glasses and put them on. He toured the room again with his gaze to save the footage. Then he retrieved various instruments from his luggage and set them up around the room: temperature distribution recorder, air analyzer, solar chronometer, and so on. The tiny gizmos whirred like dinosaur eggs about to hatch.

Eko knew that focusing on the unique Martian aesthetic represented a shortcut. Each tiny ornamental difference from Earth would give audiences at home a sense of the exotic, mysterious, and distant. This was a way to distance the scene from the observer psychologically, to reduce reality to an image in order to avoid confronting the new.

But he didn't want to shoot that way. That kind of film would no doubt please the Martian authorities. From the moment he had arrived, Martian officials had cocooned him in a kind of impenetrable friendliness, telling him in enthusiastic bureaucratese that they were absolutely delighted to have him here and couldn't wait for him to show the real Mars to Earth, hoping his art would contribute to the growing friendship and trust between the two planets. Eko had smiled and nodded, parroting back the sentiment that he was confident that Mars was full of beauty. In the hallway of the shuttle port, they shook hands, perfectly relaxed, and Eko even directed his drone to capture the scene for posterity.

Eko didn't consider his polite response a lie, though he certainly didn't take the official solicitousness at face value. He simply preferred to not express an opinion based on too little observation. He mistrusted officials, but he believed that it was absolutely vital to conserve opportunities for expressing opinions. His profession required him to travel widely, and so he understood that occasions when one had to speak one's mind and defend it were few and far between. Most of the time it was far more important to watch and listen while saying nothing.

Several other delegates from Earth had already given him their opinion of what he should shoot and how. The American delegate, Professor Jacques, gently hinted to him that it was impossible for visitors to observe the true conditions of a place under authoritarian rule. The German delegate, Colonel Hopman, was much more direct. He told Eko that he was too young to get involved in matters that he didn't fully understand. Eko understood that the colonel was referring to politics. He knew that he was only a filmmaker, too junior among the delegates to be "involved"—not just in politics, but perhaps not even in filmmaking. Film was evidence, and any recording reduced, to some extent, the potential range of explanations the future could offer for historical events.

No one had given him any suggestions that he found useful. In the little bar on *Maearth*, passersby often slapped him on the shoulders and wished him luck before turning away and lowering their voices a few decibels.

Only Theon had given him suggestion after suggestion, apparently treating the trip as just another commercial opportunity.

Drama! I tell you, the key is drama!

Theon had offered this with a dramatic expression on his face. He was a businessman, and even if he acted and dressed like he was on a beach vacation, the instinct for commerce, deeply embedded in his bones, came through. For him, the greatest failure of any art was to fall short of capturing a market. As long as the plot was exciting, he didn't care if the story valorized freedom or authoritarianism. He couldn't have cared less if the point of the film was to mock him.

Thinking about everyone who had spoken with him about his film, Eko felt like a pedestrian standing still on a median, surrounded by busy lanes of rushing traffic. He didn't care about the opinions of the other delegates, because they were like arrows aimed at the wrong target. The useless suggestions formed a constricting lasso around him, but his interest was like a soap bubble caught by the lasso, expanding in a different dimension even as the lasso tightened. He nodded as though accepting the advice of everyone because he hadn't found a theme he cared about. When he found it, he was certain that he would stand his ground.

He had not crossed ninety million kilometers to produce some clichéd drivel. He was looking for medicine—medicine that would cure what he saw as the terminal disease plaguing Earth.

Eko wasn't ready to reach any conclusions until he had gathered more information. He wanted to shoot a script that had not yet been written; he needed the future to ascertain the present. He had no ending in mind, because he still couldn't name the beginning.

After breakfast, Eko felt drowsy. Being around the delegates twenty-four seven had kept him on edge. Now that he was away from their constant feints and tests, an irresistible sense of exhaustion overwhelmed him.

He stretched out on the bed and fell asleep. He dreamed a long dream. In his dreams he often saw his teacher from the back, in that tall-backed chair, muttering to him incomprehensibly. He always tried to walk around the chair so that he could hear him better, but he never succeeded. In his dreams he would run as fast as he could, climb over mountains and hike through valleys, but no matter how much he tried, he could never get to the front of the chair.

By the time he woke up, it was four in the afternoon. Outside, the setting sun sketched out long, sharp shadows. He knew that a day on Mars was almost as long as a day on Earth, and so the welcome reception was about to begin. He didn't want to get up, so he closed his eyes and allowed the dream-scape to linger.

Will I stay here, just like him? he thought. He couldn't think of any reasons why he would, but that was the case for Arthur Davosky as well. Eighteen years earlier, when the first representatives from each planet visited the other, Arthur had come to Mars to study new filming technology. But instead of going back to Earth, he sent back the new hardware, software, and operating instructions on *Maearth*. The media on Earth was filled with speculation about his reasons and goals. Arthur was thirty-seven, at the peak of his career, winning award after award for his productions. He was well-liked by everyone and could do whatever he wanted. There was absolutely no reason for him to run or to defect. Some reports claimed that the Martian authorities had detained him because he had stumbled upon sensitive information; other reports said that he wanted to stay to learn more valuable technology.

Eko was only seven at the time, but he remembered the interminable rounds of analyses and arguments. The speculation never ceased, and in fact exploded the year Arthur finally returned to Earth, leading to daily mobs of reporters who followed him and demanded that he submit to an interview. Arthur, however, maintained his silence, even unto death.

His teacher's experience had taught Eko to be cautious

about speculating and jumping to conclusions. He knew that it was impossible for outsiders to know one's true motivations, even if they knew every other fact. He refused to even predict his own actions, because he understood that reasons changed with circumstances.

The vacuum cleaner crawled along the foot of the wall like a turtle. The room, bathed in the light of the setting sun, felt peaceful. The sun wasn't orange but a pale white. Its slanting rays limned everything in a glowing border, so very different from the light at noon through the roof.

He got up and sat at the edge of the bed, placing a hand gently against the still-life painting on the wall. The picture disappeared, replaced by a screen. A girl appeared on the screen: a red plaid skirt, a white belt with floral edging, a straw hat, a sweet smile. She was the virtual concierge doll.

"Good afternoon! The weather is perfect, isn't it? I'm Vera. What can I do for you?"

"Good afternoon. I'm Eko. I'd like to know about my transportation options—public transportation, that is. Also, how do I buy tickets and look up routes?"

The girl on the screen blinked to show that she was processing. The animation was lifelike and graceful. A few seconds later she smiled and curtsied, her skirt flaring like an opening umbrella.

"The most common way for people to get around on Mars is through the tube trains. There are no tickets to buy. Every residence is located near a community station, with a train passing through every ten minutes. You can ride the train to the nearest hub station, where you can transfer to an interdistrict express train to take you to the hub nearest your destination.

Every station has smart maps that can help you plan your trip. A circumnavigation of all of Mars City takes one hundred and fifty minutes."

"Thank you. That's very helpful."

"Is there anything else I can help you with? For example, I can provide you information on city services, museums, and shopping guides."

"Is it possible... to look up information about a person?"

"What do you have in mind?"

"How to contact a particular individual."

"Of course. Please tell me the name or the associated atelier."

"Brook. Janet Brook."

"Ms. Janet Brook is a researcher at the Third Atelier of Tarkovsky Film Archive. Her residential address is Apartment #1, coordinate seven-by-sixteen, Russell District. You may leave a message in Ms.

Brook's personal space or connect with her at her atelier."

"All right. Thank you."

"I have copied the above information to your room's memory.

Would you like to connect with her now?"

"No, not now."

"Would you like to conduct another search?"

"Let me think... oh, yes, there is someone else. I believe her name is Luoying Sloan. She's one of the students who studied on Earth."

"Ms. Luoying Sloan is a student at Dance School #1, Duncan Troupe. Her residential address is Apartment #4, coordinate eleven-by-two, Russell District. Ms. Sloan's personal space has been temporarily suspended."

"Thank you, Vera. That will be all."

"It's been a pleasure assisting you."

The girl twirled, bowed to him, and skipped away.

Eko sat on the bed and copied the information he had just gathered into his personal notepad. Having specific goals to pursue for the next few days excited him, though he wasn't sure what to expect. He sat still for a while, trying to sort through his questions and anxieties.

———

It was time to get ready for the welcome reception. The whole delegation was supposed to go to the banquet hall together. He changed, fixed his hair, and packed up his portable filming kit.

Just before leaving, he stood by the wall for a moment. With the arrival of dusk, lights were coming on all over Mars City, and everything glowed. From the shuttle, he had been amazed by the architecture of the city. It reminded him of a city constructed out of crystal, with elegant avenues and thorough-fares that connected complicated but transparent structures. The delicate houses, each made of glass and in various shapes, were scattered across the vast plain. The flat roofs, like slanted sails, glowed a deep azure. From a distance they created the illusion of sheets of water slicing into the ground. A network of glass tunnels connecting the houses twisted through the air, like crisscrossing veins or elevated highways. Looking down from the shuttle, he had felt an instinctive yearning. This was a world unlike anywhere he had been on Earth, and its alienness fascinated him.

HOME

Sunlight made Luoying squint as she emerged into the shuttle port terminal.

Having been away from sunrise on Mars for five years, she had almost forgotten how different it felt. The sky on Earth was blue, and the sun was a gentle reddish orange. On Mars, black was black, white was white. There was nothing in the way, no filter.

After deplaning from the shuttle, the students rode the seated escalator down to the ground. After passing through identity verification, they arrived in the vast open space of the terminal, the first place that felt like home.

The terminal had been built during Luoying's absence. She and her friends walked together, not speaking much. The walls, the hemispherical ceiling, and the ground were all constructed out of glass, like most things on Mars, though the floor was patterned to resemble marble. The walls were bare of ornamentation. Other than the steel girders, the only visible detail in the transparent walls was the pattern made by the insulation gas billowing between the two layers of glass, curling wisps.

Luoying walked next to Chania, and the pair smiled as they watched the confusion among the Terran delegates. The elegantly dressed Terrans, clustered after the Martian delegates but before the students, were clearly ill-prepared for navigation through the shuttle port.

The leader of the Terran delegation, Mr. Peter Beverley, strode confidently at the head of the group. But he paused in front of the fingerprint station, uncertain what to do. The retina scanner swung into his face from the side like a tentacle and made a light popping noise right in front of his eyes as it took a snapshot, which so shocked the man that he jumped backward, bumping into the radiation probe, which beeped loudly.

Everyone in the terminal turned to stare.

Red-faced, Beverley pretended to laugh and held out a hand to calm the still-beeping probe, but the probe only beeped louder in protest. His hand jerked back in surprise.

The Martian delegates ahead of him turned back, grinning, to help.

Luoying smiled and looked away politely. She pulled her luggage through the security line, easily navigating between the various probes that swung out from both sides, as though dancing a practiced routine or greeting the electronic sensors.

Beverley finally made his way through the probes as well. He held in his hand the diplomatic documents that declared his authority as the head of the Terran delegation. But there were no customs officials or passport checkpoints, and he stood in the middle of the terminal, uncertain who to show his papers to.

The terminal was shaped like a slice of pie. The narrow tip led to the shuttles, while the wide arc was where passengers boarded the tube trains for Mars City. Along the two straight walls were vending machines for gifts and snacks like fresh pastries and fruits. In the middle of the terminal floor stood a few glass boards that showed the complicated map of the tube train system, like a colorful tapestry that slowly changed. Between the entrances for the different tube trains hung small terminals. The Martian delegates were already at these, punching in the stations nearest their homes.

Luoying and Chania stood near the entrances, hesitating.

"We're home," said Chania softly. It sounded like a question for Luoying, or perhaps she was only talking to herself.

"That's right."

"How do you feel?"

"I don't feel anything."

"Really?" Chania turned to gaze at her.

"Really." She nodded for emphasis. "Strange, isn't it?"

"Not strange at all," said Chania. "I don't feel anything either."

Luoying surveyed the clean, bright terminal. "Tell me, what makes the shuttle port here different from all the airports on Earth we've been to?"

"This is a shuttle port; those are airports," said Chania.

Luoying looked at Chania's messy hair affectionately. "Get some sleep. We've still got the banquet tonight."

"You take care, too."

The students said goodbye to one another and scattered into different tubes. They were used to partings and didn't make a big deal out of it. The alcohol from the night before still lingered in their blood, and their minds were filled with memories of the spinning stars. The terminal was so bright that no one wanted to speak aloud.

Luoying was the last of the students to leave. She watched the Terran delegates clumped at the center of the terminal like a flock of lost sheep. Some were feasting on the snacks from the vending machines, unaware that their visitor accounts were being charged for each bite.

The door at the center of the curved edge of the terminal slid open, and a new group of people strode in. Luoying saw that the man at the head was her grandfather, Hans Sloan. He led a delegation of senior officials to the Terrans, stood facing Beverley, and held out his hand.

The two groups stood in two parallel lines, and hands shook as though reaching across the emptiness between two planets. The Martians, having grown up with less gravity, were much taller than the Terrans, which made the scene asymmetrical. The two groups examined each other as they went through the ritual of introductions.

This was no time to greet her grandfather, Luoying decided. She turned away from the tall, slender figure of the consul of Mars and punched in the coordinates for home.

———

Five years earlier, Mars picked the first group of students to go study on Earth.

The Boule took forever to deliberate on the matter. Three months of fact-finding were followed by three weeks of public commentary, which were followed by three days of non-stop debate in the Boule. Finally, the consul, the education minister, and the archons of all nine systems had to vote in the Boule Chamber of the Capitol, facing the bronze statues of the founders of the Martian Republic. To engage the whole citizenry and the most important governing organs of the state in the matter of the education of a few children was without precedent in the forty years since the conclusion of the war. The last time anything like it had happened was at the founding of the republic, when all the teachers had placed their hands on the name of Arsen, the great Martian educator, and swore to teach in order to create.

In the end, the vote was six for and five against. When the small gavel slammed down against the strike plate, the sound reverberated among the treelike columns situated throughout the black-walled Boule Chamber. The fate of these children became part of history.

To be honest, even those who voted in the final tally had no clear idea as to what the students would experience on Earth. The decision-makers had been born on Mars, and they had only heard accounts of the noisy bustle on Earth, legends of a previous generation. The entire Martian Republic consisted of a single city, a habitat enclosed in glass. Here the land was literally a thing of the people, managed for the commonweal. There was no private ownership in real estate, no smuggling, no buying on credit, no banking. No one knew how children who had grown up in such a place would react to the grand bazaar that was Earth, where commerce was the only rule, and advertisements would bombard the children day and night. Before their departure, the students sat through numerous lessons that tried to explain the system on Earth to them. But no matter how much the teachers tried to impress upon the children the severity of the challenges they faced, it was impossible to teach young hearts how to grow up in a classroom.

Luoying leaned against the transparent wall of the homeward-bound tube train, deep in thought.

The scenery outside was tranquil and vivid. Through the blue-tinted glass, sunlight struck the trees lining the tube, casting their shadows against her face through the glass ceiling. She was the only one in the car, and she saw no one through the wall. Everything was so quiet that it seemed unreal. The walls and floor of the car were clear as ice, and as the train glided over some houses, she looked down and saw the trees standing still in the courtyards.

The confusion she had tried to suppress for days now flooded her heart.

She didn't know why she had gone to Earth. On *Maearth*, she had discovered that she was unqualified.

One night, as the students sat chatting next to a viewport, someone brought up one of the questions on the qualifying examination that had been used to pick members of the Mercury Group five years earlier. Others soon chimed in, and they pieced together the outline of the test from collective memory. Recollection of that shared rite of passage was joyful, festive.

But Luoying soon fell silent. Based on the answers the other students recalled giving, she soon realized that she couldn't possibly have scored as high as the rest of them. She was ashamed, like a star dimmed by the bright full moon.

She wasn't sure if her suspicion was true. If she was wrong, then everything ought to continue as before. But if she was right, then it meant that she was added to the Mercury Group because someone had interfered with the selection process. The conclusion was chilling, not only because it meant that she wasn't as talented as she thought, but also because it meant that her life had been planned by someone else. She thought she had seized an opportunity, but the reality was that an opportunity had captured her.

My grandfather? He seemed the only one who could have had such influence. She didn't know why he would have done such a thing.

She wanted to go home and confront her grandfather, but she wasn't sure how. They weren't particularly close; he had moved in to live with her and Rudy only after the death of their parents. He had given her whatever she wanted, but he rarely hugged her. The Terrans called him "the great dictator." He always took walks alone.

Did she dare to ask him? Perhaps it would be better to ask

Rudy for help. As the older brother, Rudy had always protected her and tried to cheer her up. But Rudy was someone who insisted on striving for the future. She didn't know if he would understand why she cared so much about the past.

The train continued to glide silently through the glass tube, like a speeding memory. She passed by assembly halls, tree-lined promenades, the playground she had once frequented, a garden with a slide. The silence made everything seem to be a dreamscape. Occasionally she saw mothers chatting with each other, strollers temporarily stopped along the sidewalk.

Why do I care about this so much?

At first, she had felt a restlessness that she thought was driven by curiosity, but soon she realized that there was a deeper anxiety about fate. She had thought of fate as just a part of nature, something to be faced and borne, but now she realized that there was another kind of fate, a kind subject to manipulation by others, with hidden agendas and secret motivations, a kind that could be questioned and perhaps abandoned. This second kind of fate required her own participation and choice. Until she understood the truth, she couldn't move forward.

Why did I go to Earth? She had asked herself this question many times, but this time was different. She had walked many roads on Earth—so many that she was no longer fazed by roads and choices. But she never knew why she had gone there in the first place.

Music played in the train car: a faraway cello and a piano near at hand. The music made the scenery feel even richer. Gradually her home appeared in the distance. She could see the small open window upstairs, its brown frame shining peacefully under the domed glass ceiling.

She had imagined the moment of her homecoming many times: trembling excitement, eye-stinging nostalgia, maybe a bit of anxiety. But she had never imagined that she would feel nothing at all, and that very apathy made her melancholic. After five years in the noise of Earth, she had returned to home's tranquil harbor, but she seemed to have lost that primitive, heartfelt love of home permanently.

The tube train stopped precisely at the platform. Luoying gazed at the familiar red door of her house and cried.

The car door slid open, and bright, unfiltered sunlight spilled inside. Luoying squinted and shaded her eyes. The air seemed filled with golden sparkles, and she saw a gold-colored bench in front of her: smooth, gracefully shaped, and the rounded cushions and back gave off the sense that it was made out of balloons.

She looked up and saw Rudy waving at her from the second floor, looking like his usual assured self.

She smiled at him and sat down on the bench with her luggage. The bench rose into the air and flew up toward Rudy's window. She glanced around: the garden shaped like a drop of water, fan-shaped flower patches, umbrellalike trees, the spherical dome overhead, the orange trapezoidal mailbox, the wide-open window upstairs, planters suspended from the beams. Everything looked the same as when she had left.

The bench stopped by the window. Rudy unloaded her luggage and held out his arms. She leaped gracefully into his embrace, and he set her down. The moment her feet touched the floor, she felt a sense of stability.

He was much taller than the last time she saw him. His hair, still blond, no longer curled as much.

"You must be exhausted," he said.

She shook her head.

"Look at you," he said, holding out a hand at waist level. "You were just this tall when you left."

"You exaggerate," said Luoying, grinning. "Are you suggesting that I managed to gain thirty centimeters in Earth's gravity?" Her voice sounded rasping, unreal.

During the five years away, Luoying had grown only five centimeters. Upon arrival on Earth, she was taller than most girls her age there, but by the time she left, she no longer stood out. She knew very well that her body had been weighed down by that more massive world. Her growth had been stunted as her bones and heart were challenged. Every centimeter had been an effort at overcoming herself.

"How've you been?" she asked.

"Oh, I can't complain."

"What atelier did you pick?"

"Fifth Electro-Mag Atelier."

"How do you like it?"

"It's fine. I'm now a group leader."

"That's great."

Rudy noticed her expression. "What's wrong?"

Luoying looked down. "I don't know."

"As in 'I'm fine, but I don't know what to say about it'?"

"As in 'I don't know.'"

"Then something *is* wrong."

"No... I just don't know how to describe how I feel."

Luoying had lived in many places all over Earth, and the home in her heart had gradually fallen into ruin with each move.

In one of the great cities in East Asia, she had lived on the one hundred and eightieth floor of a skyscraper. The dance school she attended also trained in a studio in the same building. The building itself was a steel pyramid, like a mountain. Inside was a world complete unto itself. Elevators raced up and down the slanted edges, and people came and went like the surging tide.

In Central Europe, she had lived in an old, abandoned house in a suburb, where the metropolis met the open countryside. The land there belonged to a merchant who came there only once a year, and trespassers weren't allowed. She had gone there in search of inspiration for her dance. The fields were full of swaying golden wheat and wild birds. Flowers bloomed and wilted like the coming and going of clouds.

In the open plains of North America, she had lived in the heart of an artificial scenic park surrounded by wilderness. Terran officials had invited all the Martian students to vacation at the park. There, the prairie stretched under the big sky like a song, and loneliness showed itself in every bare tree branch, every passing bird, every cold, glinting star. From time to time, billowing clouds raced in from every direction, and lightning bolts hung from them like tree branches while trees reached up from the earth like frozen lightning.

On a plateau in Central Asia, she had lived in a tent city at the foot of snowy mountains. There she joined Reversionist friends who had gathered there in mass protest. The mountains were pure white at the top where the peaks poked into the clouds. From time to time the clouds dissipated to reveal the golden glow of the sun against the snow. The tent city had been full of passionate youths from around the world who shouted slogans while linking arms, protesting against the system until the system crushed the movement. The tent city was wiped away in a storm of violence, but the snowcapped mountains shone in the sun, unmoved.

Before going to Earth, she had never seen any of these things. They didn't exist on Mars, and perhaps never would. There were no skyscrapers on Mars, no countryside, no absentee owners of vacation villas, no lightning, no snowcapped mountains.

No blood from dragged-away protesters either. At least not in her memory.

She had experienced so much on Earth, but she didn't know how to describe it. She had gained so many memories but lost her dream. She had seen all kinds of exotic scenery, but home now seemed out of place. She had no words for any of it, all of it.

She looked into her brother's eyes, deciding to cut to the chase.

"There *is* something bothering me."

"What is it?"

"I don't think I should have been picked five years ago. I think I took someone else's place. Do you know what happened?"

She waited for his reaction. Although he said nothing, she could tell he was trying to decide how to respond. The mood between them felt odd.

"Who told you that?" he asked.

"No one. I just had a feeling."

"You can't trust random feelings."

"It's not random. We had a discussion."

"Who's 'we'?"

"The Mercury Group. On the way back, on *Maearth*, we talked about the exam. I figured out that everyone must have scored much higher than I did. They had solutions to problems that I had left blank. And all of them had been interviewed but not me. I remember how it happened. There was no notice that I was even being considered until all of a sudden I was told to get ready. It was so abrupt that I was shocked. I must have been switched in at the last minute. Do you know why?"

Rudy shrugged. She stared at him, but couldn't read his expression.

"Maybe… someone backed out at the last minute."

"Is that what happened?"

"It's possible, I guess."

In that moment, Luoying suddenly felt a vast gulf separating her and her brother. She had the feeling that he knew the truth but didn't want to tell her. His apathy in the face of her suspicions was not at all normal. The deliberate attempt to downplay her doubts, to not seek clarification, showed that he was trying to hide something from her.

They had always shared everything, she and Rudy. As children, they had been allies against the adults, and he had taken her to places they shouldn't have gone, to see things they shouldn't have seen. He had never, until this moment, allied himself with the adults against her.

She felt utterly alone. She had thought she could at least count on the help of her brother if she couldn't ask her grandfather, but she had lost Rudy, too. *What else does he know? What else isn't he telling me?*

"Why was I chosen, then?" she persisted. "You knew about the switch, didn't you?"

Rudy said nothing.

She screwed up her courage. "It was Grandfather, am I right?" Rudy still said nothing.

They had never spoken to each other like this. After five years of not seeing him, this was not how she imagined their first conversation at home would go. They each seemed to be waiting for the other to speak. The air was tense, like a taut bowstring.

Luoying sighed, thinking of giving up and changing the topic. But in a composed tone, Rudy asked, "Why do you care so much?"

She looked at him, forcing her own voice to betray no

emotion. "Even a soldier discharged from the army deserves to know why the war was fought, don't you think?"

"What's the use if the war is over?"

"Of course it's of use!"

She had drifted through so many places already and lost her faith. Didn't she deserve to know why she had been sent on her journey?

Rudy looked thoughtful. "You were too young back then... and too emotional."

"What do you mean by that?"

"You were always so sad after Mom and Dad died."

"Mom and Dad?" She held her breath.

"Yes. You took their deaths hard. So... Grandfather thought perhaps a change of scenery would lead to an improvement in mood."

After a silence, Luoying asked, "Is that the real reason?"

"I don't know. I'm just offering a possibility."

"But... they died five years before the selection process."

"Sure, but you were sad for all those years."

She tried to remember her younger self. Five years ago she had been thirteen. She couldn't even recall what she had thought or been obsessed with back then. It seemed a lifetime ago.

"Maybe you're right," she said. Her brother's suggestion wasn't unreasonable, and she decided she would accept the explanation provisionally.

They fell into an awkward silence again. Luoying gazed at her brother, at his broad shoulders, tall figure, and steady eyebrows, which no longer moved animatedly as she had remembered. He was twenty-two, an adult now, a group leader at an atelier. He would no longer run around with her, no longer tell her endless stories he made up about spaceships and rockets and war against aliens. He understood the value of being silent; he now spoke to her as one of the adults.

Rudy smiled. "Isn't there something else you wanted to ask? This is your chance."

After a moment she understood. There was indeed something she had forgotten to mention. When they were little, he had always waited for her to say something specific after he had shown her something wonderful.

"The bench—how did you do it?"

Rudy snapped his fingers. "Simple! The bench itself is made from standard molded glass, but the surface has been plated with a nickel film with strong magnetic properties. As soon as there's a sufficiently powerful magnetic field in the yard, the bench will float into the air." He pointed outside the window to show her the circle of white pipes running around the yard—a simple electromagnetic coil.

"Oh, that's fantastic," Luoying said admiringly.

That was the line he had been waiting for. When they were little, these were the words that accompanied so many incredible new toys and inventions.

Rudy laughed and told her to get plenty of rest before leaving to go downstairs. She gazed at his back, knowing that he had deliberately tried to invoke their childhood, to ignore the break in time, to pretend that everything was the same. But nothing was ever the same, even if people always tried so hard to deny it.

Her brother gone, Luoying stood by the window and looked out again.

Under the bright sun, everything was outlined in golden light and long, deep shadows. Other than the white coil, everything looked the way she remembered: the flowers, the patio furniture, the tube train station. The flowers wilted and bloomed year after year, wiping away the invisible past. She saw her younger self running alone through the garden: pink shoes, a pair of pigtails, looking up and laughing a pure, carefree laugh—she gazed up at the window and saw right through Luoying, saw right through the gloom behind her.

The garden was at peace, and the passage of time could be discerned only in a few details. She saw that the conveyor belt behind the mailbox was empty, as clean as a newborn's skin. Once, Rudy and she had secretly installed a round plate there, a sensor that allowed them to tell whether packages in the mailbox contained some interesting toy. The plate was gone now, and the curved, cylindrical surface behind the mailbox was smooth and empty, like her departure, like time's arrow.

In the afternoon, after waking from her nap, she found Grandfather in her room.

He was standing by the wall and looking out the window, holding something in his hand. He didn't hear her waking up. She gazed at his back. The sun was about to set and lit up half the room. Grandfather stood in the dark half, and his stiff, straight figure loomed like a stone tablet. This was a familiar sight to Luoying. She had thought of Grandfather many times on Earth, and each time she pictured him, she had imagined him in just such an ambivalent pose: standing next to the window, gazing into the distance, half of his body in shadows.

She sat up, hoping to ask him why he had sent her to Earth.

He turned at the noise, smiling. He was already dressed in a tuxedo for tonight, his silver hair combed neatly. The coat draped over his shoulders gave him the air of a soldier, not just of a man in his seventies.

"Slept well?" Hans sat down at the edge of her bed, his dark gray eyes staring gently into hers.

She nodded.

"You must be tired from such a long trip."

"Not too tired."

"*Maearth* is an old ship. Probably not very comfortable."

"I slept better there than on Earth."

He laughed. "And how are Garcia and Ellie?"

"They are well. They send their greetings. Oh, the captain asked me to bring you a message."

"What is it?"

"'Sometimes the fight over the treasure is more important than the treasure itself.'"

Grandfather looked thoughtful at this. After a while he nodded.

"What does it mean?" asked Luoying.

"Just an old saying."

"Our relationship with Earth… it's very tense right now, isn't it?"

He waited a beat, then smiled. "Hasn't it always been?"

Luoying waited for him to clarify, but he didn't, and she didn't ask again.

She wanted to ask the question that had been plaguing her, but the process of picking and assembling the right words was interrupted when she saw the object in Grandfather's hand. It was a photo of her parents. Her mother's hair was loosely tied back, and she held a sculpting knife in her gloved hands, streaks of clay and a relaxed smile on her face. Standing behind her, her father wrapped his arms around her, resting his chin against the curve of her neck. They both looked so happy.

Hans saw she was looking and handed her the photo.

"You came back just in time. Tomorrow is the anniversary of their deaths. Why don't we pray for them at dinner tomorrow night?" Luoying nodded, her heart heavy.

"You're growing to look more like your mother." Grandfather's voice, deep and low, seemed to leave behind a silence that did not want to be broken.

Luoying felt a tangled web of emotions. The photograph in her hand felt warm, maybe from Grandfather's hand or maybe because her parents were smiling so warmly. She had rarely seen her grandfather like this, a complicated anguish in his eyes. The four people in the room, two in the photograph, two outside, seemed to be holding a silent conversation. Her parents had been dead for ten years, and Luoying couldn't remember the last time they had been together like this. The last rays of the sun winked out, and a gentle warmth, unique to death, connected her to her grandfather.

An urgent ringing.

The red light on the wall came on, indicating an emergency call. As though shaking off a dream, Hans got up and strode to the wall to press the button to connect. The wall flickered and then the face of Grandfather's good friend Juan—Luoying had always called him Uncle Juan—appeared on the screen, his expression severe and cold.

Uncle Juan didn't even bother to start with a greeting. "Can you talk? In person."

"Before the reception?"

"Yes."

Hans nodded, his face calm. He turned off the screen, exited Luoying's room, picked up his scarf, and went downstairs.

Luoying remained sitting on the bed. The whole episode with her grandfather had taken no more than a minute or two, and the dream that had reunited her family was gone.

The door to her room gently swung shut by itself, the hallway beyond empty.

She knew that she couldn't ask Grandfather the question directly; she had to find out the truth from others, a comparatively easier task. Grandfather was the flying warrior, perpetually in motion. He would always have secrets, and she didn't know how to ask about them.

Staring at the photograph in her hand, she tried again and again to remember her self from five years ago and how she had felt after her parents had died.

The official reception for the Martian and Terran delegations, as well as the Mercury Group, was held in the Glory Memorial Hall, the site of Mars's most important ceremonial functions. The hall was a long rectangle with sixteen columns in two rows. Between the columns were miniature models and informative displays of important events in Martian history. The murals on the ceiling and the walls were projections that could be changed for each occasion.

For tonight, the hall was brightly lit, decorated in a refined manner that did not tip over into luxury. Projected lilies covered the walls, the overall effect resembling green-and-white wallpaper. Four VIP tables were set up on the raised stage at the center, and sixteen more tables were arranged around it. White tablecloths covered them all. Since cotton fabric was rare on Mars, this was a sign of high respect for the guests. Pots of African violets served as centerpieces, and poinsettias sat atop pedestals at the sides. Glass strands dangled from the ceiling, glowing in different colors.

A buffet on a slow-moving conveyor belt was set up on one side of the hall. There were no waiters at all. One corner was set up to resemble a stall that might be found at a country market on ancient Earth, with piles of vegetables and fruits. This was meant to show off the triumph of Martian agriculture.

The Terran delegates were irked by the lack of waitstaff, which to them made the banquet a shabby affair. They were used to well-dressed waiters at the ready, filling glasses with red wine as soon as they were empty and bringing out new silverware between courses, as though only through such pampering could the attendees demonstrate their elegance.

The semicircular conveyor belt, on the other hand, progressed at its own pace, neither too fast nor too slow, content to let the honored guests take care of themselves. Dishes emerged from the wall, carried on the conveyor belt until the guests had picked what they liked, and retreated back into the wall again. Wine flowed from spigots whenever guests held their glasses under them. To the Terrans, the whole setup reminded them of some third-rate country buffet, and they conversed loudly among themselves, describing how their own countries would have hosted such an important state dinner in style.

There were no waiters on Mars. Indeed, the entire service economy seemed absent. At most, one might find volunteers and interns, but no service workers, no servants, no tertiary industry at all. Everyone on Mars worked as a researcher affiliated with an atelier, and no one waited tables or took orders. The reception had been prepared and would be cleaned up by the hosts themselves.

The Martians didn't bother to explain this background to their guests, and so the cultural misunderstandings grew. A few European delegates discussed the origin of modern etiquette among the aristocrats of Old Europe; a few East Asian delegates offered praise to the cultivated manners and rites of their ancient civilizations; a few Middle Eastern delegates then proudly explained that in their countries men were strong enough that women had the leisure to host grand parties in luxurious mansions and take care of the guests themselves. The Martians listened, smiling politely. Then they got up in threes or twos to go to the conveyor belt for another serving. The Terrans, confused by the lack of embarrassment on the part of their hosts, grew even more angry, whispering among themselves and shaking their heads.

The Mercury Group took up two of the tables. Luoying sat next to Chania and Anka. They were enjoying the tastes of home and chatting happily, glad to be free from the adults for the moment. The conveyor belt brought out desserts, and Chania brought back a large plate to share with the whole table.

"This is so delicious," said Chania. "I've been missing real cooking."

None of them liked the food on Earth. To them, it was all just sustenance.

"I wonder who made these," said Anka.

Luoying took a bite. "I bet it's from Old Maury's. I love her pudding. When I was little, whenever I felt down, I begged Mom to go get some. It always cheered me up."

The joyful mood of the students contrasted sharply with the tension in the air. Luoying could feel it. Their table was next to the VIPs', and she was seated with her back right up against the stage. Snatches of conversation from up there drifted into her ears from time to time. Although she couldn't hear what everyone said, Uncle Juan's booming voice always stood out.

"Don't you dare tell me 'That didn't happen,'" he was saying. "Let me tell you, I watched as my grandmother died in one of your bombing raids. One second she was trembling in her bedroom, praying for God to save her, and the next second she was a bloody smear across the rubble. No, I'm sure they didn't teach you that in your schools. But that's what you bastards did. You murdered civilians. You rank right up there with the worst butchers in human history."

The person he was lecturing said something in a low voice, which only enraged Juan further.

"Oh, fuck off! I don't give a damn about your 'lack of involvement.' I'll toss your ass right out the airlock if you try to spew that legalistic garbage again." He paused and then added, "You've never been outside on Mars, have you? Ha! If you're out there with no protection, *pop!* and you'll be dead like a swollen octopus."

Luoying couldn't help but laugh at the image. Discreetly, she looked behind her. The man sitting next to Uncle Juan was Mr. Beverley, the head of the Terran delegation. His expression was awkward as he dabbed at his mouth with a napkin.

Luoying was fascinated. On Earth, Beverley was a big star, well-known for his elegance and fine manners. Someone else might respond to Juan's rage in kind, but Beverley couldn't. He was dressed in a retro-style fashionable suit with velvet and gold trim and two rows of brass buttons, giving him the air of an aristocrat from centuries ago. He had to look serious and thoughtful, the image of the consummate diplomat. Rage, as a mode of expression, was forbidden to him.

For a long time no one spoke again, and Luoying turned her attention back to the food. The next time she heard Uncle Juan's voice, he sounded even more excited than before. He stood up abruptly, his chair legs scraping against the stage. Everyone in the hall stopped and stared at him.

"No!" he shouted. "Absolutely not!"

The diners became agitated and whispers filled the hall, as no one was certain what had happened. Someone at Juan's table tried to pull him back down, but he refused. A Terran delegate at the table tried to get up but was held down by a friend. Finally, Hans Sloan stood up. He put a hand gently on Juan's shoulder, and the man finally sat down.

"Honored guests from Earth," Hans said, and raised his glass. "Let me say a few words. First of all, we offer our sincere welcome to you. The past is the past, but in front of us lies a long road to the future. The goals of this world's fair are our mutual benefit, mutual profit, and the pursuit of our separate goals. Exchange between our peoples will always be necessary.

"I believe that we'll find a way for both sides to be satisfied. We will take your demands into consideration, but the final deal must be approved by all the citizens of Mars. For a decision this momentous, a democratic process is vital. Moreover, I believe the Terran delegation will also behave in a democratic manner so that the final deal will be approved by all the members.

"This is a beautiful night, and it's far too early to jump to conclusions. Let's set aside our differences for now and raise a glass to our first evening together in one another's company."

Everyone raised their glass. Chania asked Luoying what had led to Uncle Juan's outburst. Luoying shook her head, saying she didn't know either.

In fact, however, she did know. Grandfather's toast was just another version of what Garcia had said: the democratic process among the Terran delegates was the fight over the treasure. Some vague outline of the situation was emerging in her mind, but she still didn't understand the nature of the treasure the Terrans were fighting over. She ate silently, her mind churning over Grandfather's ambivalent words.

THE FILM ARCHIVE

B efore paying a visit to Janet Brook, Eko went to see Peter Beverley first.

He didn't make an appointment; instead, he went up to Beverley's door and knocked on it.

It was nine thirty in the morning, and Eko knew Peter was certain to be up by then. The first formal negotiations would begin at ten sharp. It took about ten minutes to get from the hotel to the meeting hall, and he only needed a few minutes of his time.

Eko knew that Peter had had a rough time at the reception the previous night, and he wished he could have seen the expression on the man's face after he got back to the hotel. At the banquet, Eko had placed a camera under one of the poinsettias, and though he didn't make an announcement about it, he was sure Peter knew. Peter had been a movie star, and there was perhaps no one else on Earth who was more sensitive to the presence of a camera. The whole night he had presented his profile from the right side to Eko's lens, smiling in that most charming way he had. Ever since he had gotten into politics at the age of thirty-five, he posed like that for the camera.

Eko found Peter interesting. The man led a charmed life: handsome, scion of a prominent family, Ivy League–educated, friends everywhere, and though he was barely in his fifties, already many were speaking of him as the next Democratic candidate for the presidency.

His family was perhaps his most powerful asset. It was rumored that he had been selected to lead the Terran delegation because of his family's vast network of connections. Everyone understood that the job was perfect for him: high-exposure but low-risk, a great way to accumulate political capital for the next step in his career. He cared very much about how he was seen through the lens.

And that was why Eko was enjoying himself so much. After getting back to the hotel the night before, Eko had reviewed the footage of the reception and found himself quite taken with the ruddy-faced man who had sat next to Peter and screamed at him.

The door opened to reveal a perfectly coiffed Peter Beverley in a pale blue silk suit. He greeted Eko warmly, completely at ease.

"Morning," said Eko. "It's all right, I don't need to come in. I just need a few moments of your time." Peter nodded, waiting.

"Do you remember the Martian consul's speech last night about democracy? I spoke to one of the Martian legislators after the reception, and he explained that the Boule is responsible for most day-to-day decisions and engineering projects, but major decisions that affect everyone have to be put to a vote by all the citizens of Mars. That doesn't jibe with what we usually hear on Earth."

"It is rather different," Peter acknowledged.

"So… what do you make of this difference? We have a representative democracy with free and fair elections. They don't have elections at all, but they do have plebiscites involving everyone."

"You're right to point out the difference," said Peter. "It's worth pondering."

"Can I reveal this… 'difference' in my film?"

"Of course. Why shouldn't you?"

"But this seems so different from the general consensus about how Mars functions that I don't know what I'll find if I keep on digging."

"Don't worry about your conclusions. To think, to probe, to test your theories—that's what matters."

"I'm not sure you understand what I'm getting at. Right now, everyone on Earth thinks of Mars as an autocracy. My film may challenge this consensus and lead to unpredictable results."

Peter continued to smile, as though giving Eko his full attention. But Eko had noticed him fidgeting with his cuffs and brushing the hair from his shoulders. Peter reached out and clapped a hand over Eko's shoulder like a kind, older relative.

"Young man, don't worry about the consequences. To have a future, you must dare to dream."

Eko tried to tamp down his rising rage. There was no sincerity in Peter's words. He had evaded him with cliché after cliché and said nothing of substance. Eko wondered if Peter had grasped the import of his revelation at all.

But he must have. On Earth, despite the competition and distrust among nations, everyone saw Mars as the common enemy. It was like another Cold War, one based on the iron curtain of space. Mars was described as an isolated community controlled by evil generals and mad scientists, the textbook model of a society under a repressive authoritarian regime abetted by thought-control machinery, the very opposite of a free market economy and democratic governance. The media and the intelligentsia both portrayed Mars as a byword for cruelty, tyranny, and inhumanity, a massive dystopian war machine the likes of which had never existed on Earth. The Martian war for independence had been declared a suicidal act of betrayal, and the Martians were supposed to have no future except to return to the community of nations or face utter annihilation. Surely, Peter Beverley knew all this and could see what Eko was getting at.

To show democracy functioning on Mars was to challenge the very foundation of the narrative about the red planet. It would lead to admission that politicians on Earth had lied, that the propaganda against Mars was based on prejudice and envy rooted in defeat. Eko wasn't afraid of making waves, but he knew what was politically correct for a filmmaker to show. As an official member of the delegation, he knew he was subject to constraints.

But Peter had not reacted. He simply fended him off with poses and elegant, meaningless words.

Fine, thought Eko. *No matter what I end up producing, I can always say that I asked for permission first.* In fact, this was better. As a lifelong antiestablishment Reversionist, Eko delighted in shooting down conventional wisdom on Earth.

"Thank you," he said. "I guess I should have told you earlier: this conversation isn't being recorded. There's no camera here."

As Eko turned to leave, he glimpsed through the door Peter's wife putting the finishing touches on her makeup. About ten years younger than Peter, she was also a famous actress. Their romance had always been conducted in front of cameras, from the first kiss to the birth of their son. Peter was skilled at the role of model husband, romantic and appropriately spontaneous. Their marriage looked perfect, and he always made sure that she accompanied him everywhere. Eko had seen many men move from acting careers into politics, but so few of them seemed to understand the importance of the women's vote. Peter was one of the few.

The Tarkovsky Film Archive wasn't far from the hotel. Like the hotel itself, it was in the southern part of the city, two districts away. A tube train would get him there in twenty-four minutes, passing by the Capitol, site of City Hall and the Boule Chamber, as well as the Expo Center, where the world's fair was being held.

As with his visit to Peter Beverley in the morning, Eko didn't make an appointment with Janet Brook. He left no message in Janet's personal space, and didn't call the archive ahead of time either. He didn't want to alert her at all, to give her a chance to turn down his politely phrased request for a meeting, or to prepare herself to spar with him in a superficial conversation in which both sides carefully avoided the truth.

He wanted to catch her off guard; perhaps then he would see the real person. He didn't know if she was the "cause" that he sought; he had to see her first to judge.

Once aboard the tube train, Eko took out a camera patch and stuck it to the wall of the car to record the scenery along the way. He had ridden the tube train from the shuttle port to the hotel, but the ride was so short that he didn't have a chance to shoot any footage. The totally transparent structure of the train car gave the camera patch a great view.

Tube train cars were of different colors. The one Eko was in right now was beige, and he enjoyed the fantasy of sitting inside a drop of some solution as it traveled from retort to beaker to flask to funnel through twisting glass tubing. The train passed over different types of structures: clusters of small residences alternating with large public buildings. The small houses surrounded the larger edifices like satellites orbiting planets. The larger buildings were typically ring-shaped, with a glass roof over the open center. The smaller houses, on the other hand, were typically covered entirely by semispherical glass domes, including the yards, filled with flowers and other lush vegetation. Eko heard that the oxygen needs of many dwellings were mostly satisfied by the plants in their gardens, thereby saving both precious energy and the need for complex oxygen-producing machinery.

Small screens inside the train car displayed the names and brief histories of the various landmarks and districts they passed. Eko noticed that many of the buildings on Mars showed the influence of practically every architectural trend and tradition on Earth: the symmetry and harmony of the Renaissance; the complexity and excesses of rococo; the sweeping roofs and long verandas of Chinese wood-frame architecture; the hard, geometric lines of modernism; and so on. The whole city therefore resembled a natural museum of architectural history, full of layers and variety. The buildings that most drew Eko's attention, however, displayed a unique kind of fluid curves and surfaces, like gently flowing water. All the structures were made out of glass.

As the train passed by the Capitol, Eko stood up and took a few still photographs. The Capitol was the administrative center of Mars City, where all the policies affecting the republic were made. Constructed in a solemn, classical style, it wasn't a very large or imposing building. It was rectangular in plan, its front doors were located on one of the shorter sides, which were lined with bronze statues and metal, Roman-style columns. The walls were a rare dark copper interspersed with ivory-hued vertical panels, reminiscent of the Teatro alla Scala.

While the camera patch continued to film, Eko took out

his notepad and wrote to himself in shorthand. This was his habit as he wandered everywhere, whether at home or on a battlefield by the sea.

Beverley is a fool.

After a moment of thought, he deleted the note. It wasn't an objective observation and didn't quite capture what he meant. He knew that Beverley was a clever man who knew how to evaluate a situation, and he was sensitive to his own role. But he lacked *wisdom*. For Eko, opportunistic cunning wasn't the same as wisdom. Peter was an idol whose holographic image could be seen in every supermarket, his trademark million-watt smile gently nudging shoppers this way or that. That required no wisdom.

"He was not stupid. It was sheer thoughtlessness," Hannah Arendt wrote of Eichmann more than two hundred years ago, but the words remain applicable today. I don't like Beverley. There's no good reason for it—except that he seems like a wax figure sculpted by himself. He makes himself smile rather than smile because he wants to. He exudes charm, but there's nothing behind it. He doesn't even have the humor of a JFK. A man like this probably didn't exist in the past. Every age has its hypocritical politicians, but before our age, no one could be an empty shell of pasted images from the moment of his birth. Beverley is so used to being a hologram that the image has become the person, while his real self has faded into illusion.

He finished his notes just as the train pulled into the station. He despised filming politicians, though it was one of the primary sources of income for the film industry. This sort of work sapped his passion, and he would have rather filmed some urchin cursing in the streets. He stuck the notepad back into his shirt pocket, packed away the camera patch, and stood before the door.

The door slid open. An aquamarine structure resembling an oyster stood before him. The walls were opaque, so he couldn't see inside. A footpath led from the station to the building entrance, which was shaped like a conch shell.

Inside the Tarkovsky Film Archive lobby was a circular screen. Photographs scrolled across it, along with a menu of choices for visitors: self-guided tours, film viewings, atelier visits. Eko picked the last one.

Several sub-menus popped up. Patiently, Eko navigated through them until he found Janet Brook.

His heart sped up as he touched her name. The high-resolution photograph of a woman with light-blond hair appeared. One glance was enough for him to know that he had found the right person: he had seen her in Arthur Davosky's journal. Compared to the photograph in his teacher's possession, she had gained a little weight, her skin sagged a bit, and her hair was shorter. But her eyes were very distinctive, giving the appearance of always smiling. He did some mental math and determined that Janet Brook was now about forty-five, her face still as lively as that of her younger self. After a moment of hesitation, he touched the button to let her know she had a visitor.

The screen pulsed, showing that the call went through and was being processed.

A few minutes later Janet came into the lobby from a door at the other end. She wore a salmon jacket over a white blouse, with light makeup and hair tucked behind her ear on one side.

When she saw Eko, she looked momentarily confused, not recognizing him. Nonetheless, she smiled at him politely.

"Hello," she said. "I'm Janet Brook."

Eko held out his hand. "An honor to meet you. I'm Eko Lu, from Earth."

"Ah, you're with the Terran delegation."

"That's right. I'm the delegation's documentary film director."

"No kidding."

"Here's my card."

"Oh… it's not that I don't believe you. I'm sorry. I just… I had no idea they brought along a film crew."

"It's just me, actually."

"Well, this is truly wonderful. I haven't met a colleague from Earth in ages."

"Eighteen years, to be exact," said Eko.

"Really? Let me think… yes, you're right. My memory isn't as good as when I was younger."

Eko hesitated. Janet's reactions told him nothing. She looked composed, and meeting a filmmaker from Earth didn't seem to arouse any particular passions. He decided to test her some more before revealing the true purpose of his visit.

"I explained to officials at the Boule that I wanted to meet Martian filmmakers," Eko said. "They recommended you."

"That's nice of them. Why don't you come in?"

Janet pushed open the door leading to the interior of the archive building, and Eko followed, taking in everything around him. The conch-shell design motif of the entrance continued deep inside the building, and they walked through round tunnels with smooth-flowing curves full of blue-gray lines that spiraled inward.

Various videos and images scrolled over the walls as the route they took twisted around like a maze.

"Honestly, I don't know why the officials recommended you to me," said Eko after a while. "They didn't tell me much about you."

Janet laughed. "I'd guess it's because I'm the only filmmaker they know."

"Oh?"

"There was a technology developed here that they used to trade with Earth a while back. Terrans really liked it."

"What technology was it?"

"Full-fidelity holographic projections."

Eko grew excited. He had made up the excuse to continue the conversation, but Janet had brought up that exchange from decades ago herself.

"Did your atelier invent it?"

"We sure did. More than twenty years ago now."

"Please accept my gratitude, then. I have a job because of you."

"You're a holographic filmmaker?"

"Most films are holographic. Flats are almost extinct."

Janet laughed heartily, and Eko could sense the genuine pleasure behind it. "You shouldn't thank me at all. Without holographic projections, you'd still have a job. But with them, many people can no longer do what they used to do."

Eko smiled in return. He knew what she meant. Every revolution left many behind in the old world. From silent films to talkies, from flats to full-fidelity holographs—it wasn't that people were incapable of learning the new medium, only that many didn't want to. It was complicated. The more someone excelled in the old world, the more unwilling they were to start afresh in the new. They had put so much of their life into the outdated mode of expression that they could not abandon it. No one liked to abandon themselves.

"What about here on Mars?" he asked.

"We still have flats as well as holographic films. When you're recording a meeting or some industrial footage, there's no need to use 3-D. Too expensive."

"I see. We have those as well, though we don't usually count those as 'films.'"

"I understand," said Janet. "You call something a 'film' only if you can publish it."

"Isn't it the same here?"

"No. On Mars the definition is purely technical. Any kind of audio-visual record is classified as film. You publish your films on the web, divided by genre, but we don't do things that way. Our films are all stored in the central archive under each person's name. Since everyone can make dramatic narratives, factual documentaries, records of experiments, or industrial footage used as raw data, there's no need to separate them."

Carefully, Eko probed. "It sounds like you're very familiar with the way things are done on Earth."

"I wouldn't say familiar. Out of personal interest, I've picked up a few things here and there."

"Why are you interested in Earth?"

"I suppose… it's an occupational hazard. I once studied the history of film regulation on Earth. Though that's no longer an area of focus and analysis, I've maintained an interest."

"Do you have contacts on Earth, then? I wasn't aware that direct communication between citizens of the two planets is possible."

"Oh, it's not. But I've seen some official introductory material from Earth. Most stick to generalities, and so my understanding is very shallow." Janet smiled. "I'm so glad you're here. You can teach me a great deal."

Eko fell silent again. His questioning didn't seem to get

him anywhere. There was nothing unusual in Janet's answers, nothing he could seize on. Every explanation she offered was objective, carefully phrased, inoffensive. Friendly but without any trace of the personal. No, it wasn't that she was without personality. Her laughter was direct and genuine, and her expressions were sincere and curious. But she always managed to avoid revealing anything of her private life. Eko didn't know what to do. To continue the conversation this way was to meander aimlessly around the target, but to bring up what he really wanted now seemed too abrupt.

They arrived in a large, brightly lit hall. Thin pieces of glass in various shapes hung from the ceiling, breaking up the monotonous space with refractions and shadows. Words and images scrolled over the glass surfaces. Once in a while, some larger-than-life figure appeared on one of the screens to deliver a silent lecture to an invisible audience. The air was cool but felt a bit stuffy.

"Everyone shown on the screens here is an experienced filmmaker," Janet said. "If you're interested, you can wear this ceramic earplug and listen to what they're saying."

"How do these glass screens work?"

"They are plated with a thin conducting and light-emitting membrane. The membrane is so thin that it's indistinguishable from ordinary glass."

"I've noticed that Mars likes to make things out of glass. Is there some significance behind it?"

"Some significance? How do you mean?"

"Uh... I mean, why did you make this collective decision?"

"I wouldn't call it a collective *decision*; it's more a matter of necessity. On Mars, we have plenty of sand, but lack clay and stone. Other than iron, we have to rely on glass as the raw material for most things. During the war, Niles Galle invented the construction techniques we now use. Glass is easy to build with and easy to recycle."

"I see. But how do you deal with the issue of privacy? What are the rules? I noticed that many houses are not transparent, but the walls in my room are."

Janet looked surprised. "They didn't tell you? All the walls are adjustable! The virtual concierge in your hotel isn't doing a very good job if it didn't explain these basic features. The ions in the glass are controlled by electric fields, and you can twist a dial in the room to alter the degree of transparency."

Eko felt quite silly. He remembered the grand conclusions about Martian society he had drawn from the transparent walls and was glad that he didn't commit those to permanent record. He was so steeped in the context of Earth that it was natural for him to fall into the assumptions and political symbolisms prevalent on Earth. But starting the previous night, he was coming to realize the dangers in such carelessness. It wasn't just that he risked injecting subjective bias but also that he couldn't get at the objective facts. He wanted to send a message to Earth: there was nothing more dangerous than jumping to conclusions.

A glass house was just that: a glass house. It was a fact determined by the geology and technology of Mars, with no symbolism behind it, and certainly no political oppression. To capture reality, he needed to go deeper, to dig beneath the surface, until he touched the true context of Mars.

"I thought the transparency was a deliberate choice," said Eko.

"Well…" Janet hesitated. "I suppose it depends on your point of view. Whether something is transparent depends on the light."

"Can you elaborate?"

"No matter how you adjust it, the medium will always be transparent to some forms of light but not others. Total opacity is impossible."

"Are you talking about glass… or something else?"

Janet chuckled, her eyes curving in mirth. "If you stay around here for a few days, you'll hear people say there are two individuals in Russell District whose words should never be taken as plain description nor as pure metaphor. One of them is Dr. Reini, and the other is me. You can interpret what I said however you like. There's no real answer."

There was a trace of slyness in her that gave her the flightiness of youth. Eko imagined that when she was younger, she must have been very charismatic. She wasn't beautiful in the conventional sense, but there was a powerful, living authenticity in her. It was a rare quality that drew others to her. He could now understand why Davosky had fallen in love with her.

"Ms. Brook, I have a confession to make. Forgive me for keeping it from you at first. I just didn't know how to bring it up without disturbing you. But I think I have to tell you the truth."

The joy faded from Janet's face. "All right. What is it?"

"I studied under Arthur Davosky. I'm here as his representative."

Janet's face froze, as though she had heard a voice from the ancient past, distant and unreal. He stared at her. They faced each other like two statues. On the glass screens overhead, figures moved and flapped their lips, but the two of them remained still. Eko was staring at her, while Janet was staring at the air between them.

At length, Janet took a deep breath. "Why don't you come to my office? We should be sitting down for this."

"... I was twenty-seven at the time and dating a young man who liked me more than I liked him. He wanted to get married, but I dragged it out, unsure what I wanted. That was when Arthur came to Mars. At first, our relationship was purely professional. I was his designated liaison on Mars, and it was my job to explain the technology to him. And then one day he invited me to make a film with him.

"Arthur is the type that... you grow fond of over time. He was always full of strange and interesting ideas, figuring out ways to show life in a new light. Since you were his student, I'm sure you know what I mean. At first he explained to me that he wanted to practice using the new techniques, to see if he had really mastered them. I thought nothing of it and agreed to help him. It wasn't until much later that I understood it was only the first step in his long plan. His aim wasn't the technology but to realize the ideas in his mind authentically. He became engrossed in the plan for his film, and I... became engrossed in him.

"I don't know how much you understand the situation at that time. On Earth, Arthur was very successful, but he had to constantly worry about the commercial success of his next film. That isn't the case here. All of our incomes are set based on age, regardless of the atelier we've joined or our accomplishments. All of our films are uploaded to the central archive, and anyone is allowed to view them without paying for the privilege. Money isn't something we worry about. Arthur loved this arrangement. As a visitor, he received a stipend and didn't need to be concerned about making a living. He finally had an opportunity where he didn't need to worry about the market but only about expressing himself. He had waited for so long for such a chance that, once he had acquired the knowledge of holographic filming, he couldn't stop himself. Every day he immersed himself in the act of creation, like a man who no longer belonged to the real world.

"I loved how passionate he was, and he... he fell in love with me. He was like a meteor that had crashed into my life, something I had never experienced. Each day we experimented with new camera angles, new techniques, new editing styles, and then went to his hotel room to read and debate and make love. He loved thinking about light and shadows. Van Gogh's ideal was to capture the turbulence of air and light, and that was Arthur's ideal as well. He told me that the sky on Mars was different from the sky on Earth, and he loved being able to see the stars in sunlight.

"Arthur didn't want to leave. His stay on Mars was supposed to last only three months, but he asked for an extension of another three months. At the end of that, he still didn't want to leave. He asked other Terrans to bring the technology back to Earth while he stayed behind. We began to live together."

Janet held a glass but didn't drink from it. She told her story coolly and slowly. From time to time she glanced at Eko, but most of the time she looked out the window. Her atelier was on the second story of the archive, facing due south, and there was plenty of sun. Outside the window was a row of short palm trees whose tops just reached the floor of the office. In the distance they could see a domed building that resembled a mosque. The light struck Janet's face from the side, breaking into a tessellated pattern against the texture of her skin. Though eighteen years had passed, the light of reminiscence was clearly connecting her to the past.

Eko sat across a small round table from her. He also held a glass containing a reddish liquid. Listening to Janet, he could picture the young Davosky like a meteor, direct, quick. It was a different image from the old man on his deathbed, but Eko felt the core of his teacher's being.

"I've always wondered about something," he said. "Why did Mars allow him to stay? Weren't the Martians suspicious of his motives? How could they be sure he wasn't a spy here to steal technology?"

"I was his guarantor. Myself and my father. My father was Secretary General of Information at the time, and he agreed to sponsor Arthur after I begged him."

"Did you get married?"

"No. We thought about it, but in the end we didn't."

"Where did you live, then?"

"In Arthur's hotel room. Since he wasn't a Martian, he couldn't be allocated a residential unit."

Eko didn't know how to continue. He wanted to ask what had happened during the eight years they were together and why Davosky had left Mars in the end. His teacher never spoke of that time, as though it were a black hole into which words disappeared. He struggled to find the right phrasing.

But Janet spoke before he could. "Tell me: How's Arthur doing now?"

Eko was shocked. He had planned to tell her all about Arthur's life on Earth during the last decade before bringing up the end. He looked at her intent expression. Though she tried to keep the question casual, the tension was obvious in her voice and face. Her smile was frozen, like an expanding balloon stretched taut. With Eko's reply, it would either let the air out and relax, or burst. She didn't rush him, but her held breath and intense gaze put even more pressure on Eko. He couldn't lie, nor could he delay answering indefinitely.

"He died."

"Oh."

"It was lung cancer. About half a year ago."

Janet held very still for three seconds before breaking down. Her shoulders shook and tears streamed down her cheeks. She covered her mouth with both hands, but the tears continued like a river. She struggled to be quiet, but the effort only intensified her grief. She cried as though nothing could stop her. A whole morning's worth of politeness, constructed as a defense, had collapsed into nothing. Her vulnerability was laid bare. Though she continued to sit upright in her chair, the devastation in her pose forced one to look away.

Eko felt her anguish but didn't know what to do. He doubted it was his place to offer her comfort. After all, she was crying for a good reason. Handing her a tissue, he looked at her and knew that his questioning was at an end. Even the matter of the chip full of Davosky's memories had to wait for another time. For a long time he simply sat with her until she stopped crying. He sat with her through the longest noon of her life.

Before he left, Janet brought him to a small monitor. She tapped at it until the screen showed REGISTRATION SUCCESSFUL. She gave him an account number and a password, informing him that he could use them to access the Martian central archive.

"All of Arthur's films are still there. Just look for his name."

Janet's voice cracked. Her eyes were swollen and her hair was no longer neatly brushed. But Eko found her beautiful. There was nothing that enhanced a person's beauty more than genuine emotion. For most of her forty-five years of life, Janet struck those around her as invulnerable. But today she lost the most precious thing in her life. In her heart, she had always believed that Arthur would return one day, and the expectation had made her lonely but open and strong. That was all over now. Eko had ended her hope.

———————

Davosky was dead, but the world didn't stop advancing. Neither Mars nor Earth ceased to spin simply because a dreamer had died.

The Earth of the twenty-second century was a world dominated by media, which became the pillar of the world economy. Manufactured images and the personalized web altered social structure and changed the relationship between the individual and the world. As the economy based on physical goods was devalued, trade in IP saved the world.

You are the web. This was the heart of the IP economy. Everyone contributed their knowledge, and the globe was interconnected into a web so that endless commercial opportunities could be born from the exchange of knowledge. In this web of commerce, even a single sentence or a stray thought could turn into a whole array of products. Trade on this web of knowledge was a revolution, a spring without a source, a business that had effectively zero cost and nearly infinite returns.

In this revolution, every thought, every sketch, every smiling face was part of the world's GDP. Everyone sold, bought, hid their own creations, and then enticed others with revelation of these secrets for money. Any idea could generate income over the web, but without the web there was no income. The web was the locus of incessant sparks. Capital overpowered nation-states. Three giant media conglomerates vied for dominance of the world, grew into empires, lobbed propaganda back and forth, and encouraged and discouraged opinions as they sought increased profits. The description from two centuries earlier remained applicable: *Investment in media has everything to do with profit and nothing to do with value.*

On the other hand, the Mars of the twenty-second century was also a world of media. But on Mars, media weren't synonymous with the economy but represented the lifestyle everyone lived. Media created a stable electronic space connected to the various ateliers. It was like a massive cavern in which everyone was allowed to store their creations and from which everyone was free to take what others had stored. The space contained a clear record of copyright and attribution, but there was no profit to be made. To take and to give were both duties, while money was allocated to everyone without regard to their participation in this exchange of ideas.

Eko understood the concept of media on Earth very well. He was familiar with their fickleness, with tidal waves of fads and trends. He knew how to paint the treasure chest so that it aroused the desire to pay for the privilege of opening the lid. But he had no understanding of media on Mars. In his imagination, media on Mars resembled a silent beast, hidden in darkness, waiting for sacrifices from the faithful. He didn't understand how individuals related to media and who was controlling whom. Without a doubt, media on Mars freed creators from the burden of having to make a living, but media also prevented creators from obtaining riches and glory.

His teacher had been a defector, Eko was now sure. He was a courageous lover and a self-aware defector. Of the twenty billion humans on Earth and Mars, he was perhaps the only one worthy of that label. He had shuttled between two planets and observed their bilateral isolation, separate evolution, reciprocal distancing, and mutual ignorance.

After leaving the Tarkovsky Film Archive, Eko followed the road to Dance School #1, Duncan Troupe. Since the dance school was also in Russell District, he didn't have far to walk. Following the electronic map, he took a footpath through an area full of shops until he saw the diamond-shaped one-story building. Through the glass walls he could see girls, all dance students, practicing inside.

Between the footpath and the wall of the studio was a gap filled with flowers. Eko walked along the path until he was next to the building and glanced inside.

Luoying Sloan. He recognized her from *Maearth* and the welcome reception. She was practicing at one end of the dance studio by herself while the other students stretched along the barre under the direction of an instructor.

Eko observed her quietly. He didn't film. He had studied all the publicly available material on her, and now he wanted to see her in person. Luoying was dancing by herself, practicing the same set of moves again and again. A series of short hops followed by a high leap as her body spun several times in the air. Her dark leotard made her seem even more lithe and pale, and her ink-black hair was neatly pinned up in a bun. From time to time she took a break to get a drink of water, stopped to look outside, and then returned to her practice.

Eko was looking for the right subject, and he didn't yet know if she was the one. He took Theon's suggestion, though not for the reasons Theon tried to entice him with. He had little interest in following around a princess like some paparazzo. But after reviewing her public records and learning what she had done on Earth, he was curious. The reports he had read were in dry and spare prose, but the tension hidden between the lines intrigued him. He tried to imagine the girl, tried to guess where the tension had come from. She looked utterly unremarkable, like a small bottle whose bland white exterior belied the contradictory torrents of thought waging war within—a bottle that contained and concealed a turbulent sea.

The afternoon sunlight slanted to the other side of the dance school, and the long blades of grass cast shadows against the glass wall. Luoying was finished with her practice. She sat down, untied the ribbons from around her ankles, slipped off the pointe shoes, and packed them away. Smiling, she said goodbye to the teacher at the other end of the studio.

Eko was pacing back and forth some distance from the studio, trying to figure out a way to introduce himself to Luoying. At that moment a boy about Luoying's age approached the dance school along the footpath. He was tall and slender, with broad shoulders holding up a long uniform jacket, topped by a handsome face. Eko hid himself behind a tree.

The boy peeked inside the dance school, glanced at the time on his button, and waited on the lane outside. A few minutes later Luoying emerged with her backpack. The boy smiled and took the bag from her. The pair walked away together, side by side, without speaking.

The scene aroused Eko's curiosity. He saw between them a kind of simple tranquility, but he couldn't tell if they were a couple. They didn't kiss or hug, but he also didn't sense any polite distance. The way they had smiled at each other spoke of some shared understanding. The overall impression was one of being completely at ease, rather like the mood of Mars City itself. There was no sense of rush, of desperate need; rather, everything was without guile, artless.

It was such a stark contrast to the world Eko came from. He lived in a city whose prosperity was based on the entertainment industry. People rushed everywhere like fluttering birds and obsessed over their riddle-like relationships and statuses. He was used to the desperate need to be alluring and the harried sense of insecurity. But here, where everyone strolled around and paused to chat in the streets as though they had all the time in the world, he felt out of place.

Watching the two figures walking away, Eko tried to imagine Luoying's childhood, tried to imagine how one built a web of friendships and other relationships in this serene city. The idea of interviewing Luoying felt hollow. He turned and headed back toward the station.

On the tube train, Eko recalled the exhibition hall inside the archive. Crystal cubes of different sizes were scattered around the hall. Inside, he could see various scenes: three-dimensional figures moving about a miniature, vivid, living world. Next to each cube was a metal plaque explaining the film the scene was taken from. A sense of absurdity seized Eko. He realized that he was just like the tiny people inside those cubes. He also lived inside a crystal box—not just now, but since long before he had come to Mars.

THE STUDY

Side by side, Luoying and Anka walked along the glass-enclosed road. They had decided not to take the tube train from near the dance school. Instead, they'd walk directly to one of the hub stations. Both of them enjoyed walking.

The pedestrian tube was parallel to and below the tube for the train, narrow and winding. To walk through the glass tube was like walking through trouble, which naturally pushed the two closer together and forced them into the same direction. The tube was about three meters in diameter, and the bottom was suspended about half a meter above the ground. Through the transparent floor it was possible to see the red planet's surface.

The road itself was just wide enough to allow the two of them to squeeze together, shoulder to shoulder, without touching. Irises were planted along both sides. Both put their hands in their pockets, and their steps were synced. Luoying wore the dance team's uniform jacket, while Anka wore the uniform of his aerospace force squadron. The top of Luoying's head reached Anka's chin, and when she turned, she could see his firm neck and feel the rise and fall of his strong shoulders. Anka, on the other hand, could see her slender neck and smell the faint fragrance in her hair.

Luoying told Anka what was troubling her. For the first time she confessed her doubt to someone not part of her family. She had hoped to keep the secret from her friends in the Mercury Group—the very idea that she had been made one of them due to the intervention of some authority rather than because she deserved to be picked was humiliating. Since she was a little girl, she hated to be given special treatment because of who she was related to.

"Will everyone laugh at me?" she asked Anka.

Anka smiled. "Do you really think the rest of us are geniuses?"

"But you were selected because of your scores."

"It was just a test."

"Don't you think I unfairly benefited from my grandfather's power?"

"Don't be silly," said Anka. "You're still you."

Luoying felt better. Anka always had the special power to make anything that bothered her seem like not such a big deal. He wasn't talkative and disliked making grand, abstract arguments. Any problem, big or small, turned into no problem at all after he looked at it. As they talked, she began to think she was making too much of it as well. Anka simply listened as she talked, without asking many questions. This was their habit: if either had something to say, he or she said it; but if either chose to remain silent, the other didn't pry.

"Chania told me that you fainted after the banquet last night," said Anka. "Are you all right?"

"I'm fine."

"What happened?"

"Nothing. I was just too tired after the trip on *Maearth*."

"Then you shouldn't have come to practice today."

"But the recital is in twenty days! I still haven't even adjusted to the gravity."

It was the truth. Luoying had virtually no confidence in her ability to perform in twenty days. Yesterday afternoon she had tried to practice, and then she had fainted after the banquet. To adjust to the sudden change in gravity was much harder than she had anticipated.

Her solo dance was one of the headline acts at the world's fair. As a native of Mars, she was endowed with thinner bones and a strong sense of balance. Her training on Earth, on the other hand, forced her to become stronger than she would have been on Mars. A dance full of leaps and lightness under these conditions was the perfect opportunity to explore the limits of the human body. Researchers were thus very interested in her as a specimen. Terrans viewed her as an embodiment of the ancient tradition of dance developed on Earth, while the children of Mars were curious to see how a girl returning from another world had changed. She saw all these gazes—whether it was in the middle of the Boule Chamber, when she walked into the dance school, or when her image appeared on the giant screens at street corners—she saw those expectant gazes: intense, curious, judging, disapproving.

She didn't want to let Anka know how terrible the practice today had gone. Not only did she have trouble controlling her body in the air, but she couldn't even hit her takeoff or landing spots. She felt so light, and all the weight she had grown used to on Earth was gone. Her knees and ankles were sore and tired, like stories that had been retold so many times that they had lost all tension. A new gravity environment was not easy to adjust to: all the Terran visitors were wearing heavy metal shoes to help. But she had been forced to start to dance right away, before she had even relearned how to walk on this familiar-unfamiliar planet.

"Are you all finished with your training today?" she asked, trying to change the subject.

"No."

"Then won't you get in trouble for coming to meet me?"

"I just got back. I'll be fine."

"But you told me Captain Fitz is super strict."

Anka chuckled. "Don't worry about it. What's the worst that he can do? Expel me. It's no big deal. Anyway, we just had an argument."

"What happened?"

"Nothing. It was just an argument."

Luoying sensed there was more. "I thought everything was going smoothly. You even got a new uniform."

"It wasn't just for me. I just came back at the right time. All eleven squadrons of the aerospace force are getting new uniforms."

"Why? Are you planning some show?"

"No. The whole Flight System's budget got a fifty percent boost, so the budget for the aerospace force went up, too."

"But why?"

"I heard it has something to do with Ceres."

Luoying was silent for a while. "Do you think it also has to do with Earth?"

Anka was also silent for a while. Then he nodded. "I think so, actually."

He didn't elaborate, and the two continued on in silence. However, Luoying's concerns only grew. This wasn't the first time she had heard news like this. Anka belonged to the fifth squadron, whose duties normally involved industrial missions like transporting satellites and civil patrols. But in the event of a conflict, the squadron's aircraft could quickly be reconfigured as fighters. When she was seven, Luoying had once witnessed a cargo carrier rapidly transform into a fighter within five minutes. She was so astonished that she couldn't close her mouth, having been given a glimpse of the underbelly of her peaceful, ordinary life.

She couldn't tell how much Anka's information presaged the dangers of war. She didn't want war. Earth was where she had spent one of the most important periods of her life, no less important than her childhood on Mars. Regardless of who would win or lose, she didn't wish to see either world invaded by the flames of interplanetary violence.

After they got on the tube train at the hub station, it took only a few minutes to arrive at her home. Anka got off the train with her and said goodbye to her at the gate to her yard. Luoying gazed at Anka. His blue eyes often seemed a bit distracted. Seeing a tiny leaf had somehow fallen on the bridge of his nose, Luoying reached up to brush it off. He touched his nose and grinned at her.

"Get some rest," Anka said.

"I will."

"Don't trouble yourself with things that don't matter," he added. "You're still you."

He turned and got back on the train. Luoying remained alone in the garden and watched the train depart.

She knew he disliked drama. If he wanted to do something, he just did it instead of talking about it. He despised exaggerations. An "argument" with Captain Fitz was likely, in truth, an intense confrontation. *What happened?* She tried to imagine it and couldn't.

There were some words that she had never spoken to Anka, nor he to her.

She recalled what it was like five years ago when she had first emerged from the airport terminal on Earth. A tidal wave of engine noises assaulted her ears, and she was so frightened and shocked that she literally backed up several steps. The sky was filled with private aircraft of all sizes. Shuttling back and forth, the planes swept past each other, almost brushing the skyscrapers, seemingly avoiding disaster only at the last minute. She wrapped her arms around her luggage like a drowning girl clinging to a rock in the middle of a stormy sea. The sky was gray instead of the familiar dark blue of her home, nor the orange-red of a sandstorm. Everywhere was noise: rumbling, booming, buzzing, droning. Advertisements flashed no matter where she looked. Thousands of people rushed by her, as fast as flickering images on a screen. The other children had left her behind. Her friends shouted for her to keep up, as did the Terran official assigned to chaperone them, but she couldn't move. She was stuck where she was, hugging her luggage, drowning in the noise. Someone bumped into her, and her suitcase fell to the ground as though a mountain had collapsed.

Just then, a hand reached out and picked up her suitcase. His other hand grabbed hers and pulled her forward. He didn't demand to know why she was frozen in place. *We have to keep up,* he said, and pulled her along. He guided her through the crowd, parsing signs and jumping up from time to time to see where their official had gone. He looked so calm, so focused, his eyes roaming in every direction as he muttered decisively now and then. Soon they were reunited with the rest of their group. The entire process had taken no more than two minutes.

He had safely brought her into the new world.

He had smiled at her once on that day, but from then on, his was the only smile that took up space in her heart. She had never told him how she felt, and she didn't know how he felt about her.

The flowers of the garden bloomed in vibrant silence. The Barberton daisies, in particular, had grown so lush that the broad leaves practically covered the path through the garden.

_____

As soon as Luoying opened the door to the house, she heard loud, arguing voices. She paused for a minute to listen. The voices were coming from the living room; there seemed to be a large gathering in there.

She caught a few snippets of the conversation, and her heart began to beat faster. Quietly, she tiptoed up to the door of the living room and listened as she held her breath. Eavesdropping did not come naturally to her, and shame and the fear of being discovered made her stand still, not daring to touch anything.

Most of the voices she recognized. Ever since her grandfather had moved in with her and Rudy, these men—she called all of them uncles out of respect—became regular guests. The loudest voice belonged to Uncle Roowak, Archon of the Water System. He was deaf in one ear and always shouted with his good ear turned to the interlocutor, though he disliked people drawing attention to his condition. The one who spoke the fastest was Uncle Laak, the Registrar of Files, who always spoke seriously and in long paragraphs filled with dense citations. He knew so much that it was sometimes hard to understand him. The croaking voice belonged to Uncle Lanrang, Archon of the Land System, whose speech, though apparently in the common tongue, was virtually incomprehensible to Luoying, as it was filled with acronyms and numbers, sounding like a broken robot. And of course there was the booming voice of Uncle Juan, Archon of the Flight System. He was always present for these debates.

"I've told you a million times," said Juan, "what matters isn't the present but the future!"

"And I've told you just as often that the possibility they would achieve such capability within fifty years is well outside of five sigmas." That was Lanrang.

"So you're saying it *is* possible," said Juan.

"I can only say that it's not *im*possible," said Lanrang.

Roowak shouted, "By the laws of probability, *nothing* is entirely impossible. Given enough time, a monkey can produce Shakespeare. We can't just sit by and do nothing because of such a remote possibility!"

"It depends on what that possibility is!" Juan didn't back down an inch. "Even if there's only a one-in-a-million chance that they'll develop a controlled nuclear fusion engine, we can't give them the technology. Don't tell me you accept the responsibility—you can't handle it! Do you really think they come in friendship? Let me tell you, if we give them fusion tech today, tomorrow they'll be back in warships."

"Then what do you suggest?" Roowak was growing agitated. "They won't give us the plans for the hydraulic engineering hub. Without it, we can't do anything with Ceres. What's the point of devoting so much effort to get the asteroid here if we're just going to park it in space? Without water, we're doomed."

"It's simple." Juan's voice softened. "We can't get what we want without a credible threat."

Laak, who hadn't spoken for a while, broke in.

"Roowak, are you sure we have to have the plans for the hub?

They've already agreed to give us the electrical control systems, right? What if we… figure out how to build the dams ourselves?"

"Figure it out?" Roowak, who was still shouting, also made an effort to control himself. "How exactly do you propose we do that? Where am I going to get the data to run the simulations? Where do I find a lab to experiment with river-flow characteristics? Do we even have a river? I must have real turbulence impact data. I can't even run a Monte Carlo simulation without it. This is engineering, not a game. Without data, I can't promise anything."

Three seconds of silence. Three long seconds during which it seemed that the tension was going to explode like an overfilled balloon. Finally, Luoying heard the voice of her grandfather.

"Juan, nonviolence is a fundamental principle," said Hans Sloan in his deep voice. "We haven't reached a crisis point. They never mentioned fusion technology as a nonnegotiable term, and there's no reason for us to bring it up first. Let's pretend it isn't an issue and see how far we get in the negotiations."

Juan's tone seemed to relax just a bit. "Fine, but we have to reach a consensus among ourselves on where to draw the line."

"The consensus is nonviolence." After a pause, Hans continued. "Of course you are still free to voice your opinion."

A moment later Luoying heard the squeaking of chairs and shoes and the rustling of clothing, indicating that everyone was getting up. She tiptoed her way back to the entrance of the house and pretended to have just come in. Looking in the mirror, she changed out of her dance clothes and fussed with her hair.

The adults emerged from the living room. First was Roowak, followed by Laak and Lanrang, side by side. Roowak was the tallest, like a coat-tree, and the contrast with the tiny figure of Lanrang behind him made the latter seem even more shriveled. Lanrang's beard was sparse and unkempt, but his lively eyes gave him an efficient air. Laak had the kindest face of all three. He reminded Luoying of a thoughtful professor with drooping eyes and sharp lines at the corners of his mouth, indicating long hours spent contemplating difficult dilemmas.

Rudy had told Luoying that Roowak was an engineer turned military commander, Lanrang was a math genius, and Laak was a master linguist. All three were key figures in the Martian rebuilding effort after the war.

She smiled and greeted them as though she had just come in. Her heart raced, and she was worried that her trembling voice would betray what she had done. Luckily, they were so full of their own worries that none paid any attention. They walked by her seriatim, smiled at her, patted her on the shoulder to welcome her back to Mars. Then they put on their jackets and left.

As he passed her, Laak, the Registrar of Files, paused and explained apologetically that he had received her note but hadn't had a chance to respond. He was going to be in the office the next few days, and she was welcome to come find him.

"Thank you, Uncle Laak," said Luoying. "I really appreciate it."

The last one to emerge from the living room was Juan. His face, dark and leathery, and his prominent paunch made him resemble a painting of a spice merchant from India from eight hundred years before. Despite his figure, he moved with agility and efficiency. He wore a thick mustache curved up at both ends, and his dark, bushy eyebrows went some way to soften his piercing gaze. When he first came into the entrance hall, his expression was severe and wolfish; but as soon as he saw Luoying, his face cracked into a wide grin, and he picked her up just as he used to when she was a little girl.

"Look at you! My little bunny is back." He spun her once around and set her back down. "You're still so light! Did they starve you over there on Earth? Or were you too picky with your food?"

"I... I'm a dancer."

"So? A dancer must also eat! Put on some weight and you'll dance even better!"

"I won't be able to leap as high then."

"That's no big deal. What's the point of jumping like a

grasshopper? Whatever you want to eat, eat! And if you run out of ideas, come find me. Let me tell you, your Uncle Juan has turned eating into an art. Did you enjoy the desserts last night at the banquet?"

"I sure did! I ate two helpings."

"Aha! I was responsible for those. Put them in the oven myself."

"I had no idea you were such a skilled baker!... Oh, Uncle Juan, I heard you talk about your grandmother last night—"

"Did you?" Juan laughed uproariously. Luoying was befuddled by this unexpected reaction. Juan went on. "Little bunny, you have to understand that in a negotiation someone has to play the role of the reasonable adult, while someone else has to scare them a bit, like a madman. Your grandfather loves being reasonable, which means I have to go scare people. That doesn't seem fair, does it? I've complained to Hans many times that we need to switch roles once in a while."

Juan continued to laugh. He promised to have Luoying over to his house for dinner soon and then left.

Watching his departing figure, Luoying wasn't sure what to think. She saw how the laughter had slid off Juan's face the moment he turned away and how his gaze had again acquired that terrifying piercing quality. As he strode away, his back was as erect as a tree and his upper body never wavered. She remembered that Uncle Juan had always called her "little bunny" and loved to tease her, asking her what she wanted to do when she was grown up.

She knew the answer now. *When I'm grown up, I want to understand what lies behind the words, not just the words themselves.*

The entrance hall fell quiet. She turned around and saw Rudy and Grandfather at the door to the living room, chatting in low voices. Through the floor-to-ceiling window at the end of the hall, she could see that the red surface of the planet appeared almost brown with the angle of the light, and the thorn apple flowers glowed silver. The two of them seemed to be arguing, but Luoying couldn't be sure. She saw that Grandfather's expression was so severe that the blood seemed to have drained from his face. Only very rarely had she seen him so troubled. In her memory, she could recall only a scene from a news broadcast, after Grandfather had pacified a brewing rebellion in the Boule, when he had looked like this. Back then, Hans Sloan had strode into the Boule Chamber and sat down in a chair in the middle. Without saying a single word, the chamber quieted down as the legislators saw his face.

"... but a principle isn't the same as a line that cannot be crossed," she heard Rudy say.

"Of course it is," said Grandfather. "If it can be crossed, then it isn't a principle at all."

She realized then that her worries had been justified. There was a looming crisis. If the negotiations failed, war would follow. The Terrans wanted controlled nuclear fusion.

———————

Back in her room, she dropped her backpack on the floor and slid to the floor herself. This had been a long afternoon for her. The snippets of conversation she had heard were rough, technical, and abbreviated, but they were enough to give her an outline of the situation. Distracted, she took a bath. Soaking in the tub, she allowed her mind to wander as the world disappeared in the steam.

It had been some time since she had heard such frank discussion of politics. When she was little, such discussions were a part of her daily life. Many of her parents' friends gathered at their home to talk politics while gulping cup after cup of bitter coffee, filling the walls with projected maps. But on Earth it was rare to encounter real politics. Other than the Reversionist movement, which flared up in the year before her return to Mars, most of her time there had been spent in the pursuit of lighthearted diversions. It was as though she had lived in a bubble, a champagne-flavored, fun bubble. The bitter coffee aroma of political debates seemed unfamiliar to her now.

It wasn't just because she had avoided the company of policy makers on Earth. It was more a consequence of mood and atmosphere. Unlike the politicians she had met on Earth, the decision-makers on Mars had a seriousness of purpose. They often spoke of universal responsibilities and the ultimate goal of humankind, but the politicians on Earth rarely uttered such phrases. On Earth the news was dominated by events such as some government filing for bankruptcy with the World Bank, a head of state somewhere making a film to boost tourism to their country, the chief diplomat of some country making a promise to buy the government bonds of another country... It was as though countries were just large companies, and the politicians their executives. She rarely heard the kind of news that was common on Mars: a plan to divert the orbit of some asteroid or dwarf planet; an attempt to build a new model for human survival; collecting and cataloging the fruits of human civilization; ascertaining the sources of errors in simulations of human history; and so on. She often wondered if alien visitors might, based on the news broadcast on the two planets, come to the conclusion that the population of Earth was only twenty million and that of Mars twenty billion, as opposed to the other way around.

The debate in the living room just then seemed to her unreal. When she was a little girl, she had been impressed by such grand visions and heroic words. But on Earth she had lost her enthusiasm for them. There was no one who persuaded her to abandon her faith, but she had ceased to believe. Her encounter with a far larger portion of humanity, with their chaotic and selfish desires, had confused her. She no longer saw a Humanity waiting to be changed, or a Civilization that entrusted its hope to Mars. Those visions, which had once seemed full of grandeur to her, now appeared as magnificent illusions, mere windmill giants.

She understood that she was lost. There was no question that the men who had been in her house today represented the ideal of Martian life: they were the best in the fields of scientific research, engineering, exploration, and development. They stood at the peak where all the roads on Mars—solemn and honor-strewn roads—converged. But she had no idea how they could show her the way she wanted to go for her own future.

She closed her eyes and sank deeper into the warm bathwater. Through the steam-fogged walls of the bathroom, she knew that the monitor by her bed glowed with the log-in page for her personal space. She wasn't looking at it, but she couldn't escape its presence.

She had to make a choice soon. She needed to register with an atelier and establish her identity. It was a step that every child on Mars had to take to become an adult. An atelier gave one an identification number, established the credentials for acquiring the necessities of life and for expressing and living a life. All jobs, passports, documents, and credits were linked to the number. She had not logged in yet; it was as though she didn't exist, hadn't yet returned from Earth.

But she didn't want to choose an atelier. Just as a woman returning from a war didn't want to go to a regular job.

For most people on Mars, the choice of an atelier was a choice for life. Yes, some did change ateliers, but most stuck with their initial decision and climbed the career ladder year by year. Luoying didn't want to live like that, though she knew that was how everyone on Mars lived.

During her five years on Earth, she moved fourteen times and lived in twelve different cities. She tried out seven different jobs and built up five different groups of friends. She lost all certainty that she knew how to plan the rest of her life. She could no longer accept monotony, and she found hierarchy revolting. What had seemed to her the natural order of life in childhood now appeared as unbearable restraints. She wished she felt otherwise, but there it was.

The log-in screen continued to glow. She refused to go near it.

Next to the monitor, on the window ledge, was a collection of toys: a walking-singing electronic clock, a thermometer shaped like a strawberry, a mechanical doll, a lamp made from orange and green glass. Luoying stared at the collection, almost disbelieving that she had once treasured them. But there they were, a frozen memorial of the world of a thirteen-year-old girl.

She climbed out of the bathtub and dried herself in the heating booth. She put on her pajamas, and the fragrance of fresh laundry gave her some comfort. She stared at herself in the mirror as though looking as a stranger. Under her wet hair, her pale neck seemed too thin and delicate, not at all what she had hoped for herself. She wanted to be strong and clear-headed, with definite ideas about how to live, how to choose, how to live a thoughtful, determined, lucid life.

She did not want to be the confused and pale girl in the mirror.

———

Her hair pinned up, she padded out of her room. She was going down the hall to find Grandfather.

He had said yesterday that they were going to have dinner together tonight, to pray for her parents on the anniversary of their deaths. But after searching through every room, she didn't find Rudy or Hans. Inside the kitchen, a prepared dinner was being warmed in the cooker.

She sighed, staring at the glass dishes and the empty dining room. In the end, Grandfather couldn't keep his promise. She didn't blame him. He was, after all, consul of Mars, and she knew now the Terran negotiations were pushing them toward a crisis.

Leaving the kitchen, she climbed the stairs to the study on the second floor.

She wanted to talk to her parents by herself, to ask them how she ought to choose her life.

Luoying was only eight when her mother and father died. There were many things she didn't understand at the time, or perhaps she did but then forgot about them. On Earth, there was a time when she had tried to shut off her past deliberately. And unfortunately, when a door was shut for too long, it was impossible to open up again. To make herself stronger, she had cut herself off from her memories. And now, after trying to be strong for so long, she no longer had the key to go back.

The study looked just the way she had last seen it five years ago, which was the same as the way it had been ten years ago, when her parents died. This was where her father read and wrote, where her mother sculpted, and where they discussed politics with their friends. A tea service still sat on the table, with tiny spoons on saucers, as though the guests had only departed for a break and would return shortly. Her mother's tools sat on a shelf, and an unfinished sculpture rested on the workbench.

Everything was carefully maintained. But the room was too perfect. The window ledge and the corners of the window frames were so clean that it was obvious at a glance that no one lived here anymore.

The bookcases in the study were custom designed by her father. Together, they resembled some architectural wonder: tall and short, horizontal and vertical, the beams and buttresses raised frozen words into the air like some imaginary castle. The bookcases were submerged in the evening shadow. The whole room seemed to be gazing upon the past. The people were gone, but memories remained.

Luoying remembered that her parents' lives had always been connected with art. She could no longer recall the details, but that sense of art intermingling with life, with exchange and conversation, lingered.

Slowly, she walked along the walls, picking up and examining everything before setting it back down, trying to imagine what it was like when her parents had held it.

On a small table in the corner, she saw a photo album standing open. The photograph was one of her parents together.

She picked up the album, a memorial book, and flipped through it. There were photos from Mom's and Dad's child-hoods: school awards, portraits taken at a dance, records of achievements in science and art. Both of them had been accomplished youths. Dad had written, directed, and starred in a historical drama. Photographs of the production showed intricate sets projected onto the stage of a small community theater, and her father, performing the role of a hero about to be executed for his beliefs, stood in front of other teenagers with a determined expression. Mom had always loved painting and sculpting, and one of her early paintings, the winner of a competition, was still on display in the community museum. Both of them had chosen to join an engineering atelier, but their love of art continued unabated unto death.

As she looked through the photos, Luoying remembered that when she was a little girl, her favorite place in the world was with her mother in here, while she sculpted.

And just like that, she seemed to see Mom standing next to one of the bookcases. Her long hair was braided, coiled, and pinned atop her head. She gazed intently at Luoying, full of love, before rushing back to the workbench and the lump of clay. Her hands kneaded and squeezed, the sculpting knife carving away the excess to reveal the outline of what she was making. Luoying saw herself sitting in the chair, a bow in her hair and a doll in her arms, staring curiously at her mother, infected by her passion for her art.

Then she saw Dad. He was next to them, leaning against one of the bookcases, wearing a brown shirt and a wool vest. One of his feet was on top of a chair, and he rested an arm against the other leg as his hand sketched something in the air with a pen. The expression on his face was one of intense concentration as he recounted a period of history to his audience. The audience, other men and women her parents' age, discussed history and art and debated ideas that stirred the heart. She didn't understand everything they said, but she loved listening to them.

The visions awakened her memory. Bit by bit, the past sealed in her head seeped out and filled the rest of the night-shrouded room.

She realized that she had not in fact forgotten—she just hadn't thought of them for a long time.

On a page of the memorial book she saw the following: *From that day on, Adele officially became a person without an atelier.*

How could her mother be without an atelier? Luoying glanced at the date on the page: it was the year she turned six. There was no explanation elaborating the statement. She flipped back to the front of the book, where there was a copy of her mother's curriculum vitae. Indeed, there was nothing about the last two years of Mom's life. Everything simply came to an abrupt stop, like an unfinished play.

Mom didn't want to register either! A bittersweet feeling filled Luoying's heart. She felt connected to her mother's soul, despite the yawning gulf of death. She was not alone in her confusion, and her own troubles seemed suffused with her parents' influence and legacy. Her vagabond days and consequent anxiety were not so strange after all. She had wandered afar only to return to the path her mother had chosen.

But why had Mom done it? Her own confusion was the result of her time on Earth, but what had happened to her mother to make her fall into the same kind of self-doubt until she chose to belong to no set identity, no atelier?

She wanted to find out more about her mother's experiences, but there was nothing more in the memorial book. Carefully, Luoying placed the album back on the table. She turned to the bookcases, thinking perhaps they held more clues.

By the moonlight, she saw a bouquet of white flowers resting in the shadow of the legs of the semicircular table at the other end of the study. This was a traditional piece of Chinese furniture, also called a crescent table. With the flat side placed against the wall, it was intended for vases and other decorations.

The flowers were lilies, their stems wrapped in green tissue. The bouquet had been so well hidden that she had missed it when she came in earlier.

She walked over and picked up the bouquet. Below it was a card.

Forgive me.

The handwriting belonged to Grandfather. Her heart pounded.

So he had been here. Even though they couldn't have dinner together, he had kept his promise.

Luoying examined the card, perplexed. The card glowed a pale white in the moonlight, and the dark, angular strokes appeared particularly striking.

What had Hans Sloan done that he needed to beg forgiveness from her parents? She recalled how Grandfather had looked at the photograph of her parents on the day of her return. It was a look full of love and longing.

Forgive me.

She looked at the words again and froze, thunderstruck.

The scene from earlier in the afternoon, when Grandfather had looked so severe while talking to Rudy, came to her mind. Her heart seemed to stop as she finally remembered where she had seen that broadcast of her grandfather in the Boule Chamber.

It was just before she left for Earth. She was in the living room, trying to find a film she wanted to watch. By happenstance, she triggered a recording that someone else in the house had just finished playing.

She had stared, fascinated, as Grandfather strode across the Boule Chamber, full of rebellious agitation, and sat down. She saw his cold face as the chamber quieted.

And then the real Hans Sloan had appeared in the door of the living room. She rushed to turn off the recording as though caught doing something forbidden.

THE FAIR

Eko turned his hotel room into a screening room. One whole wall, smooth and clear, adjusted to be opaque, served as the perfect projection surface. Except for when he was out filming, Eko spent all his time in the room, completely immersed in the work left by his teacher on Mars.

Davosky's films were like nothing Eko had ever seen. His teacher was like a child who asked endless questions in the form of films. He had lost all interest in clichéd techniques and narrative tricks but simply showed his subjects in the most direct manner possible, displaying every detail that struck him as interesting.

To go through Davosky's films was like reading a journal of those eight years. He wasn't interested in a chronicle of what was happening to him but wielded the camera as a tool for recording thought, shot by shot. Every shot was a sentence. Many of the recordings were incomplete, and in the archives they were tagged as "unpublicized," like casual notes or sketches dashed off in a journal. There were, however, twenty completed films of various lengths. None had titles, and all were identified only with sequence numbers.

At the start of one film, the camera focused on a girl in a pink skirt. The camera roamed from left to right, from head to foot, capturing every detail. A voice-over told the audience to pay attention, because this was the last time we would see her. And then the camera rushed toward the girl and the scene faded to black, implying that the viewer had merged with the subject. After that, everything was shot from the perspective of the girl, like a soul locked into a new body, and yet the viewer was constantly aware of the girl's presence, like a transparent shell wrapped around the camera. The girl then engaged in a series of ordinary activities, but the everyday now seemed unapproachably remote. The camera was at once detached and smug, expressing with precise clarity the sensation of a self-aware consciousness that couldn't see through the superficial, a self trapped in a shell also called *self*.

Precision, yes, that was the word to describe every form of filmic expression Davosky attempted and explored.

Before coming to Mars, Eko had suffered a bout of doubt over his chosen profession. Filmmaking was gradually being drained of craft. The popularization of full-fidelity holographic technology meant that anyone was a director, not only of home videos, but also of epic series with elaborate sets that engaged all the senses, including smells, temperature, and humidity, so that a viewer with a special headset could be completely immersed. Filmmakers turned their attention elsewhere. No longer was the focus on details like framing, camera technique, movement, and so on, but all effort was devoted to complicated plots. But Davosky was showing Eko that the best way to speak the language of film wasn't to focus on novelty but on uniqueness.

Many of Davosky's films were in fact flats. The limits of two-dimensional film became for him advantages. In one film, the protagonist was a young man who suddenly got the idea of taking a photograph of himself every day right before he went to bed in order to have a record of how he changed. At first, the man needed to set an alarm to remind himself, but eventually it became a habit, a ritual to be followed without thinking every night after eating, talking, and bathing. One day, after getting off work and returning home, the man was bored and decided to look through his photographs. He prepared dinner and poured himself a glass of wine, sat on the couch in darkness, and scrubbed through the photos one by one as they were projected onto the wall. The camera followed his gaze and went to the wall, showing the viewer one photo after another. At first, it was impossible to see any change, but gradually the man aged. The sequence reached the man as he was at that moment, but didn't stop. Portrait after portrait, the man's face wrinkled and his back hunched, until finally the sequence stopped with him as an ancient, shriveled figure. Abruptly the camera pulled back to the man sitting in the dark, remote control in hand. He had died from old age, but his dinner remained on the coffee table, untouched. The camera lingered on him, and the silence was filled with the solemnity of Death.

Davosky also made plenty of holographic films. In these, he took advantage of the ability of the technology to greatly magnify minuscule details. In one of his films, the protagonist suffered from a nervous condition that forced him to obsess over the calluses on his hands, constantly fighting the urge to scratch them off. To prevent harming himself, the man tried to divert his attention elsewhere. The hissing of the furnace coming to life in the walls tortured him. He envied those who didn't seem to be bothered by the imperfection of their hands, and as a result he began to obsess over *their* hands, and the new obsession tortured him even more. To the viewer, deeply immersed in the holographic milieu, the protagonist's sensitivity and pain became oppressively magnified. In one scene the protagonist overheard two engineers discussing the potential for a big project to fail, leading to a planetary crisis; and yet, for the viewer, the soul-searing pain of helpless obsession and the calluses on the protagonist's hands were far more immediate, real, and overwhelming.

Even though Eko was spending practically all his time in the hotel room, he couldn't finish all the films. He discovered that Davosky was constantly questioning the certainty of life and personhood. With his films, Davosky strove to dissect the details of daily life and to put them back together again, and every aspect of reality was unstable, fluid, capable of being amplified or dissolved. In the process, many meanings faded away, and strange conclusions emerged unbidden.

Eko began to understand why his teacher had chosen to remain on Mars. All of these films, all of these experimental narratives and scenes, had zero market potential on Earth. Davosky was interested in the dissolution of life, an interest that no one needed. What people on Earth craved was pointers for how to live a good life, not pointers for how to live outside of life. On the web, the easiest sort of film to sell was something that satisfied a need: an illusion to provide the comfort of conversation to the lonely, for instance, or something with the fragrance of perfume, the stench of blood, an enigmatic oracle, and scenes of brave heroes saving beauties through valiant struggles. This was the sort of thing that holographic films excelled at. To be sure, films that allowed the antisocial to vent their sentiments also had plenty of consumers, but no one was going to buy Davosky's creations. It mattered little how intricately or subtly they were constructed—they couldn't survive in a world dependent on the market.

Davosky had stored all his films in the central archive. After he went back to Earth, Janet became the custodian of his personal space.

Eko wasn't very clear on the structure or design of the central archive, but he knew enough to understand that it was enormous in capacity. When he had conducted his search, he had headed directly for Davosky's personal space, but along the way, he got a peek at thousands upon thousands of side branches and passages, like the boughs of an ancient tree. He tried to calculate how much memory it held. If every Martian who had ever lived had a personal space, then there were at least tens of millions of such spaces. Add to that the spaces allocated to the hundreds of thousands of ateliers, the constantly changing public spaces, exhibition spaces, interactive spaces, and the whole central archive was another Mars City, a gigantic virtual metropolis. Everyone's personal space was like their home, and the city's electronic forums were like the public squares. The homes were used to store authored creations, while the public forums were for announcements inviting all to visit. It really was like an ancient tree that ever ramified and refreshed itself.

Eko didn't wander about the larger central archive, mostly because he lacked the time, but also because of Janet Brook's request.

Please keep this a secret, all right? she had asked him when she handed him the password. *Other than Arthur, we've never given an outsider access to the central archive. Many things stored there are free and open but important to us. As a custodian, I shouldn't do this, really. But you're Arthur's student, and I think you deserve to see his legacy. Not just his films, but also the world he lived in.* She glanced down at her hands, her voice still ragged from crying. *I want someone else to help me remember. The archive holds the eight years Arthur spent here, and I'm afraid that when I die, no one will know what he did. You can see whatever you like in his space and even copy his films. But please, keep this a secret, all right?*

Absolutely, Eko had promised.

He would tell no one. He had never mentioned his teacher's secret to anyone either. Davosky had left the most important part of his life here, and he would sustain it with his silence. His teacher had left behind these films, and Janet had unlocked the space in which they were hidden. These were the most precious gifts he had ever received. He wanted to wander through this universe slowly, to truly understand what his teacher had found, to understand the reasons why he had stayed on Mars and then left.

For Eko, Earth's unstoppable trend toward the vulgarization of everything was *the* disease of the twenty-second century. The debasement of knowledge had swept the world since the twentieth century, but back then, remnants of the classical age still survived, and there were still a brave few who lived for grand and noble ideas, for wisdom. By the twenty-second century, however, all nobility had dissolved, and no one cared about the life of ideals. Sight and imagination alike had shrunken to just a few inches in front of the nose. Without the pursuit of higher ideals, civilization itself turned vulgar. This was an illness from which everyone suffered, including Eko himself. He had come to Mars filled with doubt, uncertain if his teacher had found answers here.

Viewed from the perspective of an individual, the world was just a room. She could choose to live her whole life in one room, or she could open a door and enter another. The thought of leaving a familiar room was terrifying, but the passage between rooms took only the blink of an eye. Measured by the conventional yardstick of space, a person was much smaller than a room, but when you measured everything by the individual, a room was simply one tiny part of the stream that was life itself. On a map of time, a person was far grander than a room.

Superficially, there wasn't much to distinguish the creative life on Mars and Earth. Artists created, publicized their work, attempted to find an audience that loved their creations. But Eko understood the fundamental difference between the two. On Earth, there were also spaces where anyone was free to publish their work, and at a glance the spaces were fair and democratic. But these spaces were like supermarkets, ruled by the iron law of novelty. Every piece of art that entered such spaces was like a bottle of milk with an expiration date. Unless it found a buyer, it would be mercilessly removed from the shelves and thrown away. Three days, or maybe thirty days; commerce or death. Every warehouse aimed to have zero inventory, and every buyer craved the fresh and new. If no one paid attention to some work, then even bits could rot and decay. Theoretically, an author's work could stay quietly on the shelves indefinitely until discovered by the right audience, but in reality that never happened. Without the promise of a quick deal, there was no one willing to pay for storage. Theodor Adorno once said that "the hope of the intellectual is not that he will have an effect on the world, but that someday, somewhere, someone will read what he wrote exactly as he wrote it." The hope, some two hundred years after his death, turned out ultimately to be only a mirage.

There was no room for the pursuit of higher ideals in a world dedicated to instant commerce. Eko had survived seven years in such a supermarket, between the ages of eighteen and twenty-five. In an effort to reach for higher ideals, he had taken the risky step of separating himself from the larger market. His films belonged to a much smaller market akin to specialized stores that sold only organic fruits at high prices. By distinguishing themselves from industrial producers, sellers and buyers who transacted there found their own circle of dedicated fans and artists. Like an apple tree grown in the southern part of Kansas, he didn't bear many fruits, but what he did produce had a special flavor of nostalgia. This was his style, but it was also the result of Theon's plans. From the start, Theon had cultivated Eko and told him that having a stable base of patrons was the key to selling.

Despite his relatively stable setup, Eko still had to rush about on Earth to serve the market. He climbed skyscrapers and sat at expensive metal desks where he made his pitch to the potential sponsors of his next film. He smoked cigarettes with fashionable flavors with them and, instead of artistic vision, spoke to them of his market share. Twice a week he went on the web to do a meet and greet with netizens, where he put on a pose and hawked his latest products and productized his life. The amount of time he put into these commercial pursuits exceeded the time he spent creating.

But none of this was necessary on Mars. The creators of Mars didn't worry about making a living, didn't have to have release plans, didn't make advertisements, didn't chase after profit. It was a way of life that Eko couldn't even imagine, but he found himself deeply drawn to it. For him, to not have to worry about food and rent, to spend all day discussing creation and inspiration, was more ideal than anything else.

Eko wanted to meet with Janet again after he had made his way through all of Davosky's films. He couldn't understand why his teacher had left Mars. It was as though a man had escaped to the wilderness, where he built himself a hut and a new life out of the raw material available to him; but then, on the day he was putting the finishing touches on his new home, he decided to move back to the city he had abandoned. A new world was just taking shape as he faded back into the old.

Why? he wondered. *Is the passage between rooms a revolving door?*

In the morning, as was his habit, Eko went to the Grand Hall of the Expo Center.

The Expo Center was the tallest habitable building on all of Mars, and it was the main site of the world's fair as well. All the wonders brought by the Terran delegation were shown there, and the negotiations between the two sides took place in the Council Chamber of the building as well. The Expo Center was architecturally distinct: a five-story pyramid. The Grand Hall took up the entirety of the first floor, and each floor was smaller than the one below it, until one reached the top floor, which consisted only of the Council Chamber.

At that very moment the Terran delegates were deep in negotiations in the Council Chamber while Martians streamed through the Grand Hall, examining the goods from Earth.

Before the world's fair took over, the Expo Center served the role of a museum of science and technology. Typically the glass columns in Martian houses had pigments mixed in to hide the wires and machinery that kept the houses running. But the Expo Center was different. The Grand Hall had many thick columns, all of which were transparent to reveal the internal machinery, like tanks at an aquarium, or perhaps X-ray photographs of living organisms. Every column was accompanied by a plaque that explained the technology inside, as well as the inventor and a brief history of its evolution. Every feature of the building depended on these machines and circuits: insulation, heating, shielding against cosmic rays, water and air reclamation, and so on. The building was a miniature ecosystem. Eko read the plaques and took photographs, enjoying what he was learning.

On a typical morning Eko carried out his responsibilities as a member of the Terran delegation by shooting some footage of the Martian fairgoers and the negotiations in the Council Chamber. After that, he preferred to wander about the city and capture scenes of Martian life that he found interesting. To be honest, the negotiations bored him. Both sides kept on repeating the same points as though hoping by repetition to convince the other side. A news briefing summary that could be used every day without change would be: *Both sides exchanged their views in a friendly manner and continued discussing key points.* Anyone familiar with diplomatic negotiations would know that it meant there was no substantive progress.

The Terran delegation's impressive demands disguised its internal chaos. The wishes of the delegate from one country were often thwarted by the delegate from another. Whatever Antonov had promised one moment would be contradicted by Wang the next. Unlike the united front that prevailed among the Martian representatives, the Terran delegates had no consensus and fought as hard among themselves as they did with the Martians. The economic crisis on Earth had worsened, and technology stocks were plunging in every country, which meant that every nation hoped for Martian technology to get them out of the recession while not benefiting competing nations too much. Eko found the geopolitics tiresome and tried to spend as little time at the Expo Center as possible.

But this morning was different. As soon as he put on the camera glasses, he saw Luoying in the Grand Hall. She was dressed casually and walking together with two other girls her age. Also with them were two boys about thirteen or fourteen.

Eko grew excited. This was a rare opportunity. He knew he wanted to include Luoying in his documentary, but he didn't want to chase after her like a spy. He had a bloodhound's nose for the best shots, but he was also as stubborn as a block of hardwood. He despised the idea of filming her in secret, when she was in private spaces; even if such shots sometimes worked better, he refused to contemplate them. Three days earlier, he had seen her at the dance school, but he hadn't bumped into her anywhere else. She trained hard every day, and he didn't know how to meet her. He wasn't even sure if he would get to talk to her today.

Luoying was dressed in a pair of dark gray dance pants— not tights for practice, but comfortable and loose. Over a short blouse she wore a long tunic that swayed in sync with her pants, projecting a relaxed air.

Eko observed her from afar, trying to deduce her personality from her appearance. Her hair was loosely clipped, giving the same relaxed feel as her outfit. She looked as if she didn't care much about what was around her. Though she was walking with a group, she wasn't talking much, looking rather absentminded. He didn't know if this was how she always was or if she was preoccupied today, but he was drawn to her sense of being adrift.

Luoying walked in the middle of the group, allowing the others to steer her where they wanted. She strode lightly, in sharp contrast to the bouncing gait of the vivacious redheaded girl next to her.

Eko approached them but kept his distance. Since this was a public space, he began to film with a telephoto lens.

Of the three girls and two boys, Eko recognized one: Ruao

Beverley, Peter's son. He was something like a princeling, Eko supposed, the only one in the Terran delegation. He was playing tour guide to the other kids, showing off as he pointed to this and that and held forth. The other boy was a bit chubby and half a head taller than Ruao. He didn't look as sophisticated as Ruao, but there was a stubbornness on his face as he argued with Ruao.

Ruao appeared to be losing the argument. A look of displeasure took over his face as he strode away, his lips pursed. The other boy, dressed in a white shirt, chased after him.

"Toutou, be nice to our guest!" the redheaded girl called after him.

Eko was amused. He liked filming ordinary people going through their daily lives. He enjoyed capturing scenes that showed their pride, disdain, competitiveness, surprise. Every day at the world's fair, he got to see different types of Martians. They reacted to the wonders of Earth in their own ways, all of which were different from the kinds of reactions he was used to on Earth.

Eko sped up to get closer to the kids.

The kids stopped at the showcase for health products. The boy named Toutou pointed to a gizmo. "What's this?"

Now that he was being consulted for his expertise, Ruao perked up. "That's an ion pot. It analyzes your body to produce the ideal drink for you, guaranteeing perfect nutrition. There's also a probe that comes with it that measures your blood pH and concentrations of trace elements so that you are always at your healthiest."

Toutou laughed. "That sounds like the ramblings of a fool."

The redheaded girl hit him gently on the back. "Don't talk like that!"

Toutou refused to back down. "Of course it's nonsense.

113

Your body maintains its own homeostasis. What's the point of a gadget like that?"

Ruao answered, "You're being pretty ignorant. Experts tell us that, left alone, the human body always fluctuates around the optimal point without ever quite reaching the ideal."

"What's wrong with fluctuations?" asked Toutou. "That's how the body works!"

Ruao shook his head. "You are too full of yourself. My family owns the latest model of the pot. There was one time when I didn't use it for a month, and I felt exhausted all the time. When I caught a cold, it lingered."

Toutou laughed. "That's not hard to explain. Once you become dependent on something like that, your body loses its ability to maintain itself." His eyes turned into two slits as he grinned. "My teacher told us that Terrans love to manufacture nonexistent desires and needs."

Eko was startled. Toutou was right. The heart of commerce was desire, and when desires were satisfied, new needs must be manufactured. Whoever managed to create a new desire would own that market. The principle was familiar to everyone, but hearing it from the mouth of a child was something else. It meant that Martian education focused on the faults of a market economy from an early age. He wasn't sure how much Toutou really understood, or if he was merely parroting what he had heard.

Ruao twisted his face away awkwardly. He wanted to be like his father, who always managed to look composed regardless of the situation. But Ruao was too young to know the art of crafting himself like a chameleon for every audience, and so he managed only to look petulant. All his features were bunched up on his narrow face. He was the ideal product of a society that worshipped the sale, and he believed in advertisements like articles of truth. He honestly thought those who had something to sell wanted the best for the buyer.

"What about you, then, eh?" he said. "You suppress desires. You suppress human nature itself."

"Shut up!" Toutou was getting angry, too. "It's obvious that you make up desires."

"You suppress desires."

"You—"

"All right. All right!" the redheaded girl broke in. "Look at the two of you, resorting to playground tactics. Why don't you… let Luoying here be the judge of who's right?" She pulled on Luoying's arm, hoping she would find a way to de-escalate.

Luoying seemed to emerge from her own world. She looked at the girl and then at the two boys. Calmly she said, "I suppose desires are specific to places."

The redheaded girl seemed to feel this answer was much too ambivalent to prevent the argument from flaring up again. She tried to get Luoying to elaborate. "When you were on Earth, did you go shopping like crazy?"

"I wasn't obsessive about it. But, yes, I shopped."

"Did you buy a new pair of shoes every month?"

"I suppose."

"Even if the shoes you owned were perfectly fine?"

"Sure."

"Why?"

"No particular reason. If you lived on Earth, you'd do the same."

"But why?"

Luoying thought for a moment. "When I was part of the dance troupe on Earth, shopping was… a kind of entertainment. It's like our dance parties."

"Really?" The redheaded girl was now completely absorbed

by this new line of inquiry and had forgotten the boys. "I don't understand. Are you saying it's different buying things on Earth versus here?"

"It *is* different."

"But *how* is it different? You've never told me the details of your life on Earth. What was it like in the dance troupe? Didn't you have dance parties?"

"I did go to dance parties, but they weren't like what we have here," said Luoying. "Over there… it's just a lot of strangers. You met up; you danced. You didn't even need to bring anyone. And they weren't held every week at a set time. Sometimes we'd dance and party for several days in a row, and sometimes we'd skip a few weeks. Everyone in my troupe liked to shop. It wasn't like a planned activity or anything. The other girls liked to shop when they were free, and I sometimes went along. Once you get used to something, you no longer need a reason for it.

"And as for how shopping is different there… when we buy something, we know what we want and ask for it directly from the maker. It's not like that on Earth. Over there, they like to put everything on display, arranged in a pleasing manner. The mall was also a park. It was shaped like a mountain pierced throughout with tunnels for little trains. You got on one of these trains, and it took you past all kinds of stores. The displays showed off the clothes and shoes and gadgets like some scene in a fairy tale, and you couldn't help but stop to buy something. When couples went on dates, they also shopped. The first two years I was on Earth, I lived in a giant building, which was also a mall—no, a city in itself. It was also pyramid-shaped, like the Expo Center, except that building was two hundred floors tall. I lived on the one-hundred-and-eightieth floor, trained on the fiftieth, ate on the twentieth, and danced on the one-hundred-and-twenty-third. But you could shop on every floor. If you went there, I bet you'd shop more than I did."

"Two hundred floors!?" The redheaded girl's mouth gaped. "That's incredible."

Ruao looked full of pride, as though he had personally built the wonder Luoying was describing with his own two hands.

"But you didn't live there the whole time?"

Luoying shook her head. "Just two years."

"Why did you leave?"

"I left the dance troupe."

The girl wanted to ask more questions, but Luoying once again looked preoccupied. The two boys had walked ahead, and so the girls hurried to catch up. Eko was now even more curious about Luoying and determined to strike up a conversation. He prepared the questions in his head.

Not too long after, Eko heard the two boys arguing again.

"Now, this is a really impressive invention," said Ruao, once again lecturing the rest of the group. "IP fingerprinting was useful only as a way to prevent unauthorized transmission but couldn't do anything about transactions off the web. That was how the black market in e-books boomed. But this device here writes a bit of executable code into every book. As soon as you start to read, regardless of how you acquired the book, the code generates a signal to pay the author's web account. So now we have a complete solution to guarantee the integrity of the IP economy and to protect copyrights."

Toutou frowned. "What in the world is the IP economy?"

Ruao smirked. In a superior tone, he said, "I'm talking about the great leap from traditional industries to the creative industries."

Toutou remained confused. "Why do you need to pay to read a book?"

Ruao gawked at him as though the question were too foolish to deserve an answer.

To cover his discomfort, Ruao picked up a scroll and unrolled it. "Look at this! It's the newest personal-information processing device. It's light, small, user-friendly, and completely waterproof.

You can even use it in a swimming pool."

"That's ridiculous," said Toutou. "Who wants to look at a computer in a swimming pool?"

Ruao ignored him. "You can take it with you anywhere. The battery lasts practically forever. It can connect to the web via infrared, microwave, optical fiber, and so forth. And it's hardened against hacking. You can be on the web even in the subway."

Toutou was even more confused. "What's the point? Don't your subway trains have terminals?"

"What's a terminal?"

"A terminal! We have them at stations, museums, shops, everywhere!"

"Oh, you mean a shared computer. This is totally different. A shared computer has no space for your own stuff; you can't do anything."

"Why not? You just need to log in to your own space."

Ruao and Toutou were both growing frustrated. They couldn't understand each other at all.

Luoying broke in. "Toutou, Earth is different. They don't rely on central servers. It's just too big, and there are too many people. They link all the personal computers into a web."

Her simple explanation glossed over the vast difference between the two societies.

Eko knew she was technically correct. The difference between Mars and Earth was indeed one between central servers and personal devices, between the archive and the web. She had explained away the difference by reference to geography and population, making it no longer necessary for the two boys to argue.

But in reality the difference was far more complicated. For instance, there was the matter of the profit of hardware manufacturers. On Earth, a personal computer typically lasted no more than three years before having to be replaced. On Mars, computers were part of the infrastructure of the buildings and could not be easily replaced. Terran manufacturers would have no way to grow if people on Earth adopted the Martian approach. As another example, consider capability and responsibility. On Earth, who had the capacity to run centralized systems that served everyone? Governments or megacorps? And even more critical was the matter of ideology. The mainstream media on Earth had always been proud of a long tradition of atomistic individualism. The very idea of uniting everyone with a centralized server would be subject to vociferous criticism.

Eko didn't know if Luoying was unaware of these complexities or if she was deliberately papering them over. If she was ignorant of them, then she was lucky to have stumbled upon an easy explanation. But if she did know, then she was trying to avoid getting into a substantive discussion with the boys. He tried to guess what her unembellished face was hiding. He thought it was finally time to go greet her.

The youths began to make their way toward the food court.

Eko caught up to them. He stood next to Luoying along the counter. Luoying glanced at him and nodded.

"Hi," said Eko.

"Hello," said Luoying.

Luoying didn't seem to be particularly interested in striking up a conversation, but she was just a touch slower than the other kids and fell behind, giving Eko a chance.

"Are they your friends?" he asked, pointing to the girls ahead of her.

"Neighbors, actually."

"Do Martians move and change addresses often?"

"Almost never."

"Then you must have been neighbors for a long time."

"If I hadn't left, it would be eighteen years."

"You must know each other very well."

"If I hadn't left, yes."

"But you did leave, so…?"

Luoying didn't answer him directly. She pointed to the redheaded girl. "Gielle's dream is to be a designer. She wants to design the most beautiful wedding dress in the world." Then she pointed at the girl dressed in blue, who hadn't spoken so far. "Brenda's dream is to be a poet. She wants to be remembered like Lord Byron, to become part of the classics."

"What about you?"

"I wanted to be a botanist. A great one. Someone who discovers the secret behind petals and colors."

"Really?"

Eko chuckled without knowing why. Maybe it was because Luoying looked so serious, or maybe because these dreams sounded so weighty. He wanted to talk more with her about her childhood instead of filling his camera with silly gossip. He hoped that he sounded like a regular person trying to have a conversation, not a reporter who came at her with an agenda.

For a while Luoying didn't say anything. She picked up an apple and held on to it. Eko picked a chocolate drink from a shelf. They went to the checkout station, allowed the machine to scan their hands to pay, and walked over to a small standing table by the wall. The other kids weren't far. Luoying waved at them.

"What's your grand dream now?" asked Eko, keeping his tone light.

"I don't have grand dreams."

"Don't you want to be a great dancer? A star?"

"No."

"Why not? You have the perfect environment here."

"Perfect?"

"You have a stable life. You don't need to worry about finding a market or patrons. You have the space to practice. You have your atelier."

Luoying fell silent. Eko waited, but she didn't speak. He looked at her and thought she looked disconsolate. It was more than just perplexity or absent-mindedness. Her silence involved suppression, as though she was feeling awful but trying hard not to make a sound. He didn't know when her mood had turned. She had looked fine but a minute ago.

"What's wrong?" he asked. "I'm sorry if I said something to offend."

"No, you didn't say anything wrong." Her face was expressionless. "It's perfect here."

"What do you mean?"

"I don't mean anything."

"Do you... feel it's not so good here?"

She looked up at him, her eyes glistening. "The problem isn't whether things are good here but that you can't *think* it's not good here. Do you understand?"

Startled, Eko didn't know how to respond. Her eyes looked so sad, but he couldn't understand why. After gazing at him for a while, Luoying apologized and left. She didn't even say goodbye to the other kids. They called after her, and when she didn't respond, they turned to glare at Eko.

Eko knew that she didn't want the others to see her anguish, but he was as befuddled as the rest of them.

He had no interest in staying at the Expo Center any longer. After taking a perfunctory turn around the Grand Hall to get some panoramic shots, he left.

The world's fair here was very different from the one on Earth. Instead of eye-catching booths, colorful banners, and flashing lights, the products of Earth were arranged neatly in display cases, accompanied by short descriptions and explanations. The overall feeling was closer to a museum's. The Terran delegation had brought a roller coaster and an extreme sports simulator, but there wasn't enough space to set them up. They had brought all sorts of flashy advertising equipment and were prepared to respond to every imaginable scenario of Martian propaganda bombardment. The fact that there was no propaganda at all confused them.

A tall, magnificent stage was only partially assembled; there wasn't enough room, so it resembled a squatting giant. The high-def display carpet was only half-unrolled, which gave off an air of frustration. Advertising posters filled a whole wall, but because they were too large, the wall appeared to be full of monstrous faces. Everything seemed off-kilter, mismatched. And so it pleased neither side.

THE REGISTRY OF FILES

B y the time Luoying and Chania sat down together atop the watchtower, stars had filled the sky. They were so bright that it was painful to look at them directly, to see the Milky Way cross from left to right like a belt in the empyrean dome. The view from the watchtower included most of Mars City, now brightly lit, and the two friends seemed suspended between two starry seas, one above, one below, with the lone metallic ladder of the watch-tower at their feet. They experienced the illusion of being far away from home.

"At first, I seized on the simplest explanation. Perhaps Grandfather thought the trip to Earth would be such a wonderful learning opportunity that he had to use his authority to give me the chance."

"A wonderful learning opportunity?" Chania looked at her with a smirk. "If I had been the consul, my top priority would have been to make sure my granddaughter stayed as far from the Mercury Group as possible."

Chania was a gymnast. The two were the only female athletes in the group. She understood the pain that Luoying had gone through on Earth.

Luoying shook her head. "It's possible, isn't it? Surely the committee didn't know how hard it would be, and maybe they really hoped we'd learn something useful."

"I hope so," said Chania softly.

Chania was never afraid of following logic to a cold, heartless conclusion, but Luoying was different. It wasn't that she couldn't think of terrifying possibilities, but that she didn't want to. She didn't know why; it was just the way she was. She saw it as a weakness in herself, the way she subconsciously avoided certain facts. She hated the idea that she was just a living experiment, a specimen. She lacked Chania's strength to face the truth.

"But after I remembered that recording... I couldn't think that way anymore. Even if the organizers didn't know how difficult things would be on Earth, that wasn't why Grandfather sent me. One month after I saw that recording, I was placed in the Mercury Group. That can't be a coincidence."

"I agree with you."

"My grandfather was afraid of having me find out more... But what was it?"

"I don't think it's that hard to guess. He didn't want you to know that he was the one who sentenced your mom and dad to death."

"No! Not death. He sentenced them to mining."

"What's the difference? The mining ships on Deimos have accidents all the time."

"But I can't be sure the recording was of my parents' punishment. I didn't hear what was said, and in any event I was too young to understand it. Maybe my parents' names were mentioned."

"They were probably worried you'd dig deeper."

"If it was just my grandfather, I guess I wouldn't be so shaken. But Rudy was in on it, too. He had probably known it for a long time, but he kept it from me, along with my grandfather."

"It's possible that your brother even knew why they had been punished."

Luoying had asked to see Chania because she wanted her help in figuring out what kind of crime would result in her parents being sentenced to mining on a moon until they died. The two of them had been puzzling over the matter for some time already, but weren't any closer to an answer.

They had seen few instances of criminal punishment as they were growing up. The most that they recalled was of someone getting extra work in the workshops or being denied the right to share their creations for a period of time. Life on Mars tended to be peaceful and regular, with little crime or conflict. Luoying couldn't imagine what her parents had done. The two of them had always loved life, and there weren't any black marks in their files. They had always garnered awards and honors—until they received their sentence. They had been mining for less than a year before the accident happened.

The only thing that seemed remotely related was the fact that her mother had refused to register with an atelier.

Looking up at the stars, she asked, "Do you think not registering is a crime?"

Chania laughed. "If so, then I think I'm going to be punished."

"You haven't registered either?"

"Nope."

"Same here."

"I don't think anyone in our group has."

"Really?" Luoying was amazed. "I didn't know that... So everyone is just dragging it out?"

"Yep. Anka almost got expelled."

"What? When?"

"He didn't tell you?" Chania looked surprised. "The day he

got back, he got into a huge fight with Captain Fitz. I heard that after the banquet his squadron was supposed to fly around the hotel where the Terran delegations are staying and put on a demonstration of force. Anka refused. How can a soldier refuse a direct command? You can imagine what happened after that."

"So that's what happened…"

It was odd to hear what Anka had done from someone else. To be sure, she wasn't particularly socially active and relied on others to tell her gossip. But even so, the Anka in others' stories wasn't like the Anka she knew. She always thought of him as someone who didn't let anything bother him. Now she recalled that on Earth there was a time when he had left the group after an argument. Chania always knew what was happening with everyone and kept her in the loop.

"You know, maybe not registering really is a big deal," said Chania suddenly.

"How do you mean?"

"Let's take regular crimes: stealing, taking advantage of someone's mistake, things like that. Usually it's just an isolated incident, and everyone knows it's wrong. A simple penalty is enough. But it's different when it's a… matter of ideology. That represents a challenge to our way of life. If ideological rebels spread their ideas around, it would become a threat to the whole system. To reject the need to organize life around the ateliers could be viewed as an ideological revolution."

Luoying remained silent. Chania's words reminded her of the Reversionist friends she had met on Earth.

"I'm just guessing, mind you," said Chania.

"I was just thinking today," said Luoying, "that the biggest problem with our world is that you can't think it's not good. Everyone must pick an atelier, must live the way we're supposed to live. The more I think about it, the more scared I become. If your guess is right and refusal to register is a capital crime, then… we don't even have the freedom to leave the system. What a terrifying world."

"Did you start thinking like this only after you got back?" asked Chania.

Luoying nodded.

"It's the same with me," said Chania. "I feel awful. After everything we've been through, to finally get home, only to find out that I can't stand the place…"

"You know, if one could live only by instinct, that would be true happiness," said Luoying.

Chania chortled. "I think we said the same thing to each other four years ago."

Luoying smiled. "Exactly. I guess we're both a bit too old for that kind of sentiment now."

They had grown out of the habit of making grand summaries about life. Having seen so many perplexing and troubling things in life, it was no longer easy to summarize it. Four years earlier they had summarized the life of Terrans with the overconfidence of youth, but the mood tonight was so different.

Chania turned to regard her. "What do you want more than anything else right now?"

"To get out."

Chania laughed. "Same here."

Luoying looked up and touched the cold, hard glass dome overhead. "Too bad we'll never get out again."

The four watchtowers of Mars City were the tallest structures in the city. Like four guardian deities, they stood at the cardinal points. The two of them liked to climb up here because they could touch the glass dome that separated Mars City from the outside, could feel the border that remained intangible during their daily routines. Without a thick atmosphere, the stars appeared particularly bright and didn't twinkle.

"That's why we want to get out even more," said Chania. "When you were on Earth, did you argue with them about life here being so much better? I sure did. I told them how safe it was here, how little crime we had, how everyone on Mars was a moral person. But it wasn't until yesterday that I realized none of this had anything to do with the advanced state of Martian ethical development. No one commits crimes here because there's nowhere to run to. We're all stuck, and sooner or later we know we'll be caught." Sadness clouded her gaze. "You have to live the way you're supposed to because there's no getting out."

Both fell silent. Chania's long chestnut hair was loose and swayed gently in the air.

They hadn't talked like this, about life, in a long while. When they first got to Earth, they loved to engage in long, deep discussions after experiencing every new job, after seeing every new thing. They tried to extract principles, to declaim about the kind of life they wished to lead. But such discussions grew rare over time. They had little control over their own lives. Regardless of the variety of possible lifestyles, the choices open to the individual were so few.

Still, they had witnessed those possibilities.

On Mars, life was a matter of tradition. Every child's path was similar to every other child's: go to school at age six, volunteer for public service at nine, start to think about one's future direction at twelve, be excited with the first set of electives at thirteen. Students could choose to intern at different ateliers, and once they had accumulated enough credits, they could pick areas of interest to study in depth, write papers, assist more experienced professionals, and then decide on an atelier. They also worked in stores, workshops, mining stations—but those experiences were also part of the atelier internships. They were volunteers aiming to acquire experience. No one did anything useless; no one went off on their own. Everyone ended up at a permanent atelier, with a number, a file in the Registry, a straight road that one followed until death.

But on Earth, as Luoying drifted about, she saw people doing anything they wanted. Every time she settled in a new place, she found a new group of friends. They never signed long-term contracts with any employer but filled their time by sometimes waiting on tables, sometimes freelancing articles, sometimes making deliveries or running errands, sometimes volunteering for the government, sometimes buying and selling on the black market, sometimes selling their own IPs on the web. They lived from day to day, hopping from city to city, wolfing down fast food at airports, attending galas in fancy hotels, buying cigarettes with the last of their paychecks, getting into business with someone they had just met. Their professions were as fleeting as flirty glances: the moment there was a spark, they shifted their attention elsewhere.

Such a life of uncertainty entranced her. It was such a contrast to the life in the platonic garden of idealized creation that she had grown up in. The two collided like air masses in her heart, and a tempestuous storm was the result.

And so her experience on Earth was the combination of two kinds of adjustment, opposite in direction. While she had to adjust to a far more primitive mode of life filled with inconveniences, she also had to adjust to a far more complex lifestyle. Mars City was much more advanced than cities on Earth in infrastructure and operation, but the lifestyle on Mars was older and simpler.

In Luoying's eyes, Martians had Apollonian clarity, while Terrans had Dionysian frenzy. A ten-year-old Martian child knew Aristotelian logic, Hammurabi's code, the Jacobins and the Bourbon Restoration, as well as the rest of the development of human history and art. Everyone sat at their own desk to study or stood around a table in a coffee lounge to debate philosophy, to discuss the manifestations of the universal Will in spiritual history, to deliberate over the succession of civilizations and the role of consciousness in human history. Martians worshipped great ideas, art, and invention. Every Martian asked themselves: *Why am I doing this? What value does this action contribute to the progress of civilization?*

Terrans were not like that at all.

The first thing Luoying learned to do on Earth was how to party. She went drinking with the other girls of the dance troupe and their friends and ingested a hallucinogen that was not powerful enough to be illegal. She drifted in an altered state of consciousness, feeling closer to the divine. She listened to the others laugh, share jokes, sing loudly, and watched them twist and grind on the dance floor. No one asked anyone else who, what, where, why, but simply luxuriated in the collective release of their bodies. They hugged and kissed, followed their feelings and interests, and forgot as soon as they were done. They displayed the beauty of each individual body to its fullest extent, unified the self with the universe, and equated a moment of joy with cosmic eternity.

She was a quick student and soon was partying as hard as her friends. She never asked them *Why are we doing this? What value do our actions contribute to the progress of human history?* She understood, without asking, that such questions were meaningless in the frenzy of their passion.

There was alcohol served on Mars, but few ever got drunk. All the children of the Mercury Group had to survive the shock of encountering this new lifestyle. And they couldn't avoid the question: Did life exist in order to create grand histories and artistic masterpieces, or was life itself all the meaning it needed? They hesitated, remained silent among the crowd, sober among the frenzied, drunk while studying; they lost all faith in a flash.

Luoying had to find out why she had been sent to Earth. She didn't want to be a playing piece in someone else's game. Once she would have accepted the fate she was assigned, but no longer. She had to know if there was a *reason*.

Oh, ye gods of Olympus, she thought, *have you ever thought that one day a group of children would vacillate between your sobriety and frenzy, unable to choose?*

Before she arrived at Uncle Laak's office, Luoying tried to compose herself on the tube train. She deliberately picked the wrong destination station, twice, so that she came to the Registry by the most roundabout way possible. Otherwise, the trip would have taken only five minutes. The tube trains always picked the most optimal route, giving riders no time to think and plan.

She hesitated, trying to decide if she really wanted to pursue her inquiry.

She felt herself approaching a border, heading toward a question that did not exist in ordinary life but only appeared in the contrast of change. She was still a person who didn't officially exist.

Without registering, she had no account, no identity in the system. She was someone standing outside the system, a potential challenger.

"Refusal to register," she whispered to herself. Was this a great crime? Was this a challenge to the existing order of the world? Was this enough reason to force Grandfather to exile Mom and Dad, to make him fear her? Why did the system care so much about a nine-digit number?

She had heard certain stories on Earth, stories about something called the Age of Machines. The faces of the tellers were full of fear as they described a world in which the machines imprisoned everyone and treated individuals as interchangeable components to be exploited and discarded. Freedom and dignity had been suppressed out of existence. They told her that Mars was the example par excellence of such a world.

The tellers of these stories had never been to Mars, but they described its ills to her as though they knew her world better than she did. Eventually she grew used to these stories, knowing that the tellers were merely ignorant, not malicious. But she began to fear that they were telling the truth. She asked herself, if she truly lived in a world created by an evil regime, what should she do?

Luoying had so many questions, but most she dared not ask. Many Terrans had told her that Hans Sloan was a dictator. They spoke with such conviction. She dared not ask him, and didn't want to ask him. Her grandfather's blood flowed through her veins as well, and her doubt could never be voiced in a direct confrontation.

In the memories of her childhood, Grandfather was the protector of Mars. She did not believe that he was a dictator, but some details aroused her doubt. Grandfather was a warrior, one of the last pilots to fly during the war. He was a survivor, a victor, and a man who had done his duty. After the war he became an industrial pilot and guided mining ships between the moons of Mars and Mars itself. He had flown to Jupiter to explore, to the asteroids to gather water, to the moons to build bases. He began as a test pilot and then rose through the ranks until he led a fleet and directed the technological development of the entire Flight System.

For most of his life, Hans flew alone. Only in middle age did he go into politics as a legislator, and then a system director, until finally he became consul at the age of sixty. When Luoying was a little girl, she remembered seeing Grandfather at his desk, reading and writing until late into the night, or talking with others. Even when she and her parents visited him, sometimes he had to leave because there were urgent matters that needed his attention. His personal space stored as much material as an entire school. Luoying did not believe he was a dictator because he simply worked too hard.

But she couldn't be sure. There was evidence pointing the other way: her place in the Mercury Group, her parents' deaths, the very operation of the central archive itself.

She had to get to the bottom of her doubts.

The tube train glided through the smooth tunnels like a drop of water. Enveloped by air, it didn't even make any noise. When she was a child, Luoying had not realized how quiet the world she grew up on was. Mars had no high-speed elevators, no noisy crowds, no cars, and no airplanes. All she knew were refined, delicate houses, glass, gardens full of footpaths, shops with no cashiers, coffee lounges, cinemas with no ticket booths, and transparent tubes filled with water-drop trains. All she knew were people who studied, worked, thought, conversed. There was no marijuana; there were no screams, no naked bodies dancing in frenzy, suspended between sleep and wakefulness. No noise; only tranquility.

Around the city Luoying rode, from light into shadows,

from shadows back into light. The outline of the train car grew hazy with the shifting light. Finally, she made her decision and pressed the button for the Montesquieu Registry of Files, where Uncle Laak worked.

She needed answers. Though she didn't like facing the absurd reality, she was even more terrified of ignorance, of never knowing. To doubt one's own life was the worst of fears. She could not go on living in suspense.

As the Registrar of Files, Uncle Laak was in charge of the heart of the Martian system of files. More than anyone else, he was more familiar with those numbers that determined one's identity. The numbers were beehives arranged around him in a dense phalanx, a phalanx of lives in which he was the hub. In front of him was an ancient desk with a cracked top, but it was dustless and everything on it was arranged neatly.

"Please, sit."

Laak pointed to the chair before the desk. Luoying sat down, her back straight.

"I've read your letter and I know what you are looking for," he said.

Luoying said nothing, but her heart pounded. The sun was shining into the corner of her eye and she couldn't see everything clearly.

"Are you sure about this?" Luoying nodded.

"All right, then," said Laak. "But let me explain something. We encounter many puzzles in life, but not every question must be pursued to the bitter end."

"There's a difference between knowing and not knowing."

"Actually, there's not much difference."

"There is."

"The difference doesn't matter… once you've seen enough."

Luoying gazed at Uncle Laak. His long, slender fingers were

laced together on the desk, and his expression was somber. He sat very straight, as though a bowl of water were placed on top of his head. But for some reason, she thought his posture reminded her of prayer, with his hands together on the desk. There was a suffering look in his eyes, mysterious but clear, that came through the circular lenses of his glasses, through his laced fingers, through the air that divided them. She believed that he hoped she would see the pain.

Unlike Uncle Juan, Uncle Laak never showed his emotions. He never shouted, never laughed uproariously. His expression always resembled something carved out of an ancient stump, unchanging. She was sure that he wanted her to see the pain that was now in his eyes.

His face was long, with prominent cheekbones. The hair on his head was growing sparse and turning gray, as though singed by mental overexertion. He waited for her answer.

"I want to know."

"All right."

He stood up and touched the wall. The protective wallpaper slid away, revealing a metallic grid that filled the whole wall like filing cabinets. Each rectangle was brown in color, with a golden edge. A ringlike handle sat in the middle of each rectangle with a white placard beneath. Though it was all simulated, everything looked so real that she thought she could reach up and pull open the drawers.

The whole wall was like that, and the effect on Luoying was overwhelming. Laak walked along the wall, glancing at the markings on the white placards. He stopped and touched one of the rectangles, entering a few commands. Behind the wall, a droning noise grew.

Soon a sheet of electronic paper slid out of the slot at the side of the rectangle.

Laak picked up the sheet and handed it to Luoying. She received it carefully, like a bowl filled to the brim. She stared at it without blinking. The sheet showed her examination from five years earlier and the score. The number was incontrovertibly clear against the clear glass fiber; each stroke like a tiny knife cut into her heart.

She read over the sheet several times before looking up. She had already known what the number would tell her, but now she had confirmation.

"Why was I substituted in?"

Laak shook his head. "I can give you the facts, but I can't give you the reasons."

"I want to know who the other student was."

"What other student?"

"The one who should have gone to Earth. The one whose fate was exchanged with mine."

A moment of hesitation. "I don't know."

"That's impossible!" Luoying blurted. "You were the one in charge of administering the exam." She realized how disrespectful she sounded. She hated the way she always lost control when she was confused. She turned her face away to calm herself.

Uncle Laak's eyes now looked pitying, with a trace of anguish.

"Even if I knew," he said, "I couldn't tell you. You have the right to view your own file. I don't have the right to tell you what's in anyone else's file."

Luoying looked down at her own hands. She was sitting in an old-fashioned office chair with high armrests. Sitting in it was like being hugged by it. Luoying felt that she needed such a hug. When a suspended crag finally smashed into the sea, it would start a tsunami in the deep.

"Uncle Laak," she asked, "am I allowed to see anyone else's file?"

"You're not."

"Not even family?"

"No."

"I thought our guiding principle was that everyone's file is transparent."

"That is true, but there are two conditions. Either the subject must voluntarily disclose the file, or the law must require such disclosure. Anything a citizen has created and wishes to share with others is public, as are policy proposals they make to the government, and the financial records related to their work and management responsibilities. But otherwise every citizen has the right to privacy. Most personal files are never made public and become part of historical memory. It has always been this way in every age."

"So I can't even see my parents' files."

"Not unless they made them public."

"I tried to look for information on my mother, but all the public records stopped two years before her death, when she left her atelier. I don't know what happened to her after that. It's as though those two years never existed."

Laak looked sympathetic, but his voice remained neutral. "I'm sorry."

"But why?"

"The public records are drawn from her work at the atelier. Once she was no longer registered, there would be no more records."

"In other words, to the system, a person without an atelier is no different from a dead body."

"You can put it that way."

Sunlight slanted through the window, dispassionately slicing the wall with geometric precision. The grid of filing rectangles in the shadow resembled a bottomless sea. She knew that Uncle Laak was correct; everything he said was correct—so correct that it drove her to despair.

"Is that what it means to be registered?"

"Not entirely."

"Then what is the meaning of registration?"

"The distribution of resources. The fair, open, transparent distribution of resources. The system guarantees that everyone receives what they should—not one penny more, not one penny less. No secrets or omissions."

"We get paid according to age. What does that have to do with registration and ateliers?"

"You're talking about the living expenses stipend, which is a vanishingly small portion of the total capital in the system. That part indeed has nothing to do with registration and is based solely on age. But when you become an adult, you realize that living expenses are not the bulk of the amount of capital you may allocate in society. Most of a citizen's economic activity involves research funds, creation and production costs, the purchase of raw materials and the sale of finished goods, and so on. The flow of capital occurs strictly within the framework of ateliers, although the ateliers merely deploy capital, which ultimately flows back to the collective. This is the only way to ensure a single, consistent accounting. Without a registered account number, the system won't allow you to participate."

"Why can't anyone just conduct research on their own, outside the system?"

"You can do that if you wish, but then you may only use your living expenses stipend and can't tap into any public funding. If we allow a single breach to develop in the dam that keeps public wealth out of private hands, then corruption, hoarding, and greed will pour through like a flood."

"If someone doesn't want any public funding, is it a crime to not register?"

"No, it's not a crime."

"They won't be exiled?"

"They will not."

"Then why did my mother and father die?"

It took all of Luoying's courage to ask this last question. She bit her bottom lip, slightly dry due to her anxiety, as her heart pounded against her rib cage. Contrary to her expectation, Laak didn't look surprised. He continued to sit quietly, his posture erect, with no change in his expression or voice. He had been prepared for the question.

"They died from an unfortunate accident. I share your grief."

"That's not what I meant. I'm asking why they were punished and sent to the mining ship."

"As I've told you, I can only tell you facts, not reasons."

"Then tell me what the charge brought against them was."

"Threat to national security."

"What threat? How?"

"I can't elaborate beyond what I've told you."

Laak's voice had grown softer. Luoying felt an invisible rope suspended between them, with each pulling on one end. But the rope refused to budge even one millimeter. She choked back tears. Laak poured her a cup of tea without speaking. She shook her head, refusing to accept.

She looked into his eyes, pleading. "Uncle Laak, I'd like to ask you something else."

"What is it?"

"Is my grandfather a dictator?"

Laak gazed at her as though trying to ascertain the motivation behind her question.

At length, he spoke in a voice as dry and dispassionate as a textbook, and as unreal as an unearthed antique in the fading Martian sunlight. "We have to start from the definition. From the time of Plato's *Republic*, the meaning of 'dictator' has not changed much. If someone could enact laws and execute them at will, without any checks and balances, then by consensus, they are a dictator.

"So let's take a look at your grandfather. He cannot enact criminal laws at will because such laws must be proposed by the directors of the Security System. He cannot alter policy arbitrarily because every system has its sphere of autonomy, and cross-system policy changes require the consent of the Boule as a whole. Matters affecting the planet must be put to a vote involving the entire populace. He is under constant oversight: the central archive records and publicizes everything he says or does, every expenditure he authorizes. Do you think he is a dictator, then?"

"Then why can't I see my grandfather's file? I'm part of that oversight, aren't I?"

Laak spoke slowly. "That's different. Everyone's life has a private part, a part that belongs only to memory. That part is like the reef under the sea, while we only have the right to monitor the ships on the surface. No one has the right to pry into his life outside of his official duties."

Luoying bit her bottom lip. Laak's words were like the gridded ocean behind him, bottomless.

"What's contained in these files?"

"Memories. Time's memories."

"Why don't they have such files on Earth?"

"They do. You just haven't seen them." Laak's voice grew

even more patient and slow. "You've been to Earth, so you know how helpful our files are. When a person switches from one atelier to another, they don't need to provide any proof of identity or open new bank accounts and switch household registration records. All that is needed is a change in the atelier's record, and everything happens automatically in the background. Don't you find this convenient? The unified system of centralized record keeping makes it possible and ensures that we can establish each person's true credit history."

"Yes, that is true." Luoying knew that Laak was right. On Earth, when she changed jobs, she had to take a whole stack of documents from one office to another to prove she was who she was, to introduce herself, to be interrogated by bureaucrats, to answer the same set of questions again and again, to be surrounded by suspicion, to be drowned in form after form. She had witnessed the frauds and disguises enabled by such a system. Yes, Uncle Laak was right, but that wasn't her question.

"What I'm trying to understand is this: Why must we assign a single number to every person, a static space, an identity tied to an atelier? Why can't we move around as we please, to forget the past and to re-create the self? Why can't we be free?"

"You can do as you like, and you are free to re-create yourself," said Laak, whose voice took on an enigmatic air. "But you are not allowed to forget the past."

The rays of the setting sun were almost parallel with the ground, and deepening shadows made the ceiling seem even higher. Laak still sat erect in his gray suit jacket and his plain white shirt, the cuffs and collar neatly buttoned. Through his black-framed glasses, he looked at Luoying with pity, as though he wanted to tell her so many things while saying nothing.

His hands were flattened against the desk, and his slim fingers resembled ancient quills lying still.

Luoying noticed the columns in the office for the first time. Like other columns in Martian buildings, they concealed the electrons speeding through the wires within. But these resembled the columns in ancient Greek temples, sacred and stately. The desk, though made of glass, looked indistinguishable from wood. The penholder on the desk had enigmatic patterns on its surface. Everything in the room hinted at the weight of history, like the figure of Uncle Laak himself.

THE COFFEE LOUNGE

On Mars, coffee wasn't real coffee but a synthetic substitute. It wasn't as bitter as the real thing but was very fragrant. The drinker could choose the preferred roast and additives, including stimulating effects. Coffee lounges were open and airy, and there were no baristas or servers. Customers brewed their own beverages at machines embedded in the walls while bakers in the kitchen prepared pastries.

Since hotels and homes had their own coffee machines, people mostly came to coffee lounges to chat with friends or to discuss business. Thus, these spaces were specially engineered for audio isolation. Sound-absorbing boards hung from the ceiling; potted plants acted as partitions; the tables were set far apart from one another, ensuring a degree of privacy at each.

This particular coffee lounge was located at a busy street corner. A customer sitting next to the window could see the clothing store to the left, the framed-painting shop to the right, and the open-air theater surrounded by bushes across the street. The sides of the street were lined with statues of famous chefs through the ages because the street was dedicated to the culinary arts. On Mars, practically every street was named after a creative master: a scientist, an engineer, a painter, a chef, a fashion designer, and so on. Every street had its own collection of statues, some in formal poses, but many also portraying humorous moments. The statues of the great chefs along this street were especially vivid. Every one struck a different pose, surrounded by replicas of their signature dishes, preserving in a lasting manner the beauty of fleeting taste.

A group of children bounced past the coffee lounge to have a snack of fruits under an umbrella-shaped tree. In an empty space between the two lanes of the street, four youths played a string quartet. A few girls opened roadside display cases to put in dolls they had made—a part of their atelier internship program. Pedestrians streamed past the glass wall of the coffee lounge like hazy currents.

Janet had invited Eko here because it was close to the Tarkovsky Film Archive, and it was also where she and Arthur had gone on their first date. She didn't touch her coffee. Her gaze was focused on some nonexistent place far away as she listened intently.

Eko finished his account.

"So he didn't make any more films?" asked Janet.

"No."

"Did he ever agree to be interviewed?"

"No. He was an enigma, confiding in no one."

"Not even you?"

"Maybe a few hints here and there, but I was too young to really understand."

Janet sighed. "Arthur was stubborn as a mule. He dedicated himself to the pursuit of his vision, regardless of how others viewed him." She looked down at her hands. Softly, she added, "Did he at least explain himself to his family?"

"Family?"

"His wife and child."

"No. He and his wife divorced a long time ago, and he spent the last ten years of his life alone."

"Ten years? When did he get a divorce?"

"It was so long ago that I don't even know the exact date. I think it was when he was thirty-two, thirty-three, something like that."

"Before he had come to Mars, then."

"Definitely. You didn't know?"

Janet looked shocked. "No, I didn't."

It was Eko's turn to be shocked. How could she not know after spending eight years with Davosky? Carefully he asked, "He never spoke of it?"

Janet shook her head absentmindedly. She was lost in her memories again, her gaze unfocused. Her elbows rested on the table, fingers interlaced. Twice she seemed about to speak but stopped herself.

Eko waited patiently.

Janet sighed again. "Arthur never mentioned it. I guess I never wanted to know—or didn't have the courage to ask. I saw a photo he carried with him, a picture of him and a woman and a little boy. I asked him if that was his wife and son, and he said yes. I asked him if his family would worry that he was away for so long, but he told me they weren't getting along. I didn't pry, thinking it was something within the family. I told him that even if they weren't getting along, he had to go home sometime. He said yes, eventually. And then…

"After we were together, I never brought it up, thinking that he would leave if I did. Sometimes he would say, 'Janet, I have something I need to discuss with you.' I would ask him, 'Are you leaving?' He would say, 'No, I'm not leaving.' I would say, 'Then there's nothing to discuss.' Eventually, he stopped bringing it up.

"Arthur was like a rock, and even if you asked, you couldn't be sure he would answer. I never asked. He was engrossed in

145

his scripts and films, and I stayed with him. Year after year, I refused to let myself think about his life from before. But the whole time, I was afraid he was going to leave. I always had an instinctive feeling that he wouldn't stay on Mars forever, and so I tried to delay that day as long as possible. When Arthur finally told me he was leaving,

I wasn't surprised. I felt awful, but not surprised."

"You thought he was returning to… reunite with his wife," said Eko.

"Yes."

"He never got back together with her."

"I…" Janet's eyes moistened. "I hoped he would return. He told me he needed to take care of some things on Earth, and I thought he meant his… marriage."

Janet blinked to keep herself from crying. She tucked her hair behind her ear and took a deep breath, forcing a smile onto her face for Eko's benefit. She didn't want to look fragile, especially in front of someone who was just a kid in her eyes. She had tried to prepare herself for today, to stay detached. If she didn't allow herself to feel uplifted, then she wouldn't have to suffer the pain of tumbling back into emotional troughs.

Eko looked at her with respect. She looked a bit wan and pallid, with swollen eyes. But she was strong. Her hair was neatly combed and her clothes crisp. Eko saw in her the independence of someone who relied on herself, who took care of herself out of habit even when her mind was in chaos. She had not gotten married because she thought she would save a place for Davosky, a place that he never came back to.

"He wanted to come back," said Eko.

He didn't say it to offer some comfort to Janet, though he did want to comfort her. He simply told her the truth. Even unto death, Davosky pined to be back on Mars. The less he spoke of it, the deeper his yearning.

"He was trying to get better. For the last decade of his life, he fought against cancer, but in the end it spread." Eko didn't know if these facts would allay her sorrow in some measure. "I think the illness was the reason he returned to Earth. He tried laser and nanosurgery, chemo, everything. Maybe he found out about it on Mars but he didn't want you to worry. He was trying to get better on Earth before coming back to you, since Terran medicine was more advanced."

"I don't believe that," said Janet. "His last physical on Mars gave him a clean bill of health."

Eko was surprised. "Are you sure?"

"Absolutely. He wouldn't have been able to board *Maearth* if he had cancer. Cosmic radiation is very dangerous, even for the healthy. Had he been diagnosed with anything, we wouldn't have allowed him to leave. I know he was healthy."

Eko frowned. "Maybe the cancer was the result of the trip, then.... I guess we'll never know."

He thought he had found out why Davosky left Mars, but Janet had eliminated that possibility. He still knew nothing. He was hoping to find the answers from Janet, but she needed him to tell her what had happened. He and Janet had each offered reasons for Davosky's departure that each thought made sense, but they had disproved each other's theories. The mystery hung in the air, and he didn't know if there were any more clues to be found.

The depressive mood silenced him. The sky was like an umbrella that covered him in scattered sunlight. The counter in the middle of the coffee lounge spun, displaying tasty treats. The piano played a melancholy tune, and the keys danced as though caressed by an invisible pianist. Through the swaying leaves of the potted plants, Eko had the illusion of seeing a tuxedoed pianist at the bench.

Abruptly, he was shaken out of his reverie. He still had not completed the most important task of his trip. "Oh, I almost forgot. My teacher had some things for you."

He took out a package: a woman's comb, a button with Davosky's portrait and name, the electronic notepad that Davosky had always kept with him. He lined them up in a row on the table.

"That's mine," said Janet, caressing the objects in turn. "This was his Martian transportation pass, which I got for him. And this was his journal, which he had when he arrived from Earth."

"I saw a picture of you in it," said Eko. Then he added, "There was no photograph of his wife in it."

Janet continued to run her fingers gently over the objects.

"One last thing," said Eko, trying find the right words. "Right before his death, he had his neural patterns digitized onto this chip—that is, he stored his memories on here. He told me to bring it to Mars. I think I should give it to you. He didn't say so, but I believe this is the way he wanted to be laid to rest."

Solemnly, he cradled the chip in his palm and presented it to Janet.

Lips trembling, Janet held out her hands, trembling as well. Her fingertips brushed against Eko's hand and pulled back, as though he were holding up a ball of fire. Her swollen eyes could not move away from it.

"Arthur... he just said to bring it to Mars? No further directions?"

"No. I don't know what to do."

"Did he suffer?"

Eko thought about it. "I don't think he was in a lot of physical pain, but he had been weakening for so long that he couldn't speak. During his last window of lucidity, he tried to write but only got one letter out: *B*, the beginning of your name."

"*B*?" Janet's eyes locked with his, and her lips stopped trembling. "Ah, that's not me." She shook her head with conviction.

There was no disappointment in her voice when she spoke again, only the peace of having figured out a puzzle. "I know now where he wanted you to bring him." Eko listened intently.

"Let me tell you a secret about Arthur that no one else knows about," said Janet. "Right before his departure, he went to the First Optical-Electrical Atelier, which was responsible for maintaining the central archive's hardware. The central archive works on the principle of atomic storage, where each atom's charged transitions are treated as zeros and ones. The information density is extremely high, allowing unprecedented capacity. Arthur obtained from the atelier the plans for the central archive and brought them to Earth." Eko sat stunned. All of a sudden, everything made sense. He had found the last piece of the puzzle. This was the real reason Davosky had left.

And even Janet hadn't understood everything. Davosky hadn't just gone to the atelier to obtain the secrets of atomic storage as a last-minute impulse. It had been his plan all along. Davosky had stayed on Mars to obtain this technology.

He had hoped to construct a cave of information, a vast cave capable of holding all the wonderful thoughts of humanity, and to which all were welcome. Earth lacked anything comparable, and so he had begged and pleaded until he got the plans from the Martian researchers. The moment he did, he left. That was the business he needed to take care of on Earth.

Once back on Earth, Davosky denied all interview requests

and lived a life away from the public eye in order to realize his dream without having the technology falling into the wrong hands; perhaps guarding the precious knowledge with care had been a promise extracted by the Martian researchers before giving him the treasure in the first place. He had hoped to return to Mars as soon as the archive was constructed, but he hadn't planned for cancer.

The only question left was: What did Davosky do on Earth to build the archive?

The image of Theon came to Eko instantly. He was certain that Davosky had gotten in touch with the man. Theon and his teacher were old friends, and Davosky had collaborated with the Thales Group many times. Davosky likely thought of the Thales Group as the most appropriate executor of his plan, since there was no other institution on Earth with such coverage and influence or with so many resources at its disposal. In the second half of the twenty-second century, when the market of the web was vastly larger than the market of physical goods, the Thales Group was the biggest company in the world.

If Arthur wanted to realize his vision, he had no choice but to approach Theon.

THE GRAND THEATER

With a tumultuous heart, Luoying waited for Rudy. No matter what, she had to make her brother talk to her about their parents.

Rudy got up before she did and returned home after she was already asleep. She pretty much never saw him at home. She went to his atelier to look for him, but he wasn't in the office either. His colleagues told her that he was at the machining workshop, and so she went there and waited for him in the break room.

She didn't have the authorization to enter the workshop floor. A tempered-glass partition separated it from the break room, through which she could see the vast, uncluttered workshop floor, with walls filled with dense circuitry. The thick door of the break room was locked, and the tempered-glass partition itself was gridded with green reinforcement bars. She saw her brother, safety goggles and hard hat in place, supervising the operation of thc assembly line. Next to him stood two assistants, both of them older than he was but listening intently to his directions.

Luoying watched Rudy gesture as he issued commands with confidence. Standing before the row of gigantic machines, he was like a trainer skillfully directing a dragon to use its massive limbs to carry out his will and to fulfill the plan in his head.

The dragon was blue and white, with each segment dedicated to a single task: cutting metal, weaving fiber, welding, drilling, punching, hammering. At one end stood three giant tanks for raw materials, and at the other end emerged one golden bench after another, like soap bubbles being blown.

Luoying recognized the benches. One just like these had welcomed her home on the day she landed on Mars.

Though she'd been home for a few days, she still didn't know much about her brother's life, but she did know his ideal career path: technology researcher, industrial group leader, legislator, system director. This was the smoothest path to prominence on Mars, and Rudy was already a few rungs up the long ladder. He had always been an excellent student, with a bit of an arrogant swagger. So far he had been carrying out his plan with great success, though it was still early in the journey.

The Fifth Electro-Mag Atelier was part of the Sunlight System. Most of Mars's power needs came from the sun, and electromagnetic research was typically administratively treated as part of the Sunlight System. Sunlight System researchers were responsible for such inventions as rooftop electric panels, the power cables surrounding the city, and the magnetic particle shielding circuits installed in every house. On Mars, roofs and walls were filled with circuits of all kinds, some visible, some not. By manipulating these circuits, it was possible to generate powerful localized magnetic fields. Rudy's research focused on such effects.

While waiting, Luoying drank two glasses of juice and thought about their childhood. Back then, she and Rudy had spoken of their dreams to each other. She wanted to read next to a brightly lit window with someone she loved, while he wanted to go explore the galaxy with a girl he liked. She wanted to stay while her brother wanted to leave. But in the end it was she who had wandered afar, while he had put down roots here. They hadn't spoken to each other of their dreams in a long time.

She drained another glass, and Rudy came into the break room. Surprised to see her, he took off the hard hat and combed his messy blond hair with his fingers. He looked to be in a bad mood, with an exhausted face and red eyes. He went to the wall and got himself a coffee and two cookies before coming to sit next to her. He drank the coffee so fast that he fell into a fit of coughing.

Luoying waited until he had recovered.

"You look a bit tired," she said.

He shook his head. "I'm all right. How's your practice going?"

"All right, I guess."

Rudy waited for Luoying to explain why she had come. But she couldn't get to the point right away. Instead, she got up, glanced at the busy workshop floor, and took Rudy's mug to the wall and refilled it. She added sugar and stirred it and put the mug back in front of Rudy.

"I went to see Uncle Laak."

"What for?"

"He confirmed my suspicion."

He understood. He buried his nose in the mug as he drank. "Okay."

"But you already knew I was right, didn't you?" He didn't answer.

"And you also know why Mom and Dad died." Still nothing. "Tell me!"

"It was an accident." Rudy sat, stone-faced. "Those responsible for the technical malfunction were punished afterward."

His distant demeanor wounded her. She tried another tack.

153

"Rudy, do you think Grandfather is a dictator?"

"What kind of question is that?"

"Because that's what others say."

"Who says that?"

"Many people."

"Terrans?"

"Sure."

"You can't believe anything Terrans say. They are prejudiced."

"Not all of them."

"Then they're ignorant. You should know that."

"I *don't* know that."

"You *should*."

Rudy was frowning at Luoying, looking very serious.

"I thought they were ignorant," she said softly. "But Grandfather… he ordered the suppression of the protest movement. Isn't that true?"

She had learned of this when she protested with her Reversionist friends on Earth. How the Terrans had known this was unclear to her. It seemed as if Terrans knew many things about Mars that she had never heard about, just as Martians knew many things about Earth that many Terrans did not. They had sat around a bonfire in the protest camp and shared stories they each knew about the other world. In the end, rumors and truths were mixed together so completely that it was impossible to tell which was which.

"The protests had to be suppressed." Rudy spoke slowly but determinedly. "Mars isn't like Earth. It was too dangerous."

"Too dangerous," Luoying repeated, also very slowly. "But Mom and Dad died for that cause."

"Don't speak about things you don't understand."

"But what other reasons could possibly explain their deaths? To refuse to register is not, by itself, a crime. But to instigate an ideological revolution, to lead a massive protest movement against the atelier system—that had to be punished."

"Who told you such stories?"

Luoying ignored him. "Their ideas about freedom challenged the whole system around us, and they had to be punished. Grandfather gave the order himself, didn't he? The system cannot tolerate revolutions."

Rudy's tone was cold. "You are a romantic, but that's not how the world works."

Luoying held her tongue. The Rudy before her was nothing like the Rudy she knew as a little girl. In those days, her big brother had loved to read soul-stirring tales of idealistic revolutionaries. He told her stories about the Renaissance, the French Revolution, the anarchist movements of the twenty-first century. When he told her about these heroes, his face lit up, his words poured out like a torrent, and he waved the pen in his hand about wildly like a sword. Those young predecessors who had led young revolutions in the young history of the human race made him gaze far into the future and elevated his soul. He once told her that all systems of rules, all order, existed to be broken by the brave. The young Rudy had only two dreams: to explore afar and to join a revolution.

"Then why don't you tell me the truth as you see it?" she asked, her voice now also cold. "You should have told me everything from the start. Why are you and Grandfather so determined to keep the truth from me? Why do you think I won't understand?"

"Some things you just *can't* understand."

"I can!"

Rudy had no interest in arguing with her. It was clear that he simply wanted to end the discussion as soon as possible. In a tired voice he said, "If you really think you can understand, then stop asking these questions. I've got much bigger problems to deal with right now. You can wait until later."

"What problems?"

"The negotiations with Earth."

Luoying remembered the looming crisis. "So there's been no progress?"

"No."

"They've made fusion technology a requirement?"

"They haven't said so. But it's clear they are not going to give up on it easily."

"What's our response?"

"We also haven't said anything definite." Rudy paused, but there was a strange expression on his face: the look a hunter got when he had sighted his prey. "If I were in charge... I would go with Uncle Juan's plan and strike first. It's the cleanest solution."

"Uncle Juan wants to go to war?"

"Of course."

"But his grandmother died in the war."

"That's totally different. Uncle Juan isn't suggesting we behave like the despicable Terrans, all butchers. He thinks we should capture the Moon bases with a surprise attack, quick and bloodless. Then we'll destroy or take over all Terran satellites in orbit. Earth would then be at our mercy. He has no interest in a massacre.

We're not like them."

"How can taking over the Moon bases be bloodless?"

"We can do it." Rudy spoke with conviction. "Do you think we've been wasting our time all these years? You have no idea how much we've invested in spaceflight and weapons research. Both Sanlias and Loqia research centers have been working nonstop, and there's no way Terran research, driven by commercial interests, can compete. Our fighters, even without fusion engines, are far more powerful than theirs. I'm not exaggerating: given our guidance systems and improved lasers, I think we'll take over the Moon bases within two weeks without meeting meaningful resistance."

Luoying's heart sank. *Two weeks. What kind of war can be over in two weeks?*

She remembered that old house on Earth. She and her friends had also said something about two weeks. *Give us two weeks, and we'll take everything back!* That was Lily-Ruta, the older girl who Luoying found so fascinating. *In two weeks we'll take over this place and return it to God, to the unfallen world.* She was lying on a rotting sofa, her feet on the back, her blond tresses matted as she closed her eyes and took another hit from the marijuana-packed hookah. *Trust me. Two weeks is more than enough.*

They were faithful heretics, worshippers of a god named Nature. They viewed the claims of the rich over pieces of land as illegitimate, as the desecration of Earth itself. Luoying joined them in their effort to take over a ranch, and they achieved a quick initial victory. But two weeks later, Lily-Ruta and her friends were trapped in the old house, running out of food and water, while outside, armored police vehicles surrounded the property and loudspeakers demanded their surrender every minute. They waited for their friends in Berlin to come rescue them by air, but they didn't know that their friends were also surrounded and trapped, just like them.

In the end, everyone was arrested. The movement ended with a whimper, without even meaningful sacrifices. The three weeks they spent in jail seemed both chaotic and silly. This was, in fact, the best conclusion: it was better to be laughed at then to have anyone die. Luoying had never really believed promises involving "two weeks," and certainly not after that. She could see that a planned surprise attack could succeed, but she no longer believed that there would be no counterattack or escalation.

"Once war starts, it won't end just because we want it to," she said.

"That's true only if we're not strong enough," he said.

That was another thing that had changed in Rudy. He had despised war as a child.

"Is there any way to avoid war?" she asked.

"Sure, if we get what we want from the negotiations."

"Do we really have to have those technologies?"

"We do. To bring water to Mars isn't just a grand engineering dream; it's about the very survival of our people."

"Why must we bring water from Ceres here? Can't we—"

"What is wrong with you?" Rudy slammed his mug down on the table and stood up, agitated. "It's no longer a matter of 'we must' but 'we already have'! We've gone so far down this road that it's impossible to stop. Look up! We brought Ceres here, and it's orbiting above us. For this plan, we drove ten thousand people out of their homes on the dwarf planet. How can we stop now?" His voice trembled as emotion tightened his throat. "Why did Grandfather's friend Ronen leave? For this dream of a wet Mars! He died for it, did you know that? He didn't even get out of the Solar System before he died. He was so old that he shouldn't have been on the ship at all, but he had to leave." Rudy took a deep breath to control himself. When he spoke again, his voice was calm. "We can't stop. No matter what the price."

Luoying's mind was blank. It was as if a bomb had gone off inside.

"Ronen... Grandpa Ronen is... dead?"

"Yes."

"When?"

"Yesterday."

Grandpa Ronen is dead. Dead. Luoying couldn't process the news. Ronen, with his Santa Claus white hair and beard, who loved to tell her stories, was dead.

———————

For the past half month at home, she had been full of doubts and questions, as though on the back of an untamed horse. But the sudden news of Ronen's death plunged her deep into reminiscence, into the blue light of the past. She sat on the window ledge of her bedroom, leaning against the shell-like open window, letting a montage of her childhood scenes replay among the flowers and lawns of the garden.

Among the elders of Mars, Grandpa Ronen was the one she felt closest to. Her parents had loved her, but they had died so early that memories of them had grown hazy. Grandpa Ronen was different. Between the ages of eight and thirteen, when she was at her most depressed, he stayed by her side, told her stories, listened to her confess her fears and failures, recommended books to her, and brought her out of her loneliness with his love of nature and trust in fate. He was always full of energy and optimism, full of interest in everything. She felt closer to him than she did to her own grandfather.

Everyone dies.

Ronen had said that to her. He didn't want to avoid the fact of her parents' deaths. She was old enough then to understand death, to understand loneliness and love. She didn't understand why, only how they made her feel. Ronen was the only one who spoke with her as though she were an adult, respected her feelings.

In ancient China, it was believed that a human life is the result of concentrated qi, of energy. A few decades is how long such concentrations lasted, and the qi dissipates in the end. In ancient India, some believed that a human life is merely a brief window into the eternal cosmic light. And in ancient Greece, the mythic Silenus ridiculed mankind by saying that the best thing for a man is to not be born at all, and the second best is to die as soon as possible.

All these traditions faced our mortality directly. We have only a few decades, and no matter how we strive to extend it, a lifetime is but a brief flash in the eyes of the gods and eternal cosmos. But that is precisely where the beauty and power of life lies. All of our vitality, our beliefs, our struggles and resistance, our despair—they are endowed with splendor because of our rapid decay. Think about it: a human being flashes like a bolt of lightning, leaving no trace in the darkness. But in that brief window, they can crystalize something out of their simple soul, something that will last far beyond their death, that will reach for eternity. What a fantastical fate! Even to strike a few poses during that brief flash is among the most magnificent phenomena in the universe.

This is why we must create. Every nation's philosophy is sublimated from our sense of our impending death. This is our answer to the eternal question of why? In creation we carve traces of the soul.

And so—Ronen held her by her slender shoulders, his gaze encompassing the universe—*don't grieve too much for your parents. They lived so brightly and left behind so many wonderful works infused with their soul. They also left you. They lived the best life possible, and you should celebrate that.*

Tears flowed down Luoying's face. She was eleven at the time when Ronen said these things to her, and they fell into her heart like seeds. She was grateful to him. A sixtysomething elder had spoken to an eleven-year-old girl with genuine respect, had trusted her to understand. And she had, though it had taken her seven years to do so.

He had spoken to her of life and death, and now he was dead. His life was a bright flash that had illuminated a child's heart.

Three days later Luoying came to the newly finished Grand Theater for dress rehearsal.

She had never put so much of herself into a dance, but suddenly she began to see the act of creation in a new light. She had feared dancing, had tired of dancing, had sought recognition through dancing, but she had never treated her art with as much seriousness as she now did. This dance was hers, the crystallization of all the walks she had taken through the broad avenues and narrow alleyways of Earth, collecting the brightest flowers of two planets. The dance was composed of simple poses and unembellished leaps, not at all sophisticated or masterful, but it represented five years of her life.

She fell and climbed right back up again, as she had done so many times already. She was going to extract her soul like a bubble and hold it in her palms, and then, from the stage, fling it to the audience until it filled the space.

She never told anyone that this dance was the reason she had left the troupe on Earth. They had lived a carefree life of joy with few constraints. Outside of the required dance sessions, the instructors left them alone. The group of thirteen- and fourteen-year-old girls were free to date whomever they liked, to sell holovids of their dances and buy new clothes with the money. On weekends they went out or performed at elegant banquets, where their dancing drew applause and more money. Sometimes they accepted gigs to be extras in films. Their lifestyle was one of comfort and joy, and she could have spent all her five years on Earth in that manner.

But she always felt she was missing something.

At first she attributed her sense of anxiety to the need to adjust to a new world. But one summer night during her second year on Earth she realized that it was because of the words Grandpa Ronen had spoken to her. They had sprouted in her heart, become part of her blood. And so she said goodbye to the other girls, left the pyramid-shaped city building, and began to wander.

She learned that she could doubt everything Mars had taught her, but she couldn't forget the sense of sacredness in the act of creation, planted deep in her heart by her homeland.

Today's rehearsal was going to be attended by the Terran delegation.

The Grand Theater was one of the largest buildings on Mars. Externally, it resembled a lotus rising above ocean waves. The waves formed the entrance lobby, while the lotus flower was the performance hall itself. The hall was an oval dome with curving walls and very brightly lit. At the center of the hall was the circular stage, and above it hung spotlights shaped like snowballs. The seats for the audience surrounded the stage in concentric rings.

When Luoying arrived at the theater, Rudy was giving the Terran delegates a tour. He had been preparing for this the last few days. Now he was dressed in a crisp dark suit, and it showed off his broad shoulders and trim waist well. His name was embroidered in gold thread on the breast.

Luoying and the other performers stood at a distance from the delegates. Gielle lifted her chin as she stood among the crowd, gazing intently.

Luoying smiled. She knew why Gielle had chosen today for the dress rehearsal.

Rudy was explaining features of the theater to the Terran delegation. "A big problem facing all theaters with three-hundred-and-sixty-degree seating is that the performer can face only one direction. The usual solution is to use a rotating stage, but we went the other way. The audience moves around the performers."

Rudy gestured at the control booth in the distance, and the audience area began to move. The concentric rings of seats migrated to one side of the hall. Some of the seats moved up the ovoid walls until the curving surface pushed them into stadium formation. The farthest seats were hanging so high up the wall that they looked like balloon-shaped reliefs. A few of the delegates cried out in amazement. Luoying smiled.

"With powerful magnetic fields, we can move these seats to any part of the hall, even the ceiling. There's no need to be concerned about safety. First, here on Mars we've embedded magnetic fields in the walls of buildings as a key aspect of city design, and after decades of development the technology has a proven safety record. Second, even if something were to go wrong, causing the seats to fall, we have an independent backup system below the floor to generate a second magnetic field to levitate the seats and ensure that they descend at an acceptable rate."

Rudy gestured naturally as he lectured, his hair falling gracefully about his shoulders. As a child, he had taken first place in a public speaking contest and was experienced with such occasions.

He guided the delegates to another part of the theater, and his voice drifted away as well. "Now, as for audio engineering, the ceiling of the theater is perforated with an array of microscopic holes..."

Realizing that Rudy was about to leave, Gielle rushed Luoying onto the stage. She herself ran to the control booth.

Gielle had designed Luoying's costume. The dress rehearsal was not only Luoying's performance but also Gielle's. Indeed, Gielle was even more nervous than Luoying, and Rudy's presence made Gielle blush furiously.

Gielle had finished the costume in a single week. When she first showed up at Luoying's home, she asked her for the theme of her dance. Luoying said it was Yinghuo, which was the ancient Chinese name for Mars, and literally meant *to bewilder*.

Luoying's dance was based on an ancient Chinese myth. The planet Yinghuo, due to its erratic path and changing brightness, was seen as a harbinger of war and disaster. A young girl who from birth was under the influence of the red planet lived a life of suffering and struggle until she died in the flame and smoke of war, rising into the heavens to become the brilliant, flaming clouds of dawn and dusk.

Gielle immediately begged Luoying. "You have to wear me!"

Luoying agreed, though she wasn't sure why Gielle was so intent on helping her. When she saw the costume, she was speechless. The dress was breathtakingly beautiful, soft and elegant like cloud and mist, like her dance.

"The colors change as you touch it," said Gielle. "This is a new material from Pierre's atelier, woven from extremely thin semiconductor filaments. Pressure changes the coordination complexes within the filaments, which in turn change their light absorption characteristics." Gielle laughed. "I don't really understand the details, but it basically changes color on touch. I came up with the idea of adapting the material for clothing. When you dance, it will also change color based on your movements."

Luoying had caressed the soft material and looked at Gielle with gratitude.

She had grown up with Gielle and Brenda, played house with them, went to the same schools and neighborhood gatherings. Both of them were now also eighteen and had just chosen their ateliers. They were following life paths as smooth and clear as water, a life Luoying could no longer have. Gielle chose to join a clothing-design atelier, while Brenda chose poetry. Even as a girl, Gielle had loved to sew clothes for their dolls, and Brenda had written a book of sonnets at eleven. They both spoke of the dream of watching their citation rates rise to number one in the central archive as more and more citizens chose to quote or use their creations.

Whenever Luoying looked at them, her heart was filled with tumult.

The stage was about fifty meters in diameter. Usually it was at ground height but could be raised or lowered during performance.

Embedded in the stage was the design of a giant pentagram, and at the points of the star were the symbols for the five natural elements. The design was made from light-emitting filaments and glowed in the dark. The youth choir was at one side of the stage, where Ms. Shana, the choir director, had the children sing selections from Puccini's *Tosca* to test the sound system.

The theater quieted. Luoying walked to the middle of the stage and stood still. She crossed her arms, letting her sleeves hang naturally. The air in the hall was still, and the sleeves gently swayed like clear water, with patterns of clouds at the edges and a few lace flowers here and there. The material flowed gracefully along her body.

Luoying looked to the theater entrance. The Terran

delegation, their tour complete, was walking in a long line toward it. Eko and Theon, engrossed in a chat, walked at the very back of the line. Eko was dressed in a dark formal suit, emphasizing his height. Theon was in a navy-blue silk shirt, his collar unbuttoned. He looked particularly striking, standing between Eko and Rudy.

The music started. Four bars later the spotlights came on.

Bright blue-white light illuminated Luoying, surrounding her in blinding brightness. She uncrossed her arms and made three long leaps. Her costume was so light that she barely felt it. The long skirt swayed, spreading open as though dissolving in air. As she moved through her routine, her sleeves glowed where they came into contact with her skin. She leaped across the stage and looked back: the long train of her costume spread open like the cap of a jellyfish, with colors flowing in a spectrum from orange to indigo, like wisps of clouds at dawn.

The music flowed with her steps. She turned, pushed off, rose into the air, and spun three times before landing.

She was now one with the dance, and she was revisiting all the spots she had been to during her time on Earth. She was the girl from the myth, journeying through a war-torn land, facing down hostile stares. She wandered far, until the scenes she had witnessed became parts of herself. Every bright sunlit field, every snowbound mountain, every house, river, rock, and fence that had flashed before her eyes in this all-too-brief life; she was a montage of all of them. No, she didn't create them; they *created* her. They welcomed her in every corner, embraced her in every moment. Piece by piece, they molded her out of nothingness. She was simply realizing them for the audience, an unceasing string of moments of realization.

She saw the beautiful smiles, the genuine joy of the girls of the dance troupe who taught her how to drink and party, the lively expressions of Lily-Ruta as she recounted to her the myths she believed in, the uproarious laughter of the Reversionists around the bonfire as they warmed one another's hearts and crossed the gulf of difference, the mysterious smile on Gielle's face as she declared *You have to wear me!* All of them—*all of them*—melded into one.

She danced, devoting herself to the joys and smiles and laughter. Her ankles ached, but she refused to acknowledge the pain. She put more of herself into the movements, strained to spin, spin, spin, letting her costume turn into a halo of shifting, brilliant colors.

The drums pounded. She was at the apex of her highest leap. She fell, landed with one knee on the floor, her sleeves gently drifting down like a veil.

The music stopped. Complete silence.

She panted, and tears welled in her eyes. She kept her head down. She wasn't sure if Grandpa Ronen's spirit could see her performance from the afterlife, but she wanted to tell him *I did my best*.

"Brava! Brava!!!"

The applause from a single pair of hands echoed loudly in the vast hall. She looked up and saw it was Theon. He approached the stage, his forehead glowing in the stage lights, a kind smile on his face. He stopped before the stage and bowed deeply.

"You're truly a princess of Mars, a woodland nymph! I'm utterly devastated that I didn't get to attend one of your performances on Earth."

Luoying regarded him suspiciously.

Theon's tone was warm and charming, but the florid praise couldn't disguise his cold gaze. Luoying saw in his eyes a hint of mockery—and something much more complicated. She didn't know what he wanted.

"Please, would you tell me the name of the genius who designed your costume?"

Luoying pointed at Gielle, standing to the side.

"Oh, what a lovely young lady," said Theon, spreading his arms dramatically. "My dear, would you be interested in showing your masterpiece on Earth?"

Gielle was so excited that her eyes went wide. "Really? Are you serious? Let me tell you my—" But Luoying stopped her.

In a flash, Luoying understood what was going on. She knew that Gielle was about to tell Theon her account number and the resource locator for her designs and explanations. She was going to tell him *You can download them right now.*

She knew how much Gielle craved such attention. Theon's interest in her invention would lead to many more searches and downloads of her designs. But Luoying didn't want Theon to obtain the invention so easily. She saw it as an opportunity for negotiation.

The clothing design and material were also technologies, and technologies could be haggled over, could be the subjects of negotiations. Was there a chance to make a deal here that would bypass the technology of controlled fusion, that would avoid a war?

Luoying tried to estimate the likelihood of success. The material of her costume was attractive. It seemed transparent everywhere but was in fact transparent nowhere. She thought it would be in demand among the fashion-conscious on Earth and especially attractive to someone like Theon. Fashion was also technology, and one of Theon's most important sources of income.

And Theon was someone who could influence the whole delegation. He held the power to change a wall—a wall that was both thicker and more transparent than Martian glass.

The Thales Group was Earth's largest commercial web market operator. Countless people went to the Thales Group's platform for entertainment, business, news, and friendship; to sell knowledge; to buy information. Anyone could enter the glitzy market with a thin screen in hand. This was a wall as thick as Earth's atmosphere, one that enveloped the whole globe and crossed national boundaries. From presidents to religious fundamentalists, everyone relied on the web to sell themselves. There was no greater shared resource, and therefore Theon was the only one who could influence all the delegates.

She gazed at Theon, whose charming smile appeared on the home page of every social network. He wasn't a dull man; in fact, he looked quite intelligent. She knew that he was her only chance to influence the negotiations between the worlds.

THE ATELIER

The time that Luoying and Gielle agreed to was ten in the morning. The place: Bujuxie Garment Atelier, Russell District.

The weather was excellent today. There was no wind and no sand in the air beyond the dome. The sun glowed brightly against the dark sky; all was at peace.

Eko sat next to Theon on the tube train. They each stared out the transparent wall, not speaking. Eko was still angry with Theon. The tube train glided smoothly along the tunnel, and houses and footpaths swept through Eko's view. He, however, wasn't paying attention to the view. His mind was dominated by the unpleasant argument from the night before, ending with a slammed door.

"And so you did nothing?"

Eko had leaped out of his chair at this, consumed with rage. "Yes."

"Not even a regional test?"

"I did do a test run with the New York Film Critics Circle. Oh, also with the Royal Academy of Arts in London."

"Did you give them the technology or sell it to them?"

"They were sales. But only the chips, not the designs. One

deal was for nine million dollars, and the other for seven-point-six million pounds."

"So you made a profit."

"Not much. These are rounding errors."

Eko choked back his words. He stared at Theon, who was sunken deep in his sofa, holding the stem of his wineglass with three fingers, staring expressionlessly at the liquid within. Remembering Arthur Davosky's curled up, disease-ravaged body and Janet Brook's tearstained face, Eko's heart convulsed. He couldn't understand how Theon could be so cold, as though talking about a matter of accounting. He suppressed his anger and continued the discussion, though the muscles of his back tensed.

"My teacher gave his life for this technology."

"I had no other choice. Earth isn't Mars, and there are some things that… have no market."

"You're talking about profit."

"Don't be so dismissive of profit. The Thales Group has millions of employees around the globe. All of them depend on profit."

"How much do you make, on average, from a single IP vendor?"

"A penny, give or take."

"You won't give up even a penny?"

"Are you aware how many sellers there are on our platform?"

"But you have income from the stores, the theme parks, and advertising. Why can't you give up even a little? You know that an open artistic space, a commons, benefits everyone."

"Really? You believe every creator thinks this way?"

"Any creator worthy of that name should think this way."

A mocking smile appeared on Theon's face. He swirled his glass and looked at Eko.

"It appears that Arthur did pass on his delusions to you." Eko picked up his coat and stormed out of the hotel suite.

It was Theon's attitude that hurt him the most. The way he had dismissed his teacher's hope, like flicking the ash from the end of his cigarette, stung. He had called Davosky's dreams delusions, denigrating his life's choice as naïve. Eko could not tolerate it. In his mind he could see his teacher crossing eighty million kilometers of empty space to carry back a chip, leaving all he loved behind; he could see Davosky looking up at Mars at night while Janet Brook looked back at Earth, divided by the unbridgeable vacuum. He refused to accept that all these sacrifices were for nothing, to be dismissed in a single sentence. It was like watching a man pushing a giant black boulder up the mountain, only to have a finger nudge it off the path near the top, plunging it into the abyss.

Eko believed in his teacher's choice. True creators *would* welcome such a space. Yes, an artist would have less income, but they would also have ten times the audience. Even those who could not or would not pay would go experience their art, and such an archive would give creations a vastly greater space to exist. All real creators cared only that others cared about their art, and nothing else. How could this be wrong? How could it be a delusion?

Eko strode down the empty corridor, shouting inside himself. *Profit! Why are you thinking only of profit? Why do you call anything that doesn't care about profit a delusion? All you know is expansion, empire building, love of numbers in a spreadsheet. You have no understanding of the world; you have no right to criticize. You are nothing but a merchant!*

The lump in Eko's throat grew. He had not been so angry for a long time. He had always believed that he was there to understand the workings of the real world, and anger had no place in that process. But on this night, the emotions he had been tamping down for days finally erupted.

Theon called out after him.

"Eko, a moment, please."

Eko stopped and twisted his head around, his face stony. He saw Theon standing at the door of his suite, one hand against the frame. The harsh hallway light and the deep shadows made it impossible to see his expression.

"Are you coming to the negotiation tomorrow?"

"Yes."

In his mind Eko shouted, *Of course I'm going. Why wouldn't I?*

Abruptly he calmed down, laughing inside. This was an opportunity. *I'll go tomorrow to disrupt your plans, to ruin your trading hopes. I'll reveal you for who you are and then laugh at you, mocking you for being full of delusions.*

Instantly he felt better. He walked back to his room and fell into bed, though the dreams ensured the sleep wasn't restful.

———

The next morning Eko got up early and entered the central archive to browse the personal spaces of Gielle and Brenda.

The central archive was completely open inside. Once he had found their ateliers, everything was available: their CVs, self-introductions, productions. Gradually he formulated.

He even saw all the technical documents for Gielle's design and clothing material. If he revealed these secrets to Theon, then there was no need for any negotiation at all. But he was glad to keep his lips sealed. He had promised Janet to keep the secret, and he had no interest in helping Theon succeed. His goal was to defeat him with facts.

Churches and steep-roofed houses swept past the speeding

tube train. Neatly trimmed bushes surrounded open squares. The sun was bright and the sky clear.

Eko looked at Theon. Theon smiled at him as though there was no tension between them at all.

The argument last night had not begun as such. At first the two reminisced about Arthur. Theon told Eko about their friendship, which had begun in childhood. Arthur was four years older than Theon, and the two families were close. They went to the same school and worked in the same trade. Arthur took Theon skiing and hosted his graduation party. The two made good partners. Theon distributed the films that Arthur produced, and the two won awards and enjoyed success together. Later, when Arthur went to Mars, Theon was the only one who knew what he wanted. Indeed, Theon knew more about Mars than Eko. Under Arthur's direction, the Thales Group had better mastery of full-fidelity holographic film technology than anyone else, and that was in part the reason for its dominance in the market. Theon was grateful for everything Arthur had done for him, and they were lifelong friends.

Even so, he still betrayed Arthur's dream during the last ten years of his life.

———

At ten, Eko and Theon entered Bujuxie Garment Atelier.

The first thing that struck a visitor to the atelier was how colorful it was. It didn't feel like an art gallery; rather, the furnishing felt casual and unplanned, a place dominated by inspiration and comfort. On the left wall were giant frames of portraits and abstract doodles, while the right wall was covered by plaques, awards, commemorative scrolls, and the like. Several mannequins stood in the middle of the room, wearing various items of colorful, unfinished clothing. The sun, scattered by the beige glass, bathed the whole room in an even, warm light.

When Eko and Theon entered, several people were already in the atelier. Luoying, Gielle, and Brenda were sitting on the largest round inflated cushion in the middle of the room, reading. Brenda sat on the left and Luoying in the middle, and Gielle was lying prone next to them. She sat up as she saw Eko and Theon and leaned against Luoying as she regarded them with curiosity. Brenda was shy and quiet, her blond hair framing her pale features.

Eko and Theon sat down on the small sofa opposite the girls. A few phrases were plastered haphazardly on the wall behind them, and at first Eko had thought of it as some kind of conceptual art involving random words. But once he sat down, he realized they formed a quote:

Freedom is our desire. Therefore, we design our institutions to teach our students to be free persons, physically and mentally.

—Paul Waston, Mars, 2042

Eko found the quote intriguing. Against the smooth wall, the phrases, slanting this way and that, seemed to have been put together by a gust of wind.

Eko saw that Luoying had a photo album over her knees, which was open to a few images of mountains and bamboo groves, likely a record of her travels on Earth that she was showing to Gielle. Next to her lay a book: *Le Mythe de Sisyphe*. He was surprised. The book seemed to echo the image of the man pushing the boulder up the mountain. She wasn't looking at him.

Theon began with some small talk. Glancing at Luoying's photo album, he asked about her life on Earth.

"Did you visit London and Paris?"

"I lived in both, though just a few weeks in each."

"Then you've probably been to Dreamscape parks. London and Paris both have them, and there's one in Shanghai. Did you live in Shanghai?"

"No. I know about the parks but have never been to one."

"What's Dreamscape?" asked Gielle, still leaning on Luoying's shoulder.

"Ah, they are the pride of the Thales Group," said Luoying. "The theme parks are centered around fantastical experiences based on spaceships, pristine nature, fashion, world cuisine, everything. They are huge, and every visit is like a film, an adventure, a life."

"Wow!" Gielle was amazed. "Why didn't you go?"

"I…" Luoying shook her head. "I… just forgot."

Eko found the answer interesting. Luoying was able to practically recite their advertising slogan word for word, and yet she seemed to think nothing of the allure behind those words. He felt she was perhaps sympathetic to his own ideals. Having been to the parks himself, he knew just how powerful their draw was. On Earth, most people had either gone to the parks or wanted to but couldn't. It was rare to see anyone react like Luoying, unmoved by their appeal.

Luoying looked composed and determined. She seemed unwilling to waste time with aimless chitchat. "Mr. Thomas Theon, Gielle's design isn't just limited to dance costumes. It's generalizable to all kinds of garments. The material is light and breathable."

Theon smiled. "I can tell."

"The color-changing property is inherent in the material.

Depending on the source of light, the changes are also different."

"Even more interesting."

"It's not hard to produce or to work with."

"Great, but let's slow down a bit." Theon leaned forward, still smiling. "I have complete faith in the design, and I would love to be the agent to introduce it to Earth. But... I have to know: What are your expectations?"

"What do you mean?"

"The royalty structure, for instance. Or the terms of our agency agreement."

Luoying smiled reassuringly. "We have no special requests. We're happy to have the technology be part of the official exchange, pursuant to standard terms. Whatever the Thales Group wants to do to promote it on Earth is fine with us."

"In other words, you're willing to sell us all rights."

"Sure, if you prefer to understand it in those terms."

Theon nodded and leaned back in the sofa. He gave the appearance of being satisfied, but Luoying could see suspicion brewing under his smile. He was trying to figure out Luoying's real goal.

Theon never underestimated his opponent. Even if Luoying was just a girl, he gave her his full concentration. He couldn't yet tell what Luoying wanted, and so he said neither yes nor no.

Eko knew that one of the fundamental principles Theon followed was to give his opponent what was due. It was the only way to guarantee continued profit. When the other side claimed to want nothing in return, Theon tended to be more careful than ever. In Theon's view, such opponents came in two varieties: those who knew nothing about the big picture, and those who hid their agendas deep. Most tended to fall into the latter category, so he never accepted favors without carefully understanding the situation.

Theon was in no rush. He regarded Luoying like a principal

looking at one of his students, trying to let the conversation develop in a relaxed mood. He asked after her hobbies and inquired Gielle about her studies. He was trying to probe around the issue.

"Do you have a name for your amazing invention?" he asked Gielle.

"No, actually. I don't."

"How about Mystify? At once transparent and opaque, like the night sky, and a perfect companion to the ancient Chinese name for Mars. In advertising, we can say... *Clothes that carry you into the air. Crystalized melody and flowing painting.* How about it?"

Gielle was unfamiliar with the art of advertising, and the exaggerated phrasing made her blush like an overripe apple. "That... Do you really think it's that amazing?"

Eko knew it was time for him to say something. In the sunlit atelier, some of the young workers on the other side of the room were having dessert, and delicious aromas wafted from the coffee bar in the corner. The sweet air felt a bit unreal, like an attempt at covering up differences so that everyone would enjoy the mutual praise and press forward to a magnificent fashion banquet. Gielle was delighted by the bright visions conjured by Theon, while Luoying sat next to her quietly, making no comment. Eko didn't know what she was thinking behind her dark eyes, but he had to stop Theon from carrying out his plan, step by step, luring the girls into becoming his partners, into profit.

He stood up and cleared his throat.

Smiling at Gielle, he said, "I have a question for you: Do you make all your designs available? That is, can anyone have you make them something based on your invention?"

"Of course."

"Could I ask you to make me a suit using your process?"

"Sure! Let me get your measurements right now."

Gielle jumped up and found a measuring tape in one of the cabinets nearby. Eko stood up, raised his arms to the sides, and turned under Gielle's direction so that she could measure his shoulders, arms, chest, waist… Carefully, she noted down the numbers in her electronic notepad. The two were wholly absorbed in the act, careless of the astonished looks the others tossed their way.

While Gielle was measuring him, Eko tried to strike up a conversation with Brenda. He pointed to the book on her knees. "Do you enjoy writing poetry?"

Brenda nodded. "I do, though I haven't written many."

"Does it make you happy to have your poems sitting somewhere, waiting, until one day they're read by someone who truly understands them?"

"Absolutely. That's the greatest happiness."

Eko nodded. Brenda looked completely serious, and her hands, placed over her knees, looked pale and thin against the fabric of her dark blue skirt. Eko had read some of her poems and found them full of a youthful inquiring spirit and deeply authentic.

Eko stole a glance at Theon, who looked back at him with a cocky smirk, as though not concerned at all.

"All right. I got all the measurements I need." Gielle put away the tape.

"Thank you. When do you think you'll be finished?"

"Give me two days. I'll design the suit on my computer and then send the pattern to the workshop."

"How much do I owe you?"

"Oh, it won't be much." Gielle seemed afraid that he was going to cancel his request. "The production process is easy, and the material isn't rare either. Pierre told me that his atelier has worked out an efficient process for making the filaments and membrane, but usually they don't bother with it, since clothing isn't something they care about. It really won't cost you much. Honest."

Eko chuckled. "Do you like having lots of people using your designs?"

"Of course! My citation rate is very low right now."

"In that case, I wonder if you understand the fate awaiting your invention on Earth."

Gielle looked confused. "What do you mean?"

"I can tell you right now that very few customers on Earth will order clothes based on your invention, and even fewer will get to wear them."

"But why? I thought Earth has a huge population."

Eko's tone was like a storyteller's trying to hook an audience. "Theon is going to hide your invention and keep it away from the public. No one will know how to make the material, and they won't be able to buy it either. Theon is going to make a tiny number of garments and sell them for astronomical sums."

Gielle looked lost. "But... why?"

Eko knew he had her. "Let me ask you: How do you determine the price you charge for clothes?"

"The cost of the material plus the machine time."

"That's not how things work on Earth. He gets to decide the price, and he can charge as much as he likes."

"That's ridiculous."

"It isn't as long as he can find customers willing to pay."

"Why would anyone pay that much for clothes?"

"Oh, some will." Eko had the absurd sensation that he was telling a terrifying fairy tale to a child. "He has ways of persuading people to cough up the price he demands."

"Like what ways?"

"No other company will be allowed to produce Mystify, and he's going to make the price so high that only a small number of people will even be able to contemplate buying it. That, in turn, will turn Mystify into a status symbol and make it even more desirable. Customers will be knocking down the door. This is classic Theon."

"But it's not fair." Gielle's expression was determined. "Everyone should be equal."

"Equality is nice in theory, but if everyone were equal, who's going to buy? Disparity drives desire. It's only by keeping Mystify out of the reach of most people that they'll covet it. Theon is going to say that Mystify represents a sense of who you are. To wear Mystify clothing makes you noble, elevated, full of ideals; it turns you into a princess of Mars."

"But that's a lie!" Brenda broke in.

"I know, and I agree with you," said Eko. He felt the pleasure of denouncing something he'd long despised. "But many people, some of them girls like you, will believe the lies. They follow his direction and think only of jewelry and clothes, of famous brands. Their hearts are empty, but they think by buying and buying they will possess a soul."

"That's enough."

Eko wasn't expecting Luoying to break in.

"Mr. Lu, I think you exaggerate. I've lived with other girls on Earth. Sure, many of them love to shop, but they haven't lost their souls because of it."

"You have your perspective," said Eko, quickly recovering, "and Theon has his. Gielle, listen to me. You told me that you want more people to wear your designs, that you care the most about your citation rate. You're going to be disappointed. Theon will not allow your invention to be enjoyed by everyone.

He's going to wield it like a weapon: a weapon for manufacturing desire, a weapon for generating a sense of status envy and feelings of inadequacy. He's going to use the weapon to control the girls on Earth, to make money from them, to give himself power."

"That's despicable!" Gielle looked shocked. "It's evil. I won't allow him to have my invention."

But Luoying gazed at Eko, a stubborn look in her eyes. "I believe this invention *will* be shared on Earth, and Mr. Theon isn't going to exploit it in the manner you describe." She turned to Theon. "I have faith in this."

Eko was surprised. Sure, he had deliberately simplified the issues and spoken in an exaggerated manner, but he hadn't lied. Everyone knew the gospels of consumerism. The techniques of merchants were well understood and, in fact, they took pride in them and called them "consumer psychology."

"You have faith in him?" he asked Luoying. "Fine, let's ask him."

He gazed at Theon, confident that he would be vindicated. Theon was not the type to lie on such matters.

Theon nodded. "I will indeed inject some sense of status disparity into the marketing of Mystify. But I don't think there's anything unfair about it." He looked relaxed, as though commenting on a stage play that had nothing to do with him.

"How can you sound so cold?" Gielle turned to Luoying. "We can't give him the invention. We can't."

Eko had achieved his goal. His only plan for the day had been to throw a wrench into Theon's mercantile gears, to let him know that many creators cared more about worth than profit. He had achieved his goal but he couldn't celebrate, because at the moment of his success, he saw Luoying's eyes.

She didn't talk but she stared at him, her eyes full of

accusation, as well as exhaustion and helplessness. Under her bangs, her long lashes resembled thin reeds by a spring deep in a valley, swaying noiselessly. She bit the bottom of her lip, and her expression seemed to say, *Why are you doing this? You understand nothing.*

Eko's heart skipped a beat. He wondered if he really didn't understand. Her eyes were like ice-cold pools that cooled off his will to fight. He hesitated.

Luoying patted Gielle's hand and nodded gently. Then she sat down without saying another word.

THE GALLERY

Luoying walked very fast. She was headed in the general direction of home, but not directly toward it. She was walking by instinct, without a specific goal in mind. She knew all the roads in the district and wasn't going to get lost.

She paid so little attention to her surroundings that she didn't hear the footsteps behind her.

Why did I fail? she thought. *Have I thought of everything as too simple? Was my plan doomed? Should I have explained everything to Gielle first? But how would that have helped?*

Why did Eko prevent a deal? I thought he was Theon's friend. Was there some misunderstanding?

Maybe my whole idea is absurd. It's like trying to stop a warship with a flower, to prevent a war with a fluttering dress. Maybe these men think of me as a little girl, a naïve, ridiculous girl.

She turned onto a side road, crossed a trail, followed another narrow lane, crossed a plaza, until she was in the community park. She was surrounded by layers of green. Since it was almost noon, very few people were around. The winding footpath stayed in the shade of the pagoda trees. The park was so quiet that she calmed down, immersed in the water-like verdant light.

"Luoying!"

She stopped and turned. Eko emerged from the turn in the footpath behind her. He ran up to her and said apologetically, "I'm sorry. I called your name several times, but you were walking so fast that you didn't hear me."

Luoying nodded without saying more. The silence between them stretched awkwardly.

"I..." Eko struggled to find the words. "I think I must have offended you somehow. I'm sorry. I don't understand—"

"It's all right," said Luoying. "It's not your fault."

"You wanted a deal to be made?"

"Yes."

"Why?"

Luoying looked at him. "Why are you opposed to it?"

"Because I despise his monopolistic manipulations. Don't you?"

"I don't care about that." Luoying began to turn away.

"Wait! When you were on Earth, did you buy the fashion brands sold by the Thales Group?"

"Very few pieces."

"But many of the girls in your troupe liked them, right?"

"Yes."

"And so you have positive emotions toward his commercial empire?"

"I don't care about that!"

Luoying stared at him and then said emphatically, "The problem isn't whether someone should or shouldn't make a profit; the problem is Mars and Earth."

"But profit is the difference between how people live on the two planets."

"I don't think that's it at all."

"You should be even more aware of this than I," said Eko. "Look at the girls here, your friends: you discuss creation, prize what you can invent or compose or design. The girls on Earth, the ones you know, on the other hand, pursue nothing except the chance to buy the next outfit. Don't you consider this a great difference?"

"So what?"

"It's the religion of consumerism, where human nature has been turned away from *agape* and debased into covetousness."

"That's simplistic." Luoying was tired. She found Eko's discussion style exhausting, pointless. "You're just throwing a bunch of abstract jargon at me."

"Are you saying I'm wrong?"

"You're not wrong… but abstractions and lives are different. Fundamentally, what's the difference between designing clothes and buying clothes? Do you really think Gielle and my friends were born artists? No! There is no difference between girls on Earth and girls on Mars. No difference between people."

"Of course. We are the products of our environments."

Luoying shook her head in frustration. "No… or at least that's not all. Do you know why my friends on Earth buy clothes? To express themselves. Even though they were shaped by their surroundings, they want to be unique. Whether designing clothes or buying clothes, the fundamental impulse is the same. They can't choose the world they live in, or how that world operates, but they want to live their own lives, to find out who they are. That is all."

Her friends' faces appeared in her mind. The looks of joy, shyness, pride, anxiety—craving for praise—were so similar, and they melded into one. They lived on different planets and pursued different lifestyles, but they experienced the same pleasures and disappointments. She remembered those faces; they were her dance. She didn't want to debate him anymore and continued her walk.

But Eko followed her, unwilling to let go. The low-hanging branches almost touched the tops of their heads, and the dappled shadows caressed their faces. For a long while they didn't speak.

"Your dance troupe on Earth… they were very contemporary in style, weren't they?"

"Yes."

"I remember you telling me that you stayed with them for only two years?"

"Yes."

"You just got up and left?"

"Our instructors were hired only to give us lessons. No one cared if we stayed or not. The artistic director didn't care either. When our room-and-board contracts ran out, any of us were free to leave. I wasn't even one of the principals. There were so many other dancers who wanted to join the troupe that as soon as I left, someone else took my place."

"No, that's not what I meant. I want to understand *why* you left."

Luoying said nothing.

"You didn't like the noisy city pyramid?"

"That didn't bother me."

"Then you didn't get along with the other dancers?"

"No, I liked them."

"Then why?"

Luoying paused before answering. "Because I wanted to feel like I was creating."

"Oh… but the last time I asked you if you wanted to be a great dancer, a star, you said no."

"I want to create, but I have no interest in greatness."

"Can't you create as part of the troupe?"

"The troupe preferred to dance from a repertoire or to

prepare choreography based on specific requests, but I wanted to create my own dances."

"I understand. Didn't Camus say that to create is to live twice?" Luoying smiled at him. She no longer felt so anxious.

"You must be overjoyed to be back on Mars," said Eko, "where you're free to create."

"Not really."

"Why not?"

"I..." Luoying lowered her eyes. "I don't want to register with an atelier."

"Are you dissatisfied with something?"

"That's not quite right," said Luoying. She was thinking of her mother. "I'm just full of doubts about the world around me, unable to imagine myself living the life I was assigned to. You don't know that an atelier is for life. Though switching isn't forbidden, it's extremely rare for anyone on Mars to change ateliers. Everyone climbs the career ladder rung by rung, spending a whole life within the confines of two parallel lines. If I had never been to Earth, I suppose it wouldn't bother me. But I have been there. You know the lifestyle of everyone on Earth: free to come and go, free to hop from profession to profession. I've grown used to that kind of life, filled with fluidity and experiments. I don't want to live in a pyramid."

"I understand." Eko's voice was infused with certainty. "You grew up on Mars, and so you identify with the lofty values here. But you've also lived on Earth, where you became used to constant change. Although you seem to be arguing for both sides, in reality, you have faith in neither."

His words wounded her. She knew he was right. Lack of faith—that was her problem. She couldn't identify fully with either side. When she was on Earth, she missed home; and now that she was home, she missed Earth. This was her problem and the problem of everyone in her group.

"Why do you care so much about what I think?" she asked.

"Because I want to understand you."

She was thinking about how to respond when she noticed the button on the strap of his backpack: a glowing green light. A camera was in operation.

Instantly she realized she had been tricked. Her heart sank, and tears came unbidden to her eyes. She had not wanted to speak with him at all, but he had worn down her defenses. Everything she had told him had come straight from the heart, but he had only been trying to capture her on film.

"I don't want to be understood by you. Did you ever think of that?"

Her tone was rude, but she found his violation far worse. What right had he to "understand" her? He was curious; he spouted biting criticisms; he enjoyed probing into the minds of his subjects, like solving an intellectual puzzle. But was that enough for him to understand her, to understand her friends? How could he know their heartrending pain, their youthful anxieties, their authentic confusion, and their yearning for answers as a result of growing up on two worlds? Even if he really wanted to, how much could he empathize?

Ultimately, he stood on the other shore. What he said was correct, but he did not feel her pain. An observer never suffered like the subject. All problems in life were problems of the subject; the instant you began to observe, you had no more problems.

"Do you find it *interesting* to see someone lose her faith?" Tears welled in her eyes, but she refused to let them fall.

She turned and ran away, stranding him in the garden as he watched her vanish down the path.

It was night by the time she woke up. Luoying continued to lie in bed, turning over the encounter in her head. She was still agitated, the garden and the path still fresh in her mind.

She asked herself why she was so sensitive to comparisons between the two worlds, to the point where she couldn't live a normal life while she sought commonality between them. Humans had the capacity to adjust, and if she could just adapt to the difference in the social order, she would be fine.

But doing so wouldn't be right. She couldn't articulate the impetus in her heart that pressed her forward to consider the difference between the two worlds as not merely a difference in institutions and arrangements but a difference between two entire philosophies.

On Earth, everyone had told her that they were free and taken pride in such freedom. She had experimented with their freedom and knew that they were right; she had loved that sense of being untethered, of being adrift. But she also remembered that when she was a child in classrooms on Mars, she had been told that only Martians were free. To be free from worrying about the basic necessities of life, to have an atelier of their own, meant they didn't have to sell their creative freedom for money. Her teachers told her that when a person had to sell their thoughts for money to buy bread, then that person was doomed to be enslaved by the struggle for survival, and what they created no longer represented them but the will of money and commerce. Only on Mars was humankind free. She remembered seeing Jean-Léon Gérôme's *The Slave Market*, and the painting had made such a deep impression on her that for a long time on Earth she dared not sell herself on the web.

Now that she had lived in both worlds, she wasn't sure

which chains were heavier: the system that ensured everyone had no more and no less than what they needed, or the poverty that resulted from the struggle for survival. But she did know that all humans loved freedom, and the more their ways of life differed, the more that fundamental commonality prevailed.

Freedom! Life is art, and the nature of art is freedom.

She suddenly heard her mother's voice, that gentle, passion-infused voice. Her mother had said this to her when she was only five.

Luoying's heart melted. Her mother had always indulged her, including the little girl in all her artistic events. Luoying remembered the time when she had been in a pink dress and her mother had carried her as she laughed and talked with her friends in the study. The sun had poured through the window like a waterfall, seeped through the books, and washed all the excited adult faces. Some were holding forth while others listened politely, but even little Luoying could sense in them an unrestrained wildness. Even the arches of her mother's brows spoke to her of freedom as she laughed. Luoying had felt that she was in a different world, a world in which she was happy.

You were born with the Light, my darling. Your very birth was a miraculous act of art.

The four-year-old Luoying had been too young to really understand what that meant. She sat on her mother's lap, gazing up at her mother's smiling eyes. She knew only that she was loved, and she was full of joy and pride.

The memories came back to her bit by bit. Brightly lit fragments and scenes, they didn't cohere into a plot. They had been lying dormant at the bottom of the ocean that was her mind, untouched by light for years. But they had never vanished. As she probed and explored, the ice melted inch by inch, and the ocean was roiled by waves.

Pure white moonlight streamed through the window. Her bed, which was next to the window, seemed to meld with it. Outside, ivy draped like a natural curtain. The window was a seashell at night, and the moonlight was like the glow of an angel.

She wanted to see her parents' study again.

Jumping off the bed, she dressed, padded through the quiet hallways, and returned to the study.

The room was as dustless as the last time she had been there, but she saw that the bouquet of lilies was gone.

The study was like an empty stage, and the night was a play without actors. Slowly, Luoying walked to the middle of the stage, stepping along the wall. Against the backdrop of bookcases, she delivered a voiceless monologue.

Mom, Dad, can you hear me? Everything you've told me, I still remember. I went to Earth; I learned to walk on my own; everything that I thought I had forgotten, I still remember.

There was no answer.

She was back by the side of the crescent table, where the lilies had been placed on the floor. Nothing took the bouquet's place: no sculpture, no decoration, no secret door.

But there were two lines of writing.

She bent down. The silvery moonlight illuminated the edge of the floor, and two faint strings of symbols, perhaps carved with a pocketknife, glinted in the light. Tensing, she examined them closer. The first sequence had nine letters, and the second sequence had thirteen symbols, a mix of letters and numbers.

She sucked in a breath. Those were the required lengths for the username and password used to access someone's filed personal space.

She leaped up and retrieved pen and paper. Kneeling on the floor, she carefully copied down the symbols one by one. Then she ran to the nearest terminal and logged in to her personal space. From there, she searched for records containing the username she had copied down.

It was her mother's name. She tapped it, entered the password, and waited.

The screen showed a room, blurred. It was meant to be viewed in full fidelity.

She went to get her glasses. A personal space could be displayed in 2-D or 3-D; 2-D was easier for browsing, but 3-D gave a more immersive experience. Ateliers and academic papers typically used 2-D, while personal spaces and artistic creations often used 3-D. In a full-fidelity space, sculpture and films were shown as holographic recordings, while electronic diaries could be browsed in the form of books or voice narrations or even carved into simulated stone like a record for eternity.

Her mother's archived personal space appeared as a room with stone walls. It was nothing like the transparent walls on Mars or the spherical rooms popular on Earth; rather, it resembled the old European buildings Luoying had seen: a rectangular hall with granite walls, with a mural painted on the ceiling and plaster angels all around. The room wasn't large, but the floor-to-ceiling windows glowed between the pillars, giving a sense of depth. Over the carpeted floor stood a forest of pedestals and display cases on which sat holograms of her mother's sculptures. The whole place gave off the air of an alien and ancient past.

Luoying's heart pounded. These were her mother's memories.

She walked slowly around the room, her hand gently caressing the soul captured within each sculpture. The frozen bodies twisted and stretched toward the sky, their muscles tensed, as though yearning for something tantalizingly out of

193

reach. Simulated sunrays poured through the tall windows and washed the statues in light, making them seem like figures in some doomed tragedy.

She picked up a vase with a thin neck and a wide belly, like something from ancient Egypt or the Mayan civilization.

Examining it carefully, she noticed that it was a page from her mother's journal. Tiny letters were etched into the side of the vase.

Luoying is the light-bringing angel.

Luoying devoured the words.

Sometimes you think you've got life all figured out, but then a ray of light appears and makes you doubt everything. It's impossible for us to ever master life, and understanding is an ongoing, interminable process of self-reflection. Only connect. Conversation is soul.

No matter what happens, his coming is a big deal. Our teacher! The year I gave birth to Luoying will be forever special in the annals of Mars.

Luoying tried to remember. *What had happened eighteen years ago? And who is this teacher?*

Her heart pounded so hard that it felt like the virtual room shook with it. There was no additional explanation of her mother's journal entry. She looked around the vase and saw a porcelain bowl and a plate, and each artifact was etched with tiny letters, like ripples left by a dragonfly skimming across the water.

She wanted to read every page of her mother's journal with care. Instinctively, she knew that she was close to some great secret that she had not known.

But a noise outside the gallery told her that someone else had logged in to her mother's space. She hesitated only a moment before putting down the plate and stepping outside.

THE TOWER

Eko was not expecting to find Luoying here.

He was on a vast virtual plaza, uncertain where to go. Just then Luoying emerged from a gray door at the side of the plaza, and her red dress was striking against the gray stone wall.

He had no idea where he was. He had come here by following a link found in Davosky's journal.

We often come here to air our views, to bridge distances. Wonderful times.

Eko saw that "here" was in a slightly different color, and he had tapped his hand against the word. The next thing he knew, the world had changed around him.

He found himself in the middle of a vast rectangular plaza, and the ground was made of giant blocks of stone. Stone buildings lined the sides of the rectangle, fronted with long open galleries filled by stately statues. The plaza was deserted, though there was a fountain in the middle, dry at the moment. The buildings loomed somberly, full of sharp edges and keen angles. At the corners of the plaza, four tall towers surveyed the space like gods. Under their gazes, he felt utterly insignificant and alone.

At one end of the plaza was a narrow exit between the buildings, while at the opposite end stood an edifice resembling a Gothic cathedral, with a narrow profile, airy vaulted ceiling, tall locked doors, and flying buttresses that shot up like unsheathed swords. He started for the cathedral, but as he walked, the light beyond the exit at the other end seemed to grow brighter and pull at his attention as he looked back. Halfway to the cathedral, he changed his mind and turned around.

Luoying emerged just then.

Both of them stopped. For a long time they looked at each other, uncertain what to say or do.

"Why are you here?"

"Why are *you* here?"

Eko decided to be frank. "I came here from a link in my teacher's personal space."

"Your teacher?"

"Eighteen years ago my teacher came to Mars and lived here for eight years. I got to know the woman he loved."

"*Eighteen* years ago?"

"Yes," said Eko. "I think he was among the first group of Terrans to visit Mars after the war."

Luoying's eyes widened. She bit her bottom lip, looking astonished and a bit confused.

"What is this place?" he asked her.

"I don't know."

"Then how did you get here?"

"From my mother's space." Her eyes were still gazing at him with shock. "My mother... also mentioned a teacher."

"What's your mother's name?"

"Adele Sloan."

Eko shook his head, unfamiliar with the name. "Do you know Janet Brook?" he asked.

"Of course," she said. "She's my mother's best friend."

"She's the woman my teacher loved, and also the one who gave me the password to enter his space."

Considering the friendship between Janet and Adele, it seemed likely that the teacher Adele Sloan had mentioned was also Arthur Davosky. But given Luoying's look of consternation, he wasn't sure whether there was some more complicated history involving the three of them. Tentatively he asked, "Which atelier does your mother work at?"

"She used to work at the Third Hydroelectric Atelier," Luoying said, her voice tense. "But during the last two years of her life, she wasn't registered with any atelier."

"Oh, I'm sorry. I didn't know she had passed away."

"Both of my parents are dead. My father was at the First Optical-Electrical Atelier."

"Wait!" It was now Eko's turn to be astonished. "He was at the First Optical-Electrical Atelier?"

"Yes, before his punishment."

"What punishment?"

"He was exiled to Deimos as a miner."

"Why?"

"I don't know."

Eko felt his throat run dry. "Did they die because of the punishment?"

Luoying nodded. "Yes. A mining ship accident."

Eko was too shocked to talk. Luoying asked him what was wrong, but his mind was like a chaotic snowstorm. *First Optical-Electrical Atelier. Punishment. Death.*

He didn't know if Davosky's death and the deaths of Luoying's parents were related. He didn't know if this was a tragedy brought about by a tiny chip. A deep sense of regret arose in his heart. If Arthur Davosky's request had led to the punishment of Luoying's parents, then he didn't know how to face this girl.

She looked so delicate, but she had grown up alone in the

shadow of death. He forced himself to hold his emotions at bay as he explained to her why he had come to Mars and what he had found out.

"Arthur Davosky left with the plans and designs for your central archive," he said at the end.

Luoying looked stupefied. At length she muttered to herself. "So that's what happened…"

"I don't know what to say," said Eko. "I know it's useless, but I want to apologize on behalf of my teacher."

Luoying ignored him. "So that's what happened…" She seemed crushed by grief.

"Are you all right?"

She shook her head hard. Though her face was scrunched up, he couldn't tell if she was crying. Virtual reality could replicate the user's facial expressions, but not tears. He wanted to comfort her, but he felt as helpless as he had with Janet Brook. He approached and put a hand on Luoying's shoulder.

"Why? Why?" Luoying muttered.

Why, indeed? Eko was overwhelmed by sorrow. *Why is there no place anywhere on two worlds for a few friends united by ideals?*

"Welcome, my friends!"

The loud voice made both Luoying and Eko jump.

"Is this your first time here?"

They looked for the source of the voice and found that it came from the narrow exit at the end of the plaza. From where they stood, the plaza resembled a fish, with the exit as the fish's mouth. Outside the exit was a long alley full of toothlike protrusions. A white light shone beyond, like an ocean that was too bright for anything to be discerned within. From one side of the mouth of the alley, a tall, white-haired old man was walking toward them, his face red and grinning, his voice booming across the empty plaza. He opened his arms wide as he approached, showing his strong, welcoming hands.

"Grandpa Ronen!"

Luoying cried and ran up to him. Eko followed.

But the old man didn't appear to recognize Luoying.

"My friends, welcome! Forgive me, I don't recognize all of you yet. It's only my second day here, after all. But rest assured that I will soon know every one of you. I won't forget even if you've been here only once."

"Grandpa Ronen?" Luoying didn't understand what was going on.

"I am the guardian here, and I watch over the tower. Are you here to see the tower?"

"Tower?"

"Our tower! It's my job to point the way for you."

Luoying refused to give up. "Grandpa Ronen, why are you here?"

"Why am I here?" The old man smiled again. "Ever since my death, my memories have lived here."

Eko couldn't believe it. "What? You are—"

"That's right." The old man chuckled heartily. "I'm dead. Don't ask me how I know I'm dead, since I don't know either. You're talking to me, but you're also not talking to me. I'm a membody. Although my membody can't understand you, it can converse with you in the same manner I would have. Although I'm dead, I can fulfill my duties as guardian for years to come."

"Grandpa Ronen, don't you know me anymore? I'm Luoying!"

"Don't cry, young lady. Don't cry! What's wrong?"

The old man continued to smile kindly at Luoying with no sign of recognition. Eko admired the bright smile on the membody's face and the neat silver hair, not a strand out of place. His voice was as full and round as his belly.

Eko was at once assaulted by awe and fear, uncertain of how to face this talking figure. He was conversing with a soul already sealed away and watching the peace of the dead melding with the laughter of the living. The membody was like a cold corpse whose former owner's will was so strong that it transcended death to persist alongside memories circulating in silicon. The electrons were cold and unfeeling, but the smile was eternally warm.

Eko didn't know the old man, but he could empathize with Luoying's grief. The electronic instructions, on the other hand, could evoke tender emotions in a human interlocutor but could not understand, could not truly *listen*.

"Thank you," said Eko. "We *would* like to visit the tower. However, since we were sent here, please excuse us if we don't seem to know what to do."

"Don't worry, young man. Don't worry. There are no rules before the tower."

The old man led them toward the exit. Eko saw that Luoying seemed calmer and was following morosely.

"Would you like to know a little more about the tower?"

Luoying gazed at the old man without answering. Eko took over. "Yes, we'd like that very much."

"The tower is the heart of a set of ideals. It is the integration of generalized language."

"Generalized language?"

"That's right." The old man's voice was even and steady as he gazed at them. "Every form of expression is a language: perception, logic, painting, science, dreams, proverbs, political theories, passion, psychoanalysis—all are ways to articulate the world. As long as we still care about the form of the world, we must care about every type of language. Language is the mirror of the world." *Language is the mirror of the Light.*

Eko suddenly recalled the last words of Arthur Davosky. He took a deep breath. There was some mysterious link between this tower and his teacher's death.

The old man went on.

"Every language is a mirror, and every mirror reflects a particular aspect. Every reflection is true, but every reflection is also incomplete. Do you understand the conflict between individualism and collectivism? Do you understand the debate between logos and pathos? Do you understand to what degree they each express the truth? How do they reflect different images of the same unity? This is the Proposition of Reflections. It honors every image in every mirror but worships none of them. It attempts to shift between languages in order to reconstruct the true form of the world through reflections."

Reflections, Eko thought to himself. *Language is the mirror of the Light.*

"From reflections, you deduce the source of the light?" he asked.

"Correct. But the premise is faith that the truth exists. Incomplete reflections can be pieced together into the truth."

Don't forget the Light by focusing on the mirror. Eko nodded.

They approached the exit. Beyond the narrow alley was the ocean of white light. While the parts of the alley walls closest to them could still be seen, the walls merged into the brightness in the distance. The white light was like a thick cloud in which bright sparks flashed from time to time, giving the whole alley the appearance of a swirling galaxy.

The old man smiled and pointed to the exit. He held up three fingers.

"Every age has its own diseases. In my time, the greatest diseases were three. First, that which could not be shared prevented the sharing of that which could be shared. Second, matter, which must be fought over, constrained the freedom and free exchange of the spirit. Third, the images reflected by different mirrors were fragmented and broken and could not be pieced together or made sense of as a whole. Humans forgot about the world. They remembered only the reflections but neglected the subject before the mirrors. Proud and impatient, we divided into tribes that each laid claim to a fragment, isolated from one another. This was why we needed the tower."

The old man seemed to be chanting more than speaking, and his deep voice rumbled and resonated in his broad chest.

"Go ahead." The old man smiled and patted Luoying and Eko on their backs. Through the virtual reality rig, Eko seemed to feel the moist palm of that thick, reassuring hand. "Through this alley you'll find the tower."

Eko looked at the swirling white mist and then back at the old man. "You won't be coming with us?"

Ronen shook his head. "No. I can only guide you this far, no farther."

Eko strode forward. Luoying didn't follow. He looked back and saw that the girl was still standing by Ronen's side, as though not giving up on the hope that he would remember her.

He sighed and went back to Luoying and held her hand. Her fingers were cold and twitched in his grip, but she didn't pull away. She followed him into the alley, looking back from time to time but not stopping.

Soon they were enveloped by the white light, though the ground remained solid beneath their feet. The walls and statues to their sides disappeared, and the white light filled their vision. They seemed to be walking through an abstract tunnel of light.

Slowly and cautiously, they shuffled forward. Suddenly a sentence appeared before them, clear, serene, full of conviction, like a ray projected directly onto the retina and then into the mind and the heart. They did not seem to be parsing or comprehending so much as the sentence was imprinted straight onto their understanding by a steady and certain force.

Our theories are our inventions...

... thoughts built on sense, as windows, not as prison bars...

... objectified spirit from which everyone can take...

... multiplicity of individuals...

Eko thought he was in a tunnel in which there was no spatial or temporal order. Sentence appeared after sentence, emerging from the white light like paintings on a wall. It was impossible to look away, though there was no pressure to look.

Popper, Russell, Schrödinger, Simmel...

The faster they walked, the more sentences they encountered. The names were from two planets, across three thousand years, covering diverse fields. Some of the quotes were from men and women Eko had heard of, but others were new to him. He saw; he read; he remembered; he felt. All the quotes entwined with the words of Ronen, with the words of Davosky, like strands of different materials, of diverse colors, all twisted into a single stalk that rose into the sky. He immersed himself in the quotes, melded with the white light in the tunnel, lost all sense of direction, lost all judgment of distance.

Abruptly the tunnel ended, and he found himself in the open. It was like waking from a dream, and everything he saw was as sharp as a blade's edge. He remembered the last quote before he had emerged.

Beauty is the eternal and pure light of the One expressed dimly through matter.

—*Plotinus*

He stood rooted to the spot, as did Luoying next to him. They were in a wasteland, and in the middle of the wasteland was the tower.

The wasteland was not particularly different from other wastelands seen on Earth. Clumps of weeds popped up here and there, and the earth itself was a dry white-gray. Roiling clouds hung over the horizon.

But the tower was something else. The cylinder was broad at the base and narrow at the top, where it disappeared into the sky. The wall of the tower was made of cloud and mist, constantly rising, falling, swirling, twisting. And so the tower appeared to change form and shape from second to second. Attached to the tower were bridges and passages in every direction, in different shapes and made from different materials: mechanical arms, numbers, musical notes, watercolor-like smears. All the passages emerged from the mist-cloud cylindrical wall and then stretched far into the distance until they disappeared, as though entering other worlds.

As Eko stared at the tower, understanding sparked to life in his heart. It was as though a clear, pure stream of water had fallen from the air to wash away all his doubts in a moment. He stared at the gigantic tower, a pillar suspended between heaven and earth; he stared at the mist-cloud wall and the multiplicity of passages, all converging into one source, like pieces of a single unity. He read the five letters among the clouds: B-A-B-E-L.

It was Babel that integrated generalized language, that accommodated science, art, politics, and technology within the same spirit. Humanity was building a second Babel, a second attempt at climbing to heaven. The conversion of language and mutual understanding. Babel. The tower's name was Babel. Its first letter was *B*.

Eko raised his hands to the sky. He closed his eyes and shouted silently. His ears seemed to fill with a deafening rumbling.

Teacher, is this where you wanted to be laid to rest? Is this your last wish? Did you want to stay here, keeping watch over the unity of human languages, a guardian and guide like Ronen?

If so, I will exhaust all my power to help you achieve your wish.

He felt a breeze caress his face. He knew it wasn't real. In virtual reality there was no wind and no sand. But he preferred to believe that it was real.

YINGHUO

The wind blew through her heart, and dust swirled over the virtual sand. Luoying looked at the sky, the endless wasteland, and the roiling clouds. Shock and grief wound around each other and throbbed like plaintive violin strings in heaven. She could not describe how she felt. For the first time she saw Babel, the tower of languages, the tower of worlds, the languages of different worlds, the worlds of different languages. Words and colors swirled up the side of the tower, a magnificent music of the spheres.

The tower spun in the air, rising from nothing, reaching into nothing. The light of the tower was indescribable: there was no part of the tower that emitted light, and yet it was bright everywhere. The tower itself was light, and the symbols that covered its skin were dim, glowing only by the illumination of the tower.

In that light, visions could be dimly glimpsed. Figures and scenery entwined with one another, appearing and disappearing between the letters and numbers, as though worlds were blending with each other.

At the foot of the tower, Luoying stepped over death. She saw Ronen's smile as a winter sun. *He will not die; he has already died; he will not die again.* At the foot of the tower he had found peace.

He had guided her here so that she could understand him. *Care about the form of the world. Piece incomplete reflections together into the truth.*

She didn't fully understand what he meant, but she would remember his words, as she had remembered what he had told her when she was eleven.

Surveying the wasteland covered in sandstorms, she realized what Grandfather and his friends were defending. Grandfather, Ronen, Garcia, Galiman—they took off from the wasteland of Mars to defend this virtual tower, a tower that was more real than reality. Every world had its own myths, and Mars was no exception. When she was on Earth, she had read many myths, from the west and the east, from the arctic and the tropics. Having shuttled between worlds, she found that the myths of each world were unique to that world. In the east, the immortals came and went alone. In the west, the giants lived by tribe and race. At first, she couldn't understand such differences in spiritual nature, but later, when she saw the stark cloud-shrouded peaks of the east and the broad grasslands and forests of the west, she understood why. The peaks were suited to lone wanderers, while the broad expanses were fit for warring clans. The myths were the gifts of Nature, and all the gods were guardians of their homelands.

The myths of Mars were generated by the endless red deserts. The myths had wings that took off from dust storms. They were rough, fresh, speedy, barren, devoid of the romance of verdant hills and babbling brooks, bereft of the mysteries of dark forests. All they had was striving flight, leaving behind dust, passing through swirling sand, dodging explosions to head for the sun, to embrace the desert, as hard as iron, as light as birds. Faced with the gigantic steel warships of Earth, the Martians were like moths plunging toward the flame, tragic and resolute. Grandfather and his companions were parts of this myth, and the tower in the wasteland was their spiritual spring.

Luoying cried tearlessly. A world was always the unity of its land and its gods. Only those who had wandered through different worlds could lose that unity.

The day of the performance arrived.

The lights in the Grand Theater dimmed. Row by row, the golden seats rose up along the curvature of the wall and stopped at different heights. The domed ceiling was as dark as the empyrean until silvery lights, starlike, peeked out. The whole theater seemed suspended in space.

At one end of the egg-shaped dome appeared the image of Earth, and at the other end was red Mars. Gradually both approached the audience, becoming clearer in their view.

One planet was blue and green, veiled in wisps of white clouds; the other was red soil and shadow-limned mountains. Two giant planets loomed at the two ends of the theater while the audience between them drifted like insignificant specks of space dust, floating on gravity waves. The whole theater was solemn and dark, and music filled the hall.

Luoying was backstage, preparing for her performance. *Mars, Yinghuo*, she repeated to herself.

Red land, home in the darkness.

Her first Mars was the glowing dot in the sky, glimpsed hazily from the ground. It was a form clear on the tongue but blurred in the mind, a childhood memory that could not be pinned down, each and every dusk devoted to remembering and to the suppression of those memories.

Her second Mars was the strange description in books,

the odd world depicted in videos and images. It was blood exploding in vacuum; numbers; thunderous, continuous warfare. It was the tremble of fear in people's voices, the curious questions of children and their fantasies of evil. It was the ancient god of war, an old enemy.

Her third Mars was the window that let in starlight and sunlight, the small plaza seen through the open shutters, the fan-shaped lawn in the plaza, the white flowers on the lawn, the tube train speeding beyond the flowers, the glass houses connected by the tube train tunnels, the crystal city made from all the glass houses, the only republic in which the girls grew up, studied, dreamed, designed, created, married, made a home, chose a life. It was an ordinary life, a simple home.

Mars. Yinghuo. One thousand and eight hundred days of separation. Red land, home in the darkness.

Luoying stood backstage, just out of the audience's view. She stretched out her arms, her wrists together before her chest, fingers splayed away from each other. In the darkness, the golden threads in her cuffs glowed faintly like the Milky Way across the night sky over a wilderness. Gradually, the dark theater was filled with a soundscape: howling winds, a distant clarion, cowhide drums, and singing zither. Elders telling legends from a thousand years ago by the sea, blood and glory trembling between teeth and tongue, dead souls dancing in the wind. The clarion faded as a bamboo flute began to play. Memory traversed space, and the show began.

It was such a familiar tune. Luoying remembered every rise and fall in the melody, every hidden embellishment. She could recite every myth and truth recounted by the music.

The flute stopped. Luoying leaped and landed on the stage with the first boom of the timpani.

This was finally her dance. The world had vanished, leaving

only her. Scenes of both planets merged into her solo dance. She remembered every country she passed through. This was her fate, her soul's journey. She could no longer live within the order that governed her homeland, but she would always remember her homeland's dreams. She carved those dreams into her bones and packed all the countries into her self.

When she could no longer assimilate into any world, she wished she could live like her parents and their teacher, a vagabond at heart, gazing at home from afar.

The moment she fell, she heard a low cry. She couldn't tell where it had come from or who it was. She only knew that as she landed against the hard surface of the stage, someone held her up by the shoulders from behind.

From the moment she had leaped onto the stage, she felt off. Her body felt too light, and she couldn't exert force against the ground properly to propel herself. She seemed to be always behind the music by a fraction of a beat.

A drum section was coming up, and she knew that she had to leap into the air to spin seven times. She prepared herself and pushed off her toes.

In that instant she lost all feeling in her toes. After she spun through the air, as she landed, her right foot refused to obey her.

She crashed to the ground, and a sharp pain wracked her body.

Bright lights came on, blinding her. She saw Eko behind herself, holding her up by the shoulders. Many others were rushing onto the stage.

THE HOSPITAL

Eko and Rudy sat on the sofa in the living room of Luoying's hospital suite, waiting for her to return from her surgery. The suite was clean and neat, with soft blankets turned down in the bedroom. To help patients rest, the walls of the suite were adjusted to a milky white, and the metal pillars were painted in a soft green. Medical equipment remained out of sight in low cabinets, painted in pretty patterns to calm the patients.

Eko and Rudy didn't talk. Rudy had thanked Eko for helping Luoying when she fell on the stage, to which Eko made no reply. After that, the two sat in silence. Eko gazed at the young man, a few years younger than himself, and could sense the waves of concern that came off him. Rudy sat still without fidgeting, but Eko could see that his hands were squeezing each other so tightly that the knuckles had turned white. He was worried about his little sister and acted almost like a parent.

Eko was worried as well. He was the nearest person to Luoying when she fell. He had seen her toes bend oddly as she landed, unable to support her. At least a few bones were broken, and he hoped that, after surgery, she would fully recover and not be affected as a dancer.

Time passed slowly, and the air in the suite grew repressive.

The door opened.

Rudy and Eko stood up together. But it wasn't a doctor or

Luoying who entered. Two officials in uniforms came in. The first recognized Rudy and nodded at him.

The official turned to Eko. "Mr. Eko Lu, I presume?" His tone was polite but his face was expressionless.

"I am."

"I'm Carlson, Inspector First Grade, of the Security System. I'm charged with maintaining order and public safety in Russell District."

Eko said nothing.

Carlson waited a beat before continuing. "I'd like to ask for your cooperation in answering a few questions." Looking intently at Eko, he asked, "At the performance earlier tonight, why were you standing by the stage instead of sitting among the audience?"

"I was filming the performance and needed to be close to the stage to get a close-up."

"Did you obtain authorization?"

Rudy broke in. "I gave him permission. I'm in charge of the on-site arrangements."

Carlson glanced at him. Still stone-faced, he asked Eko, "Did you ever step onto the stage?"

"No."

"Then what was the closest you approached the dancer? Was it within one meter?"

Eko frowned. "What is this about? Are you suggesting that I—"

"We suspect that you sabotaged Luoying's performance in some way, leading to the accident."

Carlson's assistant scribbled in a notepad. Eko sucked in a breath. "I didn't do anything! I was filming the entire time, and then I ran over when she fell."

Rudy tried to defend Eko as well. "He really is a camera

operator. I checked his equipment ahead of time. I'm sure this is a misunderstanding. There's no reason for him to disrupt the performance or to harm Luoying in any way."

Keeping his eyes on Eko, Carlson walked next to Rudy and whispered in his ear. Rudy's expression changed, then he looked at Eko as though seeing him for the first time. He stopped talking.

Carlson faced Eko, cleared his throat, and continued. "I want you to think carefully about the answers you've been giving. Next, did you enter and browse the personal spaces of Luoying Sloan and Gielle Paylin?"

Eko knew then that the misunderstanding wasn't going to be easy to clear up. He nodded. "I did."

"What did you do in their spaces?"

"I read the public entries of their diaries."

"What else?"

"Nothing. That was it."

"Where else did you go in the central archive?" Eko clamped his mouth shut.

"How did you get an unlimited account for the central archive?

Terran delegates are supposed to have only hotel guest privileges." Eko said nothing.

"Were you directed to steal technical information?"

Carlson lobbed question after question like darts that unerringly found their mark. Eko could not answer, because revealing how he obtained the account could have terrible consequences for Janet Brook. Without her permission, he couldn't disclose the secret. He stayed silent and tried to find a way out.

Though he was anxious, he hadn't lost his judgment. Things looked bad for him. Not only had he gone to Luoying's personal space, but he had apologized to her on the record. To a neutral observer, this was evidence of a conflict between them. He had meant to apologize for what his teacher had done, but there wasn't enough context to absolve him of suspicion. As for the accusation of espionage against Mars, he was in an even worse position. He had browsed Gielle's technical designs and even gone to the heart of the central archive, the Tower of Babel. His motivation all along was curiosity, but that wasn't a reason that would clear him. Even if Janet Brook explained what had happened, his actions would still look suspicious. His palms grew sweaty.

The door to the suite opened again. This time a group of people came in. In the lead was a short, rotund Martian official Eko remembered from the banquet—he had a booming voice and a ruddy face—followed by two lower-ranking officials. Then came Theon and Colonel Hopman. Bringing up the rear were Peter Beverley and Martian Consul Hans Sloan.

The living room of the suite was packed full. Terrans and Martians lined up automatically on two sides. The air was extremely tense.

Hans broke the silence. "Mr. Eko Lu, I believe you're already aware of our suspicions."

"I am."

"Can you explain your activities?"

"I cannot."

"Who gave you the account to enter the central archive?"

"I cannot reveal that."

Hans waited, as though giving Eko a chance to change his answer. He stared intently at Eko; there was no threat in his gaze, only a kind of expectancy. Eko did not elaborate.

"Can you explain why you were wandering around our central archive?"

"I was… curious."

"Only curious?"

"Only curious."

"Why were you curious?"

Before Eko could answer, the red-faced short official to the side shouted, "Don't waste time with him! How could you expect to get the truth from a spy? I told you from the start: he's here to disrupt the vote."

"Juan! Don't jump to conclusions," said Hans.

Eko was at a loss. "I don't know anything about a vote."

"Oh, please!" Juan's face glowed even redder. "I've heard enough of your lies. You know that the people of Mars won't agree to give you the technology for controlled fusion, so you wanted to manipulate the vote by infiltrating the central archive. You hypocrites!"

"Not at all!" Beverley was all smiles as he tried to make peace. "This is definitely a misunderstanding. We have no intention of interfering in your political process. Eko was acting on his own, and we know nothing about his plans and gave him no orders."

Eko could see that Beverley was trying to say that he didn't care what Mars wanted to do with Eko, so long as he and the other delegates weren't dragged down with him. But he was too absorbed by other matters at that moment to be angry with Beverley. He knew controlled nuclear fusion was part of the negotiations, but now the words seemed to buzz in the air, and he sensed a sinister intent behind them.

Hans held out a hand. "Calm down, Juan. All his activities in the central archive have been recorded."

He turned to Carlson, who nodded and presented the note-pad from his assistant. Hans flipped through it quickly before handing the notepad over to Juan. After reading through the notes, Juan nodded reluctantly. Hans remained composed and in control.

"I take back what I said earlier," Juan said, but his gaze was still mistrustful. "Though you haven't gone to the voting site, I can't rule out the possibility that you intended to. I suggest you tell us everything right away. I don't want to escalate either. But if you continue to deny or keep secrets, and in the end we find out the truth, you'll be punished severely. Let me ask you one more time: Did you intend to steal one of our technologies?"

"No," said Eko. "I have no interest in acquiring any technology."

"Even if *you* had no interest, one of the other delegates from Earth might be interested. Since you Terrans couldn't get what you wanted at the negotiation table, you decided to steal it. Isn't that true?"

"I don't appreciate being accused with no evidence."

"Did you send any information to Earth?"

"No."

"But the system records show that you downloaded a great deal of data."

"I downloaded films!" Eko strained to control his voice. "Go check the records! You've logged all my activities, right? Look through everything I downloaded using my account, and you'll see they're all films—films made by my teacher, Arthur Davosky. There's nothing wrong with downloading the work of my teacher, my artistic hero."

The relentless questioning had shaken him, and he couldn't maintain his composure. He was naturally defensive about Davosky's films. They weren't some kind of political tool, though they were intensely political in origin. His head was filled with a chaotic jumble of words like "technology," "negotiation," "exchange," and "fusion." The explosive, suspicious air around him impressed on him the intensity of the conflict between the two planets. He recalled the words of Luoying: *The problem isn't whether someone should or shouldn't make a profit; the problem is Mars and Earth.*

Finally he understood Luoying's mood and her worries. Thinking back on the last twenty-some days, his mind was a mess. Thus, he didn't see Hans calling Rudy to him and whispering in the young man's ear.

Juan was unmoved by Eko's outburst. Like a cautious, prickly hedgehog, he paced around Eko. "We will review all your activities, that you may be sure of. But let's move on to the next question:

What were you doing at the tower?"

"I was curious, as I've said already. I was curious."

"Do you know the location of the tower?"

"Not really."

"Oh-ho! What a humble young spy! 'Not really,' is it? Then how were you able to get to the tower without any trouble? I bet you prepared for that visit for days. It's clear that you had a plan—perhaps under the direction of someone else—to infiltrate the innermost core of our central archive to commit acts of sabotage. Am I right?"

"You are spinning a paranoid fantasy. Not a single thing you've said is true."

"Then why did you go there? Tell me!"

Juan's shouting struck him like thunder. Eko felt his throat go dry, and his lips felt numb.

Like a ball of flames, Juan pressed his red face into Eko's, their noses almost touching. "And you went twice! The first time you can claim you were merely curious. But what about the second time?"

Eko didn't know how to explain. He had never revealed

his teacher's secret to anyone other than Luoying and Janet. The second time he went to the tower was to carry out the last wishes of Arthur Davosky, and Janet Brook had gone with him. To explain the details of his visit would necessarily implicate Janet, who had given him unauthorized access in the first place. Remembering what had happened to Luoying's parents, Eko was terrified of getting her into trouble.

He looked at Hans, who was gazing back at him. It was clear that the consul was very interested in his answer to this question. The air in the hospital suite seemed to freeze as everyone waited in silence. Eko was surrounded by looks of mistrust. Theon stood to the side, saying nothing, while Beverley was standing by Hans with a frown. Juan's burning eyes glowed like fire in the cold room.

The door opened again.

Everyone's eyes landed on the figure of Luoying in the doorframe. She was sitting over the right shoulder of a doctor. Dressed in a white hospital gown, her face looked wan and pale. Her back was straight and she kept her head high. Though she looked frail, the moment she appeared, she seemed to exert a power over everyone in the room that couldn't be ignored. On her right foot she wore a metal boot, while her left foot was bare. The doctor held her lower legs to secure her perch.

"*I* told him to go," Luoying said. Her voice was soft but steady.

"You?" blurted Rudy.

"Yes, I did. I invited Eko to my personal space, and I gave him the link to the tower."

"Why?"

"Reasons."

"Luoying, do you understand what you're saying?" Rudy's voice was full of suspicion. "This is a serious matter."

"I understand." Luoying wasn't looking at Eko or Rudy. Her eyes were locked on Juan's. "I'm very serious."

Her voice pierced the air like a needle. Everyone stared at her. Except for Eko, no one knew how to react. They waited for her to explain.

THE SKYDECK

Luoying heard the raised voices inside her suite. Dr. Reini was pushing her in a wheelchair. She stopped him and listened. Soon the point of the argument became clear to her. The voices in the room were like hammers pounding on her chest. The corridor outside the suite was long and dark, and the dry and cold air made her shiver.

She could tell that Uncle Juan was trying to probe for details, to attack Eko and the other Terrans, to create confusion, to force Eko into confessing some kind of plot, to find the excuses needed to blow up into a casus belli. He had never given up the idea of going to war. But he couldn't attack without a provocation, some reason that would make peace no longer tenable.

Details could be twisted into reasons. When the intent was to provoke a war, it was unnecessary to make every step of the deduction airtight. A small mistake committed by an individual could be the first link in a chain leading to war, and it wasn't important who that individual was or what they had done. Fortunately, Eko had not sent any data to Earth—not yet—or else the appearance of a plot against Mars would be complete.

She gripped the arms of the wheelchair. Still feeling weak after the surgery, her hands lacked strength. With each accusation

Juan made, her shoulders shook, as though Juan's questions were missiles that struck her through the door.

She didn't know what to do. She hated to see Eko being falsely accused, not just because his teacher was also her mother's teacher, but because she hated to see any innocent person falsely accused.

A hand landed on her shoulder, warm and full of strength. She felt calmer. She looked up gratefully. Dr. Reini's face, a kind presence against the dark corridor. An idea took shape in her mind. "Dr. Reini," she said, "I need your help."

"Of course." His voice was gentle and powerful.

"Can you carry me in? Carry me high so they can see me."

The doctor nodded without asking why. He crouched down and lifted her out of the chair until she was sitting on his right shoulder. Wrapping an arm around her lower legs to steady her, he stood up. Luoying felt a steadfastness in his arm that she could rely on.

Dr. Reini wasn't very tall, but he had broad shoulders and strong arms. Luoying didn't feel scared at all as he stood up. She hadn't been carried like this since she was a little girl. After her father died, no one had carried her like this. She sat on the doctor's shoulder and let her feet dangle. Her right foot was still numb from the surgery, while her left foot felt chilled. The tips of her toes trembled in the cold.

Carefully, she pushed open the door to the suite, suppressing a rising sense of panic. The adults in the room stared at her. She felt stiff and held her breath, trying to remain calm. The expressions of the people in the room were complicated—some solicitous, others confused—and, like searchlights, they all focused on her face.

She said what she had planned to say, and as she expected, she saw many more questions in the faces.

"I understand," she said. "I'm very serious."

"What were your reasons?" said a frowning Rudy. "Did you know Eko from before?"

"Yes, I knew him." Luoying blushed, as though embarrassed by her confession. "I know Eko and… I like him. I've liked him from when I was on Earth. I like his films; I like his writing. And so… once we came back to Mars, I had him visit my personal space and took him to see the tower. My mother brought me to the tower when I was little, and I always dreamed of taking someone I like there. That's what happened. You can review the system logs. I was at the tower with him, and I went there from my mother's personal space. That's the whole story."

The adults looked at one another awkwardly, their clothes rustling in the silence. She deliberately put on a serious mien to disguise the far more serious truth. She had made up a tale of girlish passion to dissolve the potential damage of a made-up crime. The adults could not speak, uncertain how to deal with a girl obsessed with her idol. Juan's dark face glowed redder as he struggled to make sense of this sudden shift. Luoying looked at him expectantly. She knew from the time she was a little girl that he could never resist her puppy-dog eyes.

Juan cleared his throat. He mumbled something about how everything was in the system and there was no need to jump to conclusions.

Since he was the one who had been most insistent on the theory that Eko was a spy, his retreat allowed everyone else to back away. The gathering of prominent individuals from both planets broke up as they departed the suite one by one, all looking preoccupied. Hans and Rudy wanted to stay with Luoying, but Luoying complained of exhaustion, asking that they return to visit her the next day. Eko said nothing but threw her a grateful look as he left.

Luoying still sat on Dr. Reini's shoulder, stiff and unmoving. Only when everyone had left and the room was empty again did she suddenly collapse, as though she had been struggling to hold up a heavy load and finally ran out of strength. Dr. Reini caught her and gently set her down.

———

The corridor was long and empty, enveloped in a comforting darkness. At the end was a curved wall of glass through which blue lights in the distance could be seen. Dr. Reini pushed Luoying along. Luoying said that she wasn't sleepy, so they decided to take a walk together. The wheels creaked in the dark passageway.

"Thank you," said Luoying.

"It's nothing," said the doctor. "Where do you want to go?"

"Doesn't matter. Anywhere is fine."

He pushed her wheelchair, and they rode up one elevator and then another. He never asked her any questions. They followed a curving hallway past a break room and a storage room filled with instruments as strange as monsters until they came to an arched door.

Reini opened the door and pushed Luoying through.

For a moment Luoying thought she was back on *Maearth*. She was under the stars, adrift in the infinite welcoming space.

They were standing on a broad skydeck. The deck was covered by a glass dome that rose out of the solar panels, leaving them with the illusion of being exposed to space directly. The hospital was located near the edge of the city, and the skydeck towered above surrounding buildings so that their view was unimpeded. Looking toward the horizon, beyond the low buildings, the vast emptiness of Mars spread out as far as the eye could see. There were no dust storms, and distant mountain ranges undulated like sleeping beasts. The skydeck was smooth and open, with a shallow pool winding past their feet. Luoying looked up at the stars and took a deep breath, not expecting to find such a space in the hospital.

"We're at the city's southernmost point. From here you can see Big Cliff directly south."

Dr. Reini's slow and gentle voice was a perfect match for the night.

Luoying gazed through the glass wall and didn't speak for a long time. Big Cliff was like a black sword in the distance. As she was enveloped by night, her anxiety gradually calmed. It was as though she were back on the dance stage. The sky above was the ceiling of the Grand Theater, and the stars were real stars. On one side was green-blue Earth, and on the other red-orange Mars. The two planets, so close in distance, felt so far apart in other ways. The stars shone around her, bright but also dark, and she danced alone in the center of the cosmos.

Luoying closed her eyes and let her worries dissipate into the night. She leaned against Dr. Reini. She had forgotten this feeling of being able to rely on a parental figure, like a tree in autumn, restrained but powerful, at peace. His movements were always steady and reassuring, like a sharpened paper cutter, simple and precise.

Finally she spoke. Her voice was like a candle's flickering flame against the vastness of the skydeck.

"Dr. Reini, will I have to stay here for a long time?"

"I don't think so." Reini sounded confident. "The broken bones will heal soon."

"Will I be able to walk?"

"Of course."

"What about dancing?" Luoying rushed to ask before she

lost her nerve. She noticed a moment of hesitation before Reini answered.

"It's too early to say right now. We have to see your progress."

"What do you mean, exactly?"

Another moment of hesitation. "I'm not worried about the fractures as much as I am about the tenosynovitis. The inflammation is quite severe. It's possible that you were over-extending yourself. As for dancing... it's possible that you can continue. But my suggestion is that you stop in order to prevent irreversible damage in the future."

Luoying's heart sank. Though Reini was trying to soften the blow, and he wasn't trying to act like her father, his meaning was clear. As soon as she heard "tenosynovitis," she knew the answer. She was never going to heal completely. For a dancer who relied on precise movements of the joints, such a condition was a nightmare. If she didn't want to end up with a permanent disability, she had to stop dancing.

Reini's diagnosis plunged into her heart like a lead ball sinking to the bottom of a pool. What she felt wasn't shock; rather, it was swirling dust settling down as the wind died.

On Earth she had had trouble with her jumps. In a gravity field three times as strong as the one on Mars, her legs felt like they were weighed down by sandbags. She had wondered if a day would come when she would lose the struggle against gravity. She imagined two outcomes. In one case, she would have to stop dancing before she could go home; in the other, she would endure the hardships and return to Mars to take flight like a bird. But she had never imagined this outcome: she was home, but she could no longer dance. She had escaped from that weighty planet, and she was just growing used to the sensation of flight, but now she had to stop. She had gritted her teeth and endured hardships motivated by hope, and now she was never going to enjoy the fruits of her labor. The curtains had fallen, and her performance was over. Sparks had come to life between the stars briefly, and now they were gone, leaving only darkness and silence. She strove to overcome the unbridgeable distance, but she failed in the end. She would never reach the sky, never touch both planets at once, despite using all her strength. In the end she fell; she had to give up. Gravity could not be overcome, and neither could distance.

She didn't even get a chance to finish her performance properly, to take a bow. Luoying looked up at the Milky Way. *I would have accepted any outcome, but you didn't even let me finish*. Tears spilled from her eyes and glided past her ears. The drops felt warm against her stiff neck. *I have nothing to strive for anymore,* she thought.

Reini knelt down next to her, his eyes compassionate and understanding through the round spectacles. He lifted Luoying's leg, cradling the boot woven from thin metal filaments.

"The boot not only secures your foot; it also contains sensors and electrodes to decode the neural impulses sent to your foot, allowing you to walk. You'll need to adjust to it over a few days. Be careful."

Luoying tried it out. She lifted her right leg and tried to flex her ankle. Although she couldn't feel anything, she saw the boot flex and bend, obeying her will.

"Feeling all right?" asked Reini.

"Yes, I can control it."

"Good. It takes most people longer to get used to it."

Luoying smiled bitterly. Who knew training as a dancer would have such a benefit? The key to dancing was control, not mere strength. It was about positioning the toes at the right angle at the right moment, about mastering every muscle so that it was neither too tense nor too relaxed. She stared at the skin-tight boot, feeling the metal filaments wrapped around skin and muscle, faithfully translating every neural impulse into movement. Reini continued to kneel by her side, not rushing her or asking questions.

As she continued practicing moving the boot, she asked, "Do you specialize in neurology?"

"In a manner of speaking."

"I've never been sure: Are there more stars in the universe or neurons in a human being?"

Reini smiled. "The stars win that contest. A person has a little more than ten billion neurons, while there are three hundred billion stars in the Milky Way alone. And there are hundreds of billions of galaxies in the rest of the universe."

"If each star were a neuron, and the whole galaxy were a whole brain, wouldn't it be much more intelligent than a human?"

"That would require stars to be able to communicate with one another, to send messages back and forth like neural transmitters. That's not easy to achieve. The stars are very far apart, separated by vacuum."

Reini's words echoed in the empty skydeck like a mystical oracle.

"Dr. Reini, may I ask how old you are?"

"Thirty-three."

"Do you remember what happened on Mars eighteen years ago, when you were fifteen?"

"Let's see, that would be year 22 of the Martian calendar, yes?"

"Yes."

"That was a pretty eventful year." Reini's voice was pregnant with meaning.

"Do you remember what happened?"

"Everyone who went through that time remembers. It was the year 2172 by Earth reckoning, the beginning of what we think of as the détente."

"The détente?"

"Back then, Earth and Mars had been completely isolated from each other for some time. During the first two decades of the war, Terrans held on to some bases on Mars, and Martians used to raid the supply convoys to those bases. Later, as Terrans pulled out of their Martian bases and began to conduct the war solely through space bombardment, Mars was completely cut off from Earth. At that point, everything Martians needed had to be produced on Mars: food, water, clothing, and so on. It was an incredibly difficult feat. Without the success of those early revolutionaries, we wouldn't be here.

"During the first decade after the conclusion of the war, there was no contact between Mars and Earth at all. Many of the leaders of the early republic argued that we must not show weakness to the Terrans by begging for aid. But Garcia insisted that we could not sacrifice our long-term future over pride. He was only thirty-three at the time, and essentially appointed himself our chief diplomat. I don't know how he managed it, but he succeeded. In year 10 of the Martian calendar, Garcia took over *Maearth*, and two years later he negotiated the first trade deal between the two worlds. In exchange for a microchip technology, Earth gave us a shipment of nitrogenous chemicals, and our two planets reestablished contact.

"In the decade after that, we bartered technology for necessary resources, but each side distrusted the other. Everything happened on *Maearth*, and no Martian set foot on Earth, just as no Terran touched the soil of Mars. This state of affairs continued until year 22 of the Martian calendar, the start of détente. The central archive has a lot of material covering that time, as it was the end of one historic epoch and the beginning of another."

"Was that when the first Terrans visited Mars?" Luoying asked.

"Yes. They came primarily to study technology. It was our decision to take the first step, to welcome them to learn about our advanced technology and to guarantee their delegates' safety. It was a risk, since our only advantage against Earth was our technology. However, decision-makers felt that if we didn't take the risk, ultimately we were the ones who would be harmed the most in a state of continued mutual isolation. Earth could survive on its own, but Mars could not. So eighteen years ago the first Terran delegates arrived. There were ten of them, focusing on five Martian technologies."

"One of them was full-fidelity holographic filming?"

"That's right. That was a key technology at the time. One of the Terrans decided to stay on Mars."

That must be Mom's teacher, thought Luoying, *and also Eko's teacher*. He wasn't a sculptor, but he talked about art with her parents. He reawakened their childhood dreams about art and brought Earth's sense of limitless freedom, of a life of movement and flow. They discussed the history of ideas in her parents' study, seeking a way to unify the different lifestyles of the two planets. The study would always contain memories of his presence, his images, his words. His coming coincided with her own birth, and that was why her mother spoke of her as light, as the coming of communication.

Without him, her parents wouldn't have died. Without their deaths, she wouldn't have gone to Earth. Without going to Earth, she wouldn't have wanted to find out about the past. Everything was already written. Thirteen years after her birth, she was fated to begin this journey to discover her own past. It was her destiny, determined at birth.

She gazed at the stars, searching for that lonely, silvery ship. The captain was on that ship, alone between a group of twenty million human beings and another group of twenty billion, neither of which understood him. But the sky was too vast for her to find the ship, and she could only imagine it in her mind's eye. She imagined Garcia shuffling alone through the passageways of the ship, his figure slowed down by age. She imagined him stopping at the bow of the ship, gazing down at the city he loved but to which he would never return.

She missed the carefree life on *Maearth*. On the ship she had also sat like this, embraced by the endless stars. Time seemed to have stopped. She and her friends ran across the ship, drinking Gio in front of the windows of the spherical observation deck, laughing at all the outdated equipment on *Maearth*. They tumbled and twisted and glided through the weightless gym, enjoying the freedom of unrestrained movement as game balls drifted by them. They kicked, turned, flew, wiped off their sweat, hugged each other, and partied without going to bed.

On the ship, she couldn't wait to go home, thinking that once she was there, she would be away from all worries and doubts; but once she was home, she discovered that the ancient ship had been a haven of tranquility. Her life there had been simple and pure. There was no fear, no conflict between one human and another, between the individual and the world, between one world and another.

"Dr. Reini, do you know my grandfather well?"

"Well enough."

"Then… can you answer a question honestly?"

"What's the question?"

"Is my grandfather… a dictator?"

"Ah, did you hear that from the Terrans?"

"Yes," Luoying replied, nodding. This was the first time she had shared this particular experience on Earth with anyone. "The first time I heard it was at a large international conference, the Symposium on the Future of Humanity. My friends and I were invited as guests of honor because we were from Mars. There were so many well-dressed men and women in a brightly lit hall. The hall had a long history, and we were told that, hundreds of years ago, revolutionaries had signed a document of great meaning there, proclaiming a new way of life. The ceiling was tall and stately, covered in religious murals, as though the gods were gazing down at us.

"We were all a bit intimidated, and we sat carefully in our seats, hoping to represent Mars well. The conference itself was quite boring. Expert after expert got up to deliver a talk, most of which we didn't understand. Just as we were discussing ways of exiting politely, a professor started to talk about Mars.

"'Everyone,' he said, 'despite the warnings of Orwell in *1984*, of Huxley in *Brave New World*, of Kafka in everything he wrote, humanity seems hell-bent on realizing their dystopian visions step by step. Humans live in blindness, not unlike the poor souls in that ancient flat classic, *The Matrix*. An Age of Machines is coming. It's no exaggeration to say that the System is going to rule over the human race. There is a powerful autonomous system taking shape, a system that treats human beings as so many fungible components. It's pressing down upon us, devouring and assimilating each individual. It's an expert at disguise, often showing itself as a beautiful, ideal garden. But whether it shows its true terror or conceals it with sweet deception, its true nature is the enslavement and extinction of human nature. Mars is our best example. Think about it, everyone: without the help of a system of machines to help him, how can a single dictator sustain his mad rebellion for so long? How can he take so many intelligent men and women and convince them to embrace betrayal, to give up survival, to march toward death?'"

Reini broke in. "Did he know who you were?"

"I think he did," said Luoying. "I saw him glancing my way a few times, even smiling. He went on: 'And so, honored guests, I want you all to remember this: we must be ever vigilant against those who would reduce humanity to components of a dictatorial system. The future of humanity lies only in such eternal vigilance. The tragedy of Mars must not be allowed to repeat on Earth.'

"I felt so cold at the time, and my lips must have turned white. Chania, who sat next to me, gripped me by the hand. Her hand was cold, too. As I looked over the audience, I thought I was looking at a featureless sea of human heads. The light was so bright, and his voice boomed at me from speakers in every direction. I was terrified, and I remained sitting only by force of habit. I think it was the longest day I could ever recall."

Reini waited until she was a bit calmer before saying, "Don't mind his nonsense too much. A man who would deliberately attack you like that is not someone whose opinion is worth listening to."

"I'm all right now," said Luoying. "After experiencing attacks like that a few times, I grew used to them. I think perhaps he wasn't trying to attack me on purpose. Instead, the pleasure I sensed in his voice was the pleasure of speaking truth. I don't care if he intended to hurt me; I only want to know if what he said was the truth." She looked up at Reini. "Tell me... did my grandfather punish my parents?"

"Yes, he did."

"Were they... convicted of treason against Mars?"

Reini didn't answer her directly. He knelt down next to her and gazed into her eyes warmly. "That was in the past. The crime they were convicted of doesn't matter. What matters is what your grandfather hoped you would learn from Earth."

"What I would learn?" Luoying was surprised.

"Your grandfather... He in fact supported many of the things your parents said. But because he's the consul, he couldn't and can't support such opinions."

"Support... what opinions?"

"Economic freedom and freedom of careers. Your parents wanted these more than anything else, but he couldn't possibly show any support. If he did, the entire unity of the central archive and the unity of our economy would collapse. He understood the necessity of ordering Martian life in this manner, but he also understood that the spiritual freedom of creation is often conditioned upon the freedom of the individual to direct their own life, their environment. Yet, as the consul, he couldn't voice an opinion like that. Do you understand?"

"Which system, theirs or ours, does Grandfather believe is better?"

"It's not a matter of which is better but a question of whether we could even choose. The only reason we won the war was centralization: we gathered all our knowledge into one space and made decisions based on total knowledge. The electronic space of the central archive is in fact older than our republic. All our arts and politics in peace have been built upon this foundation. It wasn't a question of how to choose but what path was determined by history. And your grandfather knows better than anyone that we don't get to choose our history.

"Five years ago, as the whole republic debated the question of whether to send you and the other students, your grandfather's vote was crucial to the final passage of the proposal. Can you understand why? As the consul, he presided over a crisis during which those for and against were evenly matched, and his vote virtually determined the final outcome. Indeed, he was the one who chose the name for you and your friends: Mercury. He invoked the messenger of the gods, the god of communication."

"Are you saying that my grandfather sent me to Earth… so that I could understand my parents?"

Instead of directly answering her question, Reini sighed. "I've heard him say several times how much you remind him of your mother."

Luoying remembered the first dusk in her bedroom after her return to Mars. She felt a lump in her throat.

"What kind of man is my grandfather, really?" she asked.

After a long pause, Reini said slowly, "Your grandfather… is an old man with too much on his shoulders."

Luoying could no longer hold back her tears. The doubt that had seized her heart for so many days was in those tears, as were the yearning and anxiety that had built up over one thousand and eight hundred days.

"Dr. Reini, do you make a study of history?"

"No," said Reini. "But everyone knows something about history, something unique to their experience and understanding."

"Can you tell me more?"

"It's too late tonight. Perhaps another day."

Reini hugged her and gently patted her shoulder. She held on to him, letting the tears flow silently. She had not cried like this for a long time. As she cried, she bid farewell to her doubts as she bid farewell to dancing, facing the deaths of the past as she had faced her injured leg. She looked at the sky, at the surface of her home planet, at the distant stars that she would never touch.

Reini waited until she was finally calm. "Time to sleep. Everything will be better tomorrow."

They left the skydeck, bathed in a dark blue light like the bottom of an ocean, and Reini pushed Luoying back to her suite. The winding, deserted corridors, lit by faint white lights, seemed full of mysteries. The wheels of the chair spun, gliding past the laboratories, instruments, surgical wards, through the corridors, down the elevators, past rooms full of sleeping patients.

As they turned one last corner and approached Luoying's suite, two shadows rose up.

Luoying screamed, and the two shadowy figures, shocked, screamed as well. Reini turned on the bright lights in the corridor, and as Luoying squinted, she made out Anka and Mira.

"What are you two doing here?"

"We came to visit you!" said Mira. "When we saw no one in the room, we figured you were still in surgery, so we waited."

"We haven't been here long," added Anka.

Luoying was moved. She gently chided, "Why didn't you at least turn on the light?"

Mira grinned. "We were sharing stories from when we were kids. Stories always sound better in the dark."

Anka said nothing. He and Luoying gazed at each other, and there was a warm glow in his blue eyes.

"You should eat this while it's still warm," he said, picking up a box.

"What is it?"

"Old Maury's pudding." Anka's tone was light and casual. "I happened upon it not too far from my home, so I bought a few servings before I went to your performance."

"You have no idea how hard it was to find a place to heat this up," said Mira. "We went to several shops, and they had closed just before we got there, sometimes by just a couple of minutes." He laughed heartily and held up his pinched thumb and index finger to show how close it was. His dark, round face looked adorable.

Luoying smiled at Mira. She turned and gazed into Anka's eyes, but neither said anything. His eyes were as clear as she had always remembered them to be, and it didn't matter that he said nothing. What was said wasn't as important as what was remembered. She had mentioned the pudding once; he had remembered.

She reached into the box and took out a small dessert plate. She took a bite of the pudding, and the sweetness dissolved against her tongue. Laughing, she asked Anka and Mira to join her, but they tried to leave all the pudding to her by claiming to be on diets.

"No way," she said. "I'm in charge today. You have to enjoy this with me."

The boys each picked up a piece and ate it whole.

The night was smooth as water, and the bright light lit up laughing faces that had forgotten the time. The deserted corridor extended outside the suite, echoing with the sounds and flavors of home.

THE HOTEL ROOM AT NIGHT

Eko stood at the wall of his single-occupancy hotel room and looked up at the dark sky through the transparent wall. Of the three moons, he could see two. The moonlight wasn't as bright as usual. The wind was strong. Though he couldn't hear it, he could see particles of sand being thrown against the wall, as though a storm was on its way.

It was late, but Eko didn't want to sleep. He was exhausted, but he couldn't rest. As soon as he got back from the hospital, he paced back and forth in the dark room, stood, and sat, talking to himself, talking to invisible fate. He had never doubted himself as much as he did now. On Earth he had been a successful filmmaker. At one point he thought he had found a path to follow for the future, and all that remained was to sustain the passion for fighting and advancing along it.

The trip to Mars had changed everything.

Eko had long been opposed to big business. Like his non-mainstream predecessors in generations past, he despised the blockbusters intended for the "big supermarket," where everything had the same content, the same packaging, the same themes and subjects that had been done a million times. Instead, he made his films for the "artisanal market." He called mainstream filmmakers "worker drones," because each of them was responsible for only a tiny part of the final product and had no control over the overall vision. Worst of all, they seemed content with their own repetitive, noncreative work. He almost never set foot in the web space of the "big supermarket." He mocked films that pandered to the audience in order to make a profit the same way he ridiculed animal crackers. He disdained buyers who bought on the advice of advertisements and followed trends, the same way he derided the empty-headed, status-obsessed aristocrats of the eighteenth century. He created in order to resist, with an instinctual abhorrence of the formulaic. He focused on craft, on the pursuit of the personal and unique. His films warred against the worship of money, against cloying platitudes aimed at dulling the public. He thought he was on the side of truth, critiquing the stupidity of the many to empathize with the suffering of the few.

But now he was forced to confront himself, to doubt his fundamental beliefs. This journey to the red planet had challenged his imagination. It was only now, as he was about to leave, that he saw a more complete picture, a clearer meaning.

For the first time he saw with clarity that all that he had done on Earth, instead of resisting commercialization, had only strengthened it. He hadn't challenged the logic of commerce but only provided more products for sale and purchase. He had honored the lone wolf as his totem, but now he realized that the wolf was fake, though the totemic power was real. Symbols meant imitation, and imitation meant consumption. The words he had thrown at Theon in accusation rebounded onto himself, and they struck as hard as he had meant them to. He was also a willing participant in the consumption economy, a manufacturer of desires. His creation was a language, and the language was not fundamentally very different from Theon's enticements. He had never truly departed from the mold of his commercial society. He facilitated commerce, promoted the pursuit of symbolic pleasures, and his loyal fans bought his films and mementos. He had filmed scenes of poverty, and those images had enriched the wealthy. He asked for funds from those who sat in luxurious offices in skyscrapers, and then used those funds to capture lonely souls wandering outside. With those captured images, he then generated more money, which he handed to the people inside the skyscrapers. Round after round, he played his role in making the cycle spin. The subjects of his films didn't see the films. He had never thought of showing his films for free, even though he thought the idea brilliant on Mars. But on Earth the very notion was absurd, impractical.

Eko looked at his own thin reflection. He examined his own language and analyzed how it reflected the light of the world. The result was disappointing. Formally, he seemed to have found the opposite of big business, but he had never thought about the light of the world. Isolated in a familiar language and context, he had never attempted to communicate between languages. He took delight in how different his own expressions were from the popular mode, but he didn't devote enough effort to seeking something deeper beyond mere expression. He didn't go to the big supermarket and refused to learn the language there; he and his followers took pride in such isolation and saw it as part of their own identity. But he wasn't looking for the light of the world; all he cared about was the reflection in the mirror. He had never asked himself, if he only existed in opposition to a reflection, then how could his own image have an independent existence? He had thought it impossible for one language to be converted into another, and that there was no need for such exchange.

But reflections could only be connected through the medium of light, and languages needed translation only because of the needs of the world.

Eko pressed his palms against the glass and looked outside. Dawn was approaching. The wind rose and slackened. Sand struck the glass from time to time. The night was like a roiling ocean, and in the distance the mountains outlined the mournful land, simple, somber, and deep.

Conversation. Commerce. People had lost sight of which was more important. The first commercial exchanges served the purpose of starting a conversation, and now conversation only facilitated the goal of continuing commerce. When commerce was no longer necessary, it was easy to forget about conversation. The isolation of languages was the result of collusion; it brought profit, engendered hatred, gave birth to manufactured identities, and, above all, generated the desire to buy, buy, buy. Conversation was dying, but commerce grew ever more vibrant.

Only those who cared about the world cared about conversation. Eko thought about Luoying, thought about what she had said about the commonality of all humankind. The young woman was full of doubt and confusion, and her search was running into dead end after dead end. But at the moment of confrontation, she forgot about language; faced with a web of conflicts, she lifted her chin as the strongest of princesses. He had made her cry, but she had saved him.

Eko looked at the stars overhead, gazing down on him like gods. On Earth he had never seen them so bright. The thick atmosphere weakened starlight, and urban incandescence drowned out the stars that remained. He had almost no idea what stars really looked like; he had to imagine them instead.

The sharp roofs of Mars City cut through the night like the wings of giant birds. In the distance, glass tunnels, glowing blue, crisscrossed like lines arbitrarily placed over a canvas, bright and slender. The dust storm seemed to be growing, and he could see the tunnels tremble in the wind.

Eko turned on a screen and browsed the news programs from Earth from the last few days. He kept the sound off and saw images of thousands screaming and marching through the streets. The economic crisis on Earth had worsened during the last month. He had heard about it, but it wasn't until now that he understood how serious it was.

The crisis stemmed from an economy built on language. Earth's IP stocks had collapsed within a few days because the system of IP agents and resellers had grown too complicated. A single clever sentence could be wrapped in layers of packaging to become substance, and a single idea could be registered and inflated into a vast but empty shell. Buyers were no longer buying the idea itself; they were buying the chance to sell it to someone else. As ideas churned through this economy, rising in price with every exchange, inflation set in. Higher prices meant lower worth. This was a business without substance, a glowing golden balloon inflated by the race to sell something to someone else first.

Until one day a needle poked the balloon, and a single hole led to the collapse of all packaging. The world was shaken to its roots. Everyone took to the streets to protest and complain and vent their frustration.

Eko made his decision. He would promote the central archive on Earth. As a first step, he would put all his own films in it so that his teacher's dream would advance. He wanted to construct a public space, a forum in which everyone was responsible for their own thoughts but no one would profit from their own language. Babel. What a grand and ambitious dream. When humankind was united in language, then the tower would reach heaven. All the media on Earth had been completely commercialized, and there was no more voice doubting commerce. Power and capital had reached an all-encompassing agreement in which one paved the road while the other drove everyone down it, and both profited and prospered in mutual defense. Even doubt was put into display cases for sale, while analysis and flattery competed with each other via packaging. Eko felt that he had to do something. He had never done anything like it and didn't know if it was the right answer. But he knew that his teacher had been braver than he was. The step from dreamer to doer was the hardest step of all.

Returning to his bed, he lay down with arms and legs outstretched. His hand touched the screen on the headboard and the still scene there disappeared, replaced by Vera, the virtual concierge. She looked exactly the same as the first time he met her, with the same dress and the same sweet smile.

He gave her his account and password, but instead of opening a door and welcoming him inside she shook her head, looking perplexed.

Eko understood that his account had been deleted. He would never have another chance to enter the central archive, to visit Babel, or to browse an atelier.

Still lying in bed, he raised his chin until he could see Vera, upside down, on the headboard. He tried to converse with her, but her unchanging smile contrasted sharply against the depressing night. He tried to imagine the space behind the door: nine systems, an infinite amount of storage.

The Sunlight System; the Air System; the Water System; the Biology System; the Land System; the Astronomy System; the Security System; the Art System; the Flight System. Such simple and primitive names, redolent of the nostalgia of an imagined pastoral past. Like nine thick vines, they entwined and grew and supported each other in a virtual world. In this world, every language could be read, like an impossible library. Someone had once said that if heaven exists, it must be in the form of a library.

He twisted the tiny sphere by the frame and adjusted the transparent walls of the room to a light green, then light yellow, light red, light purple, and through the cycle until they were transparent again. He looked up at the stars glowing overhead like watching gods.

He finished watching the last film of Arthur Davosky. In a voice-over, his teacher explained that he was retelling an old Chinese parable. In that parable, a man went to visit another city and saw that the people there walked with an elegance that he admired greatly. He tried to imitate their dance-like gait, but despite putting in all his effort, he couldn't copy their steps correctly. When he tried to return home, however, he found that he had forgotten how to walk the way he used to.

This is the saddest parable in the whole world, said Davosky. *It's sad because it's true.*

Eko lay still on the bed. The wind outside had stopped. He remembered that there was no rain on Mars, and no thunderstorms. It was only his imagination. He lay still without making any sound.

When the first rays of dawn peeked over the horizon, he was asleep.

AN ENDING SERVING
AS A BEGINNING

The last time Eko saw Luoying was three days after Luoying's performance, which was also the day before the departure of the Terran delegation. She was still in the hospital under the care of Dr. Reini.

The Terran delegation had dismantled their displays for the world's fair, and everyone had already packed for their impending departure. Eko took advantage of a brief break during the morning to go to the hospital to visit Luoying.

Mars City was sending off the Terran delegation in style. Balloons in the colors of the two planets hung over the streets, and the Expo Center was strewn with colorful streamers. The empty Grand Hall was being prepped as the site of the farewell banquet, and large screens lining the streets played congratulatory messages from leaders of both worlds. The superficial warmth disguised the tense crisis below the surface.

Luoying's suite, being far from the bustle of the city, was unbuffeted by these crosscurrents. A quotidian quality permeated the air. Bright sunlight limned the white lilies in gold, relaxing music played, and time seemed to stop.

Eko sat down next to Luoying's bed. He thanked her solemnly, which Luoying brushed off as nothing. He had come to her aid twice when she had fallen, she reminded him—once in virtual space, another in actual. Eko apologized for his earlier rashness, and she smiled, telling him not to worry about it. Eko explained that he had a small gift for her.

"What is it?" she asked, curious.

He took out a chip from his bag and inserted it into a pair of holographic glasses.

She put them on and entered a space at once familiar and strange. It was as though she had arrived on the other shore of time. She saw the Grand Theater, the audience, and herself. She was watching herself dance. The music was familiar, as were the steps, and she even recognized the feeling of the humid air. Her figure was in the middle of the stage, the focus of everyone's attention. Her observing self was just another member of the audience.

Slowly, step by step, she approached the dancing self, so close that she could reach out and touch her. She wanted to reach out, but in the end she restrained herself. She knew she wasn't really there.

In this drama the audience was the protagonist. Even though everyone around her was watching her dancing self, she understood that the observing self was the true center. She watched her other self. The other self had not seen herself, while the observing self had. She thought the other self was dancing so that the observing self could see. She was like a transparent soul standing with all the others around the stage, watching until the music was over. She was comforted. The performance was complete, at least once.

Luoying took off the glasses. Eko sat next to the bed, calmly looking at her. She had to take some time to adjust to the bright sunlight.

"How do you like it?"

"It's wonderful. Thank you. Really, thank you."

He smiled. "It's nothing. I'm glad you liked it."

"I've never seen myself like that."

"Me neither."

Both let the silence linger.

Eko was thinking about Theon's hint about Luoying back on *Maearth*. Theon had suggested that he manufacture some romance involving Luoying. A scene at the end involving a parting of lovers, combined with her identity, her beautiful, lovelorn face, and a translucent dress, would have guaranteed successful sales on the web, an instant classic.

He had failed to carry out Theon's instructions. Yet, he somehow managed to put her in a position where she had to claim she liked him. The whole thing was absurd. He didn't want to tell her any of this, but he was glad he had given her an authentic film that she would treasure.

Luoying, on the other hand, was thinking about memory. She had been feeling weak the last few days as she lay recuperating, but now she found a spark of strength. She was beginning to reevaluate the meaning of memory. Many had told her that, with a film of herself, she could possess the past. Anytime she wanted, she could study it, remember it, live in it. She had once also believed that memory was a way to return to the past.

But today, when she saw her holographic self, she suddenly realized that the point of memory was in fact to close off the past. Once her memory had been entrusted to something tangible, she could go on to be a different person without worrying about change, about losing the past, about negating her yesterday. Her past self had found its separate existence, and she was free to go on her own way.

They looked at each other, neither able to find a way to speak of the thoughts occupying their minds. And so they said nothing.

In the end Eko smiled. "All the footage I shot of you is on there. I'm not taking any of it with me. You don't need to worry."

Luoying wasn't sure what he meant by saying that she needn't worry. But she saw the sincerity in his face. She smiled back.

They spoke casually about the world's fair. It was a friendly conversation but not very deep. Luoying's long, dark lashes contrasted with her pale face, while Eko's curly hair covered his forehead and made his sunken eyes seem even more angular and dark.

"You're leaving first thing tomorrow morning?" she asked.

"That's right. I have to be at the press conference this afternoon and then the banquet tonight… so I probably won't have a chance to visit you again."

"Safe travels!"

"Can we stay in touch after I go back?"

"I don't know," said Luoying. "Grandfather told me that they were still discussing the terms for interplanetary communications."

"I think there must be many things about Mars that I misunderstood. I hope to have a chance to ask you more questions."

"I'd like that. There are many things I don't understand either."

They said goodbye to each other, neither mentioning the fact that they might never speak again. It was a warm and bright morning, and they both refrained from disrupting that warmth. Eko nodded at her from the door of her suite before leaving. Luoying watched as he strode down the corridor resolutely, like a sailing ship heading into the boundless sea.

———

The next morning Luoying went to the skydeck of the hospital to watch the departure of the Terran delegation. Rudy accompanied her and sat with her in the brightening dawn.

Sunlight, almost parallel with the ground, divided the red soil sharply with shadows. Half of the land was a dark brown, and the other half bright gold. The straight edges of the shadows slid inch by inch over the rough rocks like curtains being pulled aside to reveal sculptures. In the distance the edges of cliffs and mountains glinted sharply.

The peaceful air made them both forget to speak.

At length Luoying broke the silence. "What was the final result of the negotiations?"

Rudy laughed lightly. "It's very favorable to us."

"How so?"

"Well, first, two hydraulic engineers will be staying behind to teach us the technology for the sluice gates. And... we didn't have to give up much."

"They didn't demand nuclear fusion engines?"

"No. They gave up on that."

"Why?"

Rudy's smile was sly. "Because our fusion technology requires advanced technology for fission waste products and seawater processing. On Earth, nuclear energy development is most advanced in Europe, but the best seawater processing tech is controlled by the Americans. Neither wants to share their technology with the other, worried about their profits in the future. If the Chinese and the Russians were willing to cooperate, they'd probably be able to master it as well, but they can't stand each other... Delegates from the smaller countries especially didn't want the big countries to get fusion engines, since they were worried it would end up becoming a threat to them. In the end, the whole delegation gave up the request."

"So what did they ask for instead?"

"Two things: the magnetic moment walls in the Grand Theater, and the tube trains. They've been after the tube trains for a while, and it was part of the last two rounds of negotiations as well. Earth is full of skyscrapers, and tube trains would be a very efficient way to get between them compared to airplanes and cars. As for the theater walls, it was mainly the result of private contact between me and a man named Theon."

"Theon?" Luoying seemed to realize something. "So the theater visit that day—"

"Yes, I arranged that." Rudy looked very pleased with himself. "Though I think war is nothing to be afraid of, Grandfather is against it, and so I had to think of a scheme. Even I was surprised that it worked. Theon is even more influential than I thought. I almost underestimated him as merely an entertainer, but it seems that the economic crisis on Earth has a lot to do with him. Anyway, we made out like bandits by giving them the technology for the theater instead of fusion."

Luoying looked thoughtful. After a moment she asked, "What about Uncle Juan?"

"For now, he has to put his plans for war on hold." Rudy smiled enigmatically. "But as you know, in matters of foreign policy... Never mind."

Rudy was in a plain cotton shirt instead of the uniform that he had been wearing throughout the Terrans' visit. He put both his hands on his knees and tapped one foot as though following the beat of some inaudible music.

Luoying felt the distance between them. Her brother was no longer the boy she had known, and she was no longer the girl he had known. She wasn't sure if that sense of distance between them wasn't her biggest loss after her vagabond life on Earth. Politics clearly was where Rudy belonged, but she didn't know where she would feel at home.

Meanwhile, Eko had just buckled his seat belt on the shuttle. Outside, the rough, flat landscape reflected the sun's golden rays, and craters and rubble stretched all the way to the horizon. On one side of the shuttle, the slender skybridge connected the fuselage to Mars City. The bridge's frame consisted of elegant curves made up of neatly fitted metal girders, and the glass between them shined brightly in the sun. The shuttle port was a marvel of mechanical precision, and skybridges extended in every direction as aircraft and spacecraft of every description lay in silent slumber.

The shuttle began to taxi. It lifted off, and the last connection between him and the city was broken.

Eko took a last peek at the terminal. He saw Janet Brook's figure through the glass in one corner. She hadn't come with the official Martian farewell delegation but was by herself. Eko saw that she was in a loose white dress, perhaps even the same one she had worn when she had watched Arthur Davosky take off a decade ago.

Eko tried to imagine Davosky's mental state at that moment. Maybe he, like Eko, had sat next to the window and waved at Janet, thinking about his next visit. Maybe Davosky had been full of ambitious dreams, like Eko himself at this moment; and maybe Eko, like his teacher, would never return. He began to understand the complicated feelings his teacher had harbored for this planet. The more he was plunged into the despair of never being able to return, the more he yearned to return, to hope.

Janet had helped him lay his teacher to rest. After that, Eko never entered the central archive again. He didn't know if Davosky's membody was doing well and whether, like Ronen, he was joyfully carrying out his eternal watch in the tower of wisdom. Maybe he would even get to chat with Janet from time to time. Eko wouldn't witness any of that, but he hoped it would all come true.

Theon, who sat next to Eko, was occupied with some documents on a screen. Eko knew that Theon considered himself one of the greatest beneficiaries of this round of negotiations. The magnetic walls of the Grand Theater would enhance the Dreamscape parks in twenty cities immensely, giving guests an even greater sense of immersion. He had hesitated between Gielle's Mystify and the theater technology, and in the end settled on the latter.

"Why did you choose to deal with Rudy instead of his sister?" Eko asked. He knew his own interference had nothing to do with it.

Theon smirked. "Because I could tell what he wanted. He was responsible for the magnetic walls, and if a deal with Earth could be made, he would have many years of stable research funding and a growing staff under him. I could tell the kid was ambitious and wanted to climb up the ladder as quickly as possible. Dealing with that kind of person is easiest, since we both get something out of a good deal. Luoying, on the other hand, is like a black box. I couldn't tell what she wanted at all."

For Theon, someone who didn't seek to maximize their own profit was literally incomprehensible. He was knowledgeable about all kinds of economic utility functions, but all sought to maximize some kind of profit. He was skilled at reading moods and emotions, but he had to confess that he couldn't understand Arthur Davosky or Luoying Sloan. That was all right. He wasn't bothered by it. There were many people he couldn't understand, so he sought only to understand those he could. He had found the best doctors for Arthur, bought him the best house, visited him as a best friend, but never bothered to understand him.

Eko knew that he shouldn't blame Theon. Theon was a man who did what he believed was good at the moment, who calculated the price of everything with precision, who computed possibilities and optimized the result. He didn't believe the world held any ideals higher than that, and so he didn't try to understand those who pursued ideals.

There was one thing Theon had said that Eko had to agree with. When the results of the negotiations were publicized, Theon told him with a laugh that mutual suspicion was the foundation of stability. As it turned out, he was right. The Terran delegates were so obsessed with making sure that no one else got a better deal that they all ended up caving in to Theon's demands. Theon was how they crafted their images for the public, and images were what mattered to the electorate. The fall in IP stocks was a major blow for buyers and speculators and creators in every country, but Theon escaped unscathed. He was simply there to provide a platform for buyers and sellers, and collected his commission. He had long predicted such a market correction, and he foresaw that, after the fall, the governments of every nation-state would become even more reliant on his services. The trip to Mars was proving to be a golden business opportunity. From the start, he had settled on the strategy of allying himself with the Martians to keep the Terran delegates in a stable state of mutual suspicion, despite Professor Jacques's absurd idea that the Terrans should band together against the Martians.

Other than Theon, there was yet one more member of the Terran delegation who was very pleased with the trip: Peter

Beverley. He had been promised the role of global ambassador for the Thales Group's next generation of theme parks. These new parks would be based on Mars and green living. Beverley would also spread his image across the globe as a result of this trip. He didn't really understand how it had happened. He and Theon had both maximized their own utility, unaware of how narrowly they had averted war.

Eko wasn't interested in any of this. He understood that the ethics of business had its own calculating philosophy, and the world was founded upon such a philosophy. His attention was elsewhere. He wanted to gather all the mirrors in the world and piece together the broken light. Davosky's memories were at rest, but his teacher's legacy needed to be carried on. There was still a spiritual ideal in the world that waited for his approach, waited for him to collect. He observed the shrinking city through the shuttle porthole and silently said goodbye. This was a planet he had first seen when he was fifteen and was seared into his memory at age twenty-five. He was sure he would never forget it.

The golden land stretched endlessly below him. He thought he could hear the music of bagpipes.

———

"Rudy, look!" Luoying exclaimed to her brother.

Rudy stood up and turned to look where she was pointing. The sky was a dark blue, and the gigantic silvery shuttle was climbing up along a curved course. It was flying so fast that the reflection of its wings swept overhead like a meteor that was falling from the ground into the sky, heading for that invisible ancient spaceship.

Luoying's mind went blank. She knew that all her connections to Earth had been cut off at that moment. From now on, *Earth* would only be a memory. One portion of her life had come to an end, and another portion was just starting. She didn't know what the future held or where to seek her life's purpose. The stars shone in the sky, and the wide-open land was all silence.

PART TWO

CLOUD LIGHT

PROLOGUE

"Dr. Reini, why was the war fought?"

"I guess one would say... freedom."

"To free a nation?"

"I'm not sure that's right. Even now I don't think we'd be called a proper nation."

"Then... to free a class?"

"That's not quite right either. People of all classes joined in the war."

"Then what kind of freedom was it?"

"Freedom of a way of life, I suppose."

"Like the war that led to the independence of the United States?"

"It was a bit like that, but not quite the same."

"But the Terrans say we don't have freedom; only they have freedom."

"Who do you think has more freedom?"

"I don't know... What's the definition of 'freedom'?"

"What's your definition of 'freedom'?"

Luoying bit her lip and looked at Reini with anguish. "I don't know. That's the biggest question in my life."

BOOK

Looking at Mars from Mars, Mars City was like the Hanging Gardens of ancient Babylon. And like the dream of Babel, the dream of the Hanging Gardens also found a rebirth on this red planet. The city was one vast, unitary whole in which the roofs formed flowing layers and platforms and galleries connected together. Under the glass domes, blooming flowers and lush grass were everywhere, the vitality and frailty of life on full display.

Mars City's plan showed a beautiful geometry, like a series of drawings done with compass and straightedge. Looking down from above, the most prominent features were the large edifices at the center of every district. Scattered across the city, they were of different shapes and designs, like sleeping giants or birds at rest with folded wings. They towered over the other buildings like the cathedrals in every European city in the Middle Ages. Footpaths surrounded them and radiated out in every direction. Triangles and circles were inscribed within one another. Martian dwellings were often constructed on hexagonal plots that honeycombed together into a vast sea, with footpaths zigzagging along the edge, leading to the next neighborhood.

There was no single visual center of the city. To the north stood a string of towers, and to the south loomed large inclined planes. In the west stretched a big ranch, while in the east clustered nine cylindrical water towers. Tube trains arched over the clustered roofs, and, viewed from above, the city resembled a painting of dense curves that evinced planning rather than chaos.

A city like this was an homage to mathematics. Most ancient civilizations prized mathematics. Vestiges of Sumer's sexagesimal system could still be seen today, and Egyptian pyramids embodied the pinnacle of geometry. The ancient Greeks, especially, believed that mathematics was the universe, and the harmony of numbers represented the true beauty of the cosmos. Mars City was a metropolis sketched in sand, a dream ex nihilo, and the geometry on the ground was an asymptotic approach to Plato's cookies in *Sofies verden*.

Another point of commonality between Mars and ancient civilizations was the importance of astronomy. Exposed to open space, Martians turned their eyes toward the celestial dome from the start. The night sky was also the day, and darkness was also light. They understood the sky the way those who lived in valleys understood mountains and those who lived on shores understood the sea.

Mathematics and astronomy were the lighthouses of Mars, and every Martian understood their importance. But their spiritual center was different from that of the ancients. They didn't use astronomy to divine the will of the gods, and they didn't employ mathematics as a way to gain the gods' favor. They simply loved precision, loved the perfect expression of the nature of the cosmos. This was also a kind of divinity. They were an atheistic people, and they shared a faith and abiding trust only in an objective sense of accuracy.

Few spoke of the internal logic of the Martian belief system. But Reini did. He was a person who wrote history.

———————

Looking at Mars from Earth, Mars wasn't a real place but only an abstract wasteland, to be found in dry descriptions in books. Luoying could find it only in the library, where no one went. Among the tall stacks, she found books in which Mars was one of many topics like the Big Bang, the Roman Empire, steam-powered cars, and so on. In the middle of a dense wall of text, there was a cutaway diagram of the planet, its internal layers labeled with numbers and external craters pointed to by arrows. It was like seeing a dissected specimen laid out to show all its wounds.

The pages lay open. Time disappeared among the stacks; peoples and nations migrated like wild geese; weapons clashed; gears spun; frenzied fighting, betrayals, glory; soil mixed with blood. History roared between the lines and, in the quiet sunlit library, turned into fragile dust, weak, dark, untouched. The tiny font reduced the world to numbers, to abstractions, to an illusion that had no substance. Among these was Luoying's Mars. She had grown up in its embrace, but in these books it was merely a cartoonish ball of dust.

It was also a worship of the objective, a cold and arrogant sort of objectivity. With a dispassionate tone, the voice delivered its judgment, leaving no room for her to protest and no place for embarrassment. *Look*, the voice said, *this is your world, a simple and desolate place, an ugly bit of dirt.*

Few paid attention to such narratives. But Luoying did. She was a person who sought history.

———————

In one corner of the desert palace, Luoying sat in her wheelchair like a bird resting on the stately walls of a castle.

In a sense, Luoying was the princess of Mars, but unlike the princesses of ancient civilizations, she had no retinue. Unlike Amytis, who complained that life was so boring in the desert, or Bao Si of Zhou, who grew tired of mountains of gold and pearls, there was no one to build a wonder of the world for her or to light the beacon towers of border walls, summoning the armies of enraged princes just to make her smile. She was a lonely princess.

Her brother and grandfather were absorbed by the heated debates in the Boule over engineering policy, and her friends were still adjusting to the pressures of life in the ateliers.

In ancient times she would be sitting in some sunlit rose garden, an indolent smile on her face as she recounted to her faithful knights the wonders she had encountered on her adventures. But she didn't live in the legendary past; she lived on Mars, a most solid and real Mars. In front of her was a shallow pool on the hospital skydeck. The ground was smooth frosted glass, done in a pattern of white and beige diamonds. A thick column three meters in diameter held up a large glass dome. At the foot of the wall were lights, and she had to operate the controls for brightness and temperature herself.

She had no knights at her side. From time to time Dr. Reini visited her. Every evening she came here to watch the sunset, and Reini would stay with her if he didn't have other patients to attend to.

Her habit of watching sunsets had been acquired on Earth. Sunsets on Mars were much simpler: the bright white sun sank below the horizon against a dark sky. There were no clouds or the sequential disappearance of colors according to their temperatures. All that happened was the fading of everything into darkness as the distant mountains turned into silhouettes. Though the sight was different, Luoying still enjoyed it. When she watched sunsets, she felt more at peace, and even her memories grew calmer.

When Reini sat next to her, his back against the glass wall, he would listen to her recount her memories slowly and hesitantly.

"When I first heard them call Grandfather a dictator, my first reaction was shock and rage. It wasn't just the natural instinct to defend someone I loved, but, more important, Grandfather was a hero of Mars. I could understand that the Terrans would view him as an enemy but not that he would be called a cold-blooded tyrant. Here's the difference: an enemy of the Terrans could still be a hero of the Martians, but a tyrant would be an enemy of the Martians as well."

"Which do you believe?"

"I don't know. I've been puzzling over it ever since, not daring to ask anyone."

"Why not?"

"Because of fear and shame. It sounds silly when I say it, but I was afraid to be told a truth that I didn't want to hear. I couldn't deny it and didn't want to admit it. I was terrified of how I would react."

"That doesn't sound silly at all," said Reini.

Luoying gave Dr. Reini a grateful smile. She didn't know him well, but she felt comfortable telling him these thoughts because she could sense his generous spirit. He gave off a deep serenity that she wanted to possess one day herself. He was rarely impatient and explained everything to her calmly. From time to time she suffered from bouts of sorrow or anger, and he would try to explain the reasons behind various events, allowing her a chance to contextualize her emotions in the flow of history and time. His explanations felt steady and dispassionate, like trees that defied the storm on a snowy mountain.

In a way, Dr. Reini didn't seem to Luoying like a typical

doctor but a writer. She often saw him writing at a desk next to a window, empty except for a notepad and lamp. He would sit, supporting his head with one hand, deeply absorbed in some difficult question. From time to time he looked out the window, and the distant light was reflected in his round glasses. She felt that Reini was the only one who could tolerate her doubts. When she wanted to share her thoughts with someone, her ideal listener was someone like this, deep and not easily disturbed. Perhaps he wouldn't necessarily give her useful guidance, but she knew he would not judge her.

"The second month I was on Earth, something really shocked me."

Luoying paused. The first year on Earth was also the most perplexing.

"The dance troupe helped me rent my first room, in an apartment on the ninetieth floor of the pyramid tower. The apartment was spacious and comfortable, and the owner was an old woman who lived by herself, elegant and wealthy. Since she was my first landlady, I was particularly careful with my manners, treating her with great respect. The first month we lived together was uneventful.

"In the second month, during dinner one night, I mentioned something about my life on Mars. My landlady was dumbfounded.

'You're from *Mars*?'

"'I am indeed,' I said. 'I thought you knew.'

"'Not at all,' she said. 'I know you're a member of the dance troupe, but I never pry into the business of my renters.'

"After that, she did something odd. She held my hand, and I saw an expression of pity and sorrow in her eyes. She asked for all sorts of details about my life, and she had never been so solicitous before.

"From that time on, she took extra care of me. Sometimes she would hug me tightly as though I were her child, and she bought me lots of delicious treats. She even took me on sightseeing outings. I didn't know why she was suddenly so attentive to me, but I was very moved. To think that my identity was so warmly welcomed made me feel pride in my Martian heritage.

"But then one day she said something that revealed her true reasons.

"She was looking at me and muttered to herself, 'What a wonderful child. How could she be born on Mars?'

"Surprised, I asked, 'Why do you say that?'

"She looked at me, her gaze full of pity. 'Your government forces you to get jobs as child workers from the age of ten.'

"My blood turned cold at that moment as I understood the motivation behind her caring acts. She was looking at me like an orphan or a beggar, pitying my terrible fate, and unconsciously feeling herself my superior. I didn't know what to say. After thirteen years of growing up on Mars, I had always believed that my planet's civilization was more perfect, more advanced, more beautiful than that of Earth. But in her eyes I was someone to be coddled, to be pitied. I didn't understand where the error was.

"Later, I moved out of that apartment. My landlady's kindness was intolerable. I understood that she meant no harm, and I tried to be grateful. But I simply couldn't live with her pity."

Luoying looked down at her hands. When she was younger, she had feared being hated or disliked, but later she found that she was far more sensitive to pity, to condescension.

Reini listened intently to Luoying's account without interrupting. When she was finished, he asked, "I imagine she was talking about the internships as part of your electives, right?"

Luoying nodded. "Yes, it wasn't until my third year on Earth that I finally realized that must have been the case. I thought about finding her to explain the truth, but by then I was living on the other side of the globe, and I never got to see her again."

"She had probably forgotten all about it."

"Yes. Something like that probably mattered a lot more to me than her." After a moment she continued. "Actually, I'm not even sure I can explain it clearly. I know why she said what she did, but I can't judge her. I don't like what she said, but from her point of view it makes sense.

"Oh, there was another time, when the Creativity Fair came up." *The Creativity Fair.* Luoying repeated the phrase to herself.

The Creativity Fair was the most important competition for Martian youths. Held once every three years, all those between the ages of fourteen and twenty were allowed to participate. There was no limitation on form or theme, and only creativity was judged. Every team turned in one project, and the projects were judged on novelty of conception and ingenuity of execution. Great ideas from the fair could even be selected by the state as key projects to be developed for the future.

Children on Mars loved the Creativity Fair. When Luoying and her friends were young girls, they couldn't wait for the fairs.

Besides fairy-tale fantasies of princesses and princes, their greatest dream was to set foot on the stage at the Creativity Fair as competitors or as one of the laurel-presenting goddesses, the older girls who dressed up as classical Greek goddesses and solemnly pronounced who had won the golden apple. Luoying and her friends sat in front of live-broadcast screens or on the fences around the pasture, chins in hands, and imagined their own futures. They yearned for the day when they would be the focus of everyone's attention. Because their desires were so direct and united, that time felt as simple and joyful as a water-color painting.

That was the first balloon she carried with her to Earth, and also the first to be burst.

"When I left Mars for Earth, I was still so taken with the honor of the competition that I carried a notepad with me everywhere, sketching ideas and taking notes, thinking that I would gather all kinds of material that would inspire me for the fair after I got back. The hope was like a balloon trailing behind my luggage. During my first year on Earth, I was so serious about realizing my dream. I learned to use the web and found all kinds of interesting new products. I didn't understand how they worked, but I took detailed notes about them. I even sneaked into college classes to listen to lectures I only half understood, hoping to better prepare myself for the competition.

"One time I got into a conversation with a student who was just a few years older. She smoked, and talked about everything with a careless, world-weary air. I asked her about a concept from chemistry, and instead of explaining it to me, she demanded to know why I wanted to study the subject. I told her.

"She grew interested and asked me why we cared so much about the Creativity Fair and how much was the prize money. I told her that the winner didn't win any money. Then she asked me how much the champions could sell the winning projects for. I told her that winning projects weren't sold and there were no career promotions either. However, the winners got a chance to show their creations to more people, and if the projects were incorporated into the construction of the city, it would be an unparalleled honor.

"She laughed. 'So you're telling me the competition is just a chance for you to give away your ideas for free?'

"I was too startled to answer.

"The young woman leaned against the back of her chair and laughed some more as she regarded me. 'You Martians are so… interesting. Your government exploits your minds with no compensation, and you don't even seem to be aware that it's happening. Don't you want to protect your rights?'

"I was stunned, uncertain what she was talking about. At first I was merely confused, but then I became a little afraid. I felt air leaking from that beautiful balloon, and I was so sad. But I couldn't stop it. I couldn't do anything."

Luoying looked at Reini. "Doctor, why do things always turn out to be different from our first understanding of them?"

Reini, who sat next to Luoying with his arms on his knees, looked away as his eyes focused on some invisible spot, as though seeking a good answer for her. Eventually he said, "I think sometimes it happens like this: A person from one civilization looks at their surroundings as distinct objects and events and considers them separately. But when a person from another civilization looks in as an outsider, they prefer to view everything through the lens of political power and try to explain everything based on that perspective."

"Is that the way we *should* understand them?"

Reini paused. Then he said, "I can only say that normally people inside a civilization would not view their surroundings that way."

Luoying glanced at the setting sun, which seemed to be carrying a distant melancholy on the horizon. She turned and locked eyes with Dr. Reini. His eyes were in shadow, while the frames of his glasses shone bright in the light.

"Doctor, do you know how to get into the Registry of Files?"

"Why do you want to get inside?"

"I want to look up some information from the past... about my family, about Grandfather, and his father."

"Can't you find out from your family?"

"I can't. My parents died when I was too little to understand, and my brother won't talk to me about these things." After a moment of hesitation she added, "I dare not ask my grandfather at all."

Luoying had so many questions for her grandfather, but she could not ask most of them. Many Terrans had told her that Hans Sloan had become the consul because his father was also a dictator. From ancient times to now, passing the throne from parent to child was a feature shared by all dictators. They told her all this with such conviction. But she dared not ask, and didn't want to ask. Her grandfather's blood flowed in her veins as well, and she couldn't confront him.

Looking at Reini, she bit her lip expectantly.

"Procedurally, there are two ways," said Reini calmly. "First, if you have an authorization from the History Atelier, you can explain your research needs and apply for a permit with the Registry. Second, certain qualified individuals can give you a power of attorney, allowing you to access the Registry on a temporary or long-term basis on their behalf."

"Who are these qualified individuals?"

"A small group that includes the consul, the archon of each of the nine systems, and the three justices of the Security System."

Luoying's heart sank. These were all individuals she didn't want to talk to and who wouldn't likely give her access anyway. "I suppose I won't be able to go, then," she muttered.

After a moment of silence, Reini said, "I'm qualified as well."

"You?"

Reini nodded. "Your grandfather gave me permanent access."

"But why?"

"He knew that I was working on a history and needed to consult the documents and records of the Registry."

"Why would a doctor be writing a history?"

"A hobby, I suppose."

"Are you good friends with my grandfather?"

"No. But there was a time when I agreed to help him, and this was his way of thanking me."

"What did you help him with?"

"A matter of engineering."

Luoying was curious, but Reini didn't want to elaborate, and she didn't want to pry. She hadn't expected her doctor to have such connections with her family. He seemed to hint at an even more complicated past than she was aware of.

"Then... can you give me a power of attorney?" She gazed at him. "Onetime access is enough."

"In principle, yes." Reini looked at her and hesitated. "But have you thought through why you want to find out about the past?"

"I've given it some thought."

"Why?"

"I think... it's because I'm still trying to find myself." Remembering all her ruminations the last few days, she tried to be frank. "Rudy once told me that it wasn't necessary to be fixated on the past, but I just can't let it go. I want to know what events caused me to be me. And if my fate was determined by my surroundings, then I want to know what caused this world to be the way it is.

Without understanding the past, I can't choose the future."

"I understand." Reini nodded. "I can accept that reason."

Luoying let out a held breath. "Does that mean you agree?"

"Yes."

Luoying smiled gratefully at Reini, who responded with a kind look. She didn't keep on pestering him, and he didn't say more. A tranquil silence enveloped them. Reini moved Luoying's wheelchair by another few centimeters so that she could enjoy the sunlight a bit longer. Surrounded by the stars, the sun vanished millimeter by millimeter. Without clouds, there was a simple magnificence to the sight. Mars was like a lonely lover turning away, lingering but resolute, parting from the warmth, leaving light behind. Against the empty, desolate plain, Luoying seemed to discern figures of the past reenacting their deeds as if in a holographic film.

After the last sliver of the sun vanished, Luoying asked, "Doctor, I've always wanted to ask: Is it really possible to write history? I've grown to think that everyone can write a different history that sounds like the truth."

"You're right," said Reini. "But that is also what makes history important."

"Will we also one day be part of the history books?"

"Absolutely. Everyone ends up as part of the history books."

Reini pushed Luoying to the edge of the skydeck. Night had fallen, and under the starlight they had an unimpeded view of the vast land stretching thousands of kilometers in every direction. The mountains and valleys of Mars were grander than those on Earth and more angular, steeper, taller. Like their city and sky, the land was simple and direct, guileless.

Reini's history was an experiment.

There were many approaches to historiography. Chronicles by year, biographies of great figures, and narratives of events. But what Reini was working on wasn't any of those. He didn't know what to call his creation; perhaps "a history of words" would do. The protagonists of his history weren't years, figures, or events but abstract words and phrases. He didn't care about "objectivity" through the use of voluminous numerical data, nor did he think individuals provided the answers to questions he cared about. He was hoping to use logic to connect people and events into a true drama. The actors played their roles inadvertently but unexpectedly obtained a plot.

What he was working on now was the history of freedom. He had written the histories of creation and communication, but now he wanted to focus on freedom.

He had complicated feelings about his own country. The events from a decade ago left indelible marks in his heart. But he understood that the founders of his country had not intended to create an automated machine. They put their lives on the line, gave up the supplies from Earth, severed all ties to that planet, sought independence and the commons of spiritual and intellectual wealth because of a single enticement: freedom. Without the support of this belief, it was impossible that so few could have overcome so many. The republic of today was riddled with faults, but the original hope had been pure.

Reini spent much of his time reading and writing. His duties at the hospital were limited, as he was a neurology researcher, not a full-time clinician. He was responsible for studying the neural system and biomechanics and developing new instruments. But he didn't belong to a fixed laboratory and didn't have his own research group or public funding for projects. His own living stipend was too small to allow him to pursue grand projects. His isolation and limited resources had both pluses and minuses. On the one hand, his career had no advancement opportunities, but on the other hand, he had plenty of free time outside of his official duties. So he spent a great part of each day taking walks, reading, and crafting his histories.

It took about a minute on the tube train to get from his apartment to the hospital, but he preferred to walk the three kilometers every day, taking breaks along the way at parks, where he observed trees from long benches. The parks were full of lush vegetation, and he preferred to admire the marvels of nature by himself. It wasn't so much that he kept others at a distance deliberately, but there were few whose company he enjoyed. He didn't think much about it only because he didn't want to face the inevitable bitterness that would result.

Writing gave him great pleasure and allowed him to pass the otherwise bitter moments of his life with ease. Over time, he had come to rely on writing. Only when he was immersed in the vast, complicated maze of historical documents could he face the lonely days with dedication and self-assurance. He was a man who had been punished, and he could not ask for more in his life.

Reini liked to play games with words. He picked words out of life and planted them on paper, building up the drama of personalities around them. Words and their shifting uses brought about changes in life. It was a habit of thinking developed from childhood. When he was a boy, he had a set of toy blocks based on words, which influenced him greatly. During his lonely childhood, the blocks brought him endless imagined possibilities and the comforts of companionship.

Reini's father was a veteran of the war, and Reini was his only child, born in the seventh year after the conclusion of the war. Reini's mother left them when he was four. He couldn't recall her face, not even in dreams. His father was a generous, forgiving man, and he didn't complain. Under the eaves of their dwelling, he told the three-year-old Reini that the distance between events

273

wasn't like the distance between people. On that map of events, all points were equidistant. His father arranged metal dishes like a battlefield map and sang to himself in the dusk. After that, his father rarely supervised his instruction. The parting of his parents merged into all the partings during that time and, in the lingering gaze that came after sorrow, transformed into an abstract musical score with the stars as notes. Young Reini was pretty much brought up by himself.

The biggest influence in Reini's childhood was that set of toy blocks. He spent hours by himself with the blocks on the smooth kitchen floor, building castles, spaceships, whatever he fancied. The blocks were in different shapes and sizes, and could be put together in infinite ways. Each block had a word on it, meant to promote early literacy. Between the ages of two and eleven, they were Reini's constant companions. He was amazed by the way the words supported each other. *Courage* was a thin, long plank, elegant in appearance. He could put it together with *purity* and build a small tower. But when he wanted to build a bigger tower, he realized that he had to let *courage* lie flat lest it get in the way of other blocks, other words. He examined the shapes of the words, trying different combinations and usages. For a child, the process was marvelous and deeply absorbing. He put as much effort into the blocks as he put into schooling and his family.

The blocks turned into an independent game of abstractions. Even as a grown man, he still saw them in his mind. When he listened to a lecture, for instance, he saw a city onstage, out of which extended a pole of agreement, from which hung multiple mockeries, whose purpose was to disguise the tattered panic within the city and the disorderly heaps of random knowledge.

As he grew older, the games in his mind turned into deeper ruminations. He thought about how to record and narrate the experiences of his country, of how it came to be. He thought about oral histories, about using charts and figures for analysis and comparison, about noting down all the details year by year. But in the end he chose words. In his view, only by focusing on words could one see clearly the struggles and choices of every individual.

Whether history could be written was a question on which Reini reserved judgment. He knew that histories depended on whose gaze was privileged. The gaze determined the voice; the eyes governed the lips.

In books, history always exhibited the characteristics of water. For some who believed in linear progression, history was a surging river advancing relentlessly, as though the endpoint and humanity's future had been ordained by divine will. In their view, Mars represented a type of pure socialism unprecedented in human history, the inevitable revolutionary result of a certain level of scientific and technological development, the first realization of utopianism, the bright, fresh tip of time's arrow.

But for others with a cyclical view, history was like a beautiful fountain. The grandiose appearance disguised an empty interior as streams of water shot into the air only to return to the fountain, and the same story simply repeated without end. In their view, the story of Mars was just a rerun of a story that had occurred countless times before: exploration, development, independence, political consolidation. Every time, those who developed a new world rebelled, and every time, the rebels turned into new oppressors.

For yet others who leaned toward nihilism, history was only a thin shadow of reality. Reality was a deep, vast sea. What we could see was only the froth on the surface, while invisible details formed roiling currents beneath the waves.

They believed that historical events were largely accidental, contingent, fortuitous, and put no faith in the retrospective explanations of later generations. In their view, a man named Sloan committed an opportunistic murder at a fortuitous time, but those who came later decided to tell a story about a long plot with years of preparation, a story of historical necessity.

Finally, for those who believed in the law of the jungle, history was merely the result of the clash between powerful crosscurrents. In the struggle for survival, the strong persisted while the weak vanished. They believed in the truth of history, but there was no higher purpose, no teleology, no regularity. All that was was the contest between power and power, having nothing to do with philosophy or social systems. When Mars's own military power grew strong enough to overcome that of Earth's, war began. Power determined the conclusion.

No matter the form of the truth, Reini believed that a single drop of water had the hardest time explaining the appearance of water.

———————

Reini liked to read. The greatest benefit of reading was to help the lonely feel not so alone.

In a way, Reini's lonely life didn't cause him to fall into a depression because he had seen shades of himself in other historians during his study of history. No, he didn't mean the scholastically trained classical historians who had recorded the deeds of mankind to glorify God or gods, and neither did he mean the generations of bards, starting with Homer and continuing through contemporary novelists, who pleased the public with romantic epics. Rather, he identified himself with some of the historians of ancient China who wrote with a singular vision. They were lonely and disappointed, serious and objective, but their writings were filled with traces of their individual, unique consciousness.

Luoying also enjoyed reading. For her, reading was at once lonely and also not lonely.

Even as a young child, Luoying understood that her name would be forever entwined with the fate of her country because of her blood. She didn't know, however, whether this connectedness was an honor or a burden. When she read stories of other princesses in books, she found them to be more determined and pure of purpose, and their lives were happier.

She read, for instance, about Haydée, who came to be with the Count of Monte Cristo. Her father was a great hero, and despite the cruelty of foreign invaders and the betrayal of the craven, nothing could harm the eternal glory of her father. She had also read about Sulla's daughter. The Roman dictator was fatuous and shameless, a cruel oppressor of the slaves. The leader of the rebellion, on the other hand, was the embodiment of courage and justice, and so she joined the rebellion against a tyrant without hesitation. But whether it was abiding faith or dogged rebellion, they were passionate and resolute, and definitely inspiring. She could even imagine their lines: *Father, no matter how difficult the path ahead, my love for you will never diminish… No, tyrant, no matter how difficult the path ahead, I will bring you down.*

But she herself could not live like that. Instead of the life of a princess of ancient times, she lived in the real Mars of the twenty-second century. Uncertain of the nature of the world around her, she could not settle on her attitude. The feeling made her lonely.

She was sure that a look of hesitation and perplexity inspired no one, but she wanted to be faithful to the truth, which meant she had to waver on her attitude.

Although the lives of the princesses in books didn't resonate with her, she found her mind reflected in the writings of other travelers.

If the desert appears at first only as emptiness and silence, that is because it doesn't offer itself to inconstant lovers. A simple village in our homeland would hide itself from us in the same manner. If we do not renounce the rest of the world for its sake, if we do not enter its traditions, its customs, its rivalries, we cannot understand why it is someone's homeland.

It was only after leaving home that she understood the meaning of homeland, and her homeland had then concealed itself from her because of it. She understood now that she had possessed Mars only when she was a child. Back then, she had lived the same life day after day and knew of no other ways of interpreting her surroundings. She was immersed in the customs of her homeland, unforgiving to its rivals, constant in her affections, gladly giving up the whole rest of the universe for its sake. Then, and only then, was her homeland her homeland.

She understood how the writer felt between the lines. When Saint-Exupéry wrote these lines, his fate to be vagabond had already been sealed.

Luoying closed the book and gazed at its orange and dark blue cover.

Wind, Sand and Stars, by Antoine de Saint-Exupéry.

Those words encompassed all the treasures of Mars.

CRYSTAL

As Gielle entered Luoying's room, Luoying slid Dr. Reini's manuscript under her blanket and picked up a book of pictures from the nightstand. She didn't want Gielle to ask about what she was reading. It wasn't that she felt she had anything to hide; she simply didn't know how to explain.

Gielle was her usual chatty and vivacious self, as bubbly as the rising sun.

"How're you feeling?"

"All right," said Luoying.

"Can you walk now?"

"A few steps."

Luoying could see that Gielle was disappointed. In fact, she didn't really need to stay at the hospital. Reini had told her that her fracture was healing well, and it would be all right for her to recuperate at home. But she didn't want to leave. She still had so many questions for Reini, and she loved reading old books by the light of the setting sun on the skydeck. Once she went home, she would likely not enjoy such peaceful times again.

Gielle couldn't hold back any longer.

"Aren't you excited about the Creativity Fair? The preliminary rounds will be held next week. I thought you would be out of the hospital by now, which was why I signed you up as part of our team: me, you, Daniel, and Pierre."

Gielle's words brought Luoying back to her conversation with Reini a few days earlier. All at once, a flood of memories inundated her mind.

"What's wrong?" asked Gielle, noticing Luoying's distracted look. "Did you *forget* about the Creativity Fair?"

"Oh, no, not at all." Luoying shook her head. "How could I forget that?"

Gielle went on excitedly to describe their plans while Luoying listened halfheartedly.

"We *just* settled on the team name. Every afternoon we're supposed to get together at Interchange Plaza to plan. Oh, every team is supposed to have a flag, and Lily designed ours... I was thinking... But then Daniel said... In a few more days, after your leg is better, you have to join the planning discussions. We can have tea and snacks while we talk."

Gielle's enthusiastic voice drifted in and out of Luoying's consciousness. She had no interest in the fair at all. She couldn't help but remember how this all looked from Earth: an authoritarian regime using education to consolidate its rule. But she couldn't possibly explain any of this to Gielle.

Luoying sighed. Gielle's animated expressions complicated her feelings even further. She was sitting on the window ledge, telling her all the details of their preparation. Against the sunlight streaming in through the window, Gielle cut a sharp silhouette. Her round arms supported her body on the window ledge, and a few strands of loose hair fluttered in the room's air currents. The bright sun was like a halo around her. All of a sudden Luoying felt tired. Memories of Earth seemed to have become a nasty habit: she was doubting everything. She couldn't shake the taut nerves and unsettled feeling.

She shook her head, angry at herself. "What are you planning on making for the competition?"

"Another outfit!"

"What kind of outfit?"

"Still using Pierre's material, of course. One variation of his material has photoelectric properties, sort of like our roofs. I want to see if we can design an outfit that can generate electricity. Daniel is good with electronics, and he says he can embed wires to conduct the electricity out. I'll be in charge of overall design. Although this material isn't as soft or light as the material I used for your costume, we can make it into something utilitarian, like armor. It will look so gallant."

Luoying nodded. "That sounds fantastic."

"Definitely. Daniel and I already drew the patterns and the circuits. If Pierre didn't have to be at the hospital these last couple of days, we would have already started trials."

"What happened to Pierre?"

"His grandfather is ill. He has to be at the hospital to keep watch."

Luoying's heart clenched. "I hope it's nothing too serious."

Gielle nodded. "That reminds me… I should go visit, too. His grandfather is also staying at this hospital."

She jumped down, patted Luoying on the arm, and rushed toward the door. But at the door she seemed to remember something and turned around, her eyes sparkling.

"I almost forgot: we're all getting together this weekend. You should come, too."

"What are you talking about?"

"You know, the old gang. It's a party to get everyone excited about the preliminary rounds next week."

"Don't you already see each other every day?"

"It's not the same. We're having a picnic, and then we're dancing at the function hall."

"I won't be able to make it," Luoying said. "Have fun."

She knew what kind of party Gielle was talking about, but she didn't want to go. The attendees had all grown up together, gone to school together, played house and war together, entered ateliers together, and held parties together. At this party they would continue the same games that were left unfinished at the last one, joke with one another about the past, gossip when someone seemed to be dancing with someone else just a little bit differently, and plan for the next party.

It wasn't that she didn't like parties like this, but she still remembered another kind of party, a party of strangers. Lightning flashed across the sky as tiny planes landed like a flock of birds around a dance club. Men and women, sleep deprived, filled the space, exchanging charming smiles and clinking glasses. They hugged before they knew each other's names and then parted, never to see each other again. Every time a new face, every time a new introduction, every time a new pose, dancing only for herself. Scattered souls meeting by chance, never to return to the same place. Long, winding corridors filled with goods from every country: Sri Lankan mirrors, Thai pipes, German canes, Mexican knives. The loneliness of the vagabond.

Reini turned off the screen and, eschewing the tube train, walked slowly toward Hans's home. The video that he had just watched, still fresh in his mind, raised many questions.

Hans had asked Reini to review the video and give him some suggestions. It was an animation combining the rivers of Earth with the mountains of Mars. Although Hans didn't explain, Reini understood why Hans had shown him the video.

As he walked, thinking over what he was going to say to Hans, Reini's thoughts stretched like the footpath he was on.

Hans was a nostalgic man, Reini knew. He would remember a childhood wish or a good friend's ideals for the rest of his life. Reini knew few people like that. They were usually as silent as iron, but also just as solid and resolute. Out of all his contemporaries, Hans was the only one still working. His old friends had all died or become bedridden, and only he remained at his post, soliciting the advice of others with a serious expression. He persisted because certain beliefs, deep in his heart, had supported him throughout the years.

Among Hans's closest friends, Galiman was the only one who stood by him in his struggles. They had been part of the same fighter squadron during the war and, after the war, rebuilt Mars together. During those difficult years Ronen traveled far from home, while Garcia stayed on *Maearth*. For forty years only Galiman accompanied Hans, lending him his strength like a roaring lion. If one compared Hans with Diocletian, then Galiman was his Maximian, except this Augustus had no secret plan to split with the consul, and never did groom his own Caesar. For decades, he and Hans fought together for this city on a battlefield where there were no lasers or missiles, only the howling of the wind over sand. Without each other's support, neither would have lasted as long.

Hans and others his age were the founders of the Martian Republic. Mars was born in their thirties, and for the next four decades the baby grew, inch by inch. Galiman was the architect, responsible for the city's design. At the age of twenty-two, he drew up the first plan for a glass house, which defined the core structural principles for all Martian houses and became the foundation for the city's infrastructure. Their city grew and expanded on this design, and around a core of durable foundational technologies evolved an infinite variety of external forms and rich details. This was a city born from ideals. In his mind, Galiman sketched a crystal garden in the air and led his people out of the valley shrouded by the darkness of war.

Of all of Hans's beliefs, Galiman's city plan was among the most important. Hans had participated in all phases of its realization. He grew from the young pilot who flew everywhere to gather raw materials to the old consul who presided over the execution of plan after plan to perfect their vision. He gave no less of himself to this city than Galiman had. For the city he fought, and devoted his life to its protection.

Reini knew that there was no decision more difficult for Hans than the decision to give up this city, especially now, when, after two terms as consul, he was about to set down his burden and retire. The choice presented a complicated dilemma.

As Reini walked into Hans's study, Hans had just finished playing a recording of Galiman. Reini caught the very end of the video, which was from forty years ago. Galiman was an impulsive young man, and his insuppressible passion animated his smooth features, warming the air in the spacious study like a fireplace.

The sun was setting, and Hans's back cut a lonely silhouette. Reini coughed softly. Hans turned around, saw him, and nodded in acknowledgment. Hans poured a cup of tea for Reini at the table and pressed a few places on the wall. A minute later a flask of liquor and a few bowls of snacks were sent up in the dumbwaiter. Hans opened the small door and took out the tray, setting everything down on the table.

"I watched the video," said Reini.

Hans poured for Reini without speaking.

"I also reviewed the computer simulation of the plan."

"What do you think?"

"I think there are two main difficulties: air and water temperature."

Hans nodded, waiting for Reini to continue. Though his gaze appeared calm and steady, Reini could see in Hans's eyes the kind of expectancy one had when waiting for the surgeon to emerge from the operating room.

"The first problem may be the hardest," Reini said. "It's a million times harder to maintain the air in an open environment versus an enclosed environment."

"You're concerned about air pressure?"

"Yes, but that's not the key. The key is the composition of the air. A human being is essentially a balloon in equilibrium with the surrounding atmosphere, and changes in the atmosphere are reflected instantly in the body. The brain is very sensitive to the proportion of oxygen. Much of the rest must be made up by some kind of inert gas so as to prevent disruptions to the body's reactions. Since it needs to be fairly common, the only choice is nitrogen. We can't have too much carbon dioxide, lest people suffocate. The amount of water vapor also needs to be controlled, since humans are sensitive to humidity. Ultimately, we must essentially replicate the atmosphere of Earth, which is a challenge in a place with such low escape velocity."

As Reini spoke, he seemed to see thousands of thin tendrils extend out of his body to connect with the air around him, like a plant being pulled out of the soil, dangling a web of roots. He had always been cautious about grand fantasies envisioning humans scattered to every corner of the universe, because he didn't view a human being as an independent sculpture but as a membrane with air on both sides. A human being required certain conditions to survive, and without a suitable environment a human being could no more remain a human being than a jellyfish could maintain its shape out of the water.

Hans's features relaxed slightly, as though the answer was what he had anticipated.

"What about the water temperature?"

"That's the other problem," said Reini. "If we can't maintain water in a liquid state and create a true water cycle, then the idea of an open-air ecosystem is meaningless. No matter where we locate the site, the temperature at night will be below freezing. Rivers will freeze over and perhaps not even thaw completely during the day. To artificially heat the water would be incredibly costly in terms of energy, and the final result won't be better than the enclosed city."

"In other words, you don't believe the development plan can succeed."

"I can't rule out the possibility, but it will be extremely difficult."

"I understand."

"Of course, I'm basing this on rough estimates," said Reini. "I didn't perform any detailed calculations."

"That's all right," said Hans. "I was just trying to get a sense. The final result doesn't just depend on me."

Reini hesitated. "How far... has the plan progressed?"

"It's still just a proposal being evaluated. Right now the focus is on fleshing out technical details for the feasibility analysis. It hasn't yet been submitted to the Boule for debate."

"Will this be decided by the Boule or require a full plebiscite?"

"That has yet to be determined."

"Which way are you leaning?"

"I haven't decided either." Hans paused, and then added, "I have to be extremely careful here. That's probably all I can do."

There was a hint of anguish in Hans's tone that touched Reini. After a long moment he nodded. "I understand."

He understood what Hans was struggling with. Hans wanted

to stay in the city, but he didn't have much chance to see his wish fulfilled.

Hans was no longer a warrior but the consul. A warrior could cheer on the ideals of his comrades, but the consul had no such freedom. The consul had no power to dictate policy; rather, he was like a judge in court. His function was to ensure the fairness of the policy debate process and to decide the most effective way to continue the discussion. He himself, however, was not allowed to decide the outcome of the debate on his own. His interest in the technical principles of this project was like a judge's interest in the facts of the case.

The debate had grown more fierce the last few days. Since Ceres had been brought into orbit around Mars, planning for the city's future became part of the Boule's agenda. As the negotiations with Earth progressed, plans for Ceres developed from the conceptual stage into detailed reports. Following Boule protocol, every proposal must first be disclosed in the central archive's policy zone, along with supporting research and data. Rounds of open debate then followed until a final vote by the Boule or a plebiscite.

The two proposals drawing most of the attention right now were referred to as "migration" and "continuation." The former advocated moving all Martians into a crater and constructing an open-air ecosystem, while the latter advocated remaining in the crystal box that was Mars City and turning the water of Ceres into a river flowing around it. Both proposals had advantages and difficulties, and they drew about the same amount of support. Hans was in charge of presiding over this debate, and if the ultimate decision of the people was to abandon the city and move away, he had no choice but to follow their will.

"Actually, I also invited you to come because I wanted to ask you a favor," said Hans quietly.

"Of course," said Reini.

"I'd like to ask you to pay attention to what people around you are saying about this matter," said Hans, his tone cautious. "It's helpful to understand the public mood."

"I understand."

"But don't make too big a deal of it," said Hans with some hesitation. "We both know this is not entirely proper."

"You don't need to worry."

Hans nodded. Reini could tell that he was struggling with two competing impulses. One was his personal desire to prevent the accomplishments of his old friend, Galiman, from being abandoned. The other was his duty to the system to protect the fairness of the process against manipulation by selfish desires. He cared about both deeply.

As consul, Hans had the power to decide the form of the final vote, and thus could pick the form most beneficial to Galiman's crystal city legacy. Theoretically, the choice of form should be decided by the nature of the question, not the ultimate answer desired, but everyone knew that there were inevitably going to be differences between the perspective of the Boule, largely composed of elite citizens of the republic, and the views of the public as a whole. A consul who understood the public's mood accurately could thus, within the framework of the law, choose the form that most favored the outcome they desired. The influence was subtle but possibly critical in close votes. Hans had always despised such tricks, but this time he was forced to resort to them. Reini felt a pang of pity. He understood how much Hans Sloan had always prized fairness of process. The democracy of Mars was a planned democracy, and the fairness of the plan was always the heart and soul that kept the republic going.

Reini thought that perhaps the greatest irony of Hans's life was that he was forever forced to make choices that he did not want to make but had to.

He gazed at the old man sitting across from him. Hans poured for himself and drank. His brown hair, slightly curled, was combed back neatly. His dense beard was showing streaks of white, and the corners of his mouth drooped. Though he hadn't changed his look in twenty years, a careful observer would have noticed that he was aging every day, as his skin sagged and more wrinkles appeared under his eyes and on his neck. Even a body hammered out of iron was no match for the power of time.

"I think you shouldn't be too hard on yourself," said Reini, trying to keep his tone casual. "*Que será, será.* Whatever the final outcome, I don't think Archon Galiman would blame you."

Hans looked out the window as though gazing into the distant past or discerning a pessimistic future. The setting sun deepened the shadows cast by his wrinkles. When he spoke again, he sounded tired.

"I've had to live with so many regrets in my life… I'm afraid this is going to be yet another."

"You've done the best you could," said Reini.

"I've had to bid farewell to all my friends and loved ones," said Hans. He turned and regarded Reini. "All of them."

Reini had no answer for that. In Hans's dark brown eyes, there was a sorrow that he rarely expressed. It was like looking into a deep sea, only the surface of which appeared tranquil.

"Perhaps… you should have retired earlier."

"You told me that back then," said Hans. "I imagine you must be puzzled about why I've remained at my post. Since it wasn't what I wanted, why didn't I retire? I know that I shouldn't have sought another term five years ago… but I just couldn't set my mind at ease." Hans's voice cracked. "I couldn't let go. I care." He gazed at Reini, a plea for understanding in his eyes.

Reini looked back, watching as the old man struggled with himself inside. He sighed and nodded. The sun continued to shine in the distance, and the old man's wrinkles seemed to stiffen in that fading light. Hans got himself under control, and his face stopped twitching, but a sense of tragic helplessness radiated from his pose. Minutes passed. The air in the room gradually relaxed.

Hans set down his cup and refilled it with cold tea, and now he looked just as calm and cool as his beverage. A hand supporting his temple, he conversed with Reini about less contentious topics, such as the proposed reforms to the debate format in the central archive and the Sais Crater's geology and planned development. Reini listened quietly, occasionally interjecting a quick question or a bit of analysis.

At the end, Reini told Hans that Luoying seemed to have a great deal of interest in history. He didn't mention the Registry of Files, only saying that she wanted to know about the history of her family.

"What did she ask about?"

"Our life in the past," Reini said, "and also the causes of the war."

"How did you answer her?"

"I didn't say much, but I agreed to give her some books on the topic."

Hans nodded. "Do as you think is appropriate. If she wants to know, then tell her. She's old enough."

Reini agreed. He knew that Hans was more worried about Luoying than about Rudy. After bidding farewell, he got up to leave. At the door, Hans gently patted him on the arm and watched as he walked away.

At the corner, Reini turned and looked back. Hans looked his usual somber self, his face as tranquil and expressionless as the desert.

MESSAGES

Luoying thought about asking Anka to come with her to the Registry. With him by her side, she thought she would feel braver.

No matter what was hidden in the past, she thought it better to have his help than not.

Sitting up in bed, she logged in to her personal space and checked her mailbox. Surprisingly, she found six new messages. During the time she'd been hospitalized, she received on average a message a day. Scanning through the list of senders, she noticed that most were from the Mercury Group. Surrounded by the gentle lilies in the hospital room, she found the blue-hued mail listing particularly cold and attention-grabbing.

She began with the first message, sent by Chania to the whole Mercury Group.

Dear All,

Apologies in advance for the group mail, but I think what I have to say will be of interest to everyone.

Since the Creativity Fair is almost here, I imagine you've all been invited to join teams. I don't know about the rest of you, but I think we must resist a certain tendency I've detected.

I'm talking about a vain sort of enthusiasm, an overfocus

on awards and fame, on grabbing the attention of others. Many other kids our age seem obsessed, thinking not of true wisdom and knowledge but only of how to win the favor of the judges, as if trophies were the measure of life.

I think this is the result of too many competitions in our world. Mathematics, public speaking, drama, debate— everything is structured around competitions. Surrounded by this competitive air, people have forgotten the meaning of reflection, thereby straying even further from wisdom. On Earth, however, things are more practical, and they do not pine after honor the way we do here.

And so I ask that you join me in launching a revolution. We can boycott the Creativity Fair or even speak out publicly against this vanity and superficiality. What do you think? I haven't thought through the specific form of protest, but I wanted to put the idea out there for us to discuss.

Sincerely,
Chania

Luoying stared at the message for a long time.

She remembered her earlier doubts and recollections and felt sympathy as well as hesitation. Chania, like Luoying, had found the Creativity Fair problematic, but whereas Luoying questioned their government and the means by which it ruled Mars, Chania questioned the purity of the motivation of the youths joining the competition.

Luoying wasn't sure how she should respond. Chania's critique was reasonable, but the idea of a revolution gave her pause. She remembered her parents and wondered how they would have responded if they were in her place.

The next message was from Mira to the group, responding to Chania.

Count me out. If you don't like the competition, then just sit it out. I don't want to be part of the fair either. But I don't believe there's any need for a "revolution." Young people our age are all vain—who doesn't want recognition and glory? This isn't anything worth being upset over.

Mira

Then Runge's reply.

Count me in! In fact, I wish we started the revolution earlier. Those in power have taken advantage of the pure passion and enthusiasm of so many young people. People need to wake up! This crazy system has turned everyone into a fool. It sucks our intelligence like vampires sucking blood.

Runge

Luoying's heart pounded. This was what she feared the most: to discover the dark side of the system, to have to fight against it. If it was truly evil, then they had no choice but to fight. But fighting meant confronting her grandfather. She didn't want that outcome—not at all. The words on the screen stirred the conflicting emotions in her heart.

Sorin was next.

Runge, there's no reason to blindly accept the judgment of Earth. Terrans view us negatively largely due to lingering resentment from the war and ignorance. The adults are not our oppressors. They devised these institutions, at least initially, with the intent to benefit us.

Sorin

Runge struck back.

"With the intent to benefit us"? Are you serious? Everything is set up for their own benefit. They call this "the ideal education," but in reality they are interested only in indoctrinating components of the system and loyalists. Even our trip to Earth was part of the system. Do you really think that was for our benefit? No! In reality, we were nothing but hostages, a pledge to secure the negotiations with Earth so that they could obtain more resources.

Runge

Luoying was astounded. She couldn't understand how Runge had come to such a conclusion. Did he have proof? Or was this all just a guess? If his explanation was the truth, then it would represent the tip of a much larger iceberg she hadn't even imagined. The Mercury Group would no longer just be students but political chips, and not only would her own reasons for being sent to Earth be suspect, but those of all the others as well. It felt too much like a conspiracy theory.

She didn't know what to think. Staring at the screen, her mind was blank. Woodenly she clicked open the last message.

It wasn't from anyone in the Mercury Group but from *Maearth.*

Dear Luoying,

Has your leg fully healed? I'm on Maearth now, in the company of the stars.

I write to you to ask some questions that I hope you won't mind answering.

As you probably already know, ten years ago Arthur Davosky took back to Earth the technology enabling the Martian central archive, given to him by your father. What you don't know, however, is that, due to a variety of commercial reasons, his hope of promoting the use of a similar archive on Earth failed. I came to Mars in part to understand my teacher's final wishes and to continue his dream. As a filmmaker, I know the importance of a stable, responsible commons, and I want to carry on my teacher's legacy and give creators a space dedicated to art based on freedom, without having to follow the logic of commerce. (As you know, on Earth, lack of sales is the same as death.)

During the last few days, I've discovered that there are more hurdles standing in the way of my plan than I had imagined. Besides commercial difficulties, there are also complex social issues. At first I thought this was merely a matter of art that wouldn't be politically contentious, but when I tried to describe my vision to a few government officials, they all objected, though without giving me clear reasons. Only later did I realize that, for governments, creation isn't a matter of art but a matter of employment. The one concern that keeps them up at night is unemployment, and the web market, as the world's largest industry, is also a source of steady jobs. Every creator generates multiple jobs: agents, promoters, business managers, and so on. If these were no longer necessary, if the sharing and enjoyment of art were as simple as it is on Mars, then there would be mass unemployment, which would lead to social panic and threaten the rule of every government.

I suppose I didn't spend enough time studying Mars.

Pulling on a single thread affects the entire social fabric. I don't know how many people on Mars are in the creative fields or in the noncreative fields and how repetitive labor that must be done is distributed or incentivized. Such work makes up the majority of jobs on Earth, and I can't imagine Mars could function without such work. If creatives can be encouraged by honors, what is the reward for repetitive labor? Thus, I come to you for answers. You understand Earth as well as I do, and you know the power of money on our planet.

I wish you a speedy recovery and a peaceful and fulfilling life back at home.

Thank you.

Your friend,
Eko Lu

Luoying read through the message with growing unease. She hit REPLY and began to type.

Dear Eko,

It's a pleasure to hear from you, and thank you for your kind wishes. Unfortunately, I'm not at peace, and I'm far from satisfied.

In fact, I envy you, because you still have a plan for action and have the potential for action. Though you are faced with difficulties, you are on the road. I, on the other hand, don't even know the direction I should head in.

I'm uncertain about an answer for your question. Perhaps there is a standard answer, but I think it's more likely that the question has never been asked. Perhaps you can't imagine how something so fundamental can just be taken for granted. But then again, if I hadn't gone to Earth, I wouldn't be asking so many questions either.

Many jobs on Mars are done by youths: watching over a store or driving a mining rig, for instance. Sometimes these jobs are parts of a class's curriculum, and in other cases these jobs are simply done for no reward or consideration. You ask how such work is incentivized. Well, the truth is no incentive is necessary. Students volunteer for these tasks, and there are more applicants than posts. On Earth, the mainstream opinion is that the teens are being exploited by the ruling regime, but in reality, many students view the work as fun, more enjoyable than sitting in a classroom. Since no one is paid to do these jobs, no one thinks they should be paid.

I'll describe for you an example: the Creativity Fair...

Luoying stopped, unable to continue.

Earlier, when she first started writing the reply, she simply let the words flow, conveying her emotional reactions. But now that she had seen the words on the screen, she realized how they sounded. In fact, she was telling Eko that her people were unreflective, blindly following the system without thought. Such an answer was a critique and an accusation, akin to Runge's view. She couldn't tell if she should trust it.

Reviewing the messages among the Mercury Group, she found her own answer childish. Even within the Mercury Group, opinions differed greatly on the meaning of the Creativity Fair. How could she claim that they were all blindly following the system?

Composing herself, she saved the draft reply. She needed time to think through the issues before writing Eko.

The Terran delegation had left a couple of weeks earlier,

which meant that they still had eighty-some days before arriving at Earth. In her mind, she saw *Maearth* drifting farther away, on a mission toward a real ocean. The ship was lonely and slow, but its course pointed straight ahead. She read over Eko's message one more time, moved by the suppressed idealism between the lines. She saw that Eko was trying to accomplish something that he believed his world lacked but needed. Such faith had a strength, a certainty of purpose, that comforted.

This contrasted sharply with her own life for the last two weeks. She wasn't advancing anywhere, but she wasn't happy where she was. She was dissatisfied with reality but wasn't sure what was lacking. The world was like a cloud that surrounded her but evaded her gaze. There were hints of something extraordinary, but she couldn't see through the haze. Like a fish in a bowl, she swam around, eyes wide-open, but had nowhere to go.

She missed *Maearth*. It traversed the darkness like a raindrop on glass. Though its only companions were the unreachable stars, it was never distracted, never directionless. She and her friends had once called the ship Charon, ferryman of Hades, but now it seemed to her the most lively place in the universe.

She waited for Dr. Reini to return, hoping he could answer her questions.

———

After dinner, Reini went to the club. His habit was to go on Wednesdays and Sundays, a rare opportunity for him to converse with others.

There were few on Mars who followed the old religions, and a life of science or creative endeavors didn't require strict adherence to the clock. Nonetheless, the ancestral practice of counting time in seven-day cycles and resting on the weekend persisted. Sunday was reserved for family and friends, and everyone had their own favored practices. Parents, for instance, enjoyed getting together to make treats for their children, while others went to various clubs to play some sport or to share news and other gossip of interest. While Mars lacked swimming pools or golf courses, other sporting venues were abundant.

On Sundays the club was always filled with familiar faces and new conversations. Some boasted of their accomplishments and regaled listeners with blow-by-blow accounts; others let their rivalries play out in sardonic commentary; still others complained about their work. The atmosphere was not, in fact, all that different from some aristocrat's salon in old Paris, a teahouse full of patrons in old Peking, or a bar catering to those who wanted a few drinks after work in old Hokkaido.

After club members greeted one another, they gravitated toward certain age-old topics: rumors of someone getting a promotion; reports of some senior group leader being particularly impressed by a new member; hearsay of an upcoming big change or an opportunity for the ambitious.

"I heard that Martin just got made lab director."

"Oh, he got a much better position than that! He was made the executive director for one of the three research centers at his atelier, which means he's in charge of five labs!"

"How did he rise so fast?"

"It's all because he picked the right mentor. I think the mentor was just promoted to be a system director recently, and his project has ironclad funding for the future. He really likes Martin and asked him to be in charge of several key simulations. Martin's citation rate skyrocketed, which allowed him to be promoted over several researchers with much more seniority."

"No wonder! I thought he looked particularly happy last week."

"That's why it's so key to pick the right project to work on…"

The two men were having coffee as they watched a pool game in progress. One of them was balding, while the other wore bushy sideburns. The small table between them held coffee and pastries. Both acted relaxed and casual, feigning little interest in the conversation. Elegantly dressed, they smiled as though sharing a secret.

Reini had known both since they were kids. He sat next to them, holding a cue planted against the ground as he listened to the other two talk without interrupting. Since he so rarely spoke, neither of the other two men found it odd to have him listen in.

"Do you think you'll do well this round?" Balding asked.

"Hard to say. I hope so, but hard to say," said Sideburns.

"Your lab signed up for one of the plans?"

"Yes. We are Climbers, and we were assigned to assess the viability of the planned electric cable layout inside the cliffs. What about you?"

"We are Waders. Personally, I like the Climbers more, but my lab director is very stubborn and has no faith in an artificial open atmosphere. So we ended up getting the project of optimizing the transportation tube network under the ring river. I'm not excited about it, but there should be a lot of funding."

Climbers and *Waders* were terms most Martians used to refer to supporters of the migration plan and the continuation plan, respectively. The Climbers intended to make the crater that had been inhabited before the war an open-air ecosystem, while the Waders wanted to build a river around the existing Mars City.

"Aha, so we're on opposite teams." Sideburns laughed.

"That's right. May fortune smile on the winner."

"It really is a matter of fortune. If we get the project funded, the rest of my life is basically all set. But it's really hard to tell which way it will go."

"Maybe we'll both be lucky."

"That's the one outcome ruled out for sure." Sideburns laughed once more. "Shall we play again?"

They stood up and took over the pool table that had just been vacated by two other players. After one of them racked the balls into position, the other leaned over the edge of the table and concentrated. The crisp strike of the cue ball sounded like the popping of a champagne cork.

The two players who had just finished sat down where Balding and Sideburns had sat and began to talk. They loosened their collars, got their coffee, and greeted Reini with smiles. One of the two was an old man wearing glasses. He had a kind and honest face. The other was a lanky man about Reini's age with a broad forehead and an animated, joyful face.

"How's the leak in your house?" asked the young man. "Did you get it fixed?"

"I did," said the old man. His voice was very soft. "I had to disassemble the backs of the cabinets."

"Good thing you got the kind that could be disassembled," said the young man. "I should have done the same. My baby loves to throw things into the corners as he crawls around. That's all I do at home now, pick up after him."

"How many months old is he now?"

"He just turned one. He's toddling a bit."

"A year already. How time passes."

"It really is amazing. My oldest is up to my waist now, and Nana can already read."

"I can imagine how busy you must be."

The young man laughed. "You must feel pretty liberated. Does your son visit often?"

"No. After he had his baby, he doesn't come visit much."

"If the migration plan goes through, you should move somewhere close to your son. Otherwise you might get lonely all by yourself."

"I'm used to it."

The voices merged with the other murmured conversations, forming an invisible haze in the air of the club. Reini watched them, thinking of Hans's plea. He felt guilty about his mission. What could he hope to learn through conversations such as these? To Hans, Mars City was the crystallization of an ideal, but for most of its residents it was merely the backdrop of life. To them, the dilemma that troubled Hans dissolved into opportunities for more funding for their ateliers, opportunities to pick new houses, opportunities to be promoted and recognized, opportunities that could be seized and used. The city was no longer one coherent unit but fragmented into thousands upon thousands of competing desires. A single project became a million tiny projects, and each benefited someone. The crystal city had shattered so that it was impossible to discern the trend from the pieces.

Reini had a premonition that Hans's worries were turning into a directionless, dull thunder. The contest between two competing principles was no more. No matter what the ultimate decision turned out to be, the images of Galiman on Hans's wall would vanish in the fragments of daily life.

Reini was used to the types of conversations around him: atelier budgets and developments; spousal conflicts and parental concerns; the maintenance and remodeling of homes. These were fulfilling, practical lives. Work, family, house—these conversations encompassed most of a person's life. The ambitious could pursue either the pinnacle of their art or a post in the Boule, while those uninterested in politics could simply enjoy a life between their atelier, home, and club. Many people took up gardening as a hobby or spent their free time building swing sets for their children and tinkering with the circuits in their houses. It was not terribly different from life in a small town on Earth two centuries ago. As they aged, the living stipend also increased. Though the amount would never be considered luxurious, it was more than enough to meet their needs, and the gradual increase provided a sense of hope against senescence.

But Reini wasn't part of these conversations. He had no project with public funding, no family, and no house. Since he didn't live a so-called normal life, he lacked the material to join a normal conversation. His state was the consequence of a clear chain of causes and effects, and each lack had resulted in another, link by link.

More than a decade ago, after he joined his first atelier, he had been punished due to an accident. For five years he wasn't allowed to apply for research or production funding. A year after the accident, his girlfriend parted ways with him. On Mars, singles were assigned single-occupancy dorm units but could never get the chance to choose a house with a yard.

His mistake long in the past, Reini could have applied himself and made up for lost time. However, the experience of being punished changed him and made him lose interest in pursuing what others desired. Though the restrictions on him had expired, he found the idea of organizing a project team to compete with other teams for funding tedious. He would rather perform some simple experiments by himself, using readily available materials.

He also could have found another girlfriend. However, the

experience with his ex had left him baffled. Two people became involved with each other, competed to take the initiative, and then grew tired of each other. With this understanding of the process in place, to then repeat it felt to him like a deliberate performance. Two individuals, each with complicated, private thoughts, neither understanding the other, were supposed to sit together and profess their mutual love—the whole script felt inauthentic and therefore intolerable. He hoped to meet someone who began by acknowledging the unbridgeable distance between them and their mutual strangeness, but he never met anyone like that.

He disdained games of pursuit and being pursued, just as he disliked the annual competition for a piece of the overall budget among the ateliers. Motivation was the key. For someone with no interest in the game, all the techniques for winning the competition felt like useless tricks.

From a very young age Reini showed such passive tendencies. He was never a model student, but he also wasn't a rebel. As a child, he spent most of his time alone, spoke little, and didn't distinguish himself in extracurricular activities. While he got along with the other children just fine, he was never a leader. When he got into occasional fights with other children, he never allowed those fights to fester into lasting hatreds. On the playground's tiny artificial hills and rivers, he quietly went from one piece of equipment to another, like a gray comet streaking across the yellow sand and the colorful metal structures. He spoke so little that he was often forgotten, and few asked if he also led a complicated inner life full of emotions. This was a risk facing all children who disliked talking: even after years in his company, most didn't know him, not so much because understanding him was impossible but because they thought there was no need to understand.

Reini's reserved demeanor wasn't the result of some developmental problem. Rather, like many intellectually advanced children who preferred silence, he was extraordinarily sensitive to the distinction between words that were spoken and words that were swallowed. It was, in fact, another legacy of that set of word-imprinted toy blocks. Because he had constructed within himself a full city, external expression became for him an eternal reminder of the inability of speech to truly capture thoughts. He would rather stay within himself.

Reini was no longer that child who had difficulty communicating. He had learned how to live with others, to come to the club, to share leisure time unobtrusively with acquaintances as they conversed about their regular lives. He didn't require the company of others, but he didn't want to isolate himself so much that he no longer understood people.

He sat alone among the crowd, thinking about the history of Hans and Galiman and the fate of his country.

It was late by the time Reini returned to the hospital. He came by to pick up a few books, thinking everyone had already gone to sleep and the offices would be deserted. He was surprised, therefore, to find Luoying waiting for him in the small lounge outside his office, reading by herself.

She looked up and smiled at him. The ceiling light was off, and the vase on the table, which was also a lamp, provided the only illumination in the room. The green leaves in the vase softened the light against the page. Luoying's face was lit up in profile, which slimmed her nose and made her eyes appear extra bright.

"Were you waiting for me?" Reini asked. "What's wrong?"

"Nothing." Luoying hesitated. "I... just had a few questions."

"Go ahead," said Reini, curious.

"Why do the people around us work?"

"Who do you mean?"

"Everyone. Regular people. People in the ateliers. The parents. The children."

Reini thought about the people at the club. He thought about their excitement, their rage, their calculation, their joys and sorrows, their strivings and disappointments. He thought about their Sunday club gatherings, their conversations at each gathering, the children and positions and promotions discussed in each conversation. He thought about their eyes, brows, voices, gestures, their reasons and emotions. He thought and thought about the lives of the families around him.

"I think," he spoke slowly, "they work because they want a fulfilling life."

"Do all the people want to work? Or… maybe what I mean is:

Are they all working for ideals?"

"I doubt it. A world like that doesn't exist."

"Then why? Take those boring, repetitive jobs. Since people aren't working for more money the way they do on Earth, how do we find people to do them?"

Reini pondered the question. After a while he answered very cautiously. "First of all, we don't have too many dull jobs left. Most manufacturing is automated, and we have no real service sector." Reini went to the screen and brought up the interface to a database and began to type. "The amount of repetitive, unavoidable labor makes up only… nine percent of total jobs, and most of these are part-time.

"As for what motivates people to do them: it's mainly due to the competition among the ateliers for a share of the budget. Each atelier is responsible for assigning the jobs within the atelier, including the dull ones. Someone must sit there and monitor the automated workshop; someone must follow up on routine maintenance of finished products. Most of the time, people in an atelier take turns doing these boring jobs, but sometimes they have to be assigned to a dedicated person. A project's degree of success influences the share of the budget it will be allocated next year, and if there are accidents or complaints, the project may no longer get any funding. Since this affects the fate of everyone in the group, carelessness or shirking of dull tasks isn't tolerated."

"Is the competition for the budget intense?"

"'Intense' is an understatement," said Reini. "At the end of each year, the competition for the next year's budget is a critical moment for each atelier. Starting months earlier, everyone plans, prepares, persuades, organizes. Compared to Earth, the resources available on Mars are extremely limited. In a sense, you can view all of Mars as a carefully managed enterprise in which the return on every investment and the potential for loss in every eventuality are calculated to three decimal places. Most of our research, including in the creative fields, is motivated in this manner. Nothing is entirely driven by pure interest."

As he spoke, he thought of Balding Wader and Sideburns Climber at the pool club. They lived such natural lives, plotting and scheming at the club and in their backyards, organizing groups and ateliers in preparation for the end of the year.

Luoying listened to him, and her eyes widened in confusion as though listening to some fantastic tale.

Reini wasn't surprised by her reaction. Luoying's parents had died early, and she had spent most of her teens on Earth. It wasn't remarkable that she didn't have any understanding of the competition for the budget, the most important part of adult professional life.

"But why must they compete for the budget?"

"To get to be on a bigger project; to bask in the attention of everyone around them."

"Is that so important? To attract the attention of others?"

"Important?" Reini laughed. "I can only say that if it weren't important, many events in human history would never have happened."

"So what you're saying is… our world isn't built completely on deception and blind obedience?"

Reini considered Luoying's question carefully.

"No world can be built completely on the foundation of deception and blind obedience." His tone was even and controlled. "For a world to function, it must be built upon desire."

Luoying nodded. She looked out the window as if thinking over what he had said.

At length she got up to leave. Reini walked her back to her room. Silently they paced through the corridor, each lost in their own thoughts. The glass walls reflected the moonlight and cast hazy shadows. Their walking figures looked like time itself: without end, without sound, without companion, except for the inseparable shadow. They walked slowly, listening to the sound of their feet striking the ground, unwilling to break the silence.

At the door to her room, Reini urged Luoying to get some rest.

She nodded but didn't go in right away.

"Doctor, do you think people are happy?"

"Happy?"

The many possible meanings of that word moved Reini.

After a moment of hesitation he said, "Yes, I think they're happy."

He thought they were happy, or, more accurately, he felt that he had to think so.

"Why?"

"Because they have something they want."

"Is that happiness?"

"Even if it's not happiness, it's the feeling of happiness."

"What about you? Are you happy, too?"

Reini was silent for a moment. "Not in the same way."

"How are you different?"

Reini was silent again. "I'm not very interested in projects."

"Didn't you tell me living the way they do is happiness?"

"I can only say that I think they're happy."

"So what does 'happiness' mean to you?"

"Sobriety." After a moment of reflection, Reini added in a quiet voice, "And the freedom to be sober."

Luoying went inside the room and closed the door.

Reini looked at the door and thought over her questions. Yes, he thought he was happy. Although his life was lonely, he felt at peace. Superficially, he was passively enduring his fate, accepting his punishment and single status, allowing the course of his life to be determined by policies from above. But in reality his own choices played the biggest part. Anyone's life, to a certain extent, was the consequence of their own choices. He chose to not choose, which was a choice itself. He had no reason to complain or be dissatisfied, because choices had consequences. Freedom was inseparable from loneliness. Because he wanted to have freedom unconstrained by anyone else, he had to accept a lonely life uncared for by anyone else.

———

After saying goodbye to Reini, Luoying stood at the window gazing out at the desolate land shrouded in night. She turned on the sound system to play the natural music of a thunderstorm from Earth.

The patter of rain filled the room. Luoying pressed her palms against the glass and peered at Big Cliff in the distance. Neither moon was visible and only the disk of Ceres glowed overhead. Big Cliff was like a dark seam that parted sky and ground at the horizon. Stars glowed brightly above the darkened, featureless expanse. Big Cliff looked at once close at hand and unapproachably far, like a sword wielded by night. The sound of rain was so realistic that she felt the illusion of raindrops striking against the glass she leaned against.

A chill rippled through her heart as she thought through everything she had learned that day. The glass in front of her seemed to glow brightly, enveloping all the joys and sorrows and desires of humankind. The term "living space" seemed to her both oppressive and real. They had no financial sector, no tourist industry, no traffic jams and regulations, no bureaucrats examining and verifying identity documents—but that was only because they lived inside a crystal box in which everyone's lives could be uniformly planned. For Earth to imitate this way of life, everyone would have to move into the same uniform box and receive the same uniform stipend. She didn't know how to respond to Eko. He was so enthusiastic, but he was heading toward an impossible mirage.

Just as she was hesitating over the unfinished draft reply, a new message arrived, its icon blinking.

Luoying,

Tell me when you're ready to leave the hospital. I've

asked for a whole day off. I can come get you and go to the Registry of Files with you.

Take care of yourself and make sure you're fully recovered.

Anka

Abruptly, Luoying experienced a sense of peace. The calm words on the screen lit up the room with a warm light, and all the worries, conspiracies, revolutions, histories, and theoretical debates were pushed far away, leaving only the warm, calm words.

She felt very tired. Very, very tired.

MEMBRANE

The morning before she was scheduled to be discharged from the hospital, Luoying visited another patient.

Pierre's grandfather was at the same hospital, since he lived in the same district as Luoying. She looked up his room and went to the critical care unit on the second floor, among the most well-furnished wards in the hospital. Green leaf-shaped signs hung on the doors of the quiet rooms. The door to the room Luoying was looking for was open, and the walls of the spacious room were adjusted to be translucent. With sweet floral scents in the air, the place felt as peaceful as an ocean. It was almost possible to forget the depressing reality.

Pierre was sitting quietly by the bed. The sun lit up the side of his face, and his long bangs curled against his forehead, the tips of his hairs and eyebrows almost translucent. Sitting as still as a statue, it took him a while to notice Luoying. He got up in a hurry and pushed over a chair for her without speaking. Luoying sat down, and together the two watched the old man lying in a coma in bed.

Pierre's grandfather's silver hair was spread out on the pillow, framing his peaceful face, in which the wrinkles appeared smoothed out due to lack of muscle tension. Luoying wasn't sure of his condition and didn't ask Pierre. She simply sat quietly with him, watching the tiny instruments arranged about the head of the bed: graphs measuring the old man's brain activity and other biosigns scrolled slowly across the screens. The numbers were not the same thing as life, but they indicated that life held on.

"Gielle told me about your grandfather," Luoying said.

"Gielle…" Pierre's voice was mechanical, as though simply echoing her words.

"Make sure you take care of yourself, too," said Luoying. "Don't worry about the Creativity Fair."

"The Creativity Fair?" Pierre's expression was unfocused. "Right. The Creativity Fair."

Luoying glanced at Pierre, and her heart ached in sympathy. She knew that Pierre had been raised by his grandfather, and the two had only each other. Pierre had no siblings, and if his grandfather were to die, he would be all alone in the world. She recalled what he was like as a boy: scrawny, shy, quick to anger, hugging his grandfather's thighs as he looked alertly at everyone. He didn't play with the other children, but if he saw anyone being bullied on the playground, he would run over to defend the victim like a baby hedgehog with his back arched, waving his fists. He had always been a stubborn child. Even now, his gaze on his grandfather held that same heartbreaking stubbornness. His body was curled in on itself, holding his emotions tightly in check.

Luoying had seen Pierre only once since she had been back on Mars. All her memories of him were from five years ago, when he had been shorter than she was. She heard that he had turned into an excellent student, with multiple successful research projects the past couple of years—a rare accomplishment for someone so young.

After a while, Pierre suddenly turned to Luoying and said, "Sorry. I should have gone to see you earlier."

"Not at all. I'm all better now. I knew you were busy."

"There's not much for me to do here." Pierre shook his head. "Tell Gielle that I'll join you in a couple of days. I have to supervise the vacuum spraying myself. No one else can do it."

Luoying was going to tell Pierre not to worry about it and to stay by his grandfather's side, but, seeing his serious expression, she nodded. "All right. I'll let her know."

Pierre turned back to the bed and muttered as though to himself, "No one else understands. Silicon-based nano-electronic membranes, silicon quantum dots, porous silicon integrated circuits, silicon oxide superlattices—they know the jargon, but they don't really understand. Our light, our electricity... everyone knows how to use them, but no one really understands."

Luoying wasn't sure what he was going on about. Hesitantly she asked, "Gielle told me you invented a new kind of membrane?"

Pierre grinned at her, although melancholy remained in his eyes. "Not that new. I've long thought about integrating photo-electric properties into thinner, more pliable materials."

Luoying nodded. She sat with him for a while longer to be sure there wasn't something she could do and then stood up to say goodbye.

Pierre got up. "When will you be discharged?"

"This morning. I'm on my way out now."

"Right now?" He looked surprised. "Then let me walk you out."

"I'll be fine."

"I have something to discuss with you."

"What is it?"

He hesitated. "Let's wait. I'll go visit you later at your home." Luoying nodded. He stared at her back as she left.

Outside the door, she turned around to look back into the pale blue hospital room. Pierre was again sitting quietly, his thin figure leaning forward, his feet resting on the chair's footrest. He was completely still, but all his muscles were tensed. The room was so quiet.

———————

It was still early when she got back to her own room. Sunlight filled the room, and the lilies bloomed in perfect tranquility. Her bags were ready and waiting on her made-up bed. She sat by the window to have her breakfast.

Anka was the first to arrive.

He stood at the open door to the suite and knocked softly. The wind chimes over the door tinkled. Luoying turned around, and when she saw it was him, her spoon stopped in midair. Anka smiled at her without speaking. The bright sun struck his hair and made his whole body glow. Instead of a crisp uniform, he was dressed in loose sweats, which nonetheless showed off his muscular frame. Luoying didn't know what to say, and the two stared at each other in the peaceful sunlight.

Mira, Sorin, and Chania appeared behind him. The still air was broken.

"How've you been?" asked a smiling Chania. "Getting plenty of rest?"

"Not bad," said Luoying, shaken out of her reverie. "I'm fine now. I can even walk by myself."

To prove it, she stood up and walked around the room, beaming as she showed them the metal filament boot and explained its principles. As she turned and strode, she also hid her face, not wanting her friends to see her embarrassed blush. She kept her eyes away from Anka.

Once she sat back down on the bed, Chania sat next to

her. The two boys then leaned against the window as they all chatted. Chania inquired after Luoying's leg and recovery, her sensations of pain and discomfort, and compared Luoying's symptoms with her own. As they spoke, Chania lifted one leg of her pants to reveal a thick bandage wrapped around her ankle. Luoying felt a sympathetic pang and put a comforting hand on Chania's shoulder. She knew that Chania was still training hard every day for her trip report performance next month.

Luoying asked her friends what they were up to, and after glancing at one another the trio gave the same answer: writing the reports for their trip to Earth. They also wore the same expression: seven parts derision and three parts helplessness.

"Oh, there's plenty to write about," said Mira. "But the format… *grrrrr*. I spent three whole days arguing with Granny Asala over the keywords for my report. She kept on insisting that the keywords I suggested were nonstandard, which would make it difficult for future researchers to find my report in the archive. I went through five drafts."

"Why? Are they going to treat our reports like formal academic papers?" asked Luoying.

Mira shrugged. "Yep. All our reports must strictly adhere to the format of formal academic papers."

Luoying's eyes widened. "But I thought we were supposed to just write down how we felt and some notable memories."

"I thought so, too," Mira chuckled. "But remember, everyone's hoping we've brought back useful knowledge. We were an investment, and investments must have returns."

Luoying had lost all interest in even helping other students at the dance school with choreography or tutoring. If she didn't return to the school, then no one could come after her for a report. Those who went about alone were also the freest. Mira's smile was adorable, and his dark brown face glowed.

In school, he had always been fun and undisciplined, preferring play to work. He used to sleep in all the time like a hibernating bear. Luoying always thought he would never be serious about anything, but he was serious now. Their world had changed. They could be willful for a time, but they were powerless against the demands of a lifetime.

"Oh, that reminds me," said Luoying. "What about the matter we were discussing over group messaging?"

Chania smiled, her eyes giving off a proud air that was a mix of excitement, rebelliousness, and disdain for the serious and rule-bound. With a hint of mystery in her voice, she said, "It's been decided. We're going to start a revolution. Remember you and I talked about what happened to your parents? No matter why they were punished, they set an example for us. They were brave enough to challenge the system, and so should we."

"A revolution?" Luoying sucked in a breath. "What exactly do you have in mind?"

"The first thing is to get to the bottom of Runge's accusation."

"I was surprised by that," said Luoying. "Why does he think that?"

Chania lowered her voice. "Do you remember what happened our third year—"

The wind chimes over the door tinkled, and Chania stopped talking. They turned to find Gielle and Rudy at the door. Rudy was in uniform, and he had a thick folder of documents under his arm. Gielle was holding a basket of fruit, her hair in braids. After the two of them entered the room, Pierre followed.

"How are you feeling?" asked Gielle excitedly.

"I'm fine," said Luoying. "Just fine."

Luoying accepted the basket of fruit and set it down on the nightstand. Gielle picked up an orange and gave it to Luoying, then she picked out two apples and handed them to Chania and

Mira. Finally she gave Rudy another orange. While everyone else accepted the fruit, Rudy shook his head and refused. Gielle blushed awkwardly. Seeing her reaction, Luoying reached out and took the second orange as well. Rudy never paid any attention to Gielle but looked at Chania curiously.

Rudy gazed at Chania, Gielle gazed at Rudy, and Pierre, who stood at the back, gazed at Gielle. Luoying found the scene amusing. It was obvious that Rudy was interested in Chania, although they hadn't spent much time together. Luoying saw that Rudy was looking at her with the same expression that he had when he found a research topic that really excited him. Chania, on the other hand, seemed not to notice Rudy at all as she chatted in a low voice with Sorin while biting into her apple.

The atmosphere in the room was peaceful. Other than Gielle, no one spoke much. The bright sun warmed the room, and everything seemed to be going according to plan: a friendly visit, affectionate kindness, bright light, the large, round bed, pale green floors, lilies in the walls. Rudy checked over Luoying's luggage to be sure she hadn't forgotten anything, and then waited. The room was as calm as a carefully maintained meditation pool.

"Pierre," said Luoying, finally breaking the serene mood, "you mentioned that you had something to discuss with me earlier."

Pierre had been standing next to the door, away from the others, a blank look on his face. Even after Luoying's question, he didn't approach the group. He surveyed the room with a distant gaze, his bangs plastered against his forehead. The other staring faces seemed to form a tunnel with him and Luoying at either end.

"During your performance that day," said Pierre quietly, "did you notice anything unusual?"

Luoying thought back. "I... I think so." As everyone turned to her, she continued hesitantly. "The whole time I was dancing, I felt lighter than usual and I just couldn't get a good kick off the floor. It was hard to keep up with the music. I never felt like that during rehearsals."

"Isn't it good to feel lighter?" asked Gielle.

"No. The most important part of dancing is pushing off against the floor. If your body feels too light, it's impossible to get the right leverage. I tried to compensate by using brute force, which threw me off balance. I suppose I practiced too much and wore out my legs."

She looked at Pierre questioningly.

Pierre nodded as though she had confirmed some suspicion. "It's not a matter of over-practice. The problem was your costume. The fabric was lifting you up like a big parachute."

"How is that possible!?" Gielle sounded horrified. "What was wrong with the costume? I hope I didn't cause your injury. But Luoying, you'd danced in that costume before."

Luoying patted her hand, trying to comfort her. "I'm sure it's not your fault. I rehearsed with your costume several times. The fabric was so thin that I can't imagine it caused any issues." But she saw Pierre's odd expression.

"It wouldn't cause any issues normally," said Pierre, his voice cold. "But on the day of your performance, the magnetic field below the floor of the stage was turned on." Luoying's heart sank.

"Wait!" Gielle said, suddenly understanding the import of Pierre's words. "Is your material affected by the magnetic field?"

"No." Pierre's tone was certain. "My material is unaffected by magnetic fields. I measured the magnetic moment to be sure. It's zero." He swallowed, and his Adam's apple moved up and down like a drowning fish. "But someone sabotaged the costume."

With growing unease, Luoying asked, "Are you sure?"

Pierre nodded. "That night I asked to examine the costume after you were brought into surgery. I was worried that something was wrong with the material, and I discovered that the costume had been coated with a thin layer of high-magnetic-moment material."

He stopped again and looked at Rudy. Everyone in the room now understood the meaning behind his words, and even Gielle could see the suspicion in his eyes. Luoying felt as though Pierre's introspective, soft voice were as loud as a roar. The air was suddenly awkward and tense.

"Are you accusing Rudy?" muttered Gielle.

Pierre didn't answer but slowly turned to look at Gielle.

"*What proof do you have?*" Gielle shouted. She moved to stand protectively before Rudy. "*The fault lies obviously with your material—with you! How dare you throw random accusations around?*" Pierre stared at Gielle, and his brows furrowed in confusion. He clearly had not anticipated such a reaction, and he looked as though he had been punched in the stomach.

Luoying was so tense that she couldn't breathe. The very air in the room felt suffocating. She gazed at Rudy, hoping he would say something. Pierre's assertion unnerved her, not because she was being defensive about Rudy but because she knew Pierre's accusation would turn Gielle against him. Gielle craved Rudy's favor so much that Luoying's heart broke for Pierre. She could see the disappointment and terror in Pierre's eyes, and she felt sympathy for both him and Gielle. She wanted Rudy to clear the air by offering a good explanation. The injury to her leg had healed, and she didn't care about it as much as she hoped that her brother would be honest and responsible.

"It's not a random accusation," said Pierre to Gielle.

"It certainly is!" said Gielle.

"It's not."

"It is! It is!"

Rudy finally broke in.

"He's right." He spoke slowly, keeping his eyes on Luoying, as though Gielle and Pierre didn't exist. There was an awkward expression on his face as he continued to lean against the wall, his uniform crisp and neat. He kept his hands in his pockets and tried to purge the emotions from his face. "I'm sorry." Gielle's mouth hung open.

"I did it without telling you. It's my fault," said Rudy.

"But Rudy, when did you…" Luoying was at a loss for words.

"I took your costume for a routine inspection before the performance. When I was done, I coated it with a membrane that operates on the same principle as the chairs in the theater. It's only a few nanometers thick and you can't feel it, but it can generate a bit of lift in the magnetic field."

He wasn't looking at anyone else, and his voice was even more composed than usual. He struggled so hard to keep his face blank that it was as though he didn't think this was a test of his honesty but of his control. His task wasn't to offer an apology but to stay unemotional. After a pause, he added, "I'm sorry. I shouldn't have tried to help."

"Tried to *help*?" Chania broke in. "Do you understand what you've done?"

Rudy turned to her. "What do you mean?"

Chania laughed coldly. "Are you aware that Luoying may never dance again? She almost couldn't walk again. How can you act like it was nothing?"

Luoying looked at Chania, who was staring at Rudy with distaste and rage. Luoying could tell that she was angrier about his composure and seeming nonchalance than about his error.

"I just wanted to reduce the weight holding Luoying down a little," Rudy said.

"Reduce the weight!"

"Yes. I admit I was wrong. I thought she would be able to do her jumps better."

"Are you an idiot? Dancing is not high jumping."

"I thought it would be better if she could jump higher."

"Really?"

"I thought so, yes."

Chania's lips curved up in a mocking smile, and she seemed to heave an inaudible sigh. Glancing around at others in the room, she took off her coat to reveal a light yellow top and cotton pants, her usual outfit for gymnastics exercise. She stretched to loosen her limbs, her bracelets clinking against each other.

"From the moment you sent us to Earth, all I've heard is the foolish sentiment of 'jump higher.' So you want to know how to jump higher?" She stared at Rudy. "I'll show you."

She ran a few steps and leaped into the air, spinning as she landed. "Is this high?"

Without waiting for an answer, she took another two steps and leaped, kicking her legs up until they were horizontal. She landed and asked again. "What about this? Would you consider this high?"

No one answered.

"Perhaps you don't know this," said Chania in a calm voice. "In fact, just now the height of my jumps wasn't even at the level of beginners, young girls here on Mars. But since they're not here, you can't tell. You always say, 'Higher, higher!' You sent us to Earth so we could jump higher. But higher than what? A frog, a mosquito, or an alien from Andromeda? Don't pretend to be ignorant. A human being simply needs to jump at the height of a human being."

Rudy locked eyes with her. After a while he asked, "What are you trying to say, exactly?"

"I simply want to point out that you've only wanted us to jump higher. But have you thought about Luoying's suffering? What she's had to endure? To achieve the height you crave, is it worth ignoring the pain of others?"

Luoying sat on the bed, watching Chania's face from afar, her heart pounding. Chania looked cold and sad, her feet firmly planted on the ground, her back and neck straight, like a lonely crane.

A complex wave of emotions overwhelmed Luoying. She knew this was no longer an argument about an accident, or even about her. Indeed, even without Rudy's manipulation, she would have had to stop dancing sooner or later. She and the others from the Mercury Group had pushed their bodies beyond their limits in trying to adjust to the gravity on Earth, and her tenosynovitis was already very advanced, a legacy of years of overexertion. At first they had been driven by a sense of mission and hope, dedicated to the goal of reaching ever greater heights so as not to disappoint those back at home. But by the time they began to question their mission, their bodies had been injured beyond recovery.

Luoying knew that Chania wasn't arguing with Rudy over the accident but over the repressed questions below the surface. *Don't pretend to be ignorant. A human being simply needs to jump at the height of a human being.*

The air in the room felt heavy and oppressive. Chania was suppressing her pride, Gielle her wronged heart, Rudy his sense of failure. The air held down the tension. Luoying didn't know what to do. They were fighting over her, but she didn't want them to fight at all.

Reini entered the room. He nodded and smiled at the youths. When Luoying saw him, she sensed the arrival of a dependable source of strength. Reini's gaunt face, clean-shaven chin, strong and steady hands, and frameless round spectacles seemed to form a steadfast presence from which she could seek aid.

"Dr. Reini, am I ready to be discharged?" she asked hurriedly.

"Of course," said Reini, smiling.

"Don't you need to examine me one more time?"

"There's no need. I've see the scans from this morning, and you're healing well. Just come back for your periodic checkups."

"All right. Thank you. I guess we should go."

Luoying got up and put on her coat, checking the room one last time for any stray possessions. The others got up as well and helped her with the luggage. Some began to clean up the room.

All at once, the confrontational air was replaced by purposeful busyness. Everyone had their own task. The room was filled with questions like *Is this your cup?* Soon everything was ready, and they filed out. Rudy was in the front, with Gielle following immediately behind. Pierre followed Gielle. The other four came after, with Luoying bringing up the rear.

The moment they stepped out of the room, Anka moved next to Luoying and gave her shoulders a squeeze. None of the others saw it. She looked at him, but he kept his eyes forward, a smile on his face. All of a sudden Luoying felt a sense of peace drape over her.

"This afternoon...," he whispered to her.

"Two o'clock, at station three."

"All right."

They parted. Anka joined Mira and the others on one side, while Luoying went over to Rudy.

Reini emerged from the room. He had sensed the awkwardness in the room from Luoying's expression, and so he said nothing as he watched them leave. Walking up to Luoying now, he handed her an envelope.

"This is for you."

The envelope was sealed with a metallic film with red markings. It was a personal identity seal, something akin to a wax seal in the age of quills, used only for the most formal and important documents, such as powers of attorney.

Luoying looked up gratefully at him. "Thank you."

Reini nodded. "Be careful." Then he stood at the top of the stairs as the friends filed away. Luoying waved at him from the bottom of the stairs, and he waved back.

Luoying cast one last look at the room that had been her home for the last twenty-plus days, reluctant to leave. She knew that outside the hospital was a world busy with demands and activity, and she would never again experience this secluded life like a hermit's. The days in the hospital had been so peaceful, as though the last decade had dissolved into illusions, with dust settling and the surging currents turning placid. She didn't know what kind of fate awaited her, but she knew she would miss this place. Only after a long while did she make her way down the stairs, swaying a bit unsteadily.

After he watched Luoying leave, Reini returned to his study and began a new project. He was writing a history of the city, of the city itself as an idea. A city began as a city, but often it would be remembered only as a stage for history. Very few paid attention to its history as a city.

Victor Hugo once said that, before the birth of the printing press, humankind expressed itself through edifices. Reini thought that, after the birth of the space rocket, humankind again expressed its thoughts through architecture.

Most of the habitable surface of the Earth had already been covered by buildings multiple times, and new structures had to find footholds in the existing foundations like needles searching for openings in an overpopulated pincushion. Even if large swaths of cities were demolished to be rebuilt, history meant that the new buildings were surrounded by the ghosts of the old. Like the custom of a people being impressed upon generation after generation of newborns, the past gradually tamed the new. To start entirely anew with a blank page was impossible. Construction paid for by demolishing the past would be tainted from the start with the smell of death, and upon completion was no longer pure and fresh.

On the other hand, architecture on Earth was growing ever more unmoored from the ground upon which it stood. New buildings were assaulted from all sides by existing edifices but became disconnected from the land. Most resources had been extracted from the ground and circulated countless times over the surface, scattered to all corners of all continents, rising and falling with currency and stock tickers, no longer reflecting the undulating forms of mountains and valleys. Most architecture on Earth tended toward one globalized style: towering skyscrapers in metropolises, carefully manicured gardens in suburbs, devoid of local character wherever you were. Buildings reflected class but not natural geography.

But space was pure vacuum, and all construction had to start from zero. In the two and a half centuries since humans first set foot in space, countless fantastic designs had been born in the dark void of space, resulting in floating gardens unimaginable on Earth. Their multitudinous divergent forms reflected complex and ever-changing principles of operation.

These structures were nonetheless tethered to heaven and earth. They breathed air from the sky and absorbed strength from the ground. Since the resources of space were as yet under-developed, buildings were like wells drilled into the depth of nature. They relied on local materials and depended on local geography, molded by their environment. Ring-shaped cities orbiting in geosynchronous orbit, spider cities on the Moon, the crystal city and crater habitats of Mars—all were as inseparable from their environment as plants adapted to their niches.

After the religious worship of natural totems and the industrial ideal of the conquest of nature, humanity entered a third stage of the coevolution of human thought and architecture: the cosmic path of harmoniously fitting into nature. *Buildings are flowers blooming from the sand.* That was young Galiman's most famous quote.

Mars City was the product of sand. Iron, glass, and silicon chips were the most abundant yields from the planet's red earth. The first formed the skeleton, the second formed the flesh, and the last formed the soul. The whole city was refined from sand. With the rough exterior polished away, the crystal essence stood proudly, like a tide surging deep underground, erupting through thick layers of crust, emerging as springs over the surface.

As long as there had been human civilization, there had also been glass. The Phoenicians discovered glinting beads in sand, and the ancient Egyptians and Chinese made glass vessels millennia before the birth of Christ. In the Middle Ages, colorful stained glass was an offering to God, and the modern industrial age saw the rest of the universe through glass. Le Corbusier and the fashion of the twentieth century developed and refined various properties of glass as a construction material. Thus, rather than claiming Mars had developed a new heaven, it was more accurate to say that it continued a long tradition of human civilization.

However, there were differences in the way Mars used glass. It exploited the environment of Mars, used its harshness and poverty. The Martian atmosphere was thin and the temperature cold, and so the construction of houses took the form of blown glass. The semiliquid material was pumped up with air, and then the bubbles were allowed to cool in the sparse atmosphere, taking shape almost instantly without need for internal support. Details were then added via carving, engraving, inlaying, or finishing. All the techniques of glassmaking could be deployed to keep air and life within and cold and vacuum without.

The glass city was the crystallization of the ideal of humanity coexisting in harmony with nature. A house on Mars was as intimate as clothing, and the garden and the gardener were as close as water and fish. The air of each residence was mostly filtered by the plants in the garden, with the citywide air refreshing system as a supplement. The water of each dwelling was also recycled in its walls, and only a small amount of waste was piped into the centralized sewer system. Each glass bubble was a miniature ecological sphere, a unit of co-survival and cohabitation. The city began essentially as a single dwelling, and it later expanded like cellular division or crystal growth by duplicating basic but essential units.

Mars City in its current state encompassed a great deal of variation on a single theme. Most dwellings were inspired by the ideals of classical Chinese design in which living quarters were arranged around a central garden. With the transparent bubble on top, the enclosed space felt surprisingly spacious. The natural dome-shaped ceilings, on the other hand, were often decorated in the manner of classical Rome, with murals painted on the inside, or glass rods might extend down from the ceiling, fluted like Greek columns, an allusion rather than a vulgar imitation.

In Martian architecture, the concept of membranes was very important. The interiors of all buildings were coated, because by adding certain substances to the glass and augmenting them with different coatings, it was possible to give the walls and the ceiling different functions: the quarter-reflective membrane redirected all the infrared rays inside the rooms, keeping them warm; high-resistance wires provided heat; optical membranes served as displays; high-magnetic-moment membranes moved objects. More than practical conveniences, these membranes were a lifestyle: the furniture and the house were one, and one needed not take everything with them as they moved about the house.

It was a modern interpretation of the pyramid, a vast edifice erected from the wasteland, pointing from the flat ground into the dark sky.

All these were parts of Galiman's philosophy: to exploit all that nature offered and to turn poverty into jewels. The first house had been designed by him, and after it was accepted, endless variations upon the original proliferated. Led by him, a group of designers planned the city, starting with individual houses and building them up into neighborhoods. The history of the whole process was only five decades long, but for many it was the entirety of history. They were born in this city and grew up in this city. From the moment they opened their eyes, the city settled into its stable form, as though it had already been in existence for a thousand years, as though Galiman's philosophy were a law of nature.

As the inhabitants of Mars City pondered whether to abandon it, Reini observed quietly from the sidelines, a melancholic mood taking hold of him similar to the feeling one got as curtains began to descend upon a stage. If, in the end, the people decided to abandon the city, he would not be surprised. Galiman had laid such deep foundations for the principles of architecture on Mars that those who came after simply needed to replicate his basic plan, changing unimportant details here and there. Without the need to explore, they also lacked the opportunity for breakthrough advances. This left them unsatisfied. The more they envied Galiman, they more they wanted to be like him. They also wanted to be famous, to have the citation ratings of their products rise ever higher, to carve their own names into massive stones. They thus sought new plans, wishing to demolish the old city and build a new one. This wasn't quite the contest Hugo envisioned between the crowd and religion, between freedom and rules; rather, it was simply those who yearned to be great overturning those who were already great.

MEDAL

On the way to the Registry of Files, Anka told Luoying the truth about the revolution.

They sat side by side in the tube train. Anka leaned against the side of the car, an arm on the tiny table supporting his forehead, his legs extended straight ahead of him. He looked relaxed and free, his cold blue eyes as unperturbed as lake water on winter nights.

Luoying turned to him. "What did Chania mean earlier by starting a revolution?"

A gentle smile appeared on his face. "Oh, that. She's talking about a play."

"A play?"

"A comedy. It's about Earth and Mars. You have some lines in it."

"What? I know nothing about it."

"Don't worry. Your part is small." Anka's smile grew wider. "You and I are both in the chorus, which offers commentary on the action. It's easy. Once in a while we sing, '*Oh, that's wonderful, wonderful!*' or '*Ah, so great, so, so great!*' After you've recuperated a couple more days at home, you'll pick up the gist with a few run-throughs."

"Is that all?" Luoying let out a sigh of relief. "I was so nervous when she used the word 'revolution.'"

"The title of the play is indeed *Revolution*. It's a response to the Creativity Fair."

"Wait. This is *for* the Creativity Fair?"

"No. It's not part of the competition. The plan is to perform the play for the public on the day of the finals."

"So we're not boycotting the fair?"

"More like we're boycotting it *by* participating."

"Ah... okay."

Luoying relaxed and smiled. She had been worried that the others were planning some dramatic revolutionary act; it was a relief to find out the truth.

Is a revolution a good thing? She had been pondering this question since Chania's first message. She felt that her inquiries remained insufficient, leaving her uncertain if they should resist this world, and specifically which parts of this world. The whole morning she drove herself to distraction as she thought of the possibilities behind Chania's declaration, speculated on their secret plans, and guessed at the consequences of those actions and the reactions of Rudy and Grandfather. But Anka's answer had drained all the anxiety out of her. Apparently reality was more creative than all her conjectures. A play called *Revolution*—a comedy; that was it. She laughed to herself.

"I'm actually going to be in the competition proper," she told Anka.

"Oh?"

"Gielle added me to her team."

"Ah."

"I didn't want to do it, but Gielle was so enthusiastic that I couldn't turn her down."

"What are you making?"

"Clothing, an outfit that generates electricity. Pierre is an expert with photoelectricity and membrane fabrication. I think he's found a way to incorporate the technology in our roofs into a soft, wearable material."

"Really?" Anka suddenly sat straight up, his expression grave. A light came into his eyes. "What kind of material?"

"I haven't seen it," said Luoying. "Gielle told me it can be used to make transparent armor."

"Interesting," said Anka.

"Want to tell me what you're thinking?" asked Luoying.

"I can't quite explain it yet."

Luoying could see that Anka was preoccupied. He gazed outside the car for a while, his fingers gently tapping against the small table. After some time, he asked "Can you ask Pierre if others can use his invention?"

"Meaning you?"

Anka nodded without elaboration.

"Sure. I'll ask."

She saw that Anka had the same look of calm excitement he had had when he was pulling her through the crowd on Earth. It made his whole person seem sharper and more vivid, as though he had come into focus; she hadn't seen him like that in a long time.

———

As the tube train came to a stop, Luoying refocused on the goal of this trip. Her mood now was very different from the last time she was at the Registry of Files.

For a moment she stood before the door, gazing up at the gray colonnade in front of the building and the statues on both sides. They seemed to be alive, their expressions thoughtful or passionate, somber but kind, as though welcoming her. She took a deep breath and stepped through the door, her heart at peace. During the month-plus since she had been back, she had found out so many secrets that she was no longer as anxious and confused as last time, no longer doubting whether she should pursue her inquiries. Since she had come this far, she knew that the question was no longer whether she should proceed but how.

Uncle Laak was waiting for them in the lobby. Standing ramrod straight and looking grave, he shook hands with Anka and Luoying, the same way he would greet other visitors to the Registry. Though his black pullover sweater and pants were not a uniform nor formal dress, the look was equally dignified. For a moment he gazed at Luoying, his face expressionless.

Luoying handed him the envelope; Laak opened it and read the contents without speaking before folding the paper and putting it back inside the envelope. Luoying stared at his face, a bit tense.

Without changing his expression Laak nodded.

"Come with me," he said.

Relieved, she and Anka followed. But Laak stopped and politely addressed Anka.

"I'm sorry. I don't want to separate you, but the document authorizes only Luoying."

Luoying and Anka looked at each other. She wanted to argue, but Anka stopped her.

"Rules are rules," Anka said softly. "I'll wait for you here."

After a moment of hesitation Luoying nodded. Without Anka she felt much more alone and anxious. She hurried to catch up to Laak. After a retina and fingerprint scan, they passed through a glass door and entered a short, empty gray corridor devoid of decoration.

At the end of the corridor was a metal door. Laak passed his hand over the scanner, entered the password, and pressed three switches. The two thick, heavy leaves of the door swung open silently. Luoying held her breath, peering into the widening slit of light. Gradually a vast hall filled with bookcases came into view. Hungrily she looked around. The hall was approximately circular, and the rows of bookcases stretched into the distance without end. Each case was about three meters tall, made of some brown metallic material arranged in neat ranks like an army awaiting orders.

"Whose file would you like to see?" asked Laak.

"My grandfather's," said Luoying. "If possible, also my great-grandfather's. And my parents', of course."

Laak nodded and led her to the west side of the hall. She had the impression that he had known her choices before her arrival, and the question was just part of a procedure he had to follow. They walked through a main corridor between the cases, his steps steady and purposeful.

To Luoying, the tall cases around her appeared as walls inlaid with a grid of tiny photographs of smiling faces, like glowing buttons along the horizontal shelves of each case. It was like walking past a miniature world flattened into two parallel surfaces.

"Uncle Laak, does every Martian have a file here?" Her voice echoed in the vast space.

"That's correct. Everyone does."

"Why do we have to do this? Isn't all the information in the central archive already?"

Without stopping, Laak answered. "It's not a good idea to rely overmuch on any form of storage, and it's especially bad to rely exclusively on a single form of storage. On Earth the Swiss bank vaults survived long after the popularization of electronic currency for the same reasons."

"Are physical objects stored here, then?"

"That's true for some individuals. Not all."

"What kind of objects?"

"Donations from the subject or the subject's heirs. Occasionally artifacts of historical significance."

"It doesn't depend on the position or status of the subject?"

"It doesn't."

"Did my parents leave anything behind?"

Laak stopped and looked at her. His gaze softened, no longer so formal and distant. For a moment Luoying found herself looking into the face of the Uncle Laak she remembered from childhood.

"Their legacy is your responsibility," he said. "If you find… anything, you may donate it to the Registry—if you want to, that is."

Luoying looked down, slightly embarrassed. She understood what Laak was hinting at. To find the legacy of her family was her responsibility, but she had been asking questions of outsiders as though they knew her family better than she did herself. In Laak's face she read an unspoken concern for her well-being. The wrinkles on his brow and at the corners of his mouth appeared even deeper to her. Left by years of worry, they remained even in his moments of tranquility. It was as though his face were a rock that had been carved by the waves over eons, not a beach that could be easily smoothed. He looked far older than his age, and his figure faded into the sea of looming bookcases.

"Uncle Laak," she said, "I know you're right. What others say cannot be a substitute for my own judgment and continuation of the legacy of my family. But there are some facts I have to understand. Without these facts, I cannot come to a judgment."

"Such as?"

"Such as… did Grandfather kill many people?"

337

"No more than other warriors, and no fewer."

"Did Grandfather put a stop to the revolution and protests on Mars in my parents' time?"

"Yes."

"Why?"

Laak said nothing. Luoying recalled that he provided only facts, not reasons. She lowered her eyes.

After waiting a moment to be sure she had no more questions, Laak continued forward. Luoying followed.

They passed through rows of metal bookcases studded with miniature portraits like diamonds; passed through frozen smiles and the lives of the dead; passed through all the souls who had ever existed on Mars. Luoying's eyes flitted from face to face. They all had the same young, fresh faces. Whether the owners of the portraits were still hale and hearty or had been dead for decades, there was no distinction between them in this world of shelves and portraits. The names of the individuals were sorted alphabetically, wiping away all differences in rank, history, age, and personality. Everyone had a spot on the shelves, as though they had been part of the shelves from the start and, after a few decades spent in the world, returned home.

Above each portrait was a box, and the e-paper label in front of each box presented scrolling images and text. As Luoying went by, she saw familiar neighborhoods, children's classrooms, mines in the desolate wilderness, Jupiter and the galaxy. The texts were largely snippets from daily life. As her eyes roamed, she felt as if countless details were falling into her mind, swirling about, coalescing into the shapes of individual men and women. She didn't know if the details could really represent someone, how many details were necessary to piece together such a shape, and what the relation was between the shape and the person.

"Uncle Laak," she asked, "have you worked at the Registry for long?"

"Thirty years now."

"That's a long time. Weren't you the Superintendent of Education before?"

"That was only part-time."

"Do you like your work here?"

"I do."

"Why?"

"There's no answer to that." Laak caressed the photographs on the shelf next to him as he walked slowly past. "For you, perhaps it's hard to understand. You want to see all your potential choices and then rationally pick the one you want, justifying it with reasons. But in reality, if you spend your life doing something, it becomes part of your life. You will like it without having to choose it. I can tell you that I'm familiar with every shelf in here and can take you directly to whoever you want. I know this place as well as I know myself. During the thirty years I've been in charge, nothing has leaked out of here contrary to regulations; there has been no chaos, and no one has been treated any differently from anyone else. This is my life. It's a fortress. No matter what happens outside, you can find the souls of the past here without being disturbed."

Luoying looked at Laak's straight back and suddenly envied him. He spoke with such conviction, while she couldn't find a single belief in her mind that she could convey with equal certainty. The price for his conviction was decades of his time. Though he spoke calmly, she knew that no one could contradict him. This was strength, the real strength in words.

They stopped. Laak stood in front of a case and pulled off the e-paper in front of a box on the fourth shelf down, handing it to Luoying.

HANS SLOAN.

Heart pounding, she looked at the box and those around it. The whole shelf belonged to the Sloans, and there were five of them: Richard, Hans, Quentin, Rudy, Luoying. Her mother wasn't here because the boxes were arranged on the shelves by the name at birth, without regard to changes due to marriage or otherwise. She held the translucent, thin sheet, a bit uncertain.

She began to scroll through it. The text started with a simple summary of Hans's life.

"Take as long as you want," said Laak. "I'll be in my office. If you need me, use the blue button by the door."

Laak left, and Luoying was the only one in the vast circular hall. She looked up and realized that the ceiling resembled the ceiling of the Pantheon she had seen in Rome. Tall, solemn, magnificent, the translucent dome glowed stately in the sun, as though made of clouds. The homage to one of humankind's ancient sacred buildings was intentional. This was not a temple of the gods but a monument to human souls.

—————

Hans was born in an abandoned prospecting aircraft at the foot of Angela Bluff: 11°S 46°W, 2120 C.E., 30 B.R.

His birth was simultaneous with the death of his mother. Richard Sloan, a twenty-six-year-old pilot, was flying his twenty-five-year-old wife, Hanna Sloan, through Aquila Canyon to get back to Camp Sixteen so Hanna could give birth. An unexpected dust storm struck, however, and Richard's plane was forced to land at the base of the cliff due to a mechanical malfunction. There they sent out a distress call through satellite link, hoping to be rescued.

But as Hanna's contractions grew more intense and frequent, no rescuers came. Richard hailed the base multiple times, begging for aid, but never received a definitive answer. (Communication records at the base showed that during the fifty-one hours the couple was trapped, Richard spoke with the base fourteen times.)

The rescue was delayed due to legal wrangling back at the base. Richard found out that there was an intellectual property dispute over the navigation guidance system, and lawyers were evaluating the legal risk to the rescue company. Richard tried to negotiate a solution over the comms, growing more agitated and enraged as time went on. In the end, Hanna delivered the baby herself and lost consciousness after massive loss of blood. A few hours later she died.

As Richard held his wife, he felt life leaving her bit by bit as her body cooled. Helpless, he sobbed, and his grief turned into anger. He named the baby Hans to commemorate Hanna. After wiping the baby clean, he wrapped the tiny body in his flight suit, gave Hans the last of the water, and then tried to keep the baby warm with his own body heat. Father and son huddled in a corner of the plane and continued to hail for rescuers.

(The above segment was summarized from an oral account by Richard Sloan in the third year of the war. For the next forty-four years, the rest of his life, he never discussed the event again.)

By the time the rescue ship finally arrived, Richard had had no food or water for forty-eight hours. Though he was dehydrated and starving, he moved with determination and purpose. Declining to be helped, he climbed into the rescue ship by himself, refused to answer any questions or to sit with others, and turned down all medical help except food and water.

Forty years later, Lorraine Elaine, who had been a trainee nurse on the rescue ship, recalled the following: "After he handed the baby to me, he went into a corner and sat down by himself. But his eyes never left my hands as he watched me care for the newborn. Every time I turned, I could see his eyes, burning with pain, grief, and something darker. As his face darkened, the eyes only glowed brighter. Every time my eyes met his, I couldn't help but shudder.

"One time, when I was changing the newborn's diaper, my hand slipped and the blanket around the baby slid as though the baby itself were sliding. He jumped up right away, scaring the other passengers. I found it puzzling at the time that he was so concerned for the baby, and yet, instead of coming over to take care of it himself, he stayed far away. Thinking back on it now, I realize it was because he was afraid that his dark mood would affect the baby. Of course it was a bit irrational, since moods don't spread like some gas... I guess I have to say, if I had been in his position, I would have done the same.

"He sat in the corner by himself, not talking to anyone, cradling his wife's body, holding her hardened, purple hand as though she were just sleeping on his lap. I tried to imagine what it was like in that canyon, with sand and dust swirling over the sky, while the woman you loved died in your arms, the happiness you were on the verge of experiencing slipping away second by second. I thought it must have been terrible. But I was only twenty-one at the time and couldn't understand just how terrible."

The rescue ship belonged to the third Martian branch of Homeward Bound, an emergency rescue company. As soon as it landed at berth #3, Camp Sixteen, Richard got off the ship without speaking to anyone, ran into the headquarters building, and assaulted the chief executive officer, leaving him with severe injuries. Before an alarm could be raised, he managed to make his way to UPC, a computer company, and killed its president, Phillip Lyde. Then he returned to the rescue company, took his infant son, and escaped into a life of exile.

Three months later, war broke out.

"I knew that my grandfather was born in the first year of the war." Luoying paused, and then continued in a more depressed tone.

"But I never knew that he was the cause of the war."

"There's something I don't quite understand," said Anka, frowning. "Why did your great-grandfather kill the president of a computer company?"

"I found it strange when I read about it, too, so I looked into it more. The situation was complicated. The main issue involved a commercial dispute. At that time Homeward Bound's rescue ships were all out of commission as the result of a failed software upgrade of the navigation guidance system. But it wasn't an accident. The fact was all of Homeward Bound's ships ran the operating system from UPC, which charged a high price for software upgrades. Homeward Bound, unwilling to pay the cost, decided to hack the upgrade package themselves. The unauthorized action led to UPC flipping a remote kill switch that shut down all of Homeward Bound's ships until they paid a penalty.

"On the day of Richard Sloan's accident, Homeward Bound contacted UPC to explain that there was an emergency and asked UPC to grant a temporary, onetime license to the software. UPC refused, fearful that the temporary license might be hacked to enable the unauthorized use of the software indefinitely. Richard Sloan tried to call UPC during those fifty-one hours but was unable to reach a decision-maker. Initially my great-grandfather thought it was because low-level employees at UPC failed to escalate his issue properly, but later, as he attacked the executive officer of Homeward Bound to avenge his wife, the executive told him that his call *had* in fact been transferred to Phillip Lyde, the president of UPC, but Lyde personally issued the directive not to grant the temporary license.

"But why did Lyde do such a thing? It turned out that my great-grandfather was employed by SG Siliconics, a chipmaker and UPC's biggest competitor. UPC and SG Siliconics were locked in a heated battle over a particular large customer, and my great-grandfather, whose specialty was mining and refining, had been surveying the area behind Angela Bluff for a potential site for a new mine. There's probably no way to ever find definitive proof of the detailed commercial interests and private emotions behind this incident, but the executive officer told my great-grandfather that Lyde said on the phone, 'The baby isn't my problem, but my shareholders will never allow me to jeopardize three hundred billion euros.' Consumed by rage, my great-grandfather let the UPC executive go and went after Phillip Lyde instead."

"That *is* complicated," said Anka.

"You haven't heard the most complicated part yet," said Luoying. She had memorized practically everything she had read in the Registry. She had never devoted as much effort to memorizing anything in her life. "One week after Richard Sloan committed murder and became a fugitive, he was captured. But one week after that, he was rescued and made into the leader of the rebel alliance."

"What's the rebel alliance?"

"That's the predecessor to the Martian Freedom Fighters."

"What kind of people were they?"

"Just ordinary people. Pilots, engineers, scientists. They came from all the Martian bases."

Anka silently pondered what Luoying had said.

She went on. "There was a great deal of controversy about this part, and I couldn't read all the material or memorize it. All kinds of reasons were proffered for the war, and these debates filled many pages in both my grandfather's and great-grandfather's files."

Anka nodded. "I imagine that the war didn't erupt by chance. The unfortunate events surrounding your grandfather's birth might be accidents, but the rebel alliance didn't arise because of that. My feeling is that they had been waiting for a triggering event."

"I think that's right," said Luoying. "But I still can't figure out how the accident was connected to the war that erupted right after."

"Let me see…" Anka looked deep in thought. "I think there are two important clues: one is the competition between UPC and SG Siliconics, and the other is the IP dispute between Homeward Bound and UPC. Given the importance of the central archive to Mars, it seems that the latter was more likely the reason. Or maybe both were involved."

"Maybe. But do you think these two causes are enough to lead to war? I just can't see how commercial or IP disputes can lead to war—a war that killed so many."

"It's very hard to understand such large historical events from our position."

Luoying was seized by a sudden wave of emotion. She had been trying hard to describe the events dispassionately, to be objective, but grief overwhelmed her at that moment. "I hate asking these questions. To think that my great-grandmother died in such a horrible way… I wish I could be like everyone else, focused only on home and family, but I can't. I have to ask the big questions, to pursue the truth. I have to know whether what my great-grandfather did was right. Why did he lead everyone to build this new world? Was his rebellion right?"

Anka put an arm around her shoulders and caressed her hair. "I don't know about the new world or the old, but I do know it was wrong to leave two people and their newborn in the dust storm. Your great-grandfather did what he felt he had to do. The war that came after wasn't something a single man could have controlled."

He kissed her forehead, and as she gazed into his lake-like irises, tears spilled from her eyes. She leaned against his shoulders, lost to the tides of her emotions. She could see, in her mind's eye, that looming cliff with its rough red surface standing in the howling wind. The swirling dust and sand was like a mask that had been peeled off and shattered into a million fragments, covering the sun, devoid of all concern and restraint, attacking every life in sight with a naked, savage will. The fragments were like an army in which the only soul was collective, and the vortex of dust and sand surrounded the abandoned ship. Inside, two people, still ignorant of what fate held in store for them, leaned together, as she and Anka were doing now, keeping each other warm with body heat, still trusting in false hope, enduring cold, hunger, and the pangs of labor, supported by the sweet expectation of a newborn and the warm anticipation of rescue, telling each other that everything would be all right to disguise their rising anxiety, pushing the diminishing supply of food and water to the partner, knowing nothing of the tumultuous changes to come. That was the pair's final shared moment of mutual reliance.

Luoying's vision blurred. She refused to sob, and the tears swirled in her eyes until they finally returned to the depth of her heart.

She sat up and looked expectantly at Anka. "Do you think we can go visit the site of the crash?"

"I don't know." Anka hesitated before continuing. "We can ask Runge's mining group to see if there's still a mine out there."

"Does your squadron fly there?"

"No. All our training is limited to north of the cliffs."

"Can't you fly there on your own?"

"That will be hard."

"Because of regulations?"

"Only partly." Anka shook his head. "The technical challenge is a much bigger problem."

As he continued to explain, his long, bony fingers flitted through the air, imitating different types of aircraft.

"It's not hard to obtain a flight permit," he said. "But even the smallest ship I can get to is about the size of five tube train cars." His fingers sketched out the shape of a long loaf of bread. "We'll need at least three trained crew members, two to pilot the ship and one to oversee the engine. Also, something like that has to fly close to the ground and probably can't climb over the mountains."

"Why does it have to fly close to the ground?"

"These ships rely on ground effects to achieve lift. They can't go too high."

"What about shuttles?"

Anka shook his head. "They're completely different. A space shuttle is essentially a rocket, not an aircraft. The larger shuttles are restricted to flying official missions such as visits to Deimos. Also, the pilot isn't completely in control of a shuttle. Shuttles depend on ground control and guidance, and are only semiautonomous. As for the smaller atmospheric shuttles…"

Luoying waited, but Anka seemed to hesitate, unsure how to continue.

"What's wrong?" asked Luoying.

"The smaller shuttles are actually fighters," said Anka. His tone was still even, but there was a trace of a bitter smile at the corners of his mouth. "They rely on omnidirectional jets for propulsion. Piloted by a single person, they are very nimble and effective. I can certainly take mine out on private missions… except the one Fitz assigned to me is broken. I can't repair it yet because I lack the replacement parts."

"Why did you get assigned a broken fighter?"

"He claimed that he wanted me to demonstrate what I've learned on Earth," said Anka with a laugh. "The real reason is the argument I had with him. When I returned, I was supposed to get one that was in good condition, but after that night I got one that couldn't fly. I'm tired of fighting, so I'm still thinking of a way to fix it."

"How can he treat you like that?" asked Luoying. "You should file a complaint. It's not fair."

"Not fair? Nothing is ever fair."

"Then you haven't flown since you've been back?"

"No. I've been serving as a mechanic."

"Didn't you learn to fix aircraft on Earth? Maybe you can just do the same thing."

"It's not that easy," said Anka. "Aircraft on Earth generate lift from the atmosphere. Lift is directly proportional to the dynamic pressure, one half of pressure times velocity squared. Since the Martian atmospheric pressure is only about one percent of the pressure on Earth, while the gravity is around thirty-eight percent, the same aircraft from Earth essentially must fly about six times as fast to stay aloft on Mars. That translates to a velocity of thousands of kilometers per hour, which is unsustainable without special materials. Since our aircraft don't rely on the atmosphere to generate lift, they require much more power and higher energy conversion efficiency from the engines, which are far more complex than the ones on Earth. Even if I could learn everything I need to, I can't fix some of the valves and components by hand."

Luoying sighed, looking at Anka sympathetically. "You know, I'm beginning to miss that old junker of yours."

Anka laughed and gazed warmly into her eyes. "I told you so. And you wouldn't believe me at the time."

Anka had taken Luoying flying on Earth. It was unlike any of the flying taxis Luoying had taken. Anka had acquired a retired old fighter and removed all the weapons systems and other extraneous structures until it was basically a flying engine that he could pilot around for fun. Though the airplane rode turbulence about as well as a fifty-year-old donkey, it could achieve much higher altitudes than ordinary private aircraft.

As soon as Luoying landed, she threw up. Anka laughed while she berated him for not warning her about what to expect. He told her that she would miss that plane someday, but she was adamant that such a day would never come. "Never" turned out not to be so long.

She still remembered that dusk. Her stomach roiled as though there were a storm inside, but her heart was shaking with astonished pleasure. She had never seen clouds like that, as bright and colorful as rainbows, stretching from beneath the airplane's wings to the horizon. The gigantic setting sun glowed an orange-red in the distance, while the puffy clouds were lit up from within, billowing in every hue. The transition between the colors was seamless, from white to gold to crimson to deep purple, and the whole sight was as magnificent as a sacred church or temple. Once in a while, blue sky peeked out from between the colorful cloud patches.

Sitting before her in the pilot's seat, Anka pointed out

various sights outside the canopy. She clutched him from behind tightly, leaning against his shoulder, so excited that she felt she couldn't breathe.

Such beautiful clouds on that day, she thought. *I'll never see clouds like that again.* There were no clouds on Mars, so even if she were to fly again, she wouldn't see anything like it. The occasion on which Anka had taken her turned out to be the only time. They had flown once and only once.

Abruptly, Anka reached out to caress her forehead. "Don't pine after something you can't have. If I could fly, I would have done so long before now."

Luoying looked at him with a heavy heart. She knew he was telling the truth. He loved flying far more than she did, and if he told her he couldn't fly his broken fighter, then that was final. Anka was sitting on the bench in the Registry hall with a relaxed posture, one hand on the back of the seat behind her, the other resting in his lap. But she could see the defiance beneath his smile, a defiance that made her sad. She didn't know what to say to him.

She tried to change the topic instead. "I also found a medal. In the Registry, I mean."

"What sort of medal?"

"It belonged to my great-grandfather. Do you remember the medals they gave out to our heroes during the war?"

"Yes. There's an eagle on it—a desert eagle."

"That's right. But it wasn't until today that I learned that the desert eagle wasn't the original design by my great-grandfather. The desert eagle came into use only later in the war, after the other leaders of the rebel alliance decided on a change."

"So what was your great-grandfather's original design?"

"An apple."

"What?" Anka blurted, almost laughing.

"Yes, an apple." She held out her hand and opened her fingers. "See?"

Anka picked up the tiny copper-colored medal and admired it.

"There wasn't a lot of explanation in his file," said Luoying. "I don't know why Richard Sloan picked this design."

"It's a bit..." Anka paused, searching for the right word. "... unusual."

"What came to your mind as soon as you saw it?"

"Paris and the pageant of goddesses."

"Possible." Luoying nodded. "As a metaphor for the origin of the war? Using the bloody fields of Troy to comment on the present?" She paused and looked down at her own hand. "That wasn't what I was thinking. My immediate reaction was another story."

"Which one?"

"Eden."

"You think... the apple is a metaphor for mankind's rebellion against God?"

"No," said Luoying softly. "I wasn't thinking of anything grand like that. I can't tell you if Earth was meant to represent Eden, and the meaning behind Mars's rebellion. But I thought of a man looking at the woman next to him, silently saying in his heart, 'For you, I'm willing to fall.'"

Anka said nothing, but his arm tightened around Luoying's shoulders.

"My grandfather lost his mother," Luoying continued in her low voice. "My father lost his mother, and I lost mine. Maybe all the women in my family have to die young—"

"Don't be silly," Anka broke in. "During the war years, almost a third of our people died. It's nothing out of the ordinary."

"But maybe it's my fate."

"No! These are unfortunate coincidences, that's all. There's no fate."

Luoying looked at Anka, who appeared to be unusually serious. Something caught in her throat, and she felt fragile. She didn't know why she was saying such pessimistic things, but she felt that after learning the tragic history of her family, she could imagine only a tragic future to achieve some measure of balance in her mind. She felt absolutely exhausted, unable to move forward, helpless. Against the irresistible tide of fate, an individual's struggles were useless. It was so simple to wipe out a life, as easy as wind blowing away dust. She sobbed against Anka's shoulder. Without saying anything, he held her, supporting her back with his steady arm.

For a long time they sat next to each other on the bench in a corner of the magnificent empty hall. Towering bronze statues stretched before them in two rows, like living gods gazing down at them, perpetual enigmas between the thick gray columns. The hall stretched far into the distance, where Greek letters spelled out FATE, POETRY, and WISDOM. Silence enveloped the hall, devoid of the signs of any other person.

ROCK

When she was discharged, Luoying didn't think she would be returning to the hospital for a while. But at the Registry she had read something about Dr. Reini, an episode in Reini's past that he hadn't told her. She decided to go ask him about it.

Two days after she left the place, she once again pushed open the hospital doors. She cared about this episode not only because it was the reason Reini became a doctor but also because it had to do with Hans Sloan. In fact, the event was the key that linked them. Because of it, Reini chose to specialize in neurology and ended up treating her. Because of it, Reini came to know Hans and won his friendship and trust, therefore receiving the privilege of accessing the Registry of Files. Because of this connection, her grandfather entrusted her to Reini, and Reini gave her the power to see the files. Everything depended on this occurrence in the past.

And it turned out to be an error. Luoying found the situation worth pondering. Whose error was it? She couldn't say. There was apparently no villain, but Reini had been harmed and lost much in life.

Luoying read Reini's file. As a young man, he had studied in the labs of many systems, ranging from the machine center to the Classical Philosophy Atelier, until he picked biomimetic engineering as his concentration at eighteen and, thereafter, at age twenty, entered the production lab of the biomimetic engineering center, where he studied animals and machines, their structures and locomotion.

The third year after he joined the lab, a mining vehicle suffered an accident: a biomimetic quarry machine exploded and burned up during trials. Though there were no casualties, the damage to equipment was considerable. The investigators combed through the burned and broken remains slowly until they isolated the cause of the incident to an electrical leak in a sensor subsystem. Due to the extensive fire that melted many of the components, it was not an easy investigation, and the precise cause—a design flaw, a production error, or a mistake during assembly—could not be determined.

As always happened after every major accident, despite the uncertainties, a committee was formed to hold those responsible accountable. After three days of detailed testimony from dozens at all levels of the system, and another three days of discussions between the Boule investigative committee and the consul, the final result was announced: only Reini would be punished.

"How did they determine it was your fault?" asked Luoying.

"They couldn't."

"Then why were you punished?"

"Someone always has to be punished after an accident."

Reini put down the sculpting knife. His tone was placid, emotionless. More than ten years had passed since the accident, and he wasn't expecting anyone to bring it up again. He saw the expression on Luoying's face, an expression of genuine concern and confusion, which moved him. Once, many asked him about what had happened; some asked out of pity, while others asked out of politeness. Very few truly thought about his situation.

"Only the person responsible should be punished," insisted Luoying. "How could they scapegoat a random person?"

"But it was impossible, given the wreckage, to determine the precise source of the malfunction."

"I read the defense report you drafted for yourself. You offered persuasive reasons for why the design wasn't at fault."

"I suppose I did."

"Then why did you retract it later?"

Reini didn't answer right away. The events of those tense days replayed in his mind.

"Let me try to explain this to you through… accounting. At the time, it was necessary that some form of punishment be imposed. But the question was how many would be punished. If the problem was with the design, then the only one punished would be me. But if the issue was with production, then many more would have to be held accountable."

———

Reini was the designer of the component at fault, a key sensor in the quarry machine. On the day of the committee meeting, leaders from both systems involved in the quarry operation were seated solemnly at the table. The legislators presided over the meeting while a row of observers from the Security System sat to the side. On the walls, videos of the production process played, and a prototype of the destroyed machine sat at the center of the chamber, with everyone gathered around like hunters encircling a captured beast. Reini sat in the back of the gallery as everyone listened to the investigators give their reports. As analyses and summaries circled the air, his childhood habit resurfaced, and once again words and phrases began to pile up in his heart like building blocks.

On Mars, holding responsible individuals accountable was

taken extremely seriously. After every failed trial or accident, an exacting investigation followed. Reini had tried to understand the meaning behind this cultural obsession. It came not only from the meticulousness required of engineering projects but the very operation of the Martian system.

The Martian system was at once a government and an enterprise, and everyone's survival required its stable operation. Quality assurance was vital to this goal. But in a production team monopolized by the system, there were no customers to win over and no competitors to keep one honest, and it would be easy to compromise quality and to cover up mistakes and negligence without a powerful and severe accountability system. Since resources were so constrained on Mars, to ensure efficiency, ateliers only competed for funding at the planning stage. Once a project was funded, it was the only one of its kind to go into production, and the production team had to be fully accountable for the results.

The reality that the system was equivalent to the entire industry had two consequences. On the one hand, the system and every atelier in the system, like any team, had a tendency to protect its members. On the other hand, the system, as the representative of every citizen in every area of life, had to ensure the fair and just application of the law. Thus, the system imposed on every high-level administrator a double identity: insider and outsider, leader and investigator, protector and punisher. Even with the Security System in place, the duality persisted.

Accountability. The key was accountability. If one were accountable only to the team, then it was only necessary to optimize future production. But if one were accountable to those outside the team, to all the citizens of Mars, then it was necessary to pursue those responsible without regard to consequences.

At the time of the accident, to pursue management negligence, to punish the lack of care up and down the production chain, would have led to the loss of many individuals to the process, which would have been damaging to the project itself. And the leader of the project was the most authoritative expert in the field.

Accountability. To both inside and outside. In the back of the gallery, Reini pondered the subtle implications of the word. One investigator called on him and asked him a question. Still lost in his thoughts, he didn't hear the whole question, only the last part. "… do you feel you bear responsibility?"

"Responsibility?" he answered almost instinctively. "What kind of responsibility?"

Was it responsibility to the elucidation of facts or to the need for production?

The investigator asked more questions and announced more conclusions, but again he heard only the last part.

"… your manager has the responsibility to deal with you appropriately."

"What kind of responsibility?" he asked again.

Was it the responsibility to maintain the integrity of the system, or to maintain the stability of the system?

As sentence piled on sentence, forming an edifice, he didn't know where to place his steel beam. The dual meanings split *responsibility* apart. Erecting the beam or laying it flat led to completely different results. Like a child, he hesitated, toy block in hand, trying to evaluate the different possibilities.

No one paid attention to him. The discussions and decisions continued; data and charts scrolled over the walls. The investigators, engineers, and legislators whispered and debated, looking serious. As Reini gazed at them, he felt very distant. Hair and beards turned into blurred images, and he had the distinct sensation that the final result was about to be announced.

Two days later Hans Sloan, the consul, visited Reini personally. Before he had said a word, Reini knew all that he needed to know. Hans pinned the medal for valor that he had won as a young man on Reini's loose gray shirt, stating that it represented both gratitude and regret. The words on the medal spoke of *Defense of the Homeland*, not *Defense of the Truth*.

Reini was thus punished. In the end, the investigative committee concluded that the cause was negligent design, which resulted in the fewest people possible being punished. It was a critical time in Martian history, when the mining operation required every hand, and the project leader was the only one who could move it forward. Reini believed that his own design was not flawed, but he didn't argue against the conclusion. Whether his design was problematic wasn't the most important question; rather, the most important question was accountability. The fire had burned any clues left in the wreck into a tangled mess, but the Boule still had to pick a direction. They chose the responsibility to maintain the stability of the system, to protect the people needed for the greater good, to continue the production necessary for survival. Reini wasn't a fool; he understood what was needed.

Hans, sitting across from Reini, looked down and sighed. As he looked at the old man, Reini felt a sudden pang of sympathy. He could tell that Hans hadn't wanted to see such a result either, but he had come here to face Reini himself, to hand him the medal that he had earned by risking his life.

Since part of Reini's punishment was removal from the engineering lab, Hans asked him which atelier he would prefer to join next, which Reini understood to be Hans's way of apologizing. Since he had a childhood friend who was a neurologist at First Hospital in Salilo District, he decided to go join him there, switching from the senses of machines to the senses of humans.

He wasn't angry. In any event, in a complicated structure of crisscrossing beams, there was no place to insert resentment. Once in a while he did feel desolate, much as he did as a child sitting by the playground, a thicket of towering equipment that was empty of the presence of people. Emptiness was not unusual, and neither were thickets; only when his individual emptiness met with the system's thicket did he feel this sense of desolation.

In reality, Reini didn't much care where he was assigned. He had grown tired of the pressure at the engineering lab, and he thought it would be nice to go somewhere else, to have more time for reading and writing. His life at the hospital was uneventful, and Hans occasionally stopped by to visit. Gradually they grew to be friends. Reini told him that he wanted to write history, and Hans gave him access rights to the Registry of Files.

"Don't you feel unfulfilled?" asked Luoying.

Reini smiled. "To feel that requires one to fail to achieve what one wants to do or is suited to do. A piece of iron left out of the steel frame of a new edifice would feel unfulfilled, but a piece of stone would not feel the same."

He picked up a small yellow sandy rock from the table and hefted it.

"Not everyone wants to be part of a steel frame," he said. "I prefer to sculpt."

Luoying picked up the rough, irregularly shaped rock and examined it. She sat down and placed both arms on his desk and rested her head on one hand. She gazed at the rock and then at Reini. She made as if to speak then, but in the end said nothing. Behind them, a lion sculpted out of sand watched them.

An hour later Luoying pushed open the door to the rehearsal space.

She was inside a large, abandoned warehouse. Tall black steel racks lined the walls, and the ground was a featureless gray expanse. In one corner of the vast, empty warehouse was a simple stage built from old racks torn off the walls.

Spotlights lit up the stage, which seemed tiny from where she was. Some figures were reciting lines on the stage, while others busied themselves below. From a tall rack behind the stage hung the backdrop, on which were painted a cartoonish palace and a throne. Two actors were rehearsing a scene: their voices, rising and falling, fast and slow, spiraled up into the air, surrounded by the noise of the rest of the crew, and echoed in the vast, open space.

Slowly she approached the stage, her shadow stretching behind her on the floor like a long, slender train.

"Luoying!"

Leon, hurrying toward the prop area, greeted her with a smile.

Dressed in a tuxedo, he was carrying a giant cardboard box in his arms, and sweat beaded on his brow. The tux, contrasted with the tools and random objects poking out of the box, brought to mind an elegant duke who suddenly decided to sample the pleasures of manual labor.

"Did you just get here?" said Mira, sitting at the lip of the stage. "You're late!"

Like a hawker at some bazaar, Mira had spread out in front

of him a brown cloth on which were scattered broken fragments of colorful glass. Though he was in costume, he wasn't currently needed in a scene. Instead, he rested his chin in one hand and watched the stage without care, whispering from time to time with the stage manager next to him.

"You made it," said Sorin, the director, running up to her. "Let me show you around."

They kissed each other on the cheek. After asking about the progress of her recovery, Sorin pointed at the chorus standing at the back of the stage, showing Luoying her place. A hat kept his hair out of his lean face, and his bright eyes darted about with efficiency. As soon as he was done with Luoying, he ran for Kingsley, who was in charge of the lighting.

Luoying surveyed the stage. The chorus stood in two separate arcs at the back, surrounding the lead actors. One arc was dressed in white robes and the other in black, like two walls of angels observing the world. Anka's tall figure, in a white robe, stood out at the center of the group on the left. Lyric sheets in hand, he nodded at her, his eyes glowing brightly out of the dimness in back of the stage.

She walked toward her assigned place with some trepidation, because it was her first rehearsal.

Standing next to the stairs at the left side of the stage, Anita was waiting for her cue with a large bedroll in her arms. She smiled at Luoying and glanced at her ankle with an inquiring look. Luoying nodded. "I feel good."

Anita's elaborate updo and heavy, exaggerated stage makeup made it clear that she was playing the role of a wealthy woman, a grand lady used to being obeyed.

"It's a mess up there," she said, indicating the stage with her chin and grinning.

"What's happening?"

"Everyone's just making it up as we go."

"Isn't there a script?"

"Well, yes, but there have been so many revisions that no one knows what's the latest version."

"Who are you playing?"

"A lawyer. Appropriate, no?"

Anita specialized in law. Luoying nodded and pointed to the bedroll she was carrying. "What's that?"

"A corpse." Anita laughed.

Startled, Luoying was about to ask for elaboration, but Anita held up a finger to indicate that it was time for her entrance. She climbed up the stairs, swaying from side to side from the weight of the bedroll but planting each foot with determination.

Luoying followed Anita onto the stage. She edged her way to the back and joined the chorus next to Anka. He held up the lyric sheets so she could follow along.

She discovered that Anka had been right. The lyrics really were as simple as he had claimed. Most consisted of a single line: "*Oh, that's wonderful, wonderful!*" The paper was covered with repeated instances of that line, but there were notes explaining differences in emphasis and tone, the lines of the principals, and cues. Looking at Anka, she lifted a brow and smiled.

Together they looked to the center of the stage. Anita was just starting her monologue. Apparently she was a widow lamenting the death of her husband. The bedroll was unfurled on the stage, revealing a mannequin with thick eyebrows and a beard painted in black. Anita looked disconsolate and complained about how hard it was to make a living. Another actor approached, and after a few lines of dialogue her face broke into a joyous smile. She clapped her hands and circled the stage.

"*Oh, that's wonderful, wonderful!*" sang Anka and the white-robed chorus.

Gradually, Luoying became immersed in the story taking shape onstage until it was reality and the rest of the world was forgotten. Since this was the first time she was seeing the play, she was surprised by many of the jokes and almost burst out laughing. In several places she wanted to exclaim "*Oh, that's wonderful, wonderful!*" without even needing to read the cues.

On the opposite side of the stage, the black-robed chorus was mostly singing "*Ah, so great, so, so great!*" at different lines. The two sets of singers wove a distant harmony and presented a neighboring contrast.

The plot slowly developed, sliding imperceptibly from farce to realism. At first Luoying had to tamp down the urge to laugh, but gradually she didn't feel like laughing anymore. She sensed the bitterness under the surface, a rising sense of doom that seized her heart. Her voice grew a bit raspy. From the back of the stage, she saw, for the first time, a possible depiction of reality looming upon her.

At the end of the rehearsal, Luoying ran to the lip of the stage and asked the others, "What was that ending about?"

Chania, who was closest, answered calmly, "I didn't get a chance to tell you about it the other day. Runge discovered something interesting."

"What did he discover?"

"He read some notes written by his mom, who is one of the archivists for the diplomacy files, responsible for recording the details of various negotiations with Earth. Runge found out that three years earlier, when Mars was trying to purchase acetylene and methane from Earth, the negotiations reached an impasse for several months. The Terrans were concerned that it was a trick on the part of Mars, as the volatile cargo could be detonated during the delivery process to launch a surprise attack. From January to June, the negotiators just couldn't make any progress.

"But then, a series of dramatic events occurred. On July twelfth, all the students from the Mercury Group went to North America for vacation. On July eighteenth, the final agreement was signed. On August first, Mars took delivery and the shipment began to sail for home. On August tenth, we returned to our temporary homes all over Earth. We had no idea what was going on at the time. But do you really think this sequence was a mere coincidence?"

"So… Runge concluded that we were hostages to guarantee the peaceful delivery of the cargo?" asked Luoying.

Chania nodded.

Luoying muttered to herself, "Following that logic, then for five years we were only hostages on Earth to allow trade to proceed. The idea of studying on Earth was simply a cover."

Chania held her by the hand. "I know you don't want to hear this… but if our theory is right, then your grandfather added you to the Mercury Group not because of your parents' deaths but because you're the consul's granddaughter. Having you with us was a way to reassure the other parents so that they wouldn't see the risks."

"The risks…" Luoying's mind was blank. "You're saying the goal was to have me share the same risks as the rest of you."

"And should it have been necessary, all of us would have been declared heroes of Mars after our deaths."

"That's terrifying!"

"We also hope it isn't true," interjected Sorin. "That's why we changed the script and added this new ending. It's a way to gauge the reactions of the top leaders. If our theory is merely the result of hyperactive imagination, then they'll only be confused. But if our theory is true, they'll likely explode in rage."

"It's not just aimed at your grandfather," said Mira. "This is a test of the entire top leadership. It's possible that the consul didn't want to do this at all, but others did."

Luoying nodded, her heart in tumult. Once again, she heard accusations and suspicions directed against her grandfather, raising her anxiety to a new peak. She didn't want the others to see how unhappy she was, but she couldn't find an excuse to get away. Even Anka was nowhere to be found.

She tried to change the subject. "What about the rest of the play? Where did the ideas come from?"

"Based on our personal experiences, of course. I bet you can tell which ones, too."

"That part with Anita I figured is based on her note on the 'copyright of works authored by the dead,' right?"

"Ha! You're right," said Anita. "At the time I came up with that idea for fun, but just this week I heard that a representative in the U.S. Congress is bringing up a bill that essentially implements my idea! Had I known this, I would have figured out some way to secure the IP in my idea back then... Ah, I'd be so rich now, and the first holder of an 'extraterrestrial copyright' on Earth."

"See, we should put *that* in the play," said Sorin.

"Forget it," said Anita. "Aren't you tired of it yet? You've added so many scenes the last couple days."

The happy mood of her friends lifted Luoying's spirits a little. "What about the part after that? Was that based on what happened to Runge?"

Anita nodded. "That's also why the play is called *Revolution*. Runge was part of a real revolution, and we have to commemorate it."

"I don't know if that was a 'real' revolution," said Luoying. "It was just a bunch of hot-blooded young people with nothing better to do getting together. They didn't accomplish anything."

"What do you think a revolution *is*?" asked Anita, laughing. "That's the very definition."

Luoying laughed, too, finally feeling her tensed body relaxing.

"Remind me, when is our performance scheduled for?"

"On the day of the finals for the Creativity Fair. Just over a month from now."

"All right. I should be able to attend all the rehearsals from now on."

"Don't stress out over it," said Sorin, a spirited smile on his face. "Unlike those competing in the fair, we're here to have fun. Come only if you want to. Don't turn it into a chore."

Luoying nodded. The relaxed, easy atmosphere of the group made her feel a sense of belonging. Here friends were always laughing or smiling, even when they were voicing their suspicions. This comforted her, pressing her anxieties down to the bottom of the lake that was her heart.

She knew also what her friends were keeping from their faces, and why. By mocking everything around them—by acting as if they were only having fun—they concealed the desperation of their inner inquiries. They called everything around them into question but didn't resort to petty rage.

Feeling at ease in their presence, Luoying busied herself among her friends. She crisscrossed the stage made of abandoned racks, wove lies out of towels, smiled at sadness as she sat on the floor. She looked up and saw that the afternoon sun, shining through the roof, cast a transparent rainbow in the darkened air of the warehouse. Dust motes drifted through the light, as crisp as ice.

As everyone was getting ready to leave, Anka stopped Luoying. Halfway through the rehearsal, he had disappeared without alerting anyone. While Luoying was still puzzling over this, he reappeared and quietly returned to his place in the chorus. He didn't explain but simply went on as though nothing had happened. Only at the very end did he call to Luoying.

"Thanks for connecting me with Pierre yesterday," he said. "I sent him another message later."

"Good. How did the discussion go?"

"All right. I went to his lab just now to check out his membrane technology. I think I can use it."

"Use it... where?"

"To fix my fighter. Didn't I tell you that it can't fly right now? I was thinking that if I could coat the wings with his photoelectric membrane, I might give the engines more power. It's just an idea for now, though. I need to run trials."

"Did Pierre agree to help you?"

"He did, but we have to figure out how to conduct trials without Fitz finding out. I'm sure he won't approve of this attempt to get off the ground my own way."

"What are you going to do?"

Anka looked into her eyes. "Would you... help me join a team for the Creativity Fair? My squadron won't allow anyone to participate, but a team in the Creativity Fair has the right to apply to use labs and production facilities, which would be a way to hide what I'll be doing. I just don't know if there's enough time."

"In theory, teams can be organized up until the first round of the competition. But... that's tomorrow."

"I know. It's too difficult."

"Let me try," said Luoying determinedly. "Just let me."

"All right," said Anka. "Thank you."

Luoying smiled to show that it was nothing. Of course she wanted to help him. There was nothing in the world she wanted to do more than to help him. She liked seeing him act with purpose, and his dedication to his task reassured her.

"How do you plan on running the trials?"

"First, I have to assemble the modified wings, and then conduct the test flights."

"Don't run unnecessary risks. I don't want you to hurt yourself!"

"Don't worry." Anka grinned. "But only risky things are worth doing."

Anka's voice echoed in the empty warehouse. Most had already left, carrying boxes of props and costumes. The two of them were the last two to go. As they exited, Luoying gently pushed closed the heavy warehouse door. The clang of iron striking iron reverberated in their hearts.

The next morning the Russell District qualifying competition for the Creativity Fair was held at the district's children's hall.

This was the favorite haunt of all the neighborhood children. Everyone, regardless of whether they were participating in the competition, was excited. First thing in the morning, youths from all over the neighborhood filled the building like a surging flood. Though individual neighborhoods were small, each contained at least several hundred young residents of the right age for the fair; and as the teams spread apart to take their places, soon the space felt like a bustling market.

The competition site hadn't been completely made over for the occasion. No stages were erected, nor was any of the regular equipment removed. But all the desks and chairs had been painted with images from classical myths, colorful flags hung everywhere, and posters publicizing the various teams' projects scrolled across the walls.

The children's hall was the neighborhood's integrated learning center, furnished with all kinds of educational equipment: musical instruments, painting supplies, electrical and optical apparatuses, and so on. The tables and chairs made natural display pedestals for the products of the competing teams, and all that had to be done was to remove the pens and papers that normally littered their surfaces. Some of the teams had been working since dawn, and all kinds of machines, sculptures, art installations, and so on rested on the tables like soldiers standing at attention for a parade.

Among the crowd of spectators was Luoying, who experienced a nostalgic sense of familiarity. She had left Mars when she was too young to have attended many elective classes or worked in an atelier; therefore, most of her memories were from the children's hall. As she looked around, fragments of those memories seemed to be floating in the air. Next to the wall were snatches of the cowherd's ditty she had sung; on the shelves were traces of her fingers' explorations; on the desks were blotches of paint she had carelessly spilled; in the air were faded tinges of her colorful dresses. She saw herself, a much more innocent version of herself. She had spent most of her waking days between the ages of five and thirteen here. As her gaze passed over the walls and desks and other objects, the memories awakened, like dehydrated vegetables uncurling and growing vibrant again when immersed in water.

Several teachers walked about the hall—the judges for the qualifying round. A group of kids followed them around like the layers of fabric dragged behind noble ladies of yore. The opinions of the judges made up a large part of the final score, and so every competing team was prepared to give their teachers a most compelling introduction of their projects within the shortest amount of time.

"Lomar Néas, the great fashion designer of the twenty-first century, borrowed from modern dance and tried to define clothing as the relationship between the human body and space. Our design is intended to extend this concept…"

Gielle was speaking animatedly, her hands gesturing for emphasis. She had worked on this speech for a whole week, and stayed up late last night to practice the delivery.

"… Most people think of clothing as a means of staying warm or mere decoration, feeling alienated and estranged from nature and space. But we all know that the spiritual goal of every person is to break through the bonds of conventional thinking, to constantly innovate. We made this armor for this very purpose. By turning sunlight into electricity, not only is it a suitable material for space suits and mining suits, but it brings about a novel conceptual framework: our body doesn't have to hide from nature; it can embrace nature, appropriate nature…"

Gielle beamed sweetly at the teachers. She spoke with confidence and natural grace, the effort of a whole night's practice paying off. From time to time she glanced at Luoying in the crowd, who nodded back at her encouragingly. Next to her, Daniel was in a pale blue suit of armor, styled more for comic effect than practicality. As Gielle talked, he puffed out his chest and lifted his head, shifting into various poses copied from classical Greek statues.

Watching Gielle, Luoying was reminded of the old house on Earth in which she had lived for more than a year and that she shared with a group of heretics. After so much time in the company of Gielle, she discovered the other girl had a habit of using "innovation" to describe everything. It was as though her life was replete with new ideas, new concepts, new passions, just like Luoying's old housemates'.

They had also prized innovation. They pursued novel additions to a hedonistic life; members of the avant-garde, they wore strange clothes and experimented with new drugs, disdaining the tired old metropolises in their search for a completely different way of life. Luoying had partied with them and joined them in occupying the estates of the wealthy. They wove flowers and herbs into their clothes, disassembled the escalators of skyscrapers to be repurposed as slides for their old house. Gielle spoke of innovations, as did her old housemates on Earth, but neither group could have imagined the life of the other.

Among her old housemates was an Australian man whom everyone called Kangaroo. He was a kind, bald, middle-aged man and also the friend she had known the longest on Earth. He didn't dress in the unusual fashions of the other housemates or party with them in the streets. Instead, he had a job at a museum where he pretended to be a statue. Supposedly he had been hired by an artist interested in challenging the traditional conception of sculpture. Sometimes he snuck out the old hunting trophies from the museum and arranged them in the plaza to scare urbanites who had never seen wild animals. One time he even poured fresh concrete in front of an office building and left in it impressions of shoes and animal tracks. Luoying had no idea how Kangaroo managed to never be caught for these pranks, as he enjoyed a seemingly carefree existence.

While reminiscing, Luoying kept up with the roving crowd of spectators. Gielle, finished with her presentation, caught up to her excitedly. One hand on her thumping heart, sweat beading on her forehead, she gazed at Luoying inquiringly. Luoying smiled at her and squeezed her plump hand reassuringly.

Colorful exhibits greeted the teachers one after another, full of novel and interesting creations. Applause and gasps of admiration rose and fell, and more and more youths joined the group following the teachers.

Luoying saw that Brenda and two other girls had created a double-sided painting reminiscent of the old double-sided embroidery of Chinese tradition. The canvas was translucent, with a girl in deep thought on the obverse side and a strolling boy on the reverse side. From each side, only one figure could be seen, but the same stars and the moons glowed from both sides. She couldn't tell how it was made.

The procession finally wound its way through all the exhibits and returned to the center of the long hall, where the scores were tallied.

Holding up a notebook, Jean, one of the teachers, called out, "Are there any projects that haven't been shown to the judges yet?" The crowd waited expectantly.

"A total of one hundred and twelve teams have shown their projects so far," said Jean. "Unless there are any more competitors, this is the end of the qualifying round."

Behind her, the other teachers were beginning to pack up their notes.

Luoying decided that this was her only chance. Forcing herself to ignore the butterflies in her stomach, she spoke up.

"Yes, there is one more!"

Luoying heard how her own voice reverberated around the silent hall. She took a step forward and, without looking at any of the other astounded competitors and spectators, walked slowly to one of the largest desks in the center of the hall. There, she carefully nudged the projects on it aside until she had cleared out a small space, revealing the dark blue tablecloth. Then she retrieved the small rock she had taken from Reini a few days earlier and placed it in the middle of the space. The yellow rock, roughly spherical and with an unfinished surface, appeared dull and insignificant next to the other projects.

She locked eyes with Jean.

"What is this?" asked the confused teacher.

Luoying smiled. "This is my project, titled *Alone*."

The teachers looked at one another, as did the other youths in the hall. Among the colorful, complicated structures, robots, and art pieces, the rock was so primitive and clumsy that it seemed an insult. It did not fit. The other projects seemed to inch away from it the way a crowd cleared out the space around a criminal suspect. Luoying faced all of them without any expression. The astounded silence was exactly what she had expected.

After almost a full minute, Jean said, slowly, "The... idea is good."

She turned to face the rest of the crowd and, straining to keep her voice natural, said, "Luoying's project is a reminder to us all not to be limited to only high technology in our creativity. We should all broaden our minds."

Luoying sighed with relief. Gratefully she smiled at Jean.

The first round of the competition was finally over. Everyone began to clean up, and the hall was once again full of noise and laughter. The colorful flags were pulled off the walls with as much ease and joy as when they had been hung. The busy crowd filled the space, and the lonely rock was forgotten, as though it had never existed.

Gielle pulled Luoying into a side hug as they were leaving and whispered, "How did you come up with it? You never said a word!"

"Oh, the rock? I didn't think too hard."

"It's so creative!"

"Do you think so?"

Luoying smiled, thinking only: *It does not fit.* Palming the rock, she was thinking of Reini, of herself and her friends in the Mercury Group, and her mood darkened.

She had at one point contemplated bringing nothing at all and simply pointing at the empty air to declare that her creation was titled *Dream*. But in the end she thought that would be too pessimistic. After knowing Kangaroo, she didn't think of herself as creative at all. She was sensitive and felt things deeply, but that wasn't the same as being creative.

Through the whole morning, she had seen only one project that she thought was truly creative. It was a large, thin-shelled, hollow glass globe in which was suspended a slightly smaller glass globe, and another one inside that... until it was impossible to see the smallest, innermost globes. The inner surface of each shell was carved with different features: land, houses, slides, factories... and in the outermost layer, if one looked closely, it was possible to see tiny humans in the middle of all kinds of activities, their feet firmly planted against the glass, their heads pointing to the center of the concentric globes.

The whole sphere had been hung high up so that the layers of different worlds shone through the almost-invisible glass, a multilayer projection that was eye-catching. Luoying had no idea how it had been made. She spent a long time gazing up at the crystalline spheres, gazing through the infinite recursion of concentric shells, gazing at the different-scaled but self-similar worlds, gazing at the outermost layer as though seeing the upturned dome of heaven from outside, until she felt she had also been turned upside down, inside out, tossed into the depths of the infinite cosmos.

WINGS

Starting in the middle of the twenty-first century, personal aircraft became the main means of transportation on Earth. As cities grew bigger and buildings taller, surface transportation networks were overburdened, and humans had to take to the skies with winged cars.

On Earth, flying was a complicated endeavor. For children, it represented excitement and dreams; for youths, it represented the means by which to pursue dates; for adults, it was a status symbol; and for the elderly, it was a tool that they complained about incessantly but had to put up with in order to get around. For sociologists, personal aircraft led to the birth of new forms of social organization; for politicians, they represented disputes over airspace; for eco-activists, they were responsible for damage to the atmosphere; for merchants, they were just the medicine needed to prevent economic downturns. For everyone, they represented the coming of a new age.

High school students wanted to get to school; college students wanted adventure; stars wanted vacations. Everyone had different tastes, and the personal aircraft industry had to cater to them all, resulting in complicated vehicles. For high speed, they needed new solid fuels; for stability, the wings needed balancers at low airspeeds; for altitude control, they needed high-precision combustion ratio governors; for adapting to different air currents, they needed smart flow sensors; for avoiding accidents due to operator fatigue, they needed reliable autopilots; for long-distance communication and teleconferences, they needed powerful radios and high-res displays; for defense against attackers, they needed self-guided missiles; for the survival of the manufacturers, they needed advertising; for saving the life of the occupant when all was lost, they needed ejection seats and parachutes; for love, they needed lie-flat, comfortable seats. Personal aircraft evolved into a thousand forms, employing every imaginable material.

When the simple became complicated, the simple was forgotten. It wasn't too different from how children knew it was enough to eat and sleep to live, but adults claimed a hundred other "necessities." To go from the complicated back to the simple required a great deal of patience and effort.

"All we need is food," said Mira.

Sorin pored over the plans and diagrams spread out before him. "But we've taken out everything we can."

On sheets of e-paper, the various components were labeled in hasty scrawls. Some of the components had been x'd out. The three boys sat around these sheets, debating and analyzing. They planned to completely overhaul a small Martian shuttle fighter—removing all systems related to cargo hauling, mining, and war; reducing speed and altitude requirements to the bare minimum—until the plane could get off the ground with the least amount of equipment.

This was the seventh day after the qualifying round of the Creativity Fair. Since Luoying had managed to get them through that first round, the team was officially recognized and their trials could be put on the agenda. Anka explained to his friends his plans for modifying his plane, and the response was overwhelmingly enthusiastic.

Several Mercury Group members also wanted to go with Luoying to visit the crater and canyon sites that were so important to Martian history. After Runge suggested that they rent a mining ship, Chania began to organize and raise funds, and Sorin directed the secret plan along with the play. Luoying wasn't surprised by her friends' response. After all, after days spent cooped up in a glass box, struggling with their reports on their trip to Earth, the idea of an adventure to recover the truth of the Martian past held infinite appeal. Several core members of the group gathered daily to implement the details of their plan. Luoying's personal quest had grown into a yearning for the sky and a critical examination of the past.

"I think we've been coming at this the wrong way," said Anka, who was leaning against a column to the side.

"What do you mean?" asked Sorin, looking up from the plans.

"We've been starting with the plane and then taking things away, with the result that we've been struggling with every component, thinking it's necessary. But we can start from nothing and then only add in what must be added."

"Start from nothing?" Sorin furrowed his brow.

"Well, not exactly nothing. More like starting with air."

Luoying sat on the steel rack opposite them. The three engineers had already spent a night discussing the matter.

Their workshop was just a corner of the abandoned warehouse they used for rehearsals. A lone shed stood against the wall like a large mailbox, and sections of the steel racks that surrounded the warehouse lay in front of the shed diagonally, leaving a triangular area of the floor open. It was night, and the empty warehouse was dark and silent except for this lit corner. The boys sat on a few chests repurposed as furniture, and a portable projector showed images of different aircraft on the walls.

Anka leaned against the pillar, one leg crossed in front of the other. "Ultimately, our mission is just to get up the cliffs without falling. We don't need a traditional plane for that. All we care about are the wings. There's no need even for the engine. This way we can maximally simplify the structure and lessen the weight."

"How can we do without the engine?" Sorin objected. "Even if we rely on solar power, we still have to have jets. How else are we going to move? Even if the wings can vibrate, we still need minimal airspeed to stay aloft."

Anka shook his head. "That's only necessary if we have to fly against the wind and generate lift. But if we don't particularly care about the direction we fly in, then we can go with the wind, much like some insects."

Mira asked, "But I thought we went through the calculations. There won't be enough lift."

"Lift is directly proportional to wing area," said Anka. "We can make the wings bigger. Though the atmosphere is very thin, it also means that the force applied against each square centimeter of the surface is small. I've done the math. We can make the wings several times bigger than they would be on Earth."

Mira looked doubtful. "Will the wings hold? Wouldn't they bend under the weight?"

Anka shrugged. "I'm not sure. It's just an idea right now."

Sorin nodded thoughtfully. "Let's try to work out the details. I imagine we can keep the wings straight if we buttress in the right spots. The key is the lift-drag ratio, which means we have to find the right shape for the wings and the right wind conditions. I think it's feasible. We do have a lot of wind, despite the thin air."

Sketching on her notepad, Luoying listened to them but

didn't interrupt. Sorin's eyes were spirited and intense. Mira's messy hair draped around his round brown face. Anka was slouching and one of his shoes was off, but he still looked slender and handsome against the pillar.

Though she didn't follow the intricacies of the engineering discussion, she was struck by Anka's words: an airplane was nothing more than a dance between material and wind. She had a realization: to speak of flight, it was necessary to first speak of air; to speak of action, it was necessary first to speak of the surroundings.

In the quiet of the night, Luoying observed the boys in front of her and the moons visible through the domed roof. Like her, the boys had grown used to walking in the sky on Earth. Looking at them, she felt comforted. Though there were so many obstacles in their way, she felt that as long as they put their minds to it, there was nothing they couldn't accomplish. She wasn't sure where that sense of faith had come from; perhaps it was because she had grown used to drifting with them, or perhaps because she liked the way their eyes lit up with passion when they were deep in thought.

The discussion among the boys grew more animated. They listed the conditions and equipment necessary to drift with the wind. The list seemed to Luoying to pose all kinds of problems that couldn't be solved. But the boys persisted, and after attacking the problems one by one, they managed to come up with solutions for most of them. However, there were a few stubborn snags that refused to yield, like bits of fish bone lodged in the throat.

"Luoying, do you remember any descriptions of the geography around the site of your great-grandfather's crash?" asked Sorin.

Three pairs of eyes were focused on her. Apparently they

had come to an impasse in their discussion and needed her input.

"I do," said Luoying. "But there wasn't much."

"What do you have?"

"It was a turn in the canyon, where the walls went straight up and down. The gusting wind would send rocks and sand tumbling down from the cliffs."

"The wind was very strong there?"

"That's right."

"But there was a dust storm going on at the time."

"Yes."

"What about when there's no storm?"

"There's nothing about that in the files." Luoying hesitated, thinking. "Wait, I remember something about there being many wind-eroded caves on the cliffs—and gullies, also from the wind."

The boys looked at each other. Sorin nodded at Anka, who took more notes on the paper plans.

"Do you know the exact location of the site and how to get there?" asked Anka gently.

"I don't. But I know it's not far from the base camp at the time. There was one line in the files that I remember really well: *If you send out the rescue ship now, it'll take only half an hour to get here.*"

"The rescue ship can get there that quickly?"

"Yes."

"Then it should be no problem to drive our mining ship there," said Anka to Mira.

Mira nodded. It was clear that this had resolved a big part of his worries.

"Then what's the point of building or retrofitting a plane?" asked Mira. "We can just drive the mining ship over."

Luoying shook her head. "The crater and canyon we're looking for are on the ground, but most of the sites and ruins we're interested in would be up on the cliffs."

"On the cliffs?"

"The camps they built before Mars City were all up on the cliffs."

"Really?" Mira looked taken aback. "I had no idea."

"You didn't?" Now it was Luoying's turn to be surprised. "I thought everyone knew."

"I didn't." Mira turned to the other two. "You?"

"I didn't know either," said Anka.

"I think I remember hearing something about that," said Sorin, frowning. "It's weird, right? We really didn't learn much about that part of history in school. There were many details about the war, but I can't remember ever focusing on the prewar period."

"I think you're right," said Luoying, after a moment of reflection on her own schooling.

"Then how did you know about the camps?" asked Mira.

"I can't remember... maybe my parents told me about them when I was little? I really can't be sure. But I've always known."

"Can you describe the features of the camp in more detail?" asked Anka.

"I know it's in a crater, and that people lived in caves on the rim of the crater. As for more details... I can't remember."

"Anyway, you can find out more?"

Luoying was about to say that, since her parents had died when she was very young, she wasn't sure who to go to for more information, but then she remembered Reini. She had a hunch that he would be able to help. As a historian, surely he had more materials about that period. She nodded and accepted the mission.

Anka picked up a sheet of e-paper from the ground and jotted down a few more notes. After glancing over the set of plans, he said, "I think we've done as much as we can today. We've resolved many problems, though there remain two key issues: one is the geography of the area we're trying to get to, and the other is how to control the wings. Let's go back and work on these problems on our own and inform the group if there's any progress."

"What do you mean by 'control the wings'?" asked Luoying.

"It's a technical challenge," explained Anka. "We are trying to make the wings much bigger, right? Although that allows us to generate more lift, it also creates a new problem: it's very hard to control such large wings due to the turbulence. Since the airflow will be unpredictable, it'll be hard to code the control routines. The simpler we make the body of the plane, the harder it'll be to program the wings. And unless we can control the wings, we can't fly."

"Oh… that sounds bad…," muttered Luoying.

She wasn't a programmer and didn't understand the specific difficulties, but she could tell from Anka's tone how serious the problem was. The aircraft designs they inherited had resulted from decades of trials and experimentation, so any modification necessarily brought about new challenges. Though she wasn't an engineer, she understood that principle.

She saw that the boys looked solemn because of the challenges they faced, and the solemnity also made them handsome, as if the obstacles in their way energized them. As she walked with them out of the night-shrouded warehouse, she felt a warmth in her heart that she hadn't felt in many days.

———

They met at the insect lab. This was per Luoying's request; she explained that she wanted to understand the principles of insect flight. Reini agreed and brought her to the lab where he had once studied for three years as a young man.

During his stint here, Reini had studied the biosensing of motion and pressure. On Mars, many machines were based on the principles of biomimicry of insects. Mining carts, for instance, extracted ore with long, segmented arms and skittered swiftly across the rubble-strewn ground. Reini's task here was to research the coordination and motion of insect limbs, replicating them in electronics and circuitry that could be deployed in engineering design.

The lab maintained a large hothouse in which specimens of rare plants were kept in an artificial jungle. The hothouse provided habitats for bees, dragonflies, praying mantises, spiders, and many species of beetles. The moment Luoying set foot in the hothouse, a dragonfly landed on her head. Surprised, she yelped, and the dragonfly flew away, trembling.

She stood rooted in place, never having seen anything like the scene that greeted her. Every flower was blooming magnificently; every nook and cranny seemed to conceal an insect; every pair of vibrating wings gave off a vibrant allure. Lush growth filled her eyes, and butterflies fought for her attention. The translucent curled petals reminded her of the most elegant dresses. Not only had she never seen such beauty on Mars, she had never experienced it on Earth either. She had been to flower shops and grasslands on Earth, but never a garden of winged flowers.

"So beautiful!" she exclaimed.

"It is," said Reini. "This garden was why I chose to study here."

"Were all these bred on Mars?"

"Yes. About ten pairs of each species were initially brought here from Earth."

They stood in the middle of some blooming flowers. Reini gently picked up a butterfly from a flower and deposited it in Luoying's palm. While the butterfly rested calmly, its slender legs trembling, Luoying examined it carefully. As she extended a finger to caress it, the butterfly took off.

"Dr. Reini," she asked, "how do insects fly?"

Reini caught a nearby honeybee and showed its thorax to Luoying. "Do you see how its wings vibrate? This is the basic way all insects generate lift, though different species do it in slightly different ways. Bees twist their wings to change the angle of the air caught between them, while dragonflies vibrate their wings up and down to generate tiny vortices."

"Is it similar to how birds fly?"

"Quite different," said Reini. "Birds do not vibrate their wings, while insects rarely fan their wings the way birds do."

"How do insects control their wings?"

"Typically by flexing and twisting the muscles near the roots of the wings, which are very light and thin."

Luoying looked at the bee struggling in Reini's hand. It curled up until its abdomen was almost touching its thorax, kicking its tiny legs. The strange mouthparts, like components of a helmet, shifted and slid nonstop. Reini let go and the bee stumbled into the air. He held out a finger and a dragonfly landed on it.

Gazing at the dragonfly, Reini said, "If you'll allow me a bit of a digression: I think we've become too dependent on computer simulations. We no longer bother to observe. It's the opposite from the way things used to be done."

Time passed quietly in the hothouse. The afternoon was almost over, and dusk was descending.

"Dr. Reini," Luoying asked abruptly, "was there a time when people on Mars lived in a crater?"

Reini considered the question. He answered in his habitual even-tempered voice. "There was indeed a time when people on Mars lived on the walls of a large crater."

"When was that?"

"About a century ago."

"How come we don't hear much about that time?"

"Because it was a controversial experience."

"Controversial? How? What was that place like?"

Reini didn't answer for some time. When he spoke again, his voice was slow and distant, like an ancient painting taking shape in the air. "Back then, there were no glass houses. Some people lived in colonies built from the steel hulls of spaceships, but most lived in caves and underground shelters. Although the walls of the crater were cold and lacked light, they blocked harmful cosmic radiation. For human beings, survival and security always came first.

"You can imagine that the dwellings of the time were simple and crude, just holes in the mountainside. The yellow-earth walls were rough; the tiny caves were heated by electric stoves; and even during the day the inside was pitch-dark without lamps. But even so, such dwellings were not easy to build. All construction had to happen on top of steep cliffs, impossible for most ground vehicles to climb. Thus, most of the work had to be done by hand with great effort. Moreover, should any of the dwellings collapse, re-excavating them required great effort. All the goods needed to sustain life also had to be shipped in from Earth."

"Did Terrans and Martians live together then?"

Reini smiled at her. "Back then there weren't any Martians yet.

All humans were Terrans."

Luoying pondered Reini's words, like an ancient riddle. "Where is this crater?"

"The middle of Big Cliff, not far south of the equator."

"Are there surviving ruins from that time?"

"I suppose so. Anything that wasn't pulverized by the war should still be there."

"Can we still visit them?"

"That's probably difficult. No one goes there anymore."

"Can I go by myself?"

"That's even harder."

Luoying squeezed the yellow metallic apple she had in her pocket all this time. Carefully, she asked, "Why did the war start back then?"

Reini looked her in the eyes. "I think you've already looked into the causes of the war."

Luoying nodded. "But I'm asking about the goals, not the causes."

Reini nodded with understanding. "The main goal was to build a completely new society."

"Like the Mars City of today?"

"In a sense. But the goal at the time was only the prototype and core. Today's city is the result of thirty years of development during the war, and then more years after."

"What was the core at the beginning?"

"The central archive. The core of everything was the central archive; the goal was to develop a city that functioned on top of the central archive. The point wasn't to use the archive to compute the operations of the city but only to use it for storage: storage of every citizen's discoveries, every new exploration, to be shared freely, to defend the freedom of thought of each."

"But why was independence necessary? Why couldn't all this have been accomplished in the old crater-rim camp?"

"That wouldn't have been possible because the change involved the transformation of the whole economy. The envisioned city needed all intellectual and spiritual explorations to be open, unfettered from the economy. In other words, the production of goods and the production of ideas had to be separated into two distinct realms. There was no historical precedent for this."

"You mean," asked Luoying, "that the products of the spirit would not be bought and sold, right?"

"Correct. That was the vow made by the leaders of the rebellion."

"Is that a good thing?"

"I'm afraid there's no answer to that." Reini turned his gaze to the twilit horizon. "For those who started the revolution, it was a matter of faith. When it comes to matters of faith, it's impossible to judge them with labels like 'good' and 'bad.'"

"What kind of life would that be like…?" Luoying muttered to herself.

Though Reini made no judgment about right or wrong, he did explain to her, in simplified terms, some of the historical choices the early Martians made, and the lives of Luoying's grandfather and his companions when they were young. He stuck to the outlines because he was convinced that the broad trends of history were not nearly as moving as the specific acts of individuals caught in history.

Reini had once read many documents from before the war, and it was impossible not to be infected in some measure by the burning passion, as bright as sun-burnished dawn, in those words. It was a slightly impractical age, a utopia in the desert, a bubbling spring in the wasteland. Back then, without much encouragement, many would strive to make flowers bloom in the sand; indeed, the very idea moved many to throw themselves into the grand endeavor.

At the start of the war, the rebels camped in a crater, similar to the Terran forces. The only difference was that the rebels were closer to the edge of Big Cliff, closer to the plains. This was because although the rebels could obtain about half of the food and other goods they needed by raiding the Terran forces' supply ships, they still had to provide the rest through farming.

It was an age when technology developed at a dizzying speed. Perhaps in no previous era were there so many clever minds placed together under so much pressure. The rebels consisted mostly of brilliant scientists who had joined the ranks because of dissatisfaction with the way various factions on Mars had been hoarding information, erecting walls to contain knowledge. The walls had to do with politics and commerce, which they knew nothing about, but they did know that to survive in the harsh environment of Mars required the free sharing and exchange of discoveries and inventions. They had built up a platform for sharing information in order to survive. There was no thought of art, of decorative designs, of politics and plebiscites and all the rest that came after.

War gave birth to a generation. They grew up during the war, came of age in the war, and many died from the war. Hans, Galiman, Ronen, and Garcia were all children of the war. They fought as pilots, but they weren't only pilots. They grew up in the worst of times, when it was easy to lose faith. But they carried on the flame of faith and kept it alive.

Near the end of the war, Hans Sloan and his friends became the principals on the stage. Hans, young and handsome, took to the air with his wife as newlyweds and became a pilot instructor at the age of twenty-two. His father was still in the prime of his life and career as the commander of the Martian forces, and radiation sickness, though it had made him gaunt and wan, had as of yet no effect on his spirit. Galiman, his blond tresses like a lion's mane and his booming voice a lion's roar, was refining the designs that would ultimately propel the rebels to leave the crater for a new home. The sophisticated Garcia was already showing his potential as a diplomat, traveling everywhere to deliver speeches that kindled the dream of the central archive in the hearts of the new Martian people. Poetic Ronen, on the other hand, had published a series of essays, turning Habermas's communicative rationality into passionate expositions that extended to every aspect of city construction and design.

It was an age when ideals ruled. Reini knew that, regardless of the reality of the time, the people who had lived through that age had genuinely stretched their hands into space, yearning for their dreams.

———

After leaving the insect lab, Luoying suddenly wanted to dance.

She hadn't danced for days. Her mind had been preoccupied by other things, and her body had been recuperating. In her heart, she thought she had bid farewell to the dance stage, and neither her body nor her mind would ever return. But for the first time since her injury, she wanted to dance, to move all her body, to leap and turn and devote all of herself to a state of activity. She couldn't tell where the urge had come from: perhaps the flitting butterflies, perhaps the cliffs seen at the end of the horizon, perhaps the history of men and women who fought to be free of restraints; perhaps flight.

Stopping at the door of the insect lab, she turned to gaze at the wings flitting through the vibrant green of the hothouse, and the desire that had lain dormant in her body began to waken.

She went to the dance school and, without turning on the lights, danced in the blue glow of the streetlamps that came on. Stretching, going through the standard poses, spinning before the mirror. Feeling her feet strike the thick, solid floor made her feel solid. The floor was the most loyal of partners, holding her up as she felt for it with the tips of her toes.

As she danced, her thoughts rose and fell with her.

The philosophy of dance in the twenty-second century had reached an apex of complexity. Dance was seen as a relationship between the human body and space, and there were many contradictory trends. Some argued that the physical language of body movements should be used to generate new signifiers, while others propounded the use of dance to throw off the layers of signifiers imposed on the body… but Luoying wasn't interested in such abstruse theories. For her, dance wasn't about a relationship with the external world but the relationship with the self. After pondering the goal of dance at length, she had reached the conclusion that it was control. The Mercury Group's project leaders had given her the mission to learn to jump, to find the limits of the human body. But she found precision to be more important than height. The hardest task wasn't to reach higher but to set the tips of the toes in an exact position, no higher and no lower.

She raised a leg until it was at the height of her waist, set it down, and kicked back, standing still on one foot.

Only after learning to dance did she find out how limited humanity's understanding of the human body was. No one thought about how to sit, how to stand, how to walk without falling over. People carried out these incredibly complicated movements by instinct, without conscious control. How marvelous! It was as miraculous as the life energy that animated the body itself. The body had memories of its own, deeper habits that the conscious mind never understood.

A ray of light swept through the depths of her mind.

She was thinking of the night before, of the vast empty warehouse and the steel racks, of the boys locked in deep debate. All their efforts had stalled because of a crucial link, like a puzzle missing the piece that depicted the eyes. Everything was there, but it wasn't a picture.

And now she had the missing piece: control of the wings.

To control the wings, perhaps they didn't need the brain, only the instincts of the body.

SHIP

The day for the finals of the Creativity Fair had arrived.

The various districts took turns hosting the finals. This time it was the Alyosha District. The Alyosha Stadium and its environs had been spruced up for the occasion. The whole plaza was decorated to resemble the Earth of the Romantic era, classic and luxurious. The crowd at the site of the final competition was jubilant and enthusiastic. The dome of the stadium showed palaces in clouds and dancing angels, and symphonic strains filled the air. Roller-skating youths circled the stadium, taking off from various ramps to perform stunt jumps and spins, landing to waves of applause and cheering.

The audience in the seats was especially excited. To be able to witness the results of the final competition was an honor, and only the best competitors from every district were given the opportunity. All the youths were expectant, attracted not just by the competition itself but by the parties and dances that would follow. This was one of the best venues to meet young people from other districts. Everyone was looking sharp, the girls in beautiful dresses and the boys in crisp uniforms, posing elegantly. The youths who couldn't make it to the venue gathered in their own districts and watched the proceedings remotely, cheering on their friends as they consumed snacks and drinks.

Backstage was full of excitement as well. Gielle had been picked to be one of the goddesses to give out the awards to the victors. She checked herself in the mirror nervously, babbling to those around her to be sure that her hair was perfect and the floral diadem on her head straight. Thinking that she would soon have to stride confidently across the stage, the focus of the gazes of millions, she felt her palms grow sweaty. She had been reciting her lines to herself continuously, and she had drafted Luoying to check that she made no mistakes. Around them other girls in the dressing room were busy with makeup, costumes, running about and screaming "Who has seen my necklace?," and suchlike. Luoying could barely make out Gielle's recitation.

"When are you going to put on your makeup?" asked Gielle.

"I'm done," said Luoying, smiling.

"You're going up like *that*?" Gielle was too astounded to be polite.

"That's right. I'm just part of the chorus."

Luoying was in a long flowing white dress. She wore no jewelry except a small flower on her shoulder. Her long dark hair draped loosely about her shoulders, and a thin golden band was wrapped around her forehead. Her eyes and brows were not painted or lined.

Gielle found Luoying's almost casual attitude incomprehensible. Luoying didn't bother explaining herself except to say that her role was just part of the overall atmosphere of the performance. She didn't mention that she also needed to change quickly right after the finals, so the simpler her costume and makeup the better.

It was vital that Gielle know nothing about that second part.

The play they had been rehearsing would be the third

performance today. Luoying wasn't nervous at all. In her mind, the performance was for no one except themselves, a calm expression of their beliefs.

The first two performances were choreographed dances for the opening ceremony, so their play would be the first real act. While waiting for their turn to go onstage, Luoying peeked out from backstage at the bright, colorful domed ceiling of the stadium, like a nebula deep in space. The other Mercury Group members around her weren't nervous either. No one said anything except for occasional whispered reminders of instructions for how to get out quickly afterward.

It was time.

"Ladies and gentlemen, talented youths," the emcee, the education minister, spoke as fireworks exploded, "let's celebrate this feast of the mind!... To create is the highest of honors!..."

After the wild celebratory opening ceremony, it was time for drama.

———————

All the lights were focused on Mira. Dressed in a ragged brown shirt and a brown hat full of holes, he looked the very image of a vagrant down on his luck. His big toes stuck out of the gaps in his ill-fitting black boots, and he carried a small cloth bundle on a stick. He took two steps forward, two steps back, scratched his head and sighed.

—*I'm a pitiable vagabond, full of talents and dreams recognized by no one. Once, I aspired to do great deeds that would change the world, but reality smashed my ambition to smithereens. O universe, why are you so unfair? I should have been a great doctor, the vanquisher of cancer, but now I'm a homeless wanderer. Oh, what did I do wrong?*

A spotlight illuminated an area stage left, where the first

recollection of the vagabond began. A student—Mira's character's younger self—dressed in a white shirt buttoned all the way up, stood excitedly next to a rotund middle-aged man and held up a document with both hands. The middle-aged man looked serious and imposing, and the student looked at him with awe and respect.

—*Welcome to our lab. All of us are heirs to an illustrious history, and innovation is our unceasing pursuit. Our motto is: Never stop in the quest for constant innovation and eternal truths, ever maintain lively minds and progressive aims, exert all effort to keep our lab at the forefront of human exploration. Excelsior!*

The black-robed chorus chimed in.

—*Ah, so great, so, so great!*

—*Director, such lofty sentiments! I cannot agree with you more. I think my discovery will be perfectly in line with your goals.*

—*Oh? What sort of discovery is that?*

—*I've come up with a plan to streamline our production process. As soon as I arrived, I carefully examined our process chart and added a feedback procedure right here. By my calculations, we can reduce our production time by up to half.*

—*Why in the world would you want to do that?*

—*But… isn't that a good thing? This will lower our costs significantly. Wouldn't that help us get more funding in the budget?*

—*Oh, you foolish child. Do you really think victory in the competition for a share of the budget is won by such accomplishments? Have you no experience of the world? To win a share of the budget, we must make bold pronouncements and airy promises. You must never waste your energy on such useless details. Set your mind to grand blueprints.*

Once again, the black-robed chorus chimed in.

—*Ah-ha-ha, so great, so, so great.*

The light on the left side of the stage went out. Once again the spotlight highlighted Mira in the middle of the stage. He was in a boat on wheels, and he was straining to row it forward.

—*Little did I know that the improvement I suggested had long been thought of by others, but they were all too smart to bring it up. The fact was, the higher the costs of production for a project, the higher the allocated share of the budget. I was too inexperienced to understand this basic rule of the real world. But by pointing out a blatant inefficiency, I angered my colleagues, who exiled me to another continent. Oh, I am the most unfortunate soul in the world. I must learn my lesson and hold fast to my ideals. I will revitalize my career on the new continent.*

The ship wobbled ahead, passing through a sea of stars until it reached the right side of the stage. The lights came on to reveal a second version of Mira's character's younger self.

He was dressed in a glittery, silvery bodysuit, his hair in a spiky, hedgehog-like style that was very fashionable. Once again, he stood next to a middle-aged man, and his attitude was again full of respect for the man in charge. The middle-aged man here had even more severe features and slicked-back hair.

—*Welcome, young man! We welcome all good ideas and improvement suggestions, which will help us increase our profitability. Oh, profit, that most sacred word in the whole cosmos! You reflect the welfare of all humanity! We need more commerce, more trade, and more contracts to satisfy the demands of others with our supply. While benefiting them we also benefit ourselves!*

The white-robed chorus, of which Luoying was a member, sang for the first time.

—*Oh, that's wonderful, wonderful!*

—*Boss, such wonderful thoughts! I cannot agree with you more. I think my discovery will be perfectly in line with your goals.*

—*Oh? What sort of discovery is that?*

—*I've come up with a plan to streamline our production process. As soon as I arrived, I carefully examined our process chart and added a feedback procedure right here. By my calculations, we can reduce our production time by up to half.*

—*Aha, that is a fantastic discovery. This will lower our costs a great deal.*

—*And our prices, too.*

—*No, the prices will not change.*

—*But… why? If we lower our prices, there'll be many more customers.*

—*Not at all. You're too inexperienced, young man. Do you really think there is a relationship between the price and demand for cancer medication? No matter how high the price, they have to pay. Reducing the cost of production is excellent, but you must never touch our profit. Our profit is social utility! Let's devote our efforts to lowering costs, which will result in ever more profit and more social utility.*

The white-robed chorus raised their voices.

—*Oh, that's wonderful, wonderful!*

The light on the right side of the stage dimmed. Once again Mira appeared on stage, only this time he was sitting. His clothes were even more ragged, and before him, like a hawker at a market, was spread a torn blanket on which were scattered bits of broken glass. As he tried to offer his wares to invisible buyers, he spoke to the audience.

—I was enraged by their plans. They could have reduced their prices to one-eighth what they charged, but they refused to do so. I stole the ingredient list and production method for the medication and found another manufacturer who could make the drug much cheaper. Surely, trying to get medicine to the sick cheaply is a good thing? But they were absolutely outraged and tried to shut me down no matter where I went. Look at the state of my blanket! I was lucky to meet with a lawyer who took me in; otherwise I'd have nothing to eat.

Mira looked toward the center of the stage. A beam of white light from above illuminated a circular area in which Anita, dressed expensively, stood. Bathed in the bright light, she looked like an angel. A third version of Mira's younger self stood next to her.

—Ah, me, unfortunate me. I loved my husband, a great author, but he died too young. He had so many ideas that he hadn't written down.

Anita turned to the new Mira, dressed in worn but clean clothes. He held a piece of white bread and bit into it hungrily as though he hadn't eaten in days. Anita patted him on the shoulder, full of compassion.

—Did you say that you improved your predecessors' technologies?

—Yes. I optimized their production methods.

—Did the previous patent holders agree to have you improve their processes?

—Of course. Why wouldn't they? Only with constant improvement can an idea continue to live.

—Ah, such wise words! What a philosopher you are. You've just given me the solution to the problem that's been bothering me. I'm going to invent the concept of copyright by the dead. If the living can have copyrights, why not the dead? I'm going

to write down his ideas, and anyone who wishes to analyze, quote, or even mention my dead husband's work is going to have to pay me. My husband would surely agree with this. To have profit even after death! That means he will continue to live!

The white-robed chorus sang.

—*Ohhh, that's wonderful, WONDERFUL!*

At that point a large number of characters made their entrances all at once. They rushed about the stage as Anita cradled the mannequin-corpse while negotiating deals, signing contracts, and counting money. Some protested that they would stop analyzing his works if she charged for the privilege, but Anita beckoned them closer to explain that, after paying her, they could turn around and resell the license to someone else for profit. The more deals made, the more profit for everyone. She was going to divide her dead husband's representation rights into a thousand strands and auction them all off until there was a vibrant market of IP derivatives.

It was an idea that would make everyone rich.

The white-robed chorus sang with even more joy.

—*Oh, oh, oh! That's wonderful, wonderful, WONDERFUL!*

Mira, looking like a beggar, clawed his way out of the chaotic crowd on the stage. His hands were empty, having been entirely forgotten. He picked up his small bundle and looked lost. His eyes caught the small boat, as lonesome as he was. He climbed in and quietly rowed his way back to the left side of the stage, the continent where he had started from. Anita and the others disappeared in the darkness.

Despondent, Mira made his way to a small bar and complained to a woman he met there. The woman was extremely interested in his story.

—*Wait, tell me what you said again?*

—*I said that no one cared about my inventions and improvements.*

—*No, not that. What did you say before that?*

—*I was saying that they took a single piece of music and divided it into movements and chapters. By selling the rights to each piece separately, they managed to make a lot of money. They also advertised heavily on the campuses of music schools. Any student who wanted to graduate had to buy the rights owned by many dead composers.*

—*What a brilliant idea! I can do the same myself. I can divide a single article into several chapters and cite my own works. Not only will I have a much larger number of publications, but I'll also be boosting my citation rate. The director of the lab will be so pleased. And it's also a good idea to advertise among the students. If all the students I advise end up citing my papers, I'll look so smart and gain so much prestige. I wish I had thought of this earlier! Now I can gain all kinds of honor and glory, and soon I'll be the youngest, most talented researcher in the whole lab!*

The black-robed chorus, long dormant, finally sang again.

—*Ah, so great, so, so great!*

Since the woman was completely absorbed by her ever-growing dreams of glory, Mira was once again ignored. He sighed and got back on the wheeled boat and paddled his way back and forth between the two continents, alone, aimless, directionless. For a long interval he slowly paddled from the left side to the right side, and silence enveloped everything.

When he arrived on the right side of the stage once more, there was a crowd gathered around a man, interrogating him all at once. The man was having trouble fielding the questions, and when he saw Mira standing by himself, he ran up and grabbed his hand.

—Young man, you must be from the other continent. Wonderful! That therefore makes you completely impartial. These people think our company's mineral health product contains harmful substances, and they won't believe my explanations. Why don't you come and offer a testimony? All you have to do is to read from this.

Then he whispered.

—Whatever you say, they'll believe! I'll pay you a hundred when you are done.

The white-robed chorus began to sing in a mysterious manner.

—Oh, that's wonderful, wonderful.

Mira shook his head, baffled by what was being asked of him.

—You should simply publicize your ingredients and the trials you did to ensure safety. Why do you need me to read your paper?

—No way! This is a trade secret.

—But such information is always publicized on my continent.

—Absolutely not. Publishing the secret will make it impossible to sell.

As the crowd onstage listened to Mira, they shouted: *Investigate! Publish!* They pushed Mira to the front and rushed toward a cardboard skyscraper in the back, raising their fists and shouting, *Transparency! Revolution!* Pamphlets fell from the sky like snowflakes, and the frenzied crowd shouted, *Accounting irregularities! Tax dodgers!*

Mira, pushed and jostled by the crowd, stumbled around. His clothes became torn, as though he were a wild child raised in the jungle, and two pieces of cardboard somehow became attached to his back like wings. Soon the agitated crowd raised a banner with revolution on it and lifted Mira onto their shoulders as they ran into the middle of the stage in a chaotic mob. There was no direction or aim, and their voices merged into a loud cacophony in which no individual sentence could be distinguished.

Then a pointless fight broke out in the thronging mob. Mira was captured by one faction from another and then captured back again. After this happened a few times he was once again forgotten.

But he began to fly. Wires pulled him up into the air, and his cardboard wings flapped, giving him the appearance of a fairy from neverland. A spotlight stayed with him—a lonely light.

After drifting about for a while, he fell. The audience exclaimed in shock. But Mira didn't fall to the ground. Instead, he landed in a net and bounced up and down. Confused, he looked about himself, and two columns of people with serious expressions stared at him from each side.

As the lights came up, the audience realized that the net had been present throughout the show. It was behind the boat that had carried Mira between the two continents and hidden by the darkness. He had never managed to escape the net at all.

Mira sat in the net as though he were waking up in a hammock. His face was blank and innocent. While his eyes roamed from one column of serious people to the other, none of them paid any attention to him. The leaders of both sides seemed to be engaged in some heated negotiation. As they craned their necks and flapped their lips, no sound emerged. Between them was a gigantic balance scale, swaying unsteadily. A lot of weights had already been placed on both pans, but the negotiation had stalled.

One side angrily placed another large weight on the pan before them. The lever pivoted toward them. But the other side nonchalantly tipped the weight that had just been added off the pan, and the balance tilted back toward them. The two sides looked so angry that they seemed about to come to blows.

Just then, one of the leaders stepped forward and urged everyone to calm down. He looked at the other leader and then pointed at Mira, who was still entangled in the net. The other leader nodded, and both walked up to Mira, grabbed him, and tossed him toward the scale. Pulled into the air by wires, Mira tumbled a few times until he landed right on the balance. The beam tilted and then returned to horizontal and held steady. Both sides laughed in satisfaction and shook hands. As they slapped each other on the shoulders, they exchanged two huge bags of goods.

For the first time, both the black-robed and white-robed choruses sang together.

—*Oh, that's wonderful, wonderful! Ah, so great, so, so great!*

The whole stadium was silent. Members of the Mercury Group and invited extras rushed onto the stage all of a sudden and began to dance and run about in circles. After a few turns, they picked up Mira and rushed off, leaving behind an empty stage and an audience with mouths gaping.

The play had come to an end, although there was no ending. Sparse applause rang out here and there, but the actors didn't mind. They didn't even come back onstage to take a bow. The next act and the award ceremony to follow soon caught everyone's attention, and the play was forgotten.

Backstage, the Mercury Group pushed their way through the throng of other performers still waiting for their turns and stadium workers, took off their costumes and makeup, and left in a coordinated fashion. Noiselessly they went through back passages and down little-known back paths until they congregated in the ore yard where Runge was waiting for them.

As soon as Luoying walked into the ore yard, she saw an old mining ship lying in the middle of it like a hungry fish whose maw yawned open.

For the whole day Juan had been feeling unsettled.

In the morning he inspected the new transforming fighters and was satisfied with the results. The fighter model had been under development for many years, and the project had overcome multiple setbacks. At this point it was finally ready to be produced in larger numbers and put into service. Juan felt that a great burden had been lifted from his heart and replaced by a rising sense of ambition. He had been preparing for this day for a long time, and only he knew the price he had had to pay.

As the metal doors of the aerospace center slowly slid open before him, he saw rows of brand-new fighters arranged like loyal and brave warriors in gleaming armor standing at attention in a phalanx. The silvery wingtips shone in the bright sunlight, bringing to him a wave of unspeakable joy and a sense of hope. He seemed to see the curtains being pulled open on a new act in the drama that was history, silently but full of grand significance. He knew that there was no fleet in history that could surpass this one. He was already writing history.

After the inspection, he went to the surveillance center. Theoretically, the city's security was not part of the Flight System's responsibilities. But he had been insistent that an atelier under the administration of the Flight System devote its resources to researching a real-time surveillance system that was even more comprehensive and capable than the one in use. The goal was clear: to lay the foundation for the future fleet's needs and to develop the technologies necessary for espionage and counterespionage.

There was a room in this surveillance center from where it was possible to see every corner of the city on screens, just like in the control room of the official surveillance center. This was not exactly in accordance with the laws and regulations of the republic, but Juan had always protected its existence with his own power.

He had a premonition that something was wrong. Although the inspection of the new fighters had revealed nothing, he decided to come to the surveillance center to see for himself.

The newly developed "Swarm"-style electronic eye system was in operation, which transmitted to the surveillance center live footage from every part of the city. At first, as he glanced through the screens, he saw nothing out of the ordinary. Citizens were busy at work or enjoying their leisure time, each in their expected place. Silently, Juan flipped through the images. East, south, west, north. Three cargo transporters were taking off from the eastern edge of the city, and a mining ship was passing through Gate Twelve, on the southern edge of the city.

A strange hunch guided Juan's attention to Gate Twelve. He called for the feed from that area to be magnified. Every day, mining and prospecting vehicles left the city, but there was something about this ship that bothered him; maybe it was the appearance of the ship, or the youths talking silently in the video feed.

The camera zoomed in until it was possible to see the faces of the conversing youths clearly. Juan was pleased with the capabilities of the electronic eyes. As he was trying to identify the boy in the scene, who looked familiar, Luoying's face appeared. She climbed out of the mining ship and stood next to the boy, smiling sweetly as she spoke to the gatekeeper.

"Turn on the audio," Juan whispered.

The operator nodded and turned on the audio feed.

"Thank you. We'll keep that in mind."

That was all he heard. While Luoying's voice still echoed in the surveillance room, he watched as the two youths climbed back into the ship. Like a clumsy, aged dinosaur, the mining ship slowly crawled forward, passing under the raised gate.

Juan called Hans and reported what he had seen. "You are certain she mentioned nothing of this to you?"

"I really have no idea," said Hans.

"Then should I start an investigation? Or perhaps send a team after them?"

Hans hesitated. Then, calmly, he said, "Don't do anything yet. Let me do some checking and call you back."

Hans's image vanished from the screen. Juan was surprised that the consul didn't look shocked or anxious. Sitting before the control panel, Juan frowned and felt rage rising in his heart. He didn't care why the youths had left the city; the reasons weren't important. But he did care that the security regulations had been bypassed so easily. If the youths had managed to leave the city without official approval, then it was a sign that the city's security measures were much too lax. The city leaked like a sieve, without discipline or a mind-set for security. He slammed his fist onto the panel.

He had no choice but to wait for Hans. Staring at the buttons before him, he was baffled by his friend's seeming lack of concern.

For most adult citizens of Mars, the day was just an ordinary day, no different from the hundreds of other days in the year. Although young people were immersed in the excitement of the

Creativity Fair, most adults, busy with work, weren't infected by the mood.

Radio antenna arrays neatly arranged around the perimeter of the city worked tirelessly, like spinning silkworms, to send data into the storage buffers. From there, the strands of data flowed into the processing center, where they were woven into dense pictures displayed on the screens of the researchers. The researchers worked hard to stay ahead of the data, telling themselves to *hurry, hurry*. Important discoveries were hidden in the trove of data, and they had to rush to dig out the jewels. New equipment, new instruments, new methods, had returned them to a bygone, prescientific age when documents and information overwhelmed the ability of humankind to process them. The researchers wished they had been blessed with the gift of intuition and buried themselves deeper in their work.

Molecular assembly lines all over the city carried out their operations meticulously and precisely. One after another, electrons flowed through the microchannels that had been carefully crafted to guide them. Molecules danced like millions of waltzing couples, changing partners constantly. Engineers sitting before the screens, however, weren't in the mood to share in their joy. Their electronic folders were full of papers on control theory, engineering management, molecular assembly theory, and so on. To become an expert in any subject required years of dedication. They sighed inside, lamenting that they had been born in the wrong age, when it was almost impossible to improve upon what was known. Their ambitions frustrated, they decided to pay more attention to gourmet cooking and other hobbies.

The city policy makers were also busy and overworked. The leaders of the nine systems met frequently to discuss the contemplated uses of the water from Ceres, potentially the biggest policy change in postwar Martian history. Grave expressions on their faces, brimming with confidence and sense of responsibility, they debated in the shadow of history and with the aid of computer simulations of the future. The new mega-engineering project was about to start, and the key technologies were on the verge of breakthroughs. The final decision was about to emerge.

On the farms, the cows were unconcerned with anything except grazing. From time to time they looked up, contemplated the sun outside the glass dome, and shook their heads sadly. Carp in the aquaculture tanks had become used to the new plants in the tanks and no longer reacted with agitation when people passed by. Adapting to change was the key to life; this was a truth even they understood.

Such an ordinary day, when engineers were busy, when youths were absorbed by the Creativity Fair, when teachers were with their students, was perfect for escaping.

Warren Sangis was a low-ranking researcher with the Land System who had been assigned for the day to watch over the gate mainly used by mining vehicles entering and leaving the city. He was neither talented nor ambitious, and sought to do the bare minimum needed to maintain his position. No curiosity for the bigger picture lurked in his mind.

For Warren, however, today would be no ordinary day. For the first time, Martha, the woman he pined after, had agreed to go out with him on a date, and he had no idea he would be punished for the first time in his life for negligence as well. When he pressed the button to open the layers of airlocks, he had no idea of the implications of this tiny action. He was simply thinking about Martha, who was in the control room with him, and paid no attention to anything outside.

The old mining ship slowly drifted over the yellow sand. Inside, the aromas of delicious cooking permeated the air.

The ship, several generations out of date, was near retirement. The dirt-yellow hull was like a moving dune. During the first years after the war, it and its companions had been instrumental in the effort to rebuild, and a large portion of the heavy metals in the city had come out of its digging claws. Back then, a mining ship had to plan to stay out in the wild for days on each trip, and the hull was thus thick like the walls of a castle. Inside, there were cooking facilities and sleeping quarters. Though the equipment was old and outdated, everything necessary was present.

The bulkheads inside the ship had been removed so that the interior was one contiguous space used by the present crew as a feast hall. The steel racks for securing instruments had been taken off the walls and lay flat on the floor, while the partitions for the sleeping quarters had been placed atop the racks, forming two large tables that were then pushed together. The long-fringed satin tablecloth had once served as curtains at the Terran Fair but had been abandoned in the Expo Center after the Terrans left.

The table was now covered by heaping plates. The flatware, taken from the cabinets of different families, made a colorful mosaic. Those who hadn't brought plates contributed silverware, glassware, spices, and so on. The potluck meal looked as colorful and crowded as a traveling circus. Runge had stolen an internship permit to get them out of the city, and the plan was to return the permit before they were discovered.

Noise and laughter filled the ship. Bottles were opened and glasses clinked. Bubbles burst against the glass, and liquid occasionally spilled onto the tablecloth, blooming into dark flowers.

By the time Aina brought the last dish to the table and declared an official start to the feast, the crew had already consumed six bottles of Gio. Everyone got up with a loud cheer, put away the playing cards and empty bottles, and soon arranged the dishes on the table neatly.

"Cheers!"

A circle of glasses rose over their heads like a rising tide.

WIND

The crew tucked in with gusto. Aina's culinary skills had improved even more. According to her, after returning to Mars, the only activity that brought her any joy was cooking.

Aina had outdone herself this time. Fluffy golden cakes, beef and egg noodles, carrot cheesecakes, assorted vegetables flavored with fish flakes, seaweed salad, nuts and bamboo shoots, Ashala-style apple tarts, chicken soup with sweet corn... The mouthwatering flavors and aromas filled the ship, and laughter mixed with the sound of coughing from drinking too much wine too fast.

A total of twelve had made it to the mining ship: four girls and eight boys. They sat around the table in one large circle, totally relaxed. While the boys leaned over the table in debate, the girls chatted with each other as they peeled and ate fruit. Outside the portholes was the unvarying sight of the yellow sand and rocks. The ship proceeded so steadily that it was sometimes impossible to detect that they were moving.

"Are you all procrastinating on your reports?" asked Anita.

"Um... did you turn yours in already?" asked Mira.

Anita laughed. "I haven't even started. If none of you have turned yours in, then I feel better."

"Who's got time for that?" said Sorin. "I've been much too busy with the play."

"And what's the point of rushing?" said Mira. "Maybe we won't even have to finish the reports."

"What do you mean by that?" asked Anita.

"We got out of the city without proper authorization," said Mira. "If we're caught, I expect we'll each have to write a thirty-thousand-word apology report and then do community service labor for two months. Who knows what other punishments they'll impose on us after that? Maybe by then they'll forget about the Earth reports."

Chania brought out a plate of pears, and everyone exclaimed over the treat. Luoying looked on as her friends enjoyed themselves, taking delight in the familiar patterns. *This is my tribe*, she thought. Although she liked Gielle and the others, she had never felt this comfortable with them. On this ship she felt like she belonged. *Why?* she asked herself. *How do I describe this difference?*

They continued to make their way south. The afternoon sun sank lower in the western sky, and the mood turned indolent after such a feast. On the walls of the cabin hung robot arms from an earlier age, the mechanical fingers squeezed into angular fists, somber, antique witnesses of their revelry. The exposed pipes had chipped paint, and the sound of water circulating rumbled within. The oxygen circulation intakes in the ceiling gaped like mouths gulping the warm air.

Anka and Runge were in the cockpit, pulling levers and shutting valves, fingers dancing over the buttons on the instrument panels as though playing a piano. Anka was in charge of the piloting, so he remained at the front of the ship. Runge, on the other hand, was operating the instruments, so he returned to the panels only periodically to keep an eye on the dancing needles on the ancient dials.

"Do you think our play will lead to anything?" asked

Runge when he returned to the dining table from the cockpit.

"Hard to say," said Sorin. "I imagine the adults won't react at all except with silence."

"I agree," said Runge. "But even if they don't say anything in public, privately they'll find us to talk."

"How should we respond?"

"Tell the truth, of course. Everything we said in the play was based on personal experience. We have nothing to hide."

"I don't mean that," said Sorin. "I'm asking... if the adults ask what our plan is, how should we answer?"

"Still the truth. We don't plan on cooperating with them anymore."

Sorin looked at the others in the cabin.

The mood grew serious. Luoying wasn't sure what Runge meant. Runge had always been insightful but confrontational, making dramatic and exaggerated statements. She couldn't tell what exactly was involved in not cooperating with the adults. Sitting next to the window, Runge drummed his fingers against the table, a determined, defiant expression on his face. Silently the other youths looked at each other. Chania got up and stood next to him.

"I've been meaning to ask the same question, actually. What *is* our plan going forward?"

"Are you suggesting..." Luoying couldn't finish.

"Revolution," declared Chania. "A real revolution."

"I thought the play was the revolution," said Luoying quietly. "I never said that."

"*I* said that," explained Sorin to Luoying. He turned back to Chania. "But I thought you agreed at the time."

"I've always said this is only the first phase."

"So what more are we going to do?" asked Luoying.

"Break things," said Chania. "Shatter what has ossified."

"I agree," said Runge. "I can't stand it anymore. Look at the others around us: what a bunch of shameless phonies! The only thing they care about is pleasing their superiors, to get ahead by whatever means, to craft their research to fit the tastes of the system directors. Everything is corrupted by the desire for status and gain—everything!"

"How is that any different from Earth?" asked Sorin.

"At least Terrans aren't hypocrites," shot back Runge. "They are selfish, and proudly proclaim that fact. But here everyone spouts wonderful-sounding ideals: 'The pursuit of each individual for creative expression and wisdom!' But underneath, the only thing that matters is selfish gain. Phonies, every single one of them."

"I don't think that's fair," said Luoying. "I think many are genuinely motivated by and interested in exploration."

"I've never met a single person like that," said Runge. "I don't believe there's anyone not driven by self-interest."

"I think you've been brainwashed by Terran propaganda," said Sorin.

"Can you find anyone who doesn't act for their own benefit and to accrue more power for themselves?"

"There are some."

"Then they're just putting on a good act."

"How do you explain the people who spend all their time in the labs doing research and nothing else? No self-promotion, no recognition seeking."

"They just want to be admired as saints. There's always an angle."

Softly, Luoying broke in. "Why are we arguing about this? What's the point?"

"The point is," said Runge, "we must force everyone to

admit the selfish utilitarian basis for what they do, to pull off the cover of hypocrisy and discard the lies."

"Are you suggesting that we return to the system on Earth, where everything is based on money?"

Chania answered before Runge could. "At a minimum we must make the selfishness transparent. It's unbearable to live with dishonesty and self-deception."

Sorin looked into Chania's eyes. "Then you're with Runge?"

"I am."

"What specifically do you think we should do?"

"First, we should untether people from their ateliers so that they can move about freely. Housing should also become more free-flowing, like the wind. Our current system ties people permanently to one place. Superficially there is no competition, but under the surface the struggle is fierce."

"You know as well as I do that there aren't enough resources on Mars to allow people to compete for them freely. That's why there's a distribution system in place."

"The same excuse has been used for decades. Enough is enough."

"Chania"—Sorin looked at her with a worried expression—"you're too extreme."

Chania didn't respond, but she didn't look away either. She pressed her lips together and tilted her head defiantly.

A long moment of silence later, Mira said in a lackadaisical manner, "There will always be hypocrites. It's really not a big deal."

"Cynicism is easy," said Runge. "Too easy."

Mira frowned and looked as if he were thinking over Runge's words carefully. Meanwhile, Luoying felt close to exploding with words, but she didn't know where to start. Runge and Chania, standing and sitting by the window, looked more resolute than anyone else. Though they weren't moving stiffly, they seemed to be made of steel. The mood in the cabin was icy.

"Hey, Runge!"

Anka's call from the cockpit broke the tension. He turned around and beckoned at everyone.

"Come up here, all of you! I think we're almost there."

The argument was forgotten as everyone squeezed into the cockpit, gazing out the windshield and at the navigation displays.

Through the windshield, the crew could see that the mining ship was passing through a narrow, curved canyon. The rugged terrain slowed the ship down, while the towering fire-red cliffs were so high that it was impossible to see the peaks. The sun illuminated the top of the cliffs, and the jagged rocks cast deep and dark crescent-shaped shadows against the cliff faces. The youths pressed against the glass, gazing up at the sheer rock walls, excited by the prospect of slowly sailing into another world. On the contour-lined navigation display, the mining ship was a tiny dot inching between two dense clusters of curved lines.

"Do you think this is it?" Anka asked Runge, pointing to a spot on the screen.

Runge nodded.

Anka looked back at Luoying. "I'm not sure if this is the exact spot you're looking for, but it's the best we can do based on the information we've been able to gather."

As he talked, the ship emerged from the canyon and sunlight filled the cabin, haloing every head. They looked out the windshield and froze.

Before them was a delta-shaped flat expanse nestled among the plateaus and peaks all around. The long slopes were filled with deep channels, like a landscape eroded by rivers or carved by glaciers, although there wasn't a single drop of water. But eons of erosion by wind had ripped away all the regolith to reveal the angular basalt skeleton. The mountains rose into the air nearly a kilometer.

Their ship was at the entrance to the delta, like a tiny bug crawling along the foot of the mountains. The gray-brown crater was like a gigantic version of the Colosseum, open to the sky, vast and magnificent.

The northern hemisphere of Mars was dominated by broad, flat lowlands, while the southern hemisphere was full of highlands and mountains. The average elevation of the southern hemisphere was about four thousand meters higher than the average elevation of the northern hemisphere. A six-thousand-meter-tall cliff slashed across the face of the planet like a knife scar near the equator.

The young crew of the mining ship was stunned by the sight. They had never entered the mountains of southern Mars, although they had grown up on this planet. While they had seen plenty of mountains and valleys on Earth, compared to the mountains of Mars, all those geographical features looked as cute as miniatures in some theme park. Even Mount Everest was only a third as tall as Olympus Mons, and the Grand Canyon was only a fifth as long as Valles Marineris. On Mars, there were no mountains with a gentle and refined beauty. All peaks looked rough, sharp, as though they had been carved with axes out of primordial rock during Creation. Calderas and craters pockmarked the landscape, like a weary traveler's face that recorded his suffering.

They saw no obvious signs of human presence. Though the historical records told them that once this place had been full of mines and prospectors, before them now lay only the empty crater and silent, frozen lava, with no traces left of the once bustling camp. The narrow pass they had just come out of had once seen thousands of mining vehicles pass through, and the mountains around them had housed tens of thousands. A whole industry had operated here, but nothing was left of it. Their eyes roamed over the crater, searching for signs of dwellings made from spaceship hulls and abandoned ruins, but other than a few metallic fragments at the feet of the mountains, they saw nothing significant. Wind and sand had destroyed everything, until only flowing rivers of sand were left. Only forty years had passed, but already nature had wiped away the work of humankind, the landscape relapsing to an ancient, eternal desolation.

Nonetheless, they knew beyond any doubt that they had found the right place.

They saw the caves, some of them high up the mountainsides. They didn't look too different from other wind-eroded caves, but the openings had clearly been shaped and sculpted. The mouths of the caves, though half-buried in sand, still showed the smoothness of human hands. As they stared at the sand that concealed history, they seemed to see ghostly images of men and women climbing over the mountains. It was as if magical hands had swept away the rubble piled at the abandoned cave openings and blown away the sand covering the windows until the dead scene slowly came to life again. They saw people going in and out of the caves, shuttles flying overhead, a whole city built into the mountainside bustling between sky and ground.

It was finally time to fly.

The mining ship stopped at the foot of the mountain on the south side of the crater, bathed in bright sunlight.

Three boys opened the airlock and exited the ship with

oxygen supplies, helmets, comms headsets, and emergency toolkits strapped to their bodies, as well as pressure sensors secured on their backs. Carefully they confirmed the direction of the wind and spread their dragonfly-like double wings in the sun's bright rays. Everything was progressing well. Soon they turned on the high-pressure air nozzles at their feet, and as the propellers under their boots spun, they rose into the air.

As the three rose higher and higher, the others let out their held breaths and cheered.

Luoying was standing in the back of the group, feeling strange. She had been looking forward to this day for a long time, but now that it was here, she didn't feel it was different from any other moment on an ordinary day. The sun warmed her like ethereal music. The dream of flying had become reality, as unremarkable as a distant but familiar smile. She found the tranquil mood around her odd. Through the oxygen masks, the boys in the air danced like fairies in stories.

The boys drifted up, following the contours of the steep mountainside. Sorin was the most athletic, and he twisted his ankles to leap higher with the wind at every opportunity. Leon, on the other hand, moved languidly and smoothly. Anka allowed himself to be carried up by the wind, turning away from the rock face at the last minute. Contrasted with the gigantic wings, their bodies seemed even more slender as they floated with the wind.

They were flying, truly flying, with the aid of wings spread against the bright red sky. Recognition of this fact finally excited Luoying.

This was their final trial. Discarding cockpits, seats, and engines, they returned to the oldest dream of humankind: pairs of wings over the shoulders, tiny propellers underfoot. The four wings on each of their backs were equipped with a powerful photoelectric coating, and the electricity vibrated the wings at a high frequency, like a giant dragonfly's. The wings were attached to the fliers with a strong but light alloy frame. The point wasn't to break speed records but to stay aloft in the wind.

They shifted to turn into the wind. The geography of Mars was unique. Under direct sunlight, ground temperature could reach as high as the teens in degrees Celsius. But at night the temperature could plunge to a hundred degrees below zero. The clearly delineated warm and cold regions meant strong and rapid winds. A steep mountainside exposed to direct sunlight warmed up quickly, and the warm air rose along the slope, forming strong currents. In the afternoon such winds were at their strongest. The bright light excited the young crew as well as the air molecules. Even the sparse atmosphere provided enough lift.

The higher the boys rose, the stronger the wind became. When they were halfway up the mountain, the boys ascended even faster. For safety, they reduced the power to the propellers and the frequency of the wing vibrations. They fell at an even pace back down to the ground and, after a few stumbling steps, stood still.

Instantly the rest of the crew surrounded them, and inaudible cheers filled the thin air. Before the three could fold their wings back, the rest had grabbed them by the arms, knocking their helmets to congratulate them. Luoying could see the smiles under the helmet visors, as bright as the sky.

This was their second celebration of the day. The headsets filled with loud cheers.

The boys soon got out of their wings, and others took their places. The second set of fliers took off. In total there were six sets of wings.

"Girls, do you want to fly, too?" Sorin asked.

While Luoying hesitated, Chania stood up and stretched her limbs. She held her hands together and reached as high as she could, kicking her feet out as she stood on tiptoe. Then she rested her hands on her waist while she twisted and bent, loosening her muscles. She smiled at Luoying and ran over to the wings. The visor of her helmet revealed her bright eyes, an echo of the shimmering appendages.

A gust carried invisible particles of sand across Luoying's visor. The second wave of fliers had learned from the experience of the first and flew with more ease. The memory of their experience in the weightless gym of *Maearth* had returned to their bodies, and they fell back into old patterns: twisting, flexing, finding balance. The boys began a game of tag in the air while Chania zipped between them like a nimble celesta among strings and woodwinds. They seemed to have returned to those carefree nights between planets. Without the free play of those suspended days, they wouldn't have been able to fly so well so quickly. Months later, the blood and air of freedom once again surrounded them.

Against the undulating rim of the crater, light and shadow created a chiaroscuro of yellow and black.

Luoying was still gazing at the sight, a bit stunned, when Anka appeared next to her.

"Want to fly together?"

As though inviting her to dance, Anka held out one hand and took a step back.

She smiled. "Just a moment. I'm going to put on my costume."

The costume that Gielle had made for her had not been used since that disastrous performance. Luoying had held it up inside the mining ship, hesitating. In the end she put it on and carefully tied the sash, as well as the metallic filaments securing it to her wrists and ankles.

By the time she walked back into the light, she was again the dancer. She gave Anka her hand and, with a gentle push, he sent her into the air.

The moment she was off the ground, Luoying swayed a few times from side to side. The wind was light and fast, and the pressure sensors conveyed the constantly changing sensations to her body gently and intuitively. The wings were much larger than the last time she had tried them, and so at first her touch felt stiff. Gradually, as she grew used to the sensations, her movements became more fluid. She trusted herself to the air currents, letting the wind take the lead in the dance. Forgetting about directions, her body felt liberated.

Anka was right behind Luoying, a bit off to the side. The buffer between them served as a guide. Luoying adjusted the direction of the wings and the angle of the propellers so that she followed his shoulders through the air. Every gesture and movement had to be completed deliberately, as though they were in some carefully choreographed slow-motion sequence, moving in sync. She felt safe and settled. With Anka and the wind on her back, she no longer felt anxious. Joy suffused her body, and she remembered her time on Earth, when she would turn off the lights after a practice session, swinging her limbs loosely about as though she were a puppet. Through the windows of the studio she would see the giant advertising displays on the skyscraper opposite, and a million bright lights glowed in the city, with her suspended among them.

Dancing in the air had been her vision, and it was she who had suggested to Anka and the rest that, to control the wings, they didn't need complicated programs or intensive computation; instead, they could rely on the human body's instincts. Walking and dancing were skills etched into the body over eons of evolution, and they could control the wings with their muscles, the way real dragonflies did.

The boot that Reini had fitted her with also helped. The neural feedback mechanism of the boot was adapted to connect the wings to the flier's body, to amplify the movements.

Dexterously, Luoying flew through the air. She squinted and allowed her mind to be filled with visions. She saw herself standing on an endless plain, buffeted by winds from all sides, and the sand that scraped against her skin was accompanied by laughter and joyous voices. In one gust of wind, she saw the smiles of the girls from her dance troupe back on Earth, dressed in elaborate, jewel-studded costumes and waving at her from the clouds. In another gust she heard the shouts of the girls who had shared that old house with her, draped in grass-woven outfits and holding ancient shields. With yet another gust she saw Gielle and Brenda sitting on nutshell-shaped kites and painting houses in the air, blushing as they cried in surprise. Luoying wanted to stop, to freeze the scenes, but the wind was too fast, and soon they were beyond the horizon.

She seemed to sense groups of people in every current, living their own lives, but she didn't seem to belong to any of them. She felt the wind coming at her from every direction and leaving her for every quarter of the compass, but she remained rooted in place, unable to ride along on any of the winds. She belonged to none of them and didn't know how to gather others to her. She was no longer someone who could be carried away by the wind. The harder the winds blew, the less inclined she was to go with them. She wanted to fly, but only alone.

She luxuriated in the slowly slanting afternoon sun, twisting her wings to achieve the best angle in the air, feeling Anka keeping pace behind her, neither too far nor too near. She wanted to fly like this forever and never land.

———

"Someone's coming!"

The warning squawked in the headsets, as abrupt as an alarm.

"Land immediately," Runge commanded. "If you can return to the ship safely, do so. Otherwise, hide in the cliffs and we'll come get you later."

Luoying didn't have time to think. She and Anka immediately landed on a ledge jutting out of the cliff next to them and furled their wings.

They hadn't realized just how high they had flown—higher than any of the other groups. There was no time to get back to the ground. The ledge was in front of an abandoned cave, and they could still see signs of a collapsed staircase at one end. Sitting down on the ledge, they looked below. Mira and Sorin had landed at the mouth of another cave much lower down on the cliffside, while the others had successfully retreated to the mining ship, which was now slowly crawling toward a nook deep in the shadows at the foot of the cliff.

Soon they saw a gigantic ground-effect vehicle peeking out from the narrow pass they had come through earlier. Silver-hulled and red-striped, a flame emblem glowing near the tip, it moved slowly, as though searching for something.

"That's... from my squadron," said Anka.

"Why is it here?" asked Luoying.

Anka shook his head, his expression somber. Luoying was grateful that Runge had been so alert.

SAND

Hugging the rim, the big ship slowly patrolled inside the crater. Second by second, it approached their position.

Anka and Luoying concealed themselves behind piles of loose rocks on the ledge. The big ship didn't extend any visible probes, but they didn't know if it had other sensors scanning the area. From where they were, it was impossible to see Runge's mining ship. Hopefully he had managed to find some secluded hiding spot. They didn't know why the big ship was here, but instinct told them that it was best to not be found.

"Do you think it's here to look for us?" asked Luoying.

"I don't know," said Anka. "We slipped away from the city without triggering any alarms, so I don't think this is meant for us."

Luoying nodded. "I agree. I can't imagine they'd go to so much trouble for a bunch of teenagers."

"Well, I don't know if that's true," said Anka.

"Even if we're found, they'll just take us back, right? It's no big deal."

"I just don't know."

"We've had a very successful day," said Luoying. "We flew; we saw the ruins. Even if we have to go back, I don't mind."

"We don't know what the ship is doing here. Most likely it

has nothing to do with us. But it would be better if we aren't found and can go back to the city on our own terms."

"All right. Let's wait a bit."

The sun was low in the west, and the shadows on the cliffside grew deeper and sharper. The big ship made it most of the way around the crater without stopping as it passed directly below them. Continuing west, it stopped in the middle of the crater. An antenna extended out of the bow of the ship and swung around in a circle before retracting.

The ship stayed still. For Luoying, leaning against Anka, the moment seemed to last forever.

The evening wind picked up. Loose sand, swept up in the gusts, struck the hull of the ship, the only movement in the crater.

Finally the big ship began to move again. Slowly it departed the crater the way it had come. Luoying let out a sigh and relaxed. The westering sun shone on the stern of the ship, casting a long shadow ahead of the hull on the yellow sand, like a long, black sword probing over the ground.

―――――――

The wind grew—not the warm rising currents of the afternoon, but the chaotic turbulence of the cooling air of nightfall.

The swirling gusts, sweeping off the ground, filled the air with sand. Loose pebbles rolled along sloping surfaces, and sand scraped past their survival suits like streams of refugees escaping war. Red dust coated their visors. Shielding Luoying with his body, Anka guided her deeper inside the mouth of the cave. They crouched behind a pile of loose rubble. From time to time, a strong gust dislodged some pebbles from the top, and Anka would raise an arm protectively over Luoying's head.

Leaning against Anka's shoulder, Luoying suddenly thought

that her own great-grandmother probably felt just as protected and safe during that storm decades ago.

The longest half hour of Luoying's life later, Runge's voice crackled to life in their headsets.

"Luoying, Anka, Mira, Sorin, report! Are you all right?"

Anka jumped up. "Luoying and I are fine. Where are you?"

"We went through a canyon and found a whole new world—never mind, I'll give you the details later. We're coming back to get you now. Can you land safely?"

They leaned over the ledge and saw that the mining ship was swaying into view. In the twilight, the ship's outline was blurred. Anka and Runge spoke over the comm link, making preparations for opening the airlock to welcome Anka and Luoying.

Anka leaped down from the ledge and descended slowly toward the mining ship. Luoying took a deep breath and followed.

All of a sudden she felt her body pelted by a torrent of sand. Before she could react, she found herself falling, out of control as she lost all sense of balance. Her vision was a blur, and she didn't even have time to be scared.

The next minute was all chaos: strong currents gripping her legs like invisible claws; red sand; clashing winds; massive turbulence; wings out of control; being thrown; sky where the ground was supposed to be and vice versa; the red cliffside looming into view; an arm grabbing her around the waist and letting go; someone holding her up; the sensation of two feet on solid ground and the instinctive tensing of muscles as her fingers found something to grab on to.

By the time she finally recovered, Luoying found herself lying prone on a slope, hands tightly clutching protruding rocks. Her wings were hopelessly vibrating on her back. Next to her was Anka, crouching in a similar pose. Sand and gravel rolled past them in streams.

STARS

As sand flowed past her, Luoying dared not look up.

The slope she was on wasn't too steep, and her feet found purchase. She knew she could hold on for at least a while, though she didn't know how much longer the wind whipping about her would last. Like all children born on Mars, she understood the danger of dust storms.

She turned her head to the side and locked eyes with Anka, who nodded at her. His blue eyes were like the sea in the deepening twilight, and in their depths she saw serenity. Luoying snapped the switch that shut off the vibrating wings, waiting patiently for the storm to pass.

"Can you hear me?" Anka's voice crackled in her headset.

Luoying nodded. Her throat was too dry for her to speak.

"Look up and to your right," said Anka. "See that large boulder? Do you think you can climb up to it?"

Luoying looked where he was pointing, about twenty to thirty meters upslope. She squeezed her fingers to keep herself calm and strained to smile at Anka. "No problem."

Anka got up first and then helped her up. Slowly they made their way toward the boulder, deliberate step by deliberate step. Luoying made sure that three of her limbs were in contact with the side of the mountain at all times. Anka was to her left and below, not touching her, but ready to catch her if she should fall. The short climb took them a very long time. Finally, Anka climbed onto the boulder—which turned out to be another ledge—and reached down to help her up.

The two rested for a while to catch their breath. Luoying cleared her throat and asked, "I guess we're stuck up here?"

Anka pointed to the swirling sand below them. "It's too late in the day now. The wind has shifted to the wrong direction. We'll die if we try to jump down."

"What should we do?"

"Let's discuss it with Runge."

Luoying leaned over the edge of the platform. The mining ship remained where it was at the bottom of the crater. The two of them, however, had been carried to the east, closer to the pass. From this distance, the mining ship reminded her of a clumsy turtle crawling slowly toward them. The dust storm hung between them like a translucent orange curtain, and the temperature was plunging. They were about forty meters above the crater floor, too high to jump. Anka screamed into the mic, hoping that the crew of the ship could see them. The wireless system they used was extremely primitive, with a range of under a hundred meters. At first they received no answer. Only when the mining ship was directly below them did Runge's voice emerge from the headset.

"Are you all right?"

"Yes, but we're probably stuck here for the night." Anka got to the point right away.

"How much oxygen do you have left?"

Anka glanced at the display on the oxygen bottle. "Should be enough to last until noon tomorrow."

"Are you safe where you are?"

"Pretty safe. I took a quick look around. Behind us is an abandoned cave that we can use as shelter."

"I'm afraid there's no choice but to have you stay there for the night," said Runge resignedly. "We'll find a way to rescue you in the morning."

"We'll be fine," said Anka. "Why don't you head back to the city? You can send a rescue team tomorrow morning."

"What's the matter? Don't you trust me?"

Even through the headset Luoying could picture Runge's grinning face.

"I'd trust you with my life," said Anka, also smiling.

"Then don't make ridiculous suggestions. We'll wait right here tonight. If anything changes, call."

"Definitely."

"I'm really sorry about this," said Luoying. "Now we all have to be out here the whole night because of me."

"I don't want to go back anyway." The speaker this time was Mira. "It's not easy to get out here. I want to do more sightseeing."

"Mira!" said Luoying. "I'm glad you got back to the ship safely."

"I'm back… though not exactly safely."

"What happened?"

"I twisted my ankle."

Runge broke in to explain. "He and Leon basically rolled down the slope. He's lucky he didn't break a leg."

"Did you get it taken care of?" asked Luoying anxiously.

"I taped it," said Mira, his voice easy and carefree. "I'll be fine."

"It seems to be a pattern with you getting hurt every time we're out," said Anka, laughing. "Do you remember that time in Barcelona with the hot-air balloons?"

Mira guffawed. "That wasn't my fault! Who could have predicted a thunderstorm? Bad luck."

"We both fell, but only you broke a leg."

"I seem to recall you broke your leg in Tokyo, too."

"That's not the same thing at all. The next time there's an earthquake when you're trying to take off, I want to see how you handle it."

"I can't wait," said Mira. "The next time we fly, we should do it at Olympus Mons. I'm sure I'll fly higher than you."

"Listen to you! The tallest peak in the Solar System is no joke."

"Who's joking? I've been planning this. I'm going to fly through all the major sights of Mars. Valles Marineris is next. And also Hellas crater, probably a hundred times the size of this one."

"All right," said Anka with a chuckle. "If you dare to go, I'll be there with you."

Night fell. Luoying sat on the flat ledge, listening to Anka and Mira banter as the last rays of the sun disappeared behind the western rim. She drew up her knees and massaged her lower legs. The fall had hurt her kneecap and leg, and exhaustion sharpened the pain. Anka stayed busy even as he was chatting. He moved the rocks blocking the mouth of the cave out of the way until there was enough space for them to squeeze inside.

The cave had probably been eroded out of the mountainside by wind. Here the cliff curled around, and the wind, deflected into a sharp curve, carved a smooth opening between the massive rocks. Luoying followed Anka into the cave, where the faint starlight failed to penetrate the inky darkness. As Luoying felt her way along the cave wall, her fingers sensed the signs of human work. There were cubbies carved into the rock, as well as a long water basin dug along the foot of the wall. Her feet crunched over collapsed and broken furniture. The cave wall had been smoothed by tools, though it was nowhere as polished as the walls at home.

To conserve their energy supply for the night, Anka had turned off the two-way wireless with the mining ship. He unfolded his wings and secured them at the mouth of the cave as a simple barrier. Then he sat down to modify the equipment.

"It's too dim in here," he muttered as he tried to see the electric motor of the wings in the faint starlight. "This is harder than I expected…"

"What are you trying to do?"

"I was hoping to disassemble one of the wings and connect the battery to the two ends. The conducting veins in the wings can function as a heater for us during the night."

"I didn't know you're so handy with circuits."

"I wouldn't say handy, but all of us worked on the wings, so I know them well."

"What about my costume?"

Luoying took off her dance costume, which she had worn outside the survival suit, and handed it to Anka. The costume was so light that it was like handling a cloud of puffy mist.

"The material is luminescent," she explained. "Maybe there's a way to light it up."

Anka nodded. "I'll give it a try."

He stepped outside the cave, bringing a battery and the costume with him. Crouched in the moonlight, he tried to figure out how to turn the costume into a lamp. Luoying watched him crouch on one knee, his body a dark silhouette with a silvery glow on top of his head.

She shivered from the cold. The air temperature was now below zero, but she had been too nervous until now to notice. The formfitting survival suits they wore provided only the most basic protection, without heating elements. Since Anka was even more exposed and hadn't moved in a while, she began to worry that he had frozen like a statue.

Just as she was about to go out of the cave to check on him, Anka came in.

"All set," he said.

There was a glowing semispherical ball of mist in his hand, as delicate as a luminescent seashell. As he carefully stepped inside, her costume shifted through a spectrum of translucent colors, the hues flowing and swirling. The eye-catching magnificence of the stage had turned into something gentler and more lasting here, like a soft, lingering song.

After Anka placed the makeshift lamp in the middle of the room, the two took a good look at their surroundings. It had once been a living room of some kind. There was a table carved out of sandstone next to one of the inner walls, though only half of it was still standing. Hooks for hanging clothes could be seen on some of the still-intact wall sections. The decaying ruin painted a sketch of the lives that had once flourished here.

"We're lucky to have found this place," said Anka. He examined the cross section of a broken wall carefully. "There's a layer of insulation and another layer that absorbs radiation. We might not last the night if we were exposed in the open."

"Don't we need heat, though?"

"Are you cold?"

"A little."

"It's going to get a lot colder during the night." Anka lifted the bundles of folded-up wings. "Give me a hand, please."

They unfolded a pair of wings, which were too large for the narrow space and had to be twisted and bent to fit. Carefully, Anka showed Luoying how to bend the wings into arches and erect them on the ground like a tree-branch shelter on some island. Anka brought over more batteries. Sitting near the wing roots, he began to pick apart the complicated wires.

Carefully, he attached wires from the wing tips and roots to the terminals of the battery, forming a simple circuit. In a few minutes the wing tent began to give off heat. There was a faint glow in the thin, translucent material as well, illuminating the space along with the mist lamp.

Anka made sure that everything was secure before sitting down with a sigh, finally relaxing. They sat on the floor side by side, leaning against each other.

"Still cold?"

"Better now."

Anka put an arm around her shoulders.

"If we use up all the electricity for heating," said Luoying, "how are we going to fly tomorrow?"

"Let's not worry about that for now," said Anka. "We could always hang the wings out in the sun in the morning to recharge."

The cave didn't seem so shabby or terrifying with the two of them together. The wings kept the place warm and glowed like curtains. Moonlight, as clear as water, limned the mouth of the cave. The survival suits they wore sealed them from head to toe, so it was impossible for them to even touch their fingers, but the pressure sensors they wore also amplified all sensations—not only the rough texture of the rocky floor but also their mutual touches. The act of leaning against each other enveloped both in a singular sensation to be savored. Luoying rested her head on Anka's shoulder.

"We're lucky to have friends like Runge and the others," said Luoying.

"We are," said Anka. "They would rather stay out here all night than risk not being able to find us tomorrow."

"Mira worries so much about everyone... yet I feel he's the happiest of all of us."

Anka grinned. "He never takes anything too seriously, including himself."

"I'm concerned about Chania. She's never been happy."

"I don't really understand her. But I think Sorin is right: she's too extreme."

"Do you think there's something going on between them?" asked Luoying, turning to look at Anka.

Anka chuckled. "Yeah."

"But I don't think Sorin supports Chania's plan."

"I think Runge is the only one who agrees with her one hundred percent."

"Runge is also so extreme. He's always claiming that everyone is working for self-aggrandizement. I don't think that's true."

"There's an old man in Runge's lab," said Anka. "He's got a bad reputation. Since he's in charge of a big project, everyone in the lab has to try to curry favor with him. Runge refused, so the old man has been interfering with his work in petty ways."

"I had no idea."

"Runge is thinking of leaving the lab, but you know how hard that is."

Luoying sighed. "I don't know why. But it seems all of us are having trouble readjusting to life on Mars."

"You're right," said Anka. In a self-deprecating tone he added, "I suppose we all... think too highly of ourselves."

"Do you also think we should start a revolution?"

"Not really."

"Why not?"

"Because it's useless."

"Do you mistrust revolutions? Like Mira?"

"Not exactly the same." Anka paused to think. "I don't just feel that revolutions are useless; I feel everything is pointless."

"What do you mean?"

"The problems they've identified *are* problems. But I feel that no matter how the system changes, no matter what government or way of life we adopt, the problems will always remain."

"I… I've never thought about it that way."

"So how do you feel?"

"I think there are things we can do to make it better, but I don't know the best way."

"Really?"

"Do you remember the filmmaker in the Terran delegation? He wrote to me later, saying that he thought the way we live on Mars could provide the solution to Earth's problems. He was going to work on that. I liked his determination, regardless of the consequences. His idealism made you feel there's a purpose in life. I wish I had such faith in some ideal that would propel me to act. I would feel so much better then."

"Then you agree with Chania's suggestion?"

"Not exactly." Luoying chose her words carefully. "The others are all too fuzzy in their aims; they just have a lot of passion. But in the end I can't tell what actions would be useful."

Anka gazed at the costume lamp, glowing like a tiny camp-fire. "Don't you think it's funny that a Terran is trying to save Earth with lessons learned from Mars, while a bunch of Martian kids are trying to save Mars with lessons learned on Earth?"

"You're right," said Luoying. "That's the part that puzzles me the most. What is the relationship between the two worlds? Even as children, we were taught that Earth eventually would become like Mars, because when knowledge and wisdom had advanced sufficiently, it was inevitable people would crave the freedom of sharing and the community of the intellect, like we have on Mars. But on Earth, everything we heard was the opposite. They say that Mars was too primitive and simple, and progress would eventually force us to become just like Earth. Who is the primitive stage of whom?

I'm so confused."

"I think these are just empty theories."

"So you think neither is better than the other?"

"Something like that. The war caused us to diverge in our development, that's all. There's no good or bad."

Luoying also gazed at the mist light, as though seeing mirages in the darkness. "That's also one of the reasons I can't just support Runge and Chania. Whether the system is good or not, it's the result of the life's work of my grandfather and his companions. I don't want to go against them without being sure."

"I think the people of that time were very idealistic."

"That's true. I read some of Garcia's speeches and Ronen's essays. At the time, they weren't thinking of some system of controlling the population. For them, the central archive was an ideal that represented truth and communication. Knowledge was the common wealth of all humanity, and everyone had the right to approach and pick from that treasure trove, like the right to freedom and existence. They argued that only by mutual understanding could they guarantee the coexistence of all faiths, to prevent cycles of slaughter, and the central archive was the best protector of the freedom of faith and conscience by allowing each to express their true beliefs without having to compromise by the need to make a living. Politics would be enriched by such honesty for all."

"They probably never thought so many would remain hypocrites full of lies."

"Or maybe they did, but nonetheless hoped it would be otherwise."

After an interval of silence, Anka said, without any emotion, "I'm not idealistic like that."

Luoying gazed at his face through the visors, not sure what to say. Anka's dispassionate declaration made her sad.

She was about to try to comfort him, but at the last minute she changed her mind. "I wonder if the wind is still blowing."

Anka stood up and pulled her up. "Let's go see."

They emerged from the mouth of the cave. The sand and dust that had filled the sky all through dusk seemed to be gone, and the night was very tranquil. Runge's mining ship had shifted closer to the cliff.

Anka put his arms around Luoying and both leaned back to look up the cliff face. Moonlight came from the side, coating both of them in a silver sheen. The stars glowed densely overhead without twinkling. Other than the Milky Way, every other part of the sky looked about the same. Black holes from billions of light-years away were no more distinguishable than the Large Magellanic Cloud, practically close enough to touch by cosmic standards. There was no violent upheaval, no history, no stellar birth or death, only a bright web of stars quietly glowing overhead, aloof but also warm, comforting those who gazed up at them with fear and confusion.

"Do you recognize any constellations?" Luoying asked Anka. He shook his head.

"Can you find Earth?" Anka shook his head again.

Luoying sighed. "If Zeta were here, she could teach us."

"I doubt she would know either," said Anka. "She's a cosmologist, and I heard that she doesn't know any of the stars by sight or name."

Luoying began to hum an old song. After the dust storm had

abated, the yearning for peace returned. Singing, like starlight, was insubstantial but made one feel settled. Since the air was too thin to transmit sound, she sang quietly in her heart.

"I like the old folk beliefs," said Anka abruptly.

"Like what?"

"When someone dies, they turn into a star in the sky."

"I like that one, too. I've always felt that those we had known and who had passed away are stars. I think there are three hundred billion stars in the Milky Way, which is just about the number of people who have ever existed."

Anka grinned. "We may run into a bit of a problem there. There are going to be more and more people, but the number of stars isn't going up."

"But I like the thought."

"Me too," said Anka. "Wouldn't it be nice if we were put on Earth just to accomplish some mission, after which we'd return to the sky? Life would be more bearable."

"Yeah."

Surveying the night-shrouded crater, thinking of Mira's dreams of flying all over Mars, they couldn't help but imagine the future. Anka said that he really did want to visit Olympus Mons and to experience the sensation of flight at such heights. Luoying, on the other hand, wanted to visit the network of gullies in the northern plains and Ravi Vallis, just south of the equator. Rudy had said it would be ideal to take all the water from Ceres and refill these ancient channels. She wondered what that would look like. Would it be the same as a real river?

"Maybe one day we'll get to go visit other stars, like the crew of *Cerealia*."

"Do you know what's happening with the colony ship?"

"They've left the Solar System safely. Everything seems to be going well."

"Then they must be getting ready to select the next crew."

"Not much chance for us, though," said Luoying. "They're still focused on experienced astronauts and experts. I guess it will be a few decades before we'll be considered."

"Still, there's hope."

They spoke of distant stars no different from the names of ordinary streets. It didn't matter how many millions of kilometers or decades were involved, as they gave language free rein to carry them on waves of hopeless hope. In the sky, strange planets lit up one after another, like abstract pencil sketches.

The deep night gave Luoying's thoughts a kind of free-flowing freedom she hadn't experienced in a while, not since the days in the hospital, when she had read by herself on the skydeck. The feeling was like a surging sea under her skin; it had given her courage, had helped her find her direction.

The stars shined steadily overhead like diamonds of time, and in a flash they awakened a memory deep in her mind. Without hesitation, she began to recite a passage from a book she loved, *L'Homme révolté*.

Mais qui se donne...

Almost three hundred years ago, Camus spoke of facing one's destiny, of rebelling against history, of choosing the faithful land of Ithaca, of the first and last love of Earth.

Her voice echoed in the headset, like a declaration from the heart. Anka listened intently. For a long while afterward they remained silent, unwilling to break the simple determination that rose in both hearts. All other words seemed extraneous. The ancient crater and the abandoned past spread out silently beneath their feet, the best support for them in this moment.

Back in the cave, it took them a while to fall asleep. They

lay next to each other, and every movement from one was felt by the other, leading to laughter, which was amplified by both. Several times they were about to fall asleep, only to wake up laughing.

Tired out in the end, they fell asleep without noticing.

MORNING

The moment Anka got up, Luoying awakened as well. She had always been a light sleeper, and when the pressure on her shoulder was gone, her mind naturally emerged from slumber.

She saw the light glinting off the distant peaks through the golden cave mouth. She blinked a few times until her mind was fully alert. Noiselessly, she sat up, looked around, and saw that Anka had already left the cave. The empty space, with the glowing ring around the cave mouth, felt warm and secure. She lifted one of the wings blocking the entrance and went out.

Anka was standing to the right, gazing at the distant rim of the crater, a hand on his waist. In the still-dim dawn, half of his profile remained in shadows, and his visor glinted in the rising sun.

Seeing Luoying, he smiled and whispered, "Careful, it's still cold."

He held out an arm. Luoying walked over, and he wrapped the arm around her from behind, hugging her close as they stood side by side.

"You're watching the sunrise?"

Anka nodded. "It's been several years since I've seen it."

Luoying sighed. "I've never seen a real sunrise. On Earth, I once went to the beach to try to catch it, but it was an overcast day."

The world brightened bit by bit. Though the sky remained as dark as ever, the landscape was emerging from the indistinct shadows. Ray by ray, the sun climbed above the rim, but it was still blocked by a peak, so that they could see the light but not the source. The crater shucked off the disguise of night, revealing the canyons and gullies, the dust and rocks, like a curled-up child who had no memories of the tantrum it had thrown the day before. The morning breeze was gentle, and Luoying could see the fabric edging of her belt being lifted by the currents without feeling the touch of wind. The light grew more colorful. The rim was again a chiaroscuro of gold and black, and most of the crater had returned to its habitual yellow-brown. The sharp border between shadow and light sketched out smooth and full curves, like the outline for some magnificent landscape painting.

"Look over there!" Luoying pointed.

"What are you looking at?"

"The mountains. Look at the shadows! They've been shaped."

"Are you suggesting—"

"Yes, it's been worked over artificially."

"How is that possible?" Anka stared where she was pointing. "But you are right…"

The entire western and southern rim of the crater was displaying the image of a gigantic upside-down tree. The canyons high up on the rim, like gorges worn by waterfalls, formed the trunk. Lower down, the spreading network of shallow channels and gullies formed the branches and a thick canopy. Even though the outline was made from natural geography, every turn and connection showed signs of human touch. Rough corners had been smoothed and blockages cleared out until the whole mountainside served as the canvas for a magnificent painting.

In the clear morning light, the caves located next to the

canyons and gullies appeared dark and round, clearly intended to represent heavy and plump fruits hanging from the branches of the tree. Compared to the other caves unconnected to the mountain-tree, these had apparently been shaped to be more circular and uniform in size, to better approximate the appearance of fruit. Against the golden mountainside, the dark shadow limbs of the tree showed up especially well. Under the empty sky, the image was at once solemn and awe-inspiring. Luoying and Anka were entranced.

The sun continued to rise. Inch by inch, the shadow-tree sank, distorted, became harder to see. Neither of them spoke, their gazes following the incredible sight. At the last minute, as the tree was about to disappear from their view, Luoying pointed and shouted.

"Look! A signature!"

Two giant letters, *H* and *S*, were inscribed at the bottom of the crater's rim.

"My grandfather...," muttered Luoying.

"You think he—"

"Yes, it must be him!"

"It makes sense. He was a pilot, and he would have been able to carve this from the air in his plane."

"Do you remember the apple?" asked Luoying.

Anka nodded. "You think it's a memorial."

"Possibly." A sense of excitement seized Luoying. "But I just thought of another interpretation."

"Tell me."

"We were talking about Mars and Earth last night," said Luoying. "Perhaps the two worlds are like two of these apples. Neither is a stage in the evolution of the other, but both are simply fruits from the same tree, hanging on different branches grown out of the same root."

"The worlds are apples," muttered Anka.

They stood and watched until the sun had risen high enough to bathe the whole crater with light. The vanished painting continued to linger in their minds.

More sentences long buried in her heart surfaced. She couldn't understand why her memory had suddenly recovered in these last few days. It was as though these lines had been planted in her mind as soon as she read them, only waiting for this day to sprout and bloom. On this morning, they were like tears from sorrowful eyes, flowing forth naturally and unimpeded. She began to recite.

Liés à nos frères par un...

She spoke of the brotherhood of climbers, of gazing up at the same peak and being tied to the same rope, of the eternal love of those who strive to fulfill the same purpose.

Anka gazed at her. "Is it from the same book from last night?"

Luoying shook her head. "This is from Saint-Exupéry's *Wind, Sand and Stars*."

"*Wind, Sand and Stars?*"

"Yes. *Wind, Sand and Stars*."

Now that it was completely light outside, they reconnected the two depleted batteries to the wings and spread them open in front of the cave to soak up energy for a new day.

Anka turned on the wireless, and soon Runge was asking about their status. Luoying looked down over the lip of the ledge and saw the ancient mining ship emerge from the canyon in which it had taken shelter and roll toward them slowly, swaying from side to side. The ship moved with a jaunty, carefree attitude, heading directly for the spot below their cave.

Mira's voice squawked in the headsets. "Sorry you had to spend a night starving and freezing up there. I'm almost afraid to tell you that we had another feast. There was pumpkin cake, and we had bottles of chilled Gio. We stayed up half the night playing cards and listening to music. Kingsley, help me out here: What else did we do?"

"Try not to show off too much," said Anka, chuckling. "Remember, fortune is fickle."

Runge asked Anka to give a detailed report on the status of their equipment. By the time the mining ship stopped, they saw a tiny airlock open on the back of the turtle shell–like hull. Runge peeked out and waved a small flag at them, drawing their attention to the long poles sticking out of the back of the ship. "Can you see the net we've got back there?"

"Yes."

"Can you fly down on your own power?"

"That's going to be tough."

"Then can you jump into the net?"

Anka tried to estimate the distance and the size of the net. "I think the net is too small and too far."

"Do you have any other ideas?"

"I do. In a minute I'm going to toss down a battery. Watch for it."

"No problem."

"Be careful," said Anka, a hint of laughter in his voice. "Maybe you should let Sorin drive."

"Once again, you show so little faith in me." But Runge was laughing, too.

Anka got busy. Luoying watched him work, uncertain how she could help. She had not been all that concerned about getting down last night, but now she realized that it wasn't as simple as she had thought. Yesterday they had taken off with propellers driven by compressed air, which was now depleted. They couldn't take off by jumping off and gliding either. The cave wasn't high enough, and the ledge wasn't long enough for them to get a running start.

As she looked on, Anka took apart one pair of wings. Carefully he separated the membrane from the veins of the wing. The veins, made of flexible but strong material, were then twisted by Anka into a long cable, coiled in one thick pile at their feet. Finally, he connected a battery to one end of the cable and tossed it down like a sailor tossing a cable to shore at a dock. The net at the end of the mining ship, woven from thick cables and meant for crushed ore, caught it and retracted inside.

Anka then wrapped the other end of the cable around his waist and tied it to his belt. He walked over to Luoying and secured the cable around her waist. Since they had already disassembled one pair of wings to provide heat the night before and took apart another pair to make the cable, only two pairs out of the four they had worn were left. Anka took these and secured one pair to each of their backs.

"Watch me," said Anka. "All you have to do is to jump after me and follow my lead."

He waved at Runge below, who waved back in acknowledgment. A strong flagpole rose out of the mining ship, with the other end of the cable tied to it.

The mining ship began to roll away.

"Do you remember what you said about two people tied to the same rope?" asked Anka, giving her a reassuring grin.

As the slack in the cable ran out, Anka took a few steps on the ledge and leaped off, falling and being pulled along by the rope.

The ten meters between him and Luoying ran out in a moment, and Luoying instinctively followed him off the ledge. The instant she was in the air, her mind was completely blank. She fell as she felt herself being pulled along, and the ground was rushing up to her. She didn't move, thinking that she was about to die.

But her fall slowed, and the wind caught her wings as though an invisible hand were lifting her up. Gradually, Luoying breathed, no longer terrified. She saw the cable stretching down and ahead of her. Anka and she were two kites being pulled along by the cable, staying aloft.

She stretched her arms and legs. No longer worried, she allowed herself to enjoy the sensation of flight. Runge had driven into a canyon that wasn't too deep, and soon the V-shaped mouth of the canyon was ahead of them.

"I'm going to drive you along the new way we discovered yesterday, when we were trying to hide from the big ship," said Runge excitedly.

The ship rolled through the open space at the end of the canyon and turned into another canyon. The turn was sharp, and Anka and Luoying swept close by the towering cliff at the end.

"Watch it! Can't you be more careful?" shouted Anka.

Runge ignored his criticism. "Do you know where we are? We saw a stone tablet over there: Angela Bluff."

"So this is it!" Luoying shouted into the wind, shocked by the name.

"That's right," said Runge. "This is the place you were looking for."

Luoying twisted around in the air to look back at the cliff she had just swept past, the place where her grandfather had been born. A large stone tablet stood at the foot of the cliff.

They were moving away, and it was no longer possible to tell the details of the canyon. The place looked no different from all the other canyons and cliffs around the crater. The red rock face stood mutely, the same way it had stood for millions of years, remembering nothing of birth, nothing of death, nothing of the war that started because of it, nothing of the honor humans had heaped on it. She kept on twisting back to look, but it gradually faded into the distance.

She had finally seen Angela Bluff.

Runge's voice came alive in the headsets again.

"Pay attention to your right," he warned.

Angela Bluff was finally gone. They had emerged into a new crater.

This crater was bigger than the one from yesterday. Instead of the desolation of the previous crater, a circular metallic building stood in the middle of this one, looking refined and austere. It was shaped like a spider with its legs deeply planted in the soil. The steel structure was white and silver, surrounded by small aircraft of all different designs. The building and the aircraft all had flame designs painted on them.

"Anka, what is this?" asked Luoying.

Anka said nothing.

"None of us can guess what this is," said Runge excitedly. "We've never even heard of this place. It's a mystery. When we get back, we'll have to do some investigating." Anka said nothing.

"Do either of you have a guess?" asked Runge.

"No," said Luoying, answering for Anka. Her heart sank as she saw his expression.

The mining ship continued to speed ahead, leaving her no time to worry. Another warning sounded in her ears.

"We're about to reach the plains. Watch out."

While Sorin's voice still reverberated in their ears, their field of view abruptly opened up.

Luoying felt some force lift her by the waist and push her to the side. She was flying faster, and her direction changed unpredictably. As the cable tightened, she looked around her.

The golden-hued ground spread all the way to the horizon. The line that divided day from night stretched sharply to the end of the planet, where clouds of yellow sand roiled. In the distance they could see Mars City gradually growing bigger. Under the bright sun, countless glass domes glistened like a bubbly cloud over the endless ocean of sand. The blue lines of the tube trains wound around the bubbles like vines, fading into the distance like beanstalks disappearing into the sky.

In that moment, the city appeared to be a well in the desert, surrounded by green hope, the object of every gaze. Luoying suddenly began to understand the motivation behind Martian exploration. From the time she was a little girl, she had seen her elders and relatives set off on voyages into the unknown. Without a backward glance, they rushed into piles of crushed ore, they rocketed off to Jupiter, they performed incredible stunts in the vacuum of space. These weren't acts of survival; instead, they departed only because they called this city home, this transparent, ethereal city. It was warmth, brightness, safety. In the desert, it stored up the power of the sun; in the arid air, it maintained hope. As long as they could catch a glimpse of this city, the explorers had the courage to continue to fly into the unknown. As long as they could sense its presence in the distant cold, the fighters had the courage to continue the battle. Luoying didn't know if her parents had been able to gaze upon the city one last time before their deaths. She hoped that they had, and that the look diminished their pain.

This was the second time that Anka and Luoying had

danced between the open sky and the ground. The last time they had faced the burning red disk of the setting sun, looking down at ramparts made of clouds. This time they were under the space-black empyrean, gazing at a city as light as a cloud. Luoying felt herself turning into a cloud, without the need for control or strength. All she had to do was drift, this way and that, following the wind toward the distant horizon.

Sand and dust swirled through the air. Luoying's heart was open but not wanting as she spread her wings against the wind.

———

There were no clouds on Mars. As the dust storm raged, inside the Boule Chamber the gathered throng gazed anxiously into the swirling sand.

The chamber was shaped like a rectangle with a semicircle added to one end. The glass floor was treated to display imitation-marble patterns. Four classical Greek–style columns stood along each long side of the rectangle, and between the columns stood massive bronze statues, behind which hung Martian military banners. The semicircular part of the hall held a gold-colored podium emblazoned with the Great Seal of Mars. Below the seal, in seventy-five languages, were the words *Mars, My Home*.

The curved wall behind the podium was a giant screen. Right now the screen showed the desert. Four massive ships stood ready in formation, waiting for orders. Their silver hulls reflected the sun as they underwent final checks before departure. Behind them, yellow sand roiled on the horizon like clouds.

Hans Sloan stood at the podium, trying to calm the crowd. The murmuring among the crowd never ceased, though sometimes they sounded like the repressed sea before a storm, and at other times they agitated like the foam spraying from surging waves. Heels clicked against the hard floor, as rapid as a drumroll.

The audience was so caught up in their own anxiety that they had lost sense of the images on the screen. As the roiling yellow sand approached, few realized its import. A few mothers gathered together, wiping their tearful eyes, while the fathers went up in groups to demand answers from Hans, pleading for more resources to be devoted to the search.

Only when the gray shape of the mining ship loomed up on the screen and the figures of the children dancing in the air became clear did the parents gathered in the chamber suddenly approach the screen all at once.

The silence in the chamber lasted until the youths entered in a joyous and noisy gaggle. Their laughter and conversation echoed from the hallway into the chamber.

"You were driving like a drunk maniac, I swear!"

"Don't blame me! The storm was coming at us from the side. I had to drive like that to keep you airborne."

As they entered, the chattering youths took off their helmets and shook loose their hair, their animated faces full of fearless energy. It was as if a wind had blown away the clouds of anxiety, bringing with it sunlight. But then they saw the faces of their parents, and instantly they lowered their voices, their steps turned cautious and strained, and they moved away from one another, almost unconsciously standing up straighter.

The solemnity in the chamber was like an invisible force that had gently disarmed this wild wind. The youths stopped in the middle of the hall, looking at one another without speaking. The adults stood on either side of them. Some of the mothers were about to run up to embrace their children, but the fathers held them back. The air in the chamber seemed frozen.

Hans, still at the podium, cleared his throat. His gaze was steady, and his nose was like an iron that held down the exhaustion evident in his wrinkled face. His voice, like a dull knife, cut through the anxious air.

"First, I'm very glad that all of you made it back safely. You've proven your talent and courage in this unexpected adventure." His grave expression lent weight to his words. "But I must also ask each of you to reflect upon what your actions have cost others. The irresponsible, unauthorized expedition worried and frightened your parents and teachers."

Hans stopped there, looking from the youths to their parents. The chamber was completely silent. He noticed that many surreptitiously squeezed their fingers tensely.

"The biggest step on the journey from a clever youth to a mature adult is learning to be responsible for one's own actions. You broke the regulations intended to keep the city safe. By stealing the permit and leaving the city without authorization, you placed yourself and the nation both in great danger. Had any of you been injured, the consequences would have been grave. Even a young student who behaves in such a deliberately careless manner should be punished. As part of the education of future rational citizens of the Martian Republic, such punishment is necessary and proper.

"But in consideration of the fact that all of the offending youths are members of the Mercury Group, who suffered psychological harm due to the lack of appropriate explanations for certain events during their sojourn on Earth, I hereby declare that the youths shall only be isolated for a month to receive guidance and counseling. No other punishment shall be imposed.

"I would also like to take this opportunity to clarify some historical matters. Two years ago, to ensure the success of the negotiations between Earth and Mars, the students of the Mercury Group were used as hostages without their knowledge. This was our error, and I offer to the students my sincerest apologies."

Hans bowed to all the students. Every member of the audience was stunned, child and parent alike. Before this point, Luoying and her friends had speculated on every possible outcome from their little rebellion, but this wasn't one of them.

"But I hope you will believe me when I say that the effort to send you to Earth to study wasn't merely a figure in some political calculus. I hope you can believe that."

Hans saw that the students were beginning to whisper to one another. Just as he had anticipated, doubt was spreading. He pretended not to see as he continued in an even tone. "However, the adults who were involved in this incident must be held accountable for their actions. The first person who must be punished is Warren Sangis, who was on watch at the Aru District gate. He neglected his duty and permitted these students to leave the city when they didn't have the necessary authorization. He is immediately reassigned to the mining vehicle depot as a full-time maintenance worker. The exact duration of his assignment will be determined later.

"The second person who must be punished is Dr. Reini of First Hospital in Russell District. He helped these youths gain key bits of knowledge in history, biomimetics, and bio-sensing, and he even knew their plan ahead of time, but he failed to guide, supervise, or otherwise dissuade them. For such dereliction of duty, he should be punished severely. But as the students did not come to harm, the penalty is reduced. The final decision is to remove Dr. Reini from his current post at the hospital and reassign him to the Registry of Files, where he will assist the Registrar with historical files. He is also forbidden from any more scientific research or teaching without explicit authorization."

Hans allowed his gaze to roam around the crowd, pausing briefly over Luoying's shocked expression. Then he strode away from the podium toward the exit at the side of the chamber without a glance back at the chattering youths and their scolding parents.

A BEGINNING SERVING
AS AN END

On the morning Reini left the hospital for the last time, Luoying came to the skydeck of the hospital, also for the last time.

Most of Reini's belongings had already been removed, so he was only at the hospital to pick up a few last personal effects.

Luoying followed him about the office. Just like a few days before, she wanted to speak but couldn't find the words. Reini handed her a few preserved specimens that he no longer needed. She took them without looking, completely at a loss.

"Dr. Reini," she said. But when he turned to look at her, her voice weakened. "I... uh... never mind."

Reini smiled at her. "You want to ask about my reassignment."

"I'm sorry!" Luoying bowed to him again and again, her hair whipping up and down by the sides of her neck. "I'm sorry—"

"It's really not a big deal," said Reini. "Your grandfather once again allowed me to pick my new post. I'm perfectly content."

"He told me that he called you on the day we left."

"He did."

"What... did he ask you?"

"He asked me if I knew you were planning such an expedition."

"What did you tell him?"

"I said I knew."

"But I didn't tell you anything about our plans! Why did you assume the blame?"

"But I did know."

Luoying stared at Reini, whose face remained serene.

Reini took Luoying to the skydeck. It was still early, so the deck was deserted. Bright light filled the space, and water gurgled through the pool, carefree.

Luoying stood at the wall, gazing at the distant cliff. Behind the narrow band of red, Luoying knew, there was a certain crater named after Linda Sais. It was no different from any of the other thousands of craters hidden among the mountains, peacefully asleep for millions of years. The wind had shaped it. It had witnessed soil mounds being leveled by the wind, water escaping into space, lava freezing into solid rock. And at this moment, it had become an eye into the heart of Luoying, a bright eye gazing up at the stars. Because of it, the mute and dark mountains were illuminated.

"I have one last question," said Luoying, looking up at Reini's broad forehead. "Why is it that some people are always around, but I don't feel close to them? Why is that some other people are rarely with me, but I feel their warmth every moment?"

Reini pushed his glasses up the bridge of his nose. He pointed at the distant sky. "When you were out there, did you see any clouds?"

"Just one wisp. The morning of the second day."

"A wisp is about all you'll ever see on Mars. But that's enough to explain everything."

"How do you mean?"

"A cloud is actually made of liquids. The droplets are far apart from one another in the air, each moving independently.

But because they're similar in scale, they refract light similarly. That light connects them, and we see the whole constellation of droplets as one cloud."

That's how it works, thought Luoying. *Yes, we're at the same scale, and the light connects us. That's how it works.*

She had finally discovered the source of their commonality. During the three days after returning from their adventure, she had tried to tease out just why so many things she and her friends thought were natural were incomprehensible to others. She recalled the dark dance stage, the debates on the mining ship, the cave in the cold night, the orange-glowing wing tent, the bright laughter in the air; she seemed to see the very air over each youthful head shimmering with the endless search for answers and the refusal to compromise. She knew now that it was the mark left by the process of growth. The only solid support they could count on was that shared wandering through worlds more complicated than imagination. Their shared identity could all be sourced to that chaotic, common experience. It was a solid backdrop, a fact that needed no derivation from axioms.

She had found what she was looking for. There was no need for her to refuse to change, to abandon freedom, but there was also no need to worry about departures, about the lack of warmth. They had the same scale; they had the light between them.

Once, she had seen herself clearly, and that allowed her to bid herself farewell. Now she had seen her companions clearly, and she could bid them farewell as well without worry. She no longer feared the solitude of journeying afar, because they were a cloud, and light made them one. They were seeds borne by the same tree. No matter how far the wind scattered them, the same qi flowed through them.

The city was awakening in the morning light. Before the bright glass wall, Reini and Luoying were two silhouettes.

Looking at the side of his face, Luoying wondered just how much Reini understood her thoughts. Sometimes she felt he was only telling her the simplest facts, but other times she felt as though he always knew what she was trying to ask.

Reini was dressed casually today in a light green striped shirt and a gray cotton jacket. He stood with his hands in his pockets, at ease. His face, gazing into the distance, revealed little emotion at the corners of his mouth. Like the first time she had come here, Reini gave Luoying the impression of a tree. Without much movement, he kept himself upright. Even his voice was a tree: straight and gentle.

The silence and tranquility was abruptly broken. A mental patient broke in and beat his fists against the glass wall. Nurses and doctors rushed in and escorted him away. Comforting voices were interspersed with loud shouts. The whole noisy process was like a gust of wind that brought them conflict and cleaned away the story. The emptiness that remained seemed even more empty.

"Dr. Reini, will I be able to visit you in the future?"

"I'm not a doctor anymore," said Reini. "My punishment also includes not being allowed to teach. But I don't think anything in the decision forbids me from receiving visitors. You're welcome at any time."

Luoying smiled.

She looked outside the wall, knowing that one part of her life was over and another part had just begun. She didn't know what the future held. The Martian landscape was vast and silent.

PART THREE

GALE WINGS

PROLOGUE

Exile became fact only at the moment of returning home.

For more than a thousand and eight hundred days, when Luoying was away from home, she didn't realize she had been exiled. Home was an imagined place in her heart; she could only think of its warmth, its memories, its openness and acceptance, but she never thought of its shape. Imagination took what it needed based on her mood, like the air around her. Since air never conflicted with the person it surrounded, there was no seam between her and home. The distance between them was merely physical.

Before she left home, home had no shape. It was merely a presence far larger than she was. Because she was embedded within it, she could never see its limits or its borders. When she was away from home, home also had no shape. It was on the other side of the sky. Compared to the sky of the foreign land, it was too small a presence, merely a point of light. There were no details, no outlines.

Home in those moments was always a smooth and kind presence. Whether too big or too small, there were no sharp edges, no thorns or spurs, no instances where an encounter ripped away her skin and flesh to reveal the white bone beneath. She could always immerse herself in the concept of home, whether with her body or her heart.

But all the mismatches came to the fore the moment she arrived home after a long time away. In that moment, the cracks became real: visible, tangible, as clear as the distance between one person and another. She was like a puzzle piece that had fallen off the picture of home, thinking that after her sojourn abroad she would be able to fit right back in. But at the moment of return, she realized that there was no spot left for her. Her shape did not fit the hole left in the puzzle when she left. It was only in that moment that she truly lost her home.

Luoying and her friends were fated never to return home. The ship they were on was forever vacillating on the Lagrangian point between the two worlds. To vacillate was also never to belong. It was their fate to be cosmic vagabonds.

RUDY

Time for a coffee break.

The door to the Boule Chamber opened, and Rudy was the first to emerge. He strode to the wall, filled a glass with cold water at the drinking fountain, and gulped it down.

The chamber is too small, he thought. *So stuffy and cramped. What were they thinking when they built it? It lacks natural lighting and good air circulation, and the chairs are as hard as corpses. It's impossible to sit in them for a whole morning without being put into a horrible mood. The building has been in use for thirty-five years at least, hasn't it? Why don't they renovate it? The idea that it's a historical memorial is just bureaucratic nonsense. The right way to commemorate history is to turn the place into a museum and build a new capitol. They're always resisting change. Look around here: everything is old. Old building, old drinking fountain, outdated A/V system… Everything smells musty.*

He had to concede that this last bit was effective. *To squeeze so many people into such tight quarters is a great way to slow the mind down. Infected by the musty smells, it's no wonder that everyone starts to think like the aged. All the uncles and aunties are the same: forever cautious, forever hesitant, never able to decide on anything. Everything is in Mars's favor right now, but they're still hesitating! To be so conservative, so resistant to change… we'll never get anywhere. How can we possibly explore the depths of the universe like this? I should have been blunter earlier. I'm still too conciliatory, too diffident.*

The cold water did him good. His whole body felt refreshed. Rudy stood up and let out a long breath, and the tips of his burning ears felt a bit cooler.

The legislators exited the chamber by twos and threes. Coming up to the long table of refreshments, they munched on snacks and drank coffee as they chatted. For the legislators, coffee breaks were often even more productive than actual sessions, since this was when alliances could be formed and the trading of votes attempted. Legislators Chakra and Richardson passed by Rudy without a glance and headed for the lounge at the other end of the hall, whispering to each other. The dark gold veins in the floor seemed to form a carpet. The two soon disappeared down the hall.

Rudy watched their retreating figures and wondered if he had been too arrogant in the council chamber earlier. When Richardson had tried talking to him, he had turned away, pretending to be listening to Souza. Maybe he had overdone it and offended Richardson. At the time the gesture had come almost unconsciously, and he hadn't meant a deliberate insult. But thinking back on it, it did seem too disrespectful. He didn't like Richardson, a stubborn Wader who had neither the sense nor the sensibility to appreciate the importance of overcoming nature. He had mocked Rudy's enthusiasm and radicalism, and Rudy had never forgotten those insults.

I'll patch it up with him later, he thought. *After all, he's an elder, and to be so disrespectful to him in public was a mistake.* He didn't so much fear reprisal from Richardson as despise himself for losing control. Richardson, if he minded what had happened, was just one man, but his lack of control would cost him the support of many. *Smile even when you're fighting*, he repeated to himself.

He drank another glass of water and felt much better and calmer.

Legislator Franz stopped next to him and greeted him with a smile. A bald and rotund man in his forties, Franz seemed to get along with everyone. But Rudy knew how politically astute the man was. By never clearly expressing support for either the Climbers or the Waders, he made sure that his vote became something both sides fought over. Rudy felt a trace of anxiety.

"What did you think of the discussion?" Franz asked him.

Rudy tried to be cautious. "Er… I think there are multiple ways to look at it. If I were an optimist, I'd say that both sides understood the other side's position well and there's no misunderstanding. If I were a pessimist, I'd say that both sides have long understood each other's position well, perhaps too well."

Franz chuckled. "How long have you been at the Boule now?"

"About two and a half years."

"I listened to your new proposal. Interesting. Very interesting." Rudy's heart sped up but he kept his voice even. "Thank you.

Glad to hear it."

"Do you have time for a few questions?"

"Of course. Happy to elaborate on anything you want to know."

The smile disappeared from Franz's face. "The point of your proposal is to make vertical movement easier, isn't it?"

"Yes. The biggest inconvenience of the Climbers' plan is how to move between elevations."

"And you think the solution is magnetic tube cars."

"The cars will rely on magnetic levitation, but there won't be any tubes."

"What's so different about your plan compared to previous proposals?"

"Well, there's no need to dig tunnels. That's probably the biggest difference. It's like how our houses are all independent. The cars will also move independently. It will be much cheaper to build and easier to control their routes."

"But if I'm understanding this right, your plan requires a strong ground-based magnetic field. That's not going to be cheap."

"I've looked into this. It turns out that the rocks of Martian mountains have strong magnetic fields. After quarrying, if we just regulate the fields with some circuits, the material will be perfect for building what we need for the transportation system. It's not clear where the magnetic field is coming from— maybe it has to do with how the rocks were formed. Anyway, that's why I support the Climbers: we can greatly reduce the cost by using materials on hand in the mountains."

"How does your plan compare to elevators? Surely going straight up and down is the most efficient path."

"Elevators will require multiple shafts, and each shaft will have to be hundreds of meters long. Drilling through solid rock isn't trivial."

Rudy took Franz to a terminal and logged in. He navigated to his home directory and brought up several hand-drawn diagrams. They showed a tall mountainside from multiple angles. Along the steep incline were strings of caves, each equipped with walls and doors much like existing houses in the city—it was as though the city had been lifted up and then embedded in the side of the mountain. Between cave and cave—or between dwelling and dwelling—was strung a network of rails that covered the mountain face from foot to peak. Hemispherical cars, suspended from the rails like ski lifts, glided between the dwellings like pearls on strings.

This was an elaboration on the basic plan of the Climbers. The Climbers wanted to pick a crater near the equator and reuse the caves that had once housed people before the war. The floor of the crater would be turned into a lake; people would live on the rim wall. The water would be trapped within the crater to form a closed cycle of rainfall and streams, with the walls covered in lush vegetation to build a complete ecosystem. Rudy's drawings made the whole plan more vivid and provided room for imagination to roam. Each dwelling, for instance, was surrounded by a garden, and the magnetic cars moving through the jungle made the scene come alive.

As Rudy explained, he paid attention to Franz's face, which showed no expression. Rudy actually found the lack of response a good sign. Franz was one of the few people Rudy admired. As the author of numerous political essays, the man was influential despite being relatively young. As a junior legislator in the Boule, Rudy had few opportunities to make speeches or direct big policy decisions, but he had prepared detailed dossiers on all 160-plus members. To have the support of a heavyweight like Franz would do much to advance the Climbers' plan.

Franz said nothing as he flipped through the detailed proposal on the screen.

Rudy's mind spun while he observed the man. He knew that by this point the competition between the Climbers and the Waders was no longer a matter of different philosophies and theories but was focused on practical problems such as power distribution grids, transportation of goods, neighborhood organization, and detailed budgets for each step. Technical advantages and resource-use efficiency were far more persuasive than any values or principles. When both sides were arguing that their plan would bring the greatest benefit to the largest number of people, only numbers could convince. Rudy understood that any opportunity to show how his technology helped a plan was also an opportunity for the plan to help him.

Is he going to support me? he wondered. *Is he going to bring more votes to my side?*

It was a time of alliances and pacts. In the Boule, the sizes of the extreme radical and extreme conservative factions were both small. Most legislators remained neutral, unsure which plan to back. Based on numbers, the conservatives, who preferred the Waders' plan of staying put in the city, had the upper hand. But of the neutrals, a significant portion leaned toward the more radical migration plan of the Climbers. The radicals gambled that they'd win most of them. Rudy was merely a foot soldier for the Climbers, but he was radical in every sense. He gazed at Franz while Franz gazed at the screen. The longer the senior legislator stared at the screen, the more hope grew in Rudy's heart.

The wait was tense, but it didn't last forever.

Having read through the entirety of Rudy's design document, Franz looked up. "Can you take me to see your simulations?"

"Now?" Rudy struggled to keep the excitement off his face. "Of course. Anytime."

In the evening, after he came home, Rudy went straight to Hans Sloan's study.

His grandfather stood before the window, browsing through a thick book. Behind him, thick hardcover books with gilded pages filled the bookcase like some monument. Rudy didn't dare to make much noise, knowing that Hans disliked being disturbed while reading. From childhood he understood that the books meant quietude; they were the true protectors of this room. The words were high ideals, principles, his grandfather's understanding of human nature. On Mars, because paper was so expensive, few books were printed, and even fewer citizens could keep so many frozen words. Rudy took pride in the books, but he knew he had to respect them as well.

Hearing Rudy come in, Hans turned around and set down the book.

Rudy remained at the door. Softly he said, "I'm back, Grandfather."

Hans nodded. "Did you leave the afternoon session early?"

"Yes. I brought Legislator Franz to see some simulations."

Hans's voice revealed neither praise nor criticism. "What did he think?"

"He was very interested. He thought my plan was feasible. Other than the advantage of low costs from eliminating the tunnels, it also utilizes energy more efficiently. The magnetic rails could draw power from solar panels placed on the mountain-side, and eventually they could even tap into hydropower from the downflow. Also—"

Hans broke in gently. "I understand. I'm familiar with your plan." After a pause he added, "You move fast."

Rudy looked at his grandfather's face, trying to see if he meant something deeper by that. But Hans's expression was placid, revealing nothing. The silence became awkward.

The night before, Hans told Rudy that the decision would be made with a Boule vote. The decision to bring Ceres here and to engage with Earth had both been made by the Boule, so he would continue the tradition this time. Hans explained that the vote was only going to pick an engineering plan based on feasibility and potential, but no permanent decision about the future lifestyle of Mars would be made.

Rudy understood, however, that the engineering plan would essentially determine the lifestyle. He said nothing at the time, but instantly he began to plan the best way to take advantage of this knowledge. Hans was referring to his quickness of mind.

Rudy tried to break the uncomfortable silence. "Grandfather, I'm sorry to be so direct... but are you against leaving Mars City?"

"Why do you ask that?"

"I think you know that if you were to submit the decision to a plebiscite, most of the younger generation would choose to move so they'd be given a chance to shine through this historic opportunity. The Boule, on the other hand, is full of elders whose best accomplishments are already behind them. Naturally they'd lean toward preserving the status quo. To submit the decision to a Boule vote is to... maximize the chances of staying in Mars City. Am I right?"

"The reasoning you've described... is that also the basis for your own decision?"

Rudy hesitated for just a moment. "Yes. I'm not ashamed to admit it. I think most people think as I do."

"Perhaps you're right," said Hans. "But I don't think it's going to influence the final result."

"Why not? I think it will."

"As you saw today, even with a Boule vote, your side has a good chance of winning."

Rudy tried to find signs of disappointment or mockery in Hans's expression, but again he came up with nothing. Hans looked back at him as though reading a book, focused, observant, but revealing no emotion. For some reason Rudy began to fear his grandfather. He had the sense that while Hans knew every step of his plan, he couldn't make out what Hans intended at all.

Rudy suggested that Hans extend the period of debate. Hans acknowledged the suggestion but didn't say if he would implement it.

Rudy left the study and stood in the hallway alone. He was anxious, and he didn't know if his grandfather was also anxious. Even in his own mind, he had been trying to avoid the real reason he was so enthusiastic about migrating. He had imagined so many futures, and in every one of them he stood on top of the mountains, directing others to do his bidding as the new city rose around him. He could no longer accept the possibility that none of these scenes might come true. He felt ashamed for such naked ambition. When he was a little boy, he thought he would grow up to be public-spirited, making all his decisions based on what was objectively good for the collective. Today was the first time he had ever opened himself up to reveal his true desires. He wasn't sure if it was the result of the exciting success this afternoon or some power exerted by his grandfather's quiet words.

As he struggled with his conflicting emotions, he heard the crisp laughter of two girls at the other end of the hallway. The sweetness of their voices contrasted strongly with his long shadow on the floor, as crude as a rusted iron club. In the last rays of twilight, he couldn't tell who, he or the girls, was more out of place. He really had no interest in conversation right now, but out of habit he went toward Luoying's room.

He saw Gielle through the open door.

"Rudy!" she called to him happily.

Rudy nodded at her. He turned to Luoying. "How are you feeling?"

He saw that Luoying's hair was a bit messy and her forehead was sweaty. She had just come home.

"I'm good," said Luoying, smiling. "Great, even."

"Liar!" Gielle tugged on her arm and grinned at Rudy. "She's acting strange all the time. I think she's in love!"

Gielle giggled. Though she was talking about Luoying, her own face flushed.

Rudy found Gielle's theory not implausible. Luoying was at just the age to be obsessed with romance. To be honest, he had been concerned with her odd behavior lately. Sometimes she would sit by herself next to the window, her arms around her drawn-up knees, doing nothing and not answering anyone. Sometimes she disappeared for hours without telling anyone where she had been. It had been more than a month since she had come back from her adventure, and he was worried about her. He was almost glad that everything could be explained by her being in love.

"There's nothing of the sort going on," Luoying said to Gielle.

"Don't gossip."

But her denial was perfunctory, as though she lacked the interest in making it convincing.

"Oh, I don't think it's gossip." Gielle turned back to Rudy. "You'd better interrogate her. Look at how she's always busy working on that big project. I bet it's a gift for her *boyfriend*!"

Rudy looked where Gielle was pointing and saw a pile of random materials by the window: cardboard, metal frames, ribbons of various colors. Some were cut into odd shapes and already pieced together. He couldn't tell what she was making, but it was obviously something quite large. He had never noticed these things before.

"I told you, it's not a gift," said Luoying. "Then what is it?"

"Just something to publicize an event."

"What event?"

"Something for the Mercury Group."

"I thought you guys are under isolation."

"Just for a month. It's almost over."

"Hmm... Who's organizing this?" Rudy asked.

Luoying looked him straight in the eyes. "It's not a boy. Really, don't listen to Gielle. Chania wanted to host a salon, that's all. And this really isn't a gift."

"Is Chania that girl I met at the hospital?" asked Rudy.

"That's her."

"Isn't she a gymnast? What kind of salon is she hosting?"

"Yes, she's a gymnast, but she's always been interested in classic essays and papers."

"What sort of classics, exactly?"

"Oh, you know—"

Gielle interrupted: "Rudy!"

Luoying and Rudy looked at her, but she blushed, as though suddenly losing the courage to say what she had been about to say. "Um... I guess it's late. I should go home."

"You're welcome at our home anytime," said Rudy, not really paying attention to her.

But Gielle didn't get up right away. She pointed to the side. "Can you help me carry that?"

Rudy saw that she was pointing at a gigantic planter with some flowering plant inside. The plant seemed familiar, but he couldn't recall the name.

"It's from our garden," Luoying explained. "Gielle likes it, so I'm giving her some."

Rudy was annoyed but tried to hide it. He picked up the planter and walked down the stairs with Gielle. He had been hoping to seize this opportunity to have a good talk with Luoying, but now the moment was gone, as impossible to recover as dissipating smoke.

He wasn't so self-absorbed as to not understand that Gielle liked him, but in his mind he was thinking only of Chania. Few girls left such a vivid impression after just one meeting. The corners of her eyes lifted up like the wings of a bird, and he liked the proud way she held herself. She was beautiful in an unembellished way. He wasn't so much interested in what she had to say or read, but he was curious about her. Normally, he wouldn't have talked to Luoying about a girl as he had just done.

Outside the door of the house, Rudy looked up and saw Luoying gazing at the horizon, lost in thought.

"I heard that you're promoting your magnetic car technology," Gielle said.

"Uh-huh."

"That's wonderful." Gielle smiled sweetly. "I was thinking... maybe you could make the seats dangling from the rails shaped like the letter C, with a colorful veil draping over the front."

"I guess I could," said Rudy noncommittally.

"Could you also hang a small platform below the seat and fill it with flowers?"

"Uh, sure."

"How about adding a waiting area in front of every house?"

"What's the point of that?"

"So a boy could wait there as his date arrives by magnetic car, of course." Gielle grinned at him. "Maybe there's no 'point,' but life would be so boring if everything has to have a point. You have to have some creativity, right?"

Creativity. Rudy looked at her helplessly and sighed inside. He thought he had finally figured out what the greatest invention on Mars was. It wasn't the central archive or the fusion engine but the mini-maker. Programmable and easy to use, the mini-maker was capable of assembling small objects out of raw materials. By changing the programming, it was easy to get a mini-maker to output variations on the same basic object. These machines had been invented at first for isolated outposts, but other inventors had extended their capabilities. Galiman had used them in the construction of houses, and Tyler later used them for garments.

Women always think of creativity in terms of how something looks, thought Rudy. *Here they'll change the color; there they'll add a bow. Or maybe they'll make a seat look like an eggshell. And then they think they're "designing." But they don't care about the concept, the idea! Good thing we have the mini-maker to keep them busy all day tweaking appearances.*

We always have to keep women busy somehow, lest they make a mess of the world.

———

At half past eight, after his daily walk after dinner, Rudy arrived at Don Juan, a bar favored by many of the legislators lately. He pushed open the pseudo-classic style door and surveyed the inside. Richardson, Ward, Franz, and Juan were all there. He felt good. *They are all here.*

Don Juan was pretty cramped, but it was so popular because it had long tables. Most bars had small tables placed far apart, but at Don Juan it was possible for a large crowd to all gather around a long table. The long and angled bar along the walls provided another place for patrons to stand and talk. The place wasn't well lit and the drink menu wasn't impressive, but the decor gave an alluring sense of possibilities, making everyone bolder in the dimness.

Rudy found a place at the side of the long table and poured himself a drink. Soon he was drawn into the flowing conversation. He leaned back in his chair, one leg propped against the table, laughing at the racy stories being exchanged. A red-faced, balding, middle-aged man sat next to him, stuttering a bit. On the other side of the table he saw Franz engaged in a whispered conversation with another man. Richardson was at the bar, glancing at his watch from time to time as though waiting for someone.

Rudy saw Juan making his way through the crowd toward him.

His dark round face glowed from alcohol, and he guffawed loudly as he joked with the others and slapped them forcefully on the shoulders. He looked meaningfully at Rudy, and although Rudy caught his look, he pretended not to notice. Satisfied, Juan looked away.

"You asked for cod! I remember it like yesterday," Juan shouted at a man who appeared already inebriated.

"No way!" replied the man, laughing. "I haven't eaten cod in more than two years."

"Want to bet? We can go ask Lucy. She was there."

"What do you want to bet?"

Rudy continued to converse with the balding man, but he wasn't really listening. Holding his tumbler, he looked about, absorbed in his own thoughts. Amid the noise of clinking glasses and laughter, he reviewed every step he had taken during the last two years and his recent plan.

After being a member of the Boule for two years, he had complicated feelings regarding the body. He had dreamed of making an impact right away, but once he was inside, he realized that no one cared about what he had to say. No one cared that he had graduated early at the top of his class or that he was the grandson of the consul. No one was going to deviate from established procedure because he was so exceptional; indeed, no one even thought he was exceptional. All the legislators had their own proud histories of accomplishments and issues they cared about, and none paid much attention to a junior member. For the first time in his life, he was ignored. During his first year in the Boule, he had had the sensation of having fallen from the apex of life to its nadir.

But Rudy was adaptable. Soon he adjusted to the reality of his station as the most insignificant member of that august body. He spent hours in the central archive gathering background on every legislator: curriculum vitae, research, past proposals, voting records, feedback from the public, history of complaints, political leanings, and political styles. In his mind, the structure of the Boule was like a three-dimensional model of the landscape, gradually becoming clearer as he added more details. He could now see patterns in the conversation groups at the bar and deduce the general goals of each conversation partner. He had begun to manipulate in a way that he had once thought was never necessary. He told no one of these developments, not even his own grandfather.

They say I've never suffered a setback, he thought, *but that's because no one knows my setbacks. So many mope about all day, hanging their heads as though they've suffered the worst fortune has to offer, but in reality it was nothing. They think not passing a test is a big deal. So absurd. The only setback worth thinking about is the distance between one's ideals and reality. Someone with no ideals has no right to talk of setbacks.*

He raised his chin and drained his tumbler in one gulp. When he set the glass down, he saw that Juan had slipped into the seat next to him. Still laughing at some joke, Juan draped an arm over his shoulder and raised a glass, just as he did with everyone he met at the bar. Rudy felt the weight of Juan's arm, but he strained to smile easily and clinked glasses with him.

"Good thing you're here tonight," Juan whispered. "I just got a piece of important intelligence."

Rudy laughed exaggeratedly, as though he had just heard some great joke. Then he lowered his head and whispered with his lips barely moving, "What is it?"

Juan looked to the side and laughed some more. "Earth has confirmed plans to build new defensive bases on the Moon."

"So they suspect something is going on."

"Definitely."

"What do you want to do, then?"

"We have to hurry. It will be too late if they complete the bases."

"I understand. Is there anything you need from me?"

"Just wait. I'll be in touch."

Juan pulled away and laughed, slapping Rudy's shoulder as though he had just told some lewd joke. Rudy put on an awkward expression and blushed to complete the performance. Juan stood up and soon joined other conversations, his rotund body swaying as he slowly headed for the bar. He stopped next to a tall man and started to talk to him loudly about some unimportant matter. Rudy looked down thoughtfully, appearing to observers like someone drowsy from drinking.

The new engineering plan was about to take shape. Anyone could see that this would usher in a new era for Mars. Both the natural environment and the social structure would undergo complete change, like a machine being taken apart and reassembled into something new. Everyone had to think about their position in the new social order.

Rudy had no idea how future Mars would develop, but he knew they were making history. This would be the first attempt—not just in Martian history, but in the history of humanity—to terraform a planet. Everything was change and turmoil, while the future was full of possibilities and uncertainties. Rudy felt the rising tide of excitement infuse his body. He knew that it was possible that the future would deem him a villain for being part of this transformation, but those in the future would also regret not being able to participate. In a time like this, people needed powerful leaders. Whoever contributed the most would then stand at the center of the future political stage, just like his grandfather and his companions after the war. Rudy was ready for it.

CHANIA

Chania took a guarded approach to the world. She was aware that sometimes she carried her skepticism too far and appeared unfriendly, but she had no choice. She thought of herself as the opposite of Luoying. Luoying was too trusting, believing in goodwill even when it was obviously nonexistent, refusing to accept facts. Chania preferred to protect herself. She didn't believe in love, the same way she didn't believe that those in power plotted for the welfare of the people as a whole.

When Rudy found Chania, she was making posters for the salon. She didn't hear him approach, and when she looked up, he was already standing right in front of her. It was too late to hide what she was painting.

"Keep on working. I won't bother you." Rudy smiled at her in a way meant to be disarming.

"Can I help you?" Chania stared at him.

"Oh, I just wanted to chat."

Chania bit her bottom lip mistrustfully.

"What are you making?" Rudy asked.

"A poster."

"It's so rare to see people paint by hand now. Why don't you do it digitally?"

"I don't like how digital paintings look."

Chania kept her answers curt without revealing her real motivation. She didn't want to leave any signs or clues in the central archive before the gathering. Public or private spaces in the central archive were the same in her eyes, because those in charge of the system could watch over anything taking place in the system. Yes, there were regulations against invasion of privacy, but she didn't trust them.

"What are the posters for?" Rudy continued to smile, his hands jauntily stuck in his pockets.

"How did you know I was here?" Chania was unsure of Rudy's motives or the extent of his knowledge. This made her feel unsafe. "If I told you I was just passing by, would you believe me?"

"No."

Rudy laughed. "All right, I admit it. Luoying told me that sometimes you meet here in the afternoons."

"What else did she tell you?"

"Nothing! Really. I asked her about your plans, but her lips were sealed."

"Then what are you doing here?"

"I just wanted to see you."

Rudy gazed at her, his eyes burning with suppressed desire. Chania looked back, and a mocking smile turned up the corners of her mouth. She could tell that he was trying his habitual tricks on her. She found the whole thing ridiculous. She wasn't interested in being a fortress for him to storm, to conquer, and she had no desire to see him try.

She lowered her head and picked up the paintbrush again. Since she had no artistic training, she was simply adding some decorative borders on the large letters. The strokes in the letters were angular and forceful, like a column of soldiers ready to fight.

"'Give me liberty or give me death,'" Rudy read. "Why are you writing that?"

"It's for a salon. A book discussion club."

"What will you be discussing?"

"Whether we really have freedom."

"Do you think we're not free?"

"We haven't had the discussion yet," said Chania coldly. "How am I supposed to have reached a conclusion?"

"How do you define 'freedom'?"

"The ability to determine one's own fate."

"But it's impossible to ever overcome the role of chance! Often an individual can't determine everything."

"As long as someone doesn't deliberately stand in the way, it's enough."

Rudy enjoyed this conversation. He came around to Chania's side, put one hand down on the table, and leaned over her shoulder. They were in the middle of a park built around an interchange station. The two large glass tables and the cubical stools made the setting convenient for small gatherings and for painting posters. Rudy's blond hair shone in the sun, but Chania refused to look up.

"Oh, I just remembered," said Rudy. "Last time, at the hospital, you expressed some opinions about your experience studying on Earth. I wrote up a report for the Boule."

Chania looked up, alarmed. "What did you write in it?"

"I explained that the pressures of adjusting to the new environment caused a lot of psychological pain for all of you. I suggested that the educational committee reevaluate the program comprehensively. Future students should be given much more preparation and counseling beforehand."

Chania lowered her head again. "You didn't understand what I said."

"What did you mean, then?"

"I was talking about the very idea of studying on Earth, not these insignificant details."

"So you are saying you shouldn't have been sent at all?"

"There's no way for you to understand. We saw a whole other world; it doesn't matter how we adjust to it. There's no way for us to come back. We can no longer tolerate…" She hesitated, searching for the right word. "Rigidity."

"I *can* understand," said Rudy. "Techno-bureaucratism."

"Yes, that's it!"

Rudy nodded. "I despise it, too."

"Really?"

"Of course. I've written multiple articles arguing against the current system."

Chania put her elbows on the table and looked sideways and up at Rudy. After a while she said, "Then I'll tell you the truth. The salon is actually a gathering to start a movement against this kind of techno-bureaucratism. We want to advocate for the free transfer of housing and atelier affiliations so that no one has to be stuck in one place."

"Oh?" Rudy's eyes brightened. "That sounds great."

"Do you really think so?"

"Absolutely. That would be a very good change." Rudy's voice was full of conviction. "Count me in! I'll help you in whatever way I can."

After a moment of hesitation, Chania nodded. She was trying to figure out what Rudy really thought—how much of his enthusiasm was genuinely because he thought as they did, and how much of it was because he wanted to get close to her. But she realized that even if he were motivated by the latter, it was no big deal. Their goal was to get the support of as many people as possible. Since he was the consul's grandson, his support would legitimize the movement and persuade more people. Having worked this out in her mind, she grew less guarded.

Though she didn't show him any signs of being particularly welcoming, when he reached out to help her move aside the completed poster, she didn't tell him to stop.

The next day Chania told Luoying what had happened. They talked as they walked to the housing office together.

Luoying wasn't surprised by her brother's interest, but she hadn't anticipated his supportive attitude.

"A month ago, when I mentioned the idea of revolution, he was totally against it."

"I don't know what he's really thinking," said Chania, "but he did say he hated techno-bureaucratism, too."

"That's possible," said Luoying. "Rudy has always chafed under his supervisors. I remember him complaining to me about the administrative structure, too."

The two were walking slowly toward the social activity center of Russell District. Since it wasn't the weekend, few people were at the activity center. On weekends these circular rooms served as meeting places for art clubs, gourmet clubs, community dance troupes, and so forth, but during the week they were mostly empty. Through the closed windows one could see the remains of the last activity in each room, waiting to be picked up again the next weekend.

The road to the activity center led straight south. In the middle of the road was a strip of lawn lined with trees; the shaded lanes were ideal for pedestrians.

"Your brother also pledged to help us."

"What does he have in mind?"

"He didn't say. He just said that he would help in any way he could."

"That's good."

"I don't know how serious he really was."

"I wouldn't worry about it," Luoying said with a grin. "Even if he didn't mean it, he said it so he could spend more time with you. But if he actually spends more time with you, he can't go back on his word. So we've got his help no matter what."

Chania blushed. "What are you talking about?"

Luoying giggled and ran ahead. "If it works out, I suppose I'll have to call you sister-in-law someday."

"As if I want to be your sister-in-law!"

"Don't you like my brother?"

"I don't like anyone."

"Not even Sorin?"

"No."

"Why not?"

"I've told you already," said Chania in a determined voice, "I don't believe in love."

"You're much too young to say something like that."

"Well, I don't. I agree with Runge that everyone is motivated by self-interest. What we call love is always disguised selfishness in the service of some agenda."

"What do you think is Rudy's agenda?"

"I don't know," said Chania. "People can be very indirect. Maybe he's a vain man used to everyone stroking his ego. Here I am, not moved by him, so he views me as a challenge, a potential conquest to prove himself."

"At least it demonstrates the power of your allure."

"Oh, please. There are only two possibilities: one, it's a momentary impulse on his part; two, he's in love with himself."

"How did you get to be so extreme?" Luoying sighed. "Sorin is right about you."

"And you're too naïve," said Chania. "Let me ask you: Do you trust how Anka feels about you?"

Luoying, caught off guard by the question, had to collect herself before brushing off the question with a careless laugh. "Don't change the subject to me... Do you think Anka is unreliable?"

"No, it's not about him. Feelings cannot be trusted, period."

"Did you hear something?"

"No. I'm just asking you: How can you be sure he loves you? Has he ever said so?"

"No."

"Then can you be sure that he's someone who believes in love?"

"I think he is."

"We believe him only because we are familiar with him. But that's no proof."

"What proof can there be?"

"There can't be any," said Chania, shrugging. "That's the point. So-called love is no more than emotional reactions when two people are together. But after the impulses subside, there's nothing."

"How did you become such a theoretician of love?"

Luoying acted like she didn't care, but her voice betrayed a lack of confidence. She kept her eyes on the road, her lips pressed together. Chania glanced at her from the side and waved a hand before her eyes. Luoying turned to smile at her, and Chania responded with a smile, too.

The two kept on walking in silence for some time, confusion and doubt plaguing both. Chania wasn't sure if she was absolutely right. She thought that her problem was that she wanted to see through everything, while Luoying wanted to see through nothing. While she couldn't really make herself see through everything, Luoying couldn't make herself *not* see through anything. Though neither of them talked about it, both were aware of the irony.

Should I trust just once? Chania asked herself. *Should I believe just once in unselfish benevolence and sincerity?*

"No matter what," said Luoying, as though hearing Chania's silent monologue, "I choose to believe. And I hope you will also believe at least once, no matter who you choose."

Chania was silent for a beat, then she smiled gently at Luoying.

"All right, let's hope for that."

The housing registration office was on the second floor of the activity center. A middle-aged woman sat alone in the rather large space, which made the place seem especially empty. In fact, no one was on duty there on a regular basis, and only by appointment would a temporary worker show up, which explained the simplicity of the facilities and the lack of amenities. In the middle of the circular office was an empty rectangular desk. The woman sat behind it.

"Who needs to register?" the woman asked them, smiling. She looked at Luoying and Chania over her glasses, shifting her gaze from one to the other. A hint of suspicion peeked through her polite demeanor.

"We're here to apply on behalf of a friend," said Chania.

"Why isn't he here himself?"

"Er…" Chania looked to Luoying. "This is a surprise gift for him."

The woman laughed at their ignorance. "Kids, I can't help you with that. We don't allow anyone except the applicant himself to go through the process. He has to verify the contract with his fingerprints. Why do you think we have this office instead of doing everything electronically through the central archive? The physical presence of the applicant is required."

Luoying and Chania looked at each other. Neither had anticipated this being an issue.

"Can't we just fill out the forms for him first and then bring him here later?" asked Luoying.

"We just want to help him build a small house, a tiny one," said Chania.

"We'll do the work ourselves," said Luoying. "We've already been to the construction office to reserve the materials and pick out a style. They told us that we have to come here first to register a site. Once that's done, construction can begin right away."

"Please," said Chania, "you've got to help us. Our friend has been such a big help to all of us, and we want to do something nice."

"Pretty please?" added Luoying.

Throughout this appeal, the woman listened intently. From time to time she looked ready to interrupt, but stayed quiet until the girls were done and looked at her expectantly. She took off her glasses and held them, her expression full of understanding but also helplessness. She put her elbows on the table, spread her hands, and spoke in a gentle tone.

"I'd love to help you, but registration requires fingerprint authorization. Let me think. Can you bring his marriage registration certificate?"

Luoying looked abashed. "That's... I'm afraid that's not possible."

"Then I can't help you. I can use the official documentation from the marriage office to register a site, but that's the only other way."

"He's not married, though."

"Not married?"

"No."

"Then why would he need a house? He should be assigned a dorm unit for singles."

"He *is* assigned to one, but it's too small. Before, when he had his social clubs and laboratory, it was no big deal. But now he's been deprived of everything. We think he has too little space, and we just want to help him out by giving him a little more room of his own."

The woman opened her mouth, and that look of helpless understanding appeared on her face again. She seemed to be struggling to explain. A moment later she grabbed a sheet of paper and started to draw some simple circuits.

"I don't know how to explain this to you." Her voice was kind. "Let me try this way... This office is like this resistor, or this diode... sorry, my specialization is in electronics, so I think of it this way... Our job is to receive documents from the office before us and then pass the new documents to the next office, the same way electricity flows through this resistor to the next component. A resistor can't make any decision on its own to generate an electron out of nowhere. That's the job of the power source. If a resistor starts to create electrons on its own, the circuit won't work. I'm so sorry, but there's nothing I can do."

The simple but honest explanation chilled the air instantly.

Chania bit her bottom lip, still trying to find a way around this "resistor," but Luoying grabbed her by the hand and shook her head. "Forget it."

She turned to the woman. "Thank you. Do you have a suggestion for where we should go, then?"

The woman thought for a moment. "I think it's best you go

to the marriage office and make some inquiries. Helping him get married is most important. Once he's married, the couple will naturally get a house."

Luoying and Chania walked through the wide empty corridors, not paying any attention to the publicity posters all over the walls. The marriage registration office was in the same building, and they followed the gently curving corridor, went up some stairs, and hoped that the attempt would yield something.

They bumped into a shut door. No one was in. Since they hadn't made an appointment, this wasn't unexpected. They were hoping for good luck, but luck wasn't interested. Through the glass door they peeked at the office inside. A white decorative table filled with artificial flowers stood on one side of the room, and many framed photographs hung on the walls.

An old woman came down the stairs behind them.

"Hello!" Luoying called to her. "Can you help us? Do you know if this office…"

She looked over at Chania, uncertain how to continue.

The old woman smiled at them kindly. "What are you interested in?"

Chania jumped in. "Do you know if this office can make introductions to potential marriage partners?"

The old woman looked at them curiously. "You?"

"No! Not for us," Chania said hurriedly. "For a friend."

"Oh. Why doesn't he just go to one of the singles parties? There's one every weekend."

"He doesn't like that sort of thing."

"Hmm, let me think." The old woman was apparently taking up this task enthusiastically. "What atelier is he with?"

"He doesn't have an atelier right now."

"Doesn't have one?" The old woman frowned at this impossible fact.

"He's helping out at the Registry of Files."

"I see." The old woman pondered the matter for a moment. "Young lady, based on my experience, I must say this is a very, very difficult task. Not impossible, mind you"—she paused, then added—"but very difficult."

The old woman's gaze embarrassed them. Luoying looked at Chania, and Chania looked at Luoying.

———

Later in the afternoon, as the pair walked toward First Hospital, Chania had entirely forgotten the tiny concession she had made to the possibility of love earlier that day. Once again she had returned to her cold and steadfast refusal to believe. She had in the past vacillated between the two positions, and refusal to believe made her feel safer. To be without expectations was also to be without disappointment and worry. She was her old self, convinced that behind all protestations of love there was only the pursuit of material gain.

"Haven't you heard enough?" she asked Luoying. "A stable marriage is just a way to get a house."

Luoying was feeling rather low as well. But she persisted. "I don't think that's true for everyone."

Chania could feel the chill in her heart as she spoke. "Why do you think no one on Mars gets divorced? It's because they can't. Remember how I explained to you that our low crime rate has nothing to do with our supposed superior moral development? It's the same with our low divorce rate. Married couples here are no more loving than couples on Earth, and we don't value family more either. The only reason people stay together is because of the house. After divorce, they would

493

both have to move back to singles' apartments. That's all the explanation there is."

Their conversation with the old woman had affected Chania deeply. Although she had vaguely sensed the truth, it had never been stated to her so clearly. A marriage, a family, a set of vows—none of these were as strong or sacred as she had believed when she was a little girl. On Earth, most people had long since abandoned the institution of marriage, and even on Mars, marriages were not so much driven by tender love as practical economic concerns. The old woman had told them that in order to resolve marital problems, two married couples would sometimes swap partners. After two divorces and two new marriages, there would still be two families and two houses. How much of such an exchange involved love? Chania had no idea, but she was sure her disbelieving position was the right one.

They were almost at the hospital. The pure white walls and simple design, half-revealed behind a row of short, cone-shaped pines, gave off a solemnity composed of cleanliness and lightness. They stopped. Chania looked up at the building, trying to find the small room near the top, which Luoying had described to her.

"Does Dr. Reini know our plan?" she asked.

"I don't think so. I never mentioned it to him."

"I still don't think our small gift is enough. We should try to get something more practical."

"But you've seen there's nothing we can do," Luoying said with a sigh.

Chania was about to say something more, but at that moment they saw something fall from the top of the hospital: the figure of a man.

Shocked, they stared at the falling figure, unable to make any noise as their hearts pounded wildly. The figure disappeared in a second behind the trees, and a dull thud came to their ears like an earthquake. Before they could even react properly, a man had plunged to the ground like a dropped package. A life had ended.

Chania felt a heavy weight press down on her heart. She couldn't breathe. Shuddering, she glanced over at Luoying, whose bloodless lips told her that they were thinking of the same memory.

They began to run. Many people emerged from the hospital, racing to the site of the fall. As they stared at the bloody, twisted limbs, Luoying stood still. She whispered to Chania that she had seen the man before. It was the mental patient she had encountered on the skydeck, the man who had slammed his fists and his body against the glass wall.

REINI

This was the 272nd day of the fortieth year of the Martian Republic, and also Reini's thirty-third birthday.

Reini got up early that morning, as was his habit. After vacuuming the Registry of Files, he stood in the reading room on the second floor and looked outside. Other than the large hall for the files, this was his favorite place in the Registry. It faced the lawn in the back, and the view was peaceful and comforting. He stood between the tall rows of bookcases, facing the window, the bright sun overhead. He didn't turn down the transparency of the glass. The decorative columns were bathed in the pellucid early-morning light. He loved to watch the light, which reminded him that life could still be bright.

Coming to the Registry was Reini's own choice. After so many years of writing history, he was familiar with the place. Laak, the Registrar, was someone he respected. The old man needed a younger assistant, while Reini needed inner tranquility.

The windows of the room were tall and narrow, with panes that slid up and down. Above the windows hung rolled-up cloth curtains, a rarity on Mars. The green tassels draped down, an echo of the green lawn outside. Since it was his birthday, he fell into reminiscence and stood longer than usual by the window. Memories overwhelmed him like the tides, and so he didn't realize he was no longer alone in the room.

"Dr. Reini," said a soft voice.

Reini turned around and saw Luoying. She was dressed in black, which made her appear even more pale.

"What a surprise!" He smiled at her.

"I came to wish you a happy birthday," said Luoying, walking up to the window.

"Thank you. I didn't know you remembered."

Reini was genuinely grateful. No one had wished him a happy birthday in a long time. Other than Luoying, he really couldn't imagine who else would visit him. His acquaintances at the various sports clubs preferred to spend their leisure time at home with their families, not visiting an old bachelor like him. He didn't like to organize parties, and anyway he had no room for guests. For years he had spent his birthdays alone. It touched him that someone had remembered.

"How've you been?" he asked.

"Pretty well."

"Keeping yourself busy?"

"Very busy. With a big project." Luoying paused and didn't elaborate, as though deliberately adding to the mystery. Her expression was a mixture of mischievousness and pride. Then she asked, "Dr. Reini, if you get the chance to go back to an atelier, would you prefer a hospital or an engineering research institute?"

Reini was surprised. "Why are you asking?"

"Because we're trying to find an atelier for you. There's some hope."

"Find an atelier for me?"

"Yes. Last week we inquired at two hospitals, in Galileo District and Watson District. Yesterday we spoke with an exploratory group within the Land System and gave them a brief description of your technology. They seemed really interested."

Reini looked awkward. "Thank you for all your efforts… but I'm afraid there's no possibility of me joining any of them."

"Why not?"

"Because my file has been frozen. I'm not allowed a transfer."

"But when we spoke with these ateliers, they all showed a lot of interest. Your technology can bring them renown and a bigger share of the budget. If they agree to have you, why won't it work?"

Reini shook his head. "It's not that simple. With my file frozen, it's impossible for me to register to use their equipment or to apply for funds with them."

"What if I ask my grandfather to unfreeze your file?"

"He's the consul," said Reini, smiling. "If he reversed himself just a month after he issued the order to punish me in the first place, the people would lose faith in him."

Luoying refused to give up. It was as though she had anticipated his answers. "What if we started a movement to abolish the file and atelier system?"

"What?" Reini was shocked.

"We've been thinking about it for a while. The system unreasonably locks every person down. If someone wishes to switch ateliers, they must first receive the system's approval to transfer their file. Without that, nothing can be done. This gives the system directors and the atelier heads too much power, and everyone has to obey them. And since the budget allocated to each atelier often depends on whether the atelier is responsible for some part of a large engineering project, the result is that everyone is dependent on their direct supervisor to assign them good projects. This becomes a problem for the whole republic. Society ossifies, loses initiative and liveliness. Techno-bureaucratism rules all."

Reini listened carefully. Luoying explained herself in precise, deliberate phrases, her expression serious. She was like a different person from the Luoying of two months earlier, when she had first returned from Earth. Back then, she had been more confused than determined, and her expressions showed much hesitation. Now she seemed far more purposeful, and the light of conviction glinted in her eyes. She seemed thinner and paler, perhaps the result of her injury and the time spent indoors, but her bright eyes gave her whole person more spirit. She was speaking slowly and precisely, so that the unfamiliar words flowed from her smoothly and naturally. Reini wasn't sure where her theories had come from, but he realized the youths were learning about and understanding the world at a rapid rate.

"You're trying to change the system, then?" asked Reini when Luoying was finished.

"Yes, I suppose we are."

"But have you thought that every system exists for specific reasons?"

"What reasons do you mean?"

"Historical ones, and ones imposed by the natural environment. There are always limits to how resources can be fairly distributed."

"We understand. But we don't believe we should ignore the faults of the system due to these reasons."

"It's impossible to construct a perfect system."

"But our system has severe flaws. It requires the individual to submit to the system, and those who refuse cannot survive. Those who rebel are imprisoned, perhaps driven mad until they seek the solace of death. A couple of days ago I saw a man jump to his death."

"I didn't hear about that. Where was this?"

"There's been no report," said Luoying. "You've met the

suicide: the mental patient we saw on the skydeck at the hospital, striking at the glass cage."

"Him!"

"Do you know him?"

"Yes. I've known him for a long time."

"Then do you know what happened?" asked Luoying. "We tried to find out more, but no one would tell us anything. We speculated that he was trying to break free from all the bonds around him."

Instead of answering, Reini was lost in thought. Luoying's news left a great emptiness in his heart. The trials and tribulations of years past surfaced in his mind all at once, and he felt the full force of the unpredictability of fate. The man's death was so unexpected. It was always hard to foretell a person's fortune and misfortune; indeed, sometimes it was impossible to even ascertain which category an event fell into. Compared to death, the struggles that occupied the minds of most seemed so petty.

He sighed. "I'm very grateful to all of you, but please don't trouble yourselves anymore on my behalf. I need your friendship, but that is all. I'm fine where I am."

Luoying looked perplexed and unwilling to give up. She nodded reluctantly but added, "I respect your decision, but I still want to urge you to reconsider. I know that you're indifferent to fame or gain, but that isn't the same as just giving in. You're a good man and you deserve better."

"Thank you," said Reini, smiling again. "I'll think about what you said."

Luoying lowered her gaze. "I don't believe that a just world should exploit a man like you."

Reini was deeply moved. When he first told Hans that he was willing to accept the responsibility for the youths' offense and thereby reduce their punishment, he didn't think he was doing them some kind of favor. He simply thought there was nothing wrong with the young to have an adventure. To punish them severely and ruin their prospects for the future was not a good result. He had not thought that his act would bring about such gratitude or care. He didn't know how to express how he felt. For too long he had not expressed such tender emotions.

After a moment he recovered and asked, "What happened to you recently? You seem to have become a radical."

"Do you really think I'm very radical?"

"A bit," said Reini. "Last month you were still skeptical about the value of revolution."

"That was true," said Luoying. "But recently I've come to appreciate the meaning of starting a movement. I think life requires action, otherwise there is no direction. I've been thinking a lot about Camus's *L'Homme révolté*, one of the books you gave me. It talks about the soil, the people, and the furious love of the heart strung like a tight bow. These things give life meaning. I want to do something. We're in search of targets, and this is the only action we feel has meaning."

"You're doing the right thing," said Reini.

Luoying looked at him. "Tell me the truth: Don't you think our system is too rigid, too lacking in freedom?"

Instead of answering her directly, Reini asked another question. "Do you remember what you said to me about the distance between one person and another on Earth? The unfamiliarity, the loneliness, the mutual distrust?"

"Of course."

"In reality, there are only two systems in the world: the solid and the liquid. A solid system features stable structure, in which every unit is fixed in its position. Between the atomic units the bonds are strong. A liquid system, on the other hand, features

501

freedom of movement, and the units are relatively independent. Between them there is no fixed bond, and little strength."

"Are you saying..." Luoying pondered this. "... that there is no way to have freedom and attachment both?"

"There are many values that are mutually exclusive."

Reini understood that Mars was the very embodiment of the crystal. The city was as stable as a crystal lattice. Every family had a house, and every house, with its yard, was similar in size. Houses were arranged in neat chains like periodic necklaces. Martians rarely moved. Children grew up in the houses of their parents until they got married, when they registered for their own houses elsewhere. A whole life was spent in two houses, and people were as rooted as plants. The neighborhood was the most important social structure, a child's whole world. Everyone they knew were the people who grew up with them and the people who, after their choice of atelier, accompanied them for the rest of their lives. While the city expanded as the population grew, each new residential district looked exactly the same as the rest of the city: the same neat chains of houses, the same peace and equality. Each house could be decorated in thousands of variations, but all of them together belonged to the same whole. Twenty million people were distributed evenly, and there was no structural center to the city.

Stability was premised on fixed bonds.

"But didn't you speak of clouds? There's both freedom and connection."

"Clouds, yes." Reini nodded. "But clouds require an external source of light and cannot last."

"I don't know," said Luoying, her gaze lowered. "I just think that if you avoid all conflict, where is your direction in life? If you accept everything and see through everything, doesn't that feel nihilistic?"

"Me?" Reini looked down, thinking, and then pointed to the other side of the reading room.

He took her through the long rows of bookcases. Old-fashioned books were arranged neatly on them, the gleaming golden letters against the red spines evoking another land. The paper had yellowed with age, like ancients living in the past. In the slanting sunlight, the room felt especially quiet. Overhead, the ceiling was decorated with the constellations turning almost imperceptibly, a reminder of unstoppable time. Reini walked through the stacks like a man walking through layers of illusions toward the heart of reality, facing the simple truth hidden in the memory banks. They walked without talking, the clicking of heels on floor the only sound in the room.

Reini stopped in front of a shelf labeled EARTH CLASSICS. He pointed at one of them. "*L'Homme révolté*." Then he took down a thin volume right next to it, flipped through until he reached the page he was looking for, and began to read aloud.

When he was finished, he closed the book, and, as always when he read these passages, his heart became storm torn. In his mind he saw the black sea facing the characters in the book, as well as the rough and vast desert of this planet. They showed his direction, he always knew. He could see all the people passing over this world, coalescing out of the swirling sand before scattering into dust again, busily coming and going, noisily shoving and pushing. He walked among them, their joys and sorrows surrounding him. He gazed at their faces. In his heart, what they wore, what customs they followed, what system they made, what acts they committed, were unimportant; what was important was whether they stopped to face each other, to look at each other. This was what he was truly interested in.

"Not heroism, not sainthood," Luoying muttered. "… you're more interested in being a human being?"

"Yes," Reini said. "That's what I want."

"But what does it mean to be a human being?"

"It means to be able to face another human being."

Luoying pondered the meaning of his words without asking more questions. Her absorption made her black eyes seem like two deep pools. She took the book from him and gently caressed the cover, gazing at it carefully.

"*La Peste*," she read.

"*La Peste*," Reini repeated. "Nowhere to go."

Luoying turned to the first page and began to read: "'It is as reasonable to represent one kind of imprisonment by another, as it is to represent anything that really exists by that which exists not.' Daniel Defoe…"

Reini did not explain, letting Luoying read on by herself.

Reini knew that, given how little time they had, it was impossible for her to read very far or for him to explain very clearly. More truths about life hidden in the depths of the cosmos were not even comprehensible to him. He contemplated the meaning of the movement Luoying mentioned, questioning himself whether he was too passive or reluctant to act. When he had suffered in life, he had asked himself the same kinds of questions, wondering if he had deviated from the appropriate course one should follow.

Normally, he viewed action pessimistically. In the endless ocean, he felt that hunkering on a barge that drifted with the current was a better choice than taking arms against a sea of troubles. But sometimes he berated himself for the pain he suffered as a contemplative and passive observer. Luoying's question struck at the very conflict in his heart.

A burst of music broke the silence among the stacks. Someone was visiting.

"Oh, it's time," said Luoying, closing the book.

"What is it?"

Luoying looked around for a clock. "Time passes so quickly!" Reini was still confused. Luoying beckoned him to follow her.

They walked down the curving corridor on the second floor, turned at the corner with the statues of angels, descended the broad, fanning stairs until they were in the lobby of the Registry. Luoying took a deep breath and smiled enigmatically at Reini. Then she pressed the button on the wall and watched as the heavy, curved bronze doors slowly slid open. She gestured outside.

Reini looked where she was pointing and stood still in surprise. A group of youths was smiling at him, beckoning him closer. Before them were arrayed the statues he had crafted over the years, as solemn as an army ready for inspection. In the middle was the lion that he had worked on for more than a year without finishing. Someone had roughed out the tail so that, though not perfect, at least the overall structure was complete. The crouching lion, stately and powerful, its earthy exterior as rough and worn as the skin of a battle-worn chief, wore a sash like a decorated soldier. Surrounded by the smaller statues around it, the lion resembled the leader of a caravan from afar bearing wondrous gifts, even its large, bell-like eyes emitting a lifelike light. Reini had never imagined his own sculptures would look so alive. The statues supported a banner: happy birthday.

Even though there was no wind, the banner seemed to be flapping.

Luoying had returned to her friends and joined their loud cheers for his birthday. Someone explained that, since they didn't think Reini alone could move so many things, they had moved all his sculptures and tools here so that he would be able to continue his hobby. Two of the youths in headbands danced with modeling tools, while another waved at the lion and other sculptures like a general directing a march. There was much laughter and cheer under the bright sun.

Reini didn't know what to say. There were no words to express his emotions; it had been years since he could recall such a warm memory.

A life force that he had not felt in a long time moved him.

———————

Reini had been born in year 7 of the Martian calendar, a year of divisions. He was now thirty-three, and whenever he looked back at the break that happened thirty-three years ago, he felt regret and sorrow. He knew that of all the choices that Hans Sloan had to make in his decades-long career, the division in year 7 was his most reluctant one.

Mars had not always been a crystallized world. The founders had chosen the central archive without settling on any specific social arrangement. In their idealistic fervor, they imagined a completely free world in which everyone was free to explore and discover, free to share their creations in the central archive, free to use the creations of others, supported by a stipend. But in the seventh year after the founding of the republic, the set patterns by which the world functioned pushed them to another extreme, leading to a structure that prioritized stability, regularity, and efficiency.

Usually, as a machine's design was optimized and its construction refined, thermal motion within the system became a greater source of noise and wasted energy. It was the same with a society. A world in which everyone was free to do as they liked sounded wonderful in theory, but in practice would result in the waste of a great deal of resources. Thus, in that year, the system crystallized in the city, and the random movements caused by freedom were reduced to a minimum. Layers stacked upon layers of supervision; departments and administrative organs interconnected into chains; the system reintegrated and re-formed. In other words, the system was bureaucratized.

The decision wasn't made by a plebiscite but in the Boule. Which matters would be submitted to a plebiscite was always a subtle decision, and the first consul of Mars, Richard Sloan, had decided on the Boule vote alone. Hans and his friends, all legislators, debated the issue heatedly. Several of his friends opposed the idea of sacrificing freedom in the name of efficiency, with Ronen and Garcia the loudest voices. Hans and Galiman, on the other hand, argued that ideals had to make compromises with reality.

Since the Boule was composed of the individuals from each system who were most dedicated to building and policy making, natural supporters of system consolidation, it was believed that support for the reforms would be overwhelming. But the result of the vote turned out to be extremely close. The bureaucratization faction won by only a very slim margin. A system inspired by circuit design in which the individual units were ateliers offered great conveniences for management and overall planning. No one could tell just what role Hans and his friends played in that vote.

In the face of such a momentous choice, everyone's character was starkly revealed. Different individuals chose different worlds, and some entered the system, while others left.

Hans disliked the systemization. He preferred the preconsolidation arrangement in which individuals freely joined small groups to conduct cross-discipline research. But he also understood that a combination of specialization, departmentalization, and process management was the most reliable way to improve efficiency in any era. In the end, he voted for the system. He remained a part of the system, specializing in flight, and won the trust of his peers with his wartime experience and exploration of remote sectors. A decade later he was promoted to Archon of the Flight System.

Galiman, the designer of Martian housing, had already achieved much as an inventor and researcher during the war and was well known by the public. After the reform, he didn't leave the system. Instead he became part of the glass research atelier under the Land System. He focused on scientific research as well as politics and was responsible for turning his atelier into the top research institute on the planet. Eventually he became Archon of the Land System.

Ronen and Garcia, on the other hand, refused to accept the change quietly. Ronen had a deep distaste for the new schools, which tried to specialize pupils based on their talents. Forever a generalist, there was no ready-made position for him. He turned down all management and political responsibilities and spent his time traveling between Mars and the dwarf planets, building a deep bond with Ceres.

For two years Garcia tried to work within the system, thinking that he could learn to collaborate with bureaucrats, but the effort came to naught. He couldn't live with the system, and the system rejected him. Thus, he asked to be given the mission of developing diplomatic relations with Earth, a task that nobody else at the time wanted.

These events ultimately led to results that no one could have predicted. Hans became consul of Mars, but the system's allocation of power led to opposition from his son, forcing Hans to punish him. Ronen's wanderings turned into permanent exile, with no corner of his home planet able to hold his proud figure. Galiman's system needed Ceres, and so he had to allow Ronen to take his stories with him to a grave among the stars. Garcia lived on *Maearth*, never setting foot on a planetary surface. He opened a window for Mars but also brought to Hans's son the spirit of rebellion from another land and, ultimately, death. He also set Hans's granddaughter on a spiritual journey as a perpetual vagabond.

The decision changed Reini's life as well. After Garcia finally knocked open the door to Earth and established diplomatic relations, the first demand from Earth was the release of war prisoners. Reini's mother thus left. She was so overjoyed at the news that she put down Reini, only three years old at the time, and returned to her home without looking back.

When Reini worked on the old files, he would from time to time read snippets from that momentous era. He would then look out the window, sighing over how a single moment could change the course of all the other moments in the river of time so irrevocably. The crystal city spread before him, at once fragile and glowing. Human forms, trapped in time, turned into silhouettes with open arms and frozen expressions, tracing out the paths of unpredictable fate step by step.

———

Reini emerged from the Registry of Files and got on the tube train heading for the Tarkovsky Film Archive.

From the train, he looked back at the Registry, wondering whether staying here was the right choice. He decided it was. Sometimes Reini felt that he was more comfortable with the people and events of the past; they were the constant presences in his life. The cobblestone streets of old Earth, lit by dim streetlamps and strewn with trash, and the ancient bridges and plazas of London, filled with bronze statues, though the memories of another planet, felt to him as real as the small red circular tables in the corners of the Registry, more familiar than the sights and sounds of his life. The wisdom of the past was always with him, giving him faith that the silent and lasting sentiments weren't wrong.

He hadn't been to the Tarkovsky Archive in a long time. Earlier in his life he had gone there twice a year, but more recently he had stopped doing that. Those worthy of memorializing weren't remembered as often. Still, the way to the archive was etched in his mind, and even with a different origin station, he knew how to get there quickly by train. He called ahead so that Janet would be expecting him at her atelier.

He didn't know how to start the conversation with her; each year, when they saw each other, he didn't know what to say at first. Janet was twelve years older than he was, but a group of people bound them together. They never spoke of the source of their friendship. There was no need when the bond was as solid as the ground itself.

Reini never told Luoying that he had once studied under Adele, her mother. For three and a half years she taught him the art of sculpting at a community studio. Those were the most important three and a half years of his life.

When Reini saw Janet, he felt sorry for her. When the young man from Earth brought the news that Arthur had died, she had seemingly aged ten years overnight. Faith provided support to the spirit, and spirit provided support to the body. For a decade Janet had lived on a belief, a hope, but now she was without its sustaining strength.

Nonetheless, she strove to be friendly, even with the sadness that couldn't be hidden. She led him to her atelier and poured him a cup of tea. He got to the point right away, informing her of Luoying's description of their plan for a revolution.

As Reini had anticipated, Janet fell into a thoughtful silence as she stared out the window, her eyes unfocused.

"It's been ten years," said Reini with a sigh.

"Yes, it has."

"Sometimes I think history is repeating itself." Janet said nothing.

"Their passion and sense of justice... so familiar."

Janet turned back to the room and drained her teacup in one gulp. She gazed at Reini. "If you think you're seeing history replay itself, how do you think I feel?"

LUOYING

As death fell to the ground before their eyes, Luoying and Chania were thinking of the same memory. It was a terrifying moment on Earth, a moment that persisted for a long time in their still-childish hearts.

It was a public holiday, when many people had gone to the beach. Few were left in the city, and a dozen or so members of the Mercury Group gathered in Bangkok from around the world, where they rented a cheap cargo airship and cruised over the city for fun. The cargo airship was very slow and not terribly stable, but there was plenty of space in the gondola for the group to sit around in a circle and play cards. Luoying was at the back while the other kids laughed and joked, creating a joyous mood. Outside the gondola, the steel-girded skyscrapers passed one by one. They were flying fairly low, so that many of the skyscrapers towered over them.

That lazy afternoon was torn apart in a moment. Luoying happened to be glancing outside the gondola when the man fell. A few others saw him as well, and everyone stopped the game. The man, his limbs flailing, swept past the gondola in a flash. His clothes billowed in the wind, and his face, twisted features frozen into a grimace like a deformed portrait, seared itself into their minds. Luoying rushed to the porthole, but all she could see was a seemingly bottomless chasm. On Earth, it was impossible to see the ground from the top floors of buildings, and impossible to see the sky from the ground. She was so terrified that Sorin had to hold her and gently cover her eyes.

A few minutes later they saw from the network bulletins that the suicide had been a medicinal chemist who had discovered the cure for the KW32 virus. Investors, hoping to make a killing, bid his stock up to stratospheric levels. However, he kept on missing deadlines, and though much of the funds raised by investors had been spent, there was no result. Two days earlier his stock had collapsed, trapping many investors. Besieged by angry shareholders, he finally couldn't take the strain anymore. With the news of his death, the bulletins automatically showed contextually relevant warnings that investors should be cautious with cutting-edge research. It was possible to lose everything.

Luoying and her friends stayed out all night. They sat in a small bar until it was midnight, and then they wandered around the deserted and dark streets. Runge took off his jacket and draped it around Luoying to keep her warm. Near dawn, hungry and tired, they found a twenty-four-hour restaurant and wolfed down some breakfast. The other patrons of the restaurant, clearly denizens of the city's seamier side, looked at them oddly. None of them brought up what they had witnessed, but a cloud of depression hung over the group. They understood how scientific research worked: it was a matter of luck. There was no way to guarantee return on investment, and they couldn't imagine how anyone survived if research had to produce results according to a fixed schedule.

They missed home so much in that moment. At home, research and exploration were not subject to such inhumane pressures. They had believed that nothing of the sort would ever happen at home. But they were wrong.

That memory had returned to Luoying in such an unexpected manner. Before she had had time to sort out her past, her reality had collided with her memories, forcefully extracting a moment she had witnessed and endowing it with new meaning.

What did Luoying believe about her home? She never expected it to be as lush or rich as Eden, full of fruits and honey and milk. She knew it was a poor planet, limited in livable space, beset by danger, where everyone lived on the edge of death every day and had to carefully conserve the resources they had, all of them precious. She knew all that, but she had held on to a fantasy of her home as a pool of tranquility, a place where you felt at peace, not overwhelmed by stress. She recalled that at home no one needed to worry about food, clothing, or shelter. Everyone was free to pursue their interests and dreams. There was no employer who exploited your every productive moment, and you were free to spend your time as you wished. What a free and carefree place home was in her recollection!

But now her surroundings had intruded on her memories. Home was not simple or tranquil. It was full of competition, invisible restraints, oppression that had to be submitted to. It locked everyone in place like components on a circuit board. Inside, there were deaths, power struggles, the just who were deprived of happiness due to false accusations. What kind of world was this? Why was it as hard to survive here as in the other world?

Dr. Reini said that he wants to be a human being who can face another human being, thought Luoying. *What about me?*

Dr. Reini was not an activist, not a doer. Luoying wasn't sure if she should be one. She hesitated over whether to join the movement. It was a momentous choice. At first she had not wanted to join, and then she changed her mind. She had even prepared her props. But after the conversation with Reini, she was leaning toward staying out of it again.

Sitting at the window, Luoying gazed up at the sky, vacillating between her choices. The death she had seen was like a knife that sliced open the curtain over her life, that unsealed the storage sack of her memories. Moments spilled out like a flood, and she watched her own hesitation like a consciousness detached from the world.

She recalled the last time she had participated in a collective movement. That was back on Earth, with her Terran friends. She had joined a group of Reversionists, fanatical environmentalists who yearned for the world to revert to ancient ways of living and tried to dismantle the modern metropolis. In the twenty-second century, when all the authentic, so-called primitive ways of life had disappeared and died out, their passion was clearly tinged with an exoticizing gaze. Because what they yearned for was so unattainable, they craved and believed in it all the more. All of them were very young, and they launched resistance movements across the globe, trying to halt the irresistible tide of sprawling urbanization. At the time, cities on Earth were still growing as remaining pockets of rural population were being absorbed. Concentrating the human presence on Earth was a response to the growing cost of energy and a way to reduce humanity's impact on the environment. But the Reversionists disagreed.

"It's nothing more than bottomless greed!" they shouted. "We don't need cities!"

They sat before tents pitched in the highlands, surrounding a bonfire. Luoying listened to the speeches.

"Can you imagine how much energy it takes to construct a mega-metropolis?" asked one of the older boys. He was lecturing Luoying. "Can you imagine how much energy it costs to maintain the abandoned land? In the old days, people lived in small towns scattered around the country, and that was the best! Some claim that small-town life was unsatisfying, and that was why everyone tried to go to the big cities the first chance they got. Lies! All lies! It's all motivated by greed. Desire is the fall of humankind. Earth was at first a paradise, but we fell because of unchecked desire.

Look at what a hell we've made of our planet!" Luoying nodded, not sure she really was following.

"We must fight against all extravagant desires and destroy dreams of luxury while the blood of purity still flows through our veins!"

They seemed to be always speaking with exclamation points.

"We must protest, march, demonstrate! We must tear down those buildings and return to nature! We must shout our rage and let our voices be heard!"

Luoying looked thoughtful and then asked, "Why can't you just talk to the governments?"

"How can you trust governments?" They laughed. "You're the granddaughter of a dictator. You may have faith in governments, but we don't."

At the time Luoying asked these questions, she didn't care about the answers. She had journeyed with them for many days until they reached this uninhabited plateau, where they cooked over open fires surrounded by snowy fields that hadn't be disturbed in ages, where they could gaze up at night and see the stars, usually invisible in the bright glow of Earth cities. She had no clear understanding of their purpose, but she was glad to chant their slogans and wave their banners. She was like a kid who had come along to have fun, not caring where they were headed or why, running ahead in her excitement without wavering.

Thinking back now, she realized how happy she had been in those days. Fully absorbed, with no need for reflection, she had followed her determined and passionate friends into marches and protests, screaming and shaking her fist—oh, such unfettered joy!

In the end they had been arrested on account of the damage they had done to the airport on the plateau. After three days in a crowded detention center, the protesters were released to be deported back to their countries. It wasn't the most glorious ending, but they certainly made a lot of noise while it lasted. Laughing and hugging, they said goodbye to one another and scattered to the ends of the earth.

Luoying shook herself out of her reverie. She jumped onto the floor and ran barefoot to the screen on the wall, where she opened her mailbox.

Dear Eko,

> *I hope you're well.*
> *What's happening with the movement you were going to start?*
> *I admire you and wish you all the best.*
> *I wanted to ask you about the situation of the Reversionists on Earth. Do you know if they've launched any new movements or published any new manifestos? I once marched with them, and now I miss that time.*

> *Thank you,*
> *Luoying*

Luoying pressed send and watched as the animation showed a letter flying away. She realized that she needed action. In fact, she didn't even care about the system that much. The distinction between various systems didn't seem all that important to her, and she didn't share Chania's visceral distaste for what she termed "the evil inherent in the system." She was attracted by the idea of action itself. She liked the pure life force that came to the fore when one was devoted to some movement, a flash of release, in stark contrast to the habitual care, restraint, and self-consciousness of daily life. When one was acting as part of a movement, a person was full of life and unified with one's will. She envied that state.

She thought about the movement they had discussed and made her decision. No matter what, she was going to try. She was only eighteen, standing at the threshold of the world. They were unsatisfied with the world, and this was perhaps their only opportunity to fight it. She thought and thought, and said *yes*.

––––––

The location selected for the final meeting before they launched the movement was a place Luoying both craved to be in and wanted to avoid at all costs: her parents' study. Rudy was the one who invited Chania, Luoying, and all the other participants to come. Luoying was surprised at how seriously her brother seemed to be taking all of this.

She did have some reservations. After so many days back, the study had become a vast and intricate garden in her mind. She had stayed away from the room, uncertain what she was afraid of—no, certainly not the objects that served as memorials to her parents—but she was reluctant to face the objects whose significance she had devoted so much energy to pursue. Perhaps because she had been so relentless in her initial quest, the obstacles she had encountered had pushed her to the other extreme. After Rudy pushed open the door and entered, she followed without speaking. Dragging her feet a bit, she passed Chania, Runge, and Sorin. No one noticed her hesitation.

The room was still as quiet as she remembered.

On the long desk next to the wall lay paintbrushes, sculpting knives, and a tea set that hadn't been cleared away, as though a noisy party had just concluded. Everything in the room appeared hazy, like antiques. The slanting rays of sunlight, filtered through the turquoise curtains, refracted into a cold arc. Where sunlight didn't reach, shadows stretched deep, making the lit area next to the window even brighter by contrast, endowing it with an otherworldly glow.

"Sit! Please, sit!" Rudy gestured to everyone.

Luoying watched as everyone took their seats around the low bookcases in the middle. Her brother was next to Chania, while Sorin and Runge sat opposite them. There was one person leaning against the bookcases, another who had their feet on a shelf, elbows supported on their legs.

She shuddered, startled. Everything, the postures and expressions, seemed to match the hazy memory in her head. When she was little, she had witnessed a scene just like this as she sat quietly to the side. Those enthusiastic figures had been sitting around this room, excitedly discussing topics that transcended reality.

Luoying watched them. Chania cocked her head as she surveyed the paintings hanging around the room, her long hair draping behind like a waterfall, her face curious and eager. Sorin and Runge were reading the titles on the bookcases and whispering to each other. Rudy stood leaning against a bookcase. Casually dressed, he appeared handsome and confident as he smiled at them.

"Have you decided on a day for the protest?" he asked Chania. "Not yet. We're thinking four or maybe five days from now."

"How about Sunday?" Rudy asked. "There's a session of the Boule on that day, which will gain us more attention."

"Wouldn't that seem a bit too provocative?" Sorin looked concerned.

"Don't worry," said Rudy. "I guarantee you'll be safe. The question is whether you have the courage to face them head-on."

Chania lifted her eyebrows challengingly. "What's there to be scared of?"

Luoying said nothing. She had no desire to speak at all. In fact, she found herself trapped in a sensation of being in two places and times at once. The scene around her felt unreal. The beige bookcases were veiled in a gossamer woven from golden sun rays, while the photos on the walls came to life as reflections of reality. Her mother was making a speech in the air, her black eyes and black hair aglow from her fervor. On the other side, her father sat with his elbows on his knees, explicating something deliberately. Their figures overlapped with her friends', and they looked right through her. There was another person in the room, the man named Arthur. He was quiet and had curly hair, and Luoying had few memories of him—though she did recall how he had once patted her head and told her the story of Sinbad the Sailor. Their faces and figures floated in the air like transparent ghosts surrounding them. On a shelf next to the window stood the unfinished sculptures, time travelers who had traversed ten years.

"I don't care what day we hold the protest," said Chania, staring at Rudy. "But I want to know, why are you helping us?"

Rudy smiled. "Do you want to hear the truth?"

"Of course."

"One reason is that I think I'm falling in love with you."

Chania smirked. "I don't believe you, but thanks."

"Another reason is that I agree with you." Rudy continued to smile confidently. "For some time now I've been thinking of reforming the system, but I've always kept those thoughts to myself out of fear of giving offense. All the problems you've pointed out—institutional inflexibility, excessive conformity to one approach, lack of individual freedom, and so on—I agree with all the critiques! For instance, you mention the administrative system that operates like a fixed circuit. But in my view, it's not just the administration but all of our institutions that are controlled like circuits. There is no freedom for the individual. From one atelier to another, we are just interchangeable components functioning according to our specifications, without the need for souls. In order to achieve a better world, we can't pretend to be blind to its faults."

Sorin frowned. "But… you're expanding on our proposals. We weren't thinking of getting involved in areas we don't understand. The engineering institutions, for example, are too complex for us. Actually, isn't there a system in place now that allows the various labs to associate freely and apply for project funding together?"

"There is such a system," said Rudy. "But I don't think you fully appreciate the implications. If you imagine each lab as an electronic component—resistor, capacitor, quantum transistor, or whatever—then so-called free association is just each component melding itself into the circuit, hoping to become a part of the next big circuit. And once the project is funded, all that's left is repetition and obedience. Do you know who benefits from a system like this? Only the aged who already have fame and accomplishments. Once they gain the power to design the next generation of social circuitry, they'll use their authority to force others to travel along paths they plan out. They have too much power! The problems you've identified aren't limited to administration but touch upon the very philosophy of the functioning of society. If we're to start a movement, we can't be too timid. We must be direct and forceful, plunging into the heart of this world like a sharpened knife."

No one spoke in the ensuing silence. Chania squinted and gazed at Rudy thoughtfully. Sorin and Runge looked at each other.

Runge spoke up first. "I think the problem you're describing stems from the disease of 'great accomplishments dementia'— an unreasoning obsession with doing great deeds."

"So do you agree?" asked Rudy cautiously.

Runge didn't answer him directly. "But we don't know what you want to do about it."

"What I want to do about it?" A dark glint flashed in Rudy's eyes. Slowly he paced to the other side of the study and activated a small wall panel. He selected a few options on the screen, swung his hand down forcefully, and then pushed a button. Then he swept his arm across the blank wall as though sketching out some burning mural of change before turning to say in a cold voice, "What I want to do is the same thing my parents did: start a revolution."

Luoying gasped.

She stared at the wall that Rudy had swept across. The whole wall showed an old photograph of their parents. The pair were dressed formally but with their collars and cuffs unbuttoned to show an air of careless grace. They stood shoulder to shoulder, their expressions full of fervor. Behind them were two immense mining vehicles like monsters at rest, waiting for orders. From the vehicles draped giant posters the size of theater curtains, filled with images of banners, gods, and crowds of people. On the bottoms of the posters, in jumbo letters, appeared the slogan WE DON'T WANT CORRUPT REPRESSION!

Other photographs appeared on the wall. More people: some running in a crowd; some making speeches before audiences; some raising banners with animated images; some standing around Quentin and Adele, their eyes on the pair. In all the photos, there were signs saying fairness and the like, some of which were even humorous. The crowds were never very big, but the ardor, like boiling water, bubbled out of the images.

Luoying was amazed. She approached the wall slowly, as though trying to walk into the pictures. Rudy had already forgotten the photographs as the discussion continued. Chania was talking, but Luoying heard nothing. She pressed a hand against the wall, trying to caress the faces of her parents through time.

Abruptly, she ran out of the study to get her holographic glasses. She hadn't entered the full-fidelity virtual world in a while, but never before had it held such allure for her. She put on her glasses and tried to overcome the vertigo as she looked around, trying to identify where she was and who she was with.

She didn't see the place where her parents had gathered with the other protesters. In fact, she didn't see her parents. Whether due to an error in her selection or because the photographs weren't associated with a full-fidelity data source, the program automatically placed her elsewhere. Instead of the scene she was hoping to see, she found herself in a stately but slightly dim hall with tiers of seats around, filled by many silent people. She recognized it as the Boule Chamber. The silence around her felt oppressive.

Uninterested, she was about to depart the replay to search

for more scenes involving her parents in the directory, but at that moment she saw her grandfather. He entered from a side door and strode onto the raised dais with confident steps. A column of elders followed him.

Hans began to make a speech, but she couldn't hear what he was saying. The scene had no sound—or maybe there was but she couldn't find a way to turn it on. She could see that his expression was very calm, but occasional traces of sorrow, exhaustion, or remorse flickered across his face. The speech seemed like an explanation, or perhaps a confession. Then he took off the gleaming medal he wore on his chest, set it down gently on the podium, and looked around the hall.

Next she saw Uncle Juan. She wasn't sure what was happening, but the scene shifted abruptly. Uncle Juan stood up from his seat and gestured with his hands. Everyone in the hall looked where he was pointing. Luoying couldn't see what had attracted their attention, but she saw that Juan's expression was somber, even angry. His dark face was filled with a cold strength that no one dared to challenge. He held up his hands and pressed them downward as though bringing a weight over the whole chamber.

Luoying wanted to see more, but the scene blacked out abruptly.

She took off the glasses and saw Rudy standing in front of her. He had turned off the control screen, and the wall behind her was empty. He took the glasses from her. She tried to grab them back, but he held her at bay and put the glasses away. There was no anger on his face, but his determined attitude brooked no disagreement. He shook his head at her, his expression gentle but superior, as though saying, *I'm doing this for your own good.*

She shook her head angrily. Ever since the incident with

her dance costume, she hated Rudy's condescending attitude more than anything else. She looked at him pleadingly, but he had already turned around and was walking out of the study.

Only then did Luoying realize that the study was empty. The others had already left.

She chased after him. At the bannister she called out, "Rudy! What was that?"

Rudy paused on the stairs and looked up at her. "What are you talking about?"

"The recordings, the photographs, everything I saw!"

"I have no idea what you saw."

"What happened to you? Why did you change so suddenly? Two months ago you said you were against revolution."

"Did I?"

"You did! I asked you why Grandfather suppressed the protests.

You said they were too dangerous and that suppression was the right thing to do."

"Hmm." Rudy looked thoughtful for a moment. "Maybe I did say that. I can't remember."

Luoying hesitated for a beat. "I think you've changed."

A smirk. "I know what I'm doing."

They descended the stairs quietly. Chania and the others were already at the door and waving goodbye to them. Rudy approached them and seemed to make more plans, but Luoying was in no mood to pay attention. Confused images circled in her mind, more real than the reality around her.

The next day Luoying came to the First Flight Center of North District.

She had never been here. The flight center was a grand and

magnificent building with few visitors. The ceiling of the vast circular hall was held up by forty silver-gray columns, and the floor was crisscrossed by moving walkways that were still at the moment. Around the edge of the hall, various pieces of equipment and instruments beeped and chirped quietly. Everything was the model of order and discipline.

Luoying saw Anka from a distance. He was busy with something and didn't see her. Luoying had looked up the schedule ahead of time and knew that today he was on duty alone. As she approached, she saw that Anka was trying to repair something in front of him, and his broad back resembled a little hill.

Gently, she crossed the vast hall. Two brand-new aircraft rested next to each other. Silver in color, with aerodynamic curves and smooth hulls, they resembled two elegant dolphins lying on a beach. Steel racks stood around the hall, with robotic arms folded neatly at rest, exuding a stately presence. There was no one else here except Anka, and the blinking lights on the walls—indicating surveillance cameras—were his only companions.

Anka was on one knee next to a shelf at the wall, elbows on the ground, trying to put something together. Before him, a white object lay in two pieces like the two halves of a broken eggshell. One half was almost empty, while the other half was filled with electronic components.

"Anka," Luoying said softly.

Anka turned around, surprised. He wiped away a bead of sweat from his nose with the back of one hand, which left a smudge.

"Are you still repairing your fighter?"

"Yeah. Working on the navigator now. Almost done."

"You'll be able to fly it after?"

"I hope so."

He looked exhausted but still focused. She wasn't sure how to encourage or comfort him.

"You have to fix everything by hand like this?"

"No. I can't open the sealed integrated components. For those I have to reserve time at the repair station and use the waldos."

"Sounds hard."

"There's no choice."

"Captain Fitz still won't give you a working plane?"

"He said he would if I apologized publicly."

"I see."

Anka smiled at her, as though Fitz's harassment didn't bother him. He knelt down again and returned to his task. Luoying sat down on a tool chest next to him, watching him quietly.

"What made you come to visit?" Anka asked as his hands remained busy.

"I have... two questions," Luoying said. "The first is: What kind of person is Uncle Juan? I mean, how do people see him in the Flight System?"

Anka's hands stopped. "Why do you want to know?"

Luoying described the recording she had seen. Then she added, "I don't know how to describe it. But... every time I see him, I get a different impression. Sometimes he seems so kind, but at other times he seems terrifying. I don't know what happened in the scene I told you about."

"I haven't heard anything like that either."

"So what's his reputation in the Flight System?"

"Hmm." Anka paused to think. "He's a man with ideas. But... he seems like an anti-moralist."

"How do you know that?"

"It's just an impression." After a beat Anka added, "He doesn't give many speeches, and I don't see him often."

Luoying nodded. Then she asked, "Can the Flight System deploy troops?"

"Yes. It has that power."

"But why? I thought the Flight System normally has authority only over transportation and civil missions."

"Theoretically, that's true. But the design of the Flight System has always been highly militarized, and resources can be shifted over to military deployment at any time." Anka paused to think. "Do you remember the base we saw when we came out of the crater?"

Luoying tried to remember. "You mean the one we saw when you and I were flying like kites? The one that's not too far from Angela Bluff?"

"Yes. I found out that it's a secret military research station after I got back."

"Military?"

"That's right. And it's administered by the Flight System. I heard it was set up by Juan personally, as the archon."

"I've never even heard of it. I can't imagine my grandfather would have approved."

"I wouldn't know anything about that."

Luoying was quiet. Lately she had found out so much more about the world, things she had never known before, that she didn't have time to process it all. All she knew was that the world seemed far too complicated to be seen clearly. Anka also stopped his work and stared at the floor, his gaze unfocused as he pondered something.

"Are you coming this Sunday?" Luoying asked.

"What's happening on Sunday?"

"It's our protest rally."

"What protest rally?"

"The one that Chania wanted to start: the march for the free flow of housing and identities. We've been talking about it over electronic group messaging. I thought you were part of the thread."

Anka looked unconcerned. "Oh, I've been getting the messages. I just haven't paid much attention."

"So are you going?"

"Don't know yet. I guess we'll see."

Anka looked absent-minded as his slender fingers busied themselves again. Luoying suddenly felt that he was very far away. She had come today to find him, hoping to talk about her anxiety and confusion, hoping for some comfort, not just to talk about some abstract grand ideas about the world that neither of them really understood. But now she didn't know how to continue. Anka was sitting right across from her, but she couldn't tell him of her perplexity and unease.

She wanted to return to that warm night in the cold cave, but it seemed so distant that it was unreal. After their return, they were each in isolation for a month, and then they were too busy to exchange more than a few words. Luoying had the sudden sense that there was nothing special between the two of them, and the warmth that she had felt with him was just a momentary emotional surge. She recalled the words of Chania, her pessimism toward all lasting attachment.

"Do you care about what I do?" she asked impulsively.

Anka looked up, a bit confused. "What do you mean? The march on Sunday?"

"No. I don't care about that."

"Then what do you mean?"

"Nothing specific or concrete. I'm just asking if you care. About me."

Anka looked at her, a trace of anguish flickering through his eyes. Then he looked distant again. "What do you want me to say?"

Luoying choked on a lump in her throat. "What do I want you to say? What can I have you say?" Anka said nothing.

"Do you believe in lasting love?" she asked.

"No," said Anka. "I've never believed in anything like that."

Luoying got up and said that she needed to be on her way. Anka nodded and told her to take care of herself. He was on duty and couldn't walk her out. She hoped that he would ask her to stay longer, or say something comforting, but he didn't. Quietly she left, walking straight out of the vast circular hall without looking back.

GIELLE

What does Rudy have in mind?

Gielle's emotions had been in turmoil for the last few days. Rudy's behavior was so strange. She thought he was giving her hints, or even confessing his feelings, but other things he did seemed to contradict these guesses. *There's nothing so complicated as love in the world, is there?* she thought. She wanted to believe in her instincts, but she also feared that she was too emotional, too likely to make mountains out of molehills.

"Most people can't tell how pessimistic I am," she muttered to herself. She craved happiness, but the instant that the possibility of happiness approached her, she was too scared to believe it.

She tried to sort through her tangled thoughts.

There had been no warning for what happened. Rudy simply walked over and invited her to visit his lab the next day. Gielle's heart raced. He asked her right in front of everyone, just as books described it. She and her friends were sitting on the edge of the raised flower bed while he and his friends were coming out of the tube train station. He saw her, walked over, said hi to her friends, and then asked her if she would like to come to see the work on the new hydraulic engineering plan. He was polite and confident, smiling brightly. She almost couldn't believe her own ears.

Gielle didn't know if she had blushed at the time, but she certainly felt the heat in her cheeks now. Though she was alone in her room, she covered her face with her hands and bit down on her lip to prevent the grin from being seen.

He asked me to see him! Even if it's not a date, it has to show he likes me. As to why he didn't ask me to go to a concert... maybe he wants me to understand his work better. But why did he look so aloof when I asked him how I should dress for the visit? And he was looking at Lily... I wonder if he likes Lily instead, and was asking me to make her jealous?... No, my Rudy isn't that kind of boy. But when I looked at him, he really did look a bit awkward... I wonder why he's never had a girlfriend.

Gielle sighed.

What can I do? I can't help being so sensitive and noticing details others would have missed. She sighed again and looked at herself in the mirror. The girl facing her looked disconsolate, her round face evincing a melancholy no one else could understand.

Growing up with Luoying, Gielle was familiar with Rudy's habits, and Rudy had taken care of her like he had his little sister. She often thought the seeds for her feelings for Rudy had been planted back then. Later, after Luoying left, she didn't have as many chances to see him, and so the seeds did not sprout and grow but remained buried and dormant. In her heart she concealed a dream like a secret garden, always believing that someday a man would come and brighten her life.

The moment she was waiting for arrived when she was sixteen. At a community ball, she saw Rudy dance. It was a celebration in honor of all the twenty-year-olds in the community for achieving formal adulthood. Rudy was in the middle of the crowd, the center of all attention. His smile wasn't just confident; it was arrogant. In his half-open shirt, he looked powerful and elegant. She became obsessed with him from then on, her mood dependent on his attitude, willingly changing herself for him.

Gielle wanted to know what sort of girl Rudy liked: someone poised and quiet, or someone vivacious and outgoing. She showed Rudy her sketches and designs. If he even offered one bit of praise, she spent the rest of the day floating on a cloud, feeling herself clever and original. Since he liked the costume she had made for Luoying, Gielle had been focusing on dance costumes and formal wear.

Because Rudy was so exceptional, she wanted to be exceptional herself. As a new designer, she had little name recognition. The citation rate for her designs was low and few ordered her clothes, and she worked extra hard to change the situation. Fashion was unlike most other arts; it was as competitive as the restaurant industry. Unlike the production of some metallic membrane or precision probes, which involved competing for the budget through engineering, clothing was all about the click rate. There was no fudging the click rate. Whatever design the customer chose was the design that got made, and the production rate directly reflected the designer's success and appeal. So far, Gielle had not been able to distinguish herself from the competition, and she felt rather discouraged. Her lack of exceptional accomplishments made her worry that she wasn't good enough for Rudy. To stave off the fear, she worked even harder, changing her posted designs constantly.

Gielle often tried to guess why Rudy never showed particular interest in any girls. She figured that he had very high standards; or maybe he was focused on his career; or maybe he wasn't as superficial as most boys and didn't know how to express his deep feelings. Every one of these possibilities attracted Gielle even more to him. She thought Rudy must have stayed alone for so long because he valued romantic attachment more than others.

———————

There wasn't a lot of time for her to be alone with her thoughts. Today was the scheduled day for the trial run of the hydrology model of the crater. As an active volunteer, Gielle was supposed to participate. She was already very interested in the project, and now, buoyed by the thought of the date tomorrow, she was even more energized. Humming happily, she fairly skipped her way out of her house. The sun seemed even brighter than usual, and the flowers more colorful in their bloom.

The trial was to take place on Golden Light Avenue, in front of the history museum. As Gielle headed to the site, she thought of the name of the street as a good omen for her date the next day. By the time she arrived, many people were already at work. Everyone was dressed in a white vest with a cartoonish logo, busily preparing the site for the trial.

"Hi, Warren!" Gielle waved.

"Gielle." The boy greeted her with a nod of the head, his hands occupied as he was carrying a box.

"What are you working on?"

"Assembling the model waterwheels. We're almost ready."

"Can I help with anything?"

The boy pointed at the history museum with his chin. "Mr. Holly is in charge of assignments. You should go before everything is done."

Gielle rushed in the direction he pointed. Outside the front door of the history museum, a crowd of people gathered on the steps. Mr. Holly, standing in the middle with his e-notebook, was shouting out the jobs that still needed to be done and how many volunteers were needed for each. Even with so many people, the scene was orderly. Every large event on Mars required many volunteers to help out at the last minute, and they were all used to it. Each time Mr. Holly called out a new assignment, a group volunteered and walked up. An adult researcher then came to take them to where the work had to be done. Gielle joined the jostling crowd at the back, hoping she wasn't too late to get an assignment.

A model crater had been built in the sunken plaza in the middle of Golden Light Avenue. Surrounded by statues of generals, the sandstone construction replicated the slopes of the crater, studded with caves like a beehive. Every detail of the real crater was reproduced in miniature, and the yellow rocky cliffs seemed as glorious as the real thing. Carved channels wound down the mountainsides from rim to floor, with ramifying branches and tributaries winding past every cave dwelling, until all the streambeds congregated at the very bottom of the crater. Above the crater hung a giant spherical bulb like an unlit sun.

"Monitoring the sluice gates!" Mr. Holly called out.

A few youths raised their hands and pushed through the crowd. Gielle moved closer. Standing on her tiptoes, she shifted between paying attention to Mr. Holly and looking at the crater model. The roughness of the mountainsides in the model terrified her a little, but she was nonetheless moved by the grand scale of the endeavor.

She began to imagine life in the crater in the future, what the cave houses would look like, how to go out on dates, how to browse and shop. Her thoughts, like a drifting cloud, soon stopped over Rudy. She had always had a fantasy of picking out the house she would share with Rudy. It was her most secret wish, something she had never shared with anyone. She didn't know much about architecture, but she felt that she had good aesthetic taste and an eye for details. She had always been able to discover some neat idea in common objects that no one else paid attention to. Her favorite pastime was to stroll along while pondering the beauty of a perfect garden, imagining the discussions she would have with Rudy about how to arrange and decorate their home.

Galiman was the inventor she most admired. He had come up with the design of the Martian house, as well as the mini-makers that were so convenient to use. He must have invented these things so that lovers could work together to make a beautiful home. What a sweet process this was: to create a nest for love where the pair would always be together.

"Laying out agricultural models!" Mr. Holly shouted.

Shaking herself out of her fantasies, Gielle saw that there weren't many people left. She waved her hand high in the air and shouted, "Me! Me!" Mr. Holly picked her, and along with the other volunteers she followed a woman in her thirties in a white lab coat to the side of the crater model. The woman kindly handed each of them a bag of model trees and flower bushes and directed them to plant them along a mountainside. Excitedly, Gielle dug through the soil, carefully planting each model.

"We'll need the help of more volunteers in the coming days," Mr. Holly shouted over the crowd. "One important duty will be to monitor the test fields and farmwork. If anyone is interested, please see Ms. Mathews."

He was pointing at the woman in the lab coat. Gielle stood up, brushed off the dirt on her dress, and told her, "I volunteer!"

Ms. Mathews laughed. "Thank you, dear. But we're looking for adults."

"I'm eighteen!"

"Really? All right. Why don't you leave your name on the sign-up sheet later? We'll do the interviews in a few days."

"Interviews?" Gielle looked at her pleadingly. "Won't you let me in right now, please?"

"Young lady, this is hard work that requires a lot of dedication. Some parts of the experiment require around-the-clock monitoring."

"That's no problem!" she said. Then, after a moment, she added, "I'll definitely give it my all."

Ms. Mathews chuckled and talked with her some more. Gielle asked a ton of questions, and Ms. Mathews responded patiently. Gielle wanted to know what sort of experimental field it was, and Ms. Mathews told her it was possibly the first field on Mars that would be exposed instead of enclosed in a glass dome. Gielle cried out in excitement, certain that she would be part of history for participating in such a glorious step forward.

All the volunteers worked hard as the sun rose to its highest point and then began its descent. The mountainside was now looking like a living community, full of fields, electrical stations, neighborhoods, and gardens. A few models of animals were scattered in the woods and fields, peeking out from between the trees.

Tiny models of people in the crater echoed the real people laboring outside the crater, a scene of creation in which the myth and the reality were each other's ideals.

At three in the afternoon, as all the volunteers stepped back to watch, a heavy water cart arrived at the scene like a lofty titan of old whose monstrous steel body held the sweet nectar of life. The massive storage tank tilted slowly, and the clear water flooded into the model crater like a blessing from the gods, turning the bottom of the crater into a roiling lake. The water level rose slowly while the bulb suspended above the crater finally came alight. Directed by a lampshade, the yellow rays of light slanted toward one side of the crater, lighting up part of the lake and the mountainside. The whole process was carried out slowly and ceremoniously, transcending the limits of the model's scale.

"My dear friends," declared Mr. Holly from the top of the steps, "we are truly fortunate to witness one of the most memorable and bright inflection points in the history of humanity. For the first time humans, utilizing their intelligence, will remake nature at a planetary scale in a single stroke. The melding of the strength of humankind and nature is the glory of Mars, the first step we take toward our future as an independent people, a most important step! To be able to participate in and to contribute to such a campaign is the greatest honor of all who live in this age!"

As Gielle listened to the rousing speech, joy and fervor filled her heart. Watching the newborn lake and the magnificent ring of mountains, watching the mist already gathering over the lake and the sunbathed slopes, she seemed to already feel the refreshing breeze on her face, smell the fragrant flowers, and hear the chirping birds. The corners of her eyes became moist.

The lake was now fairly deep. Simulated algae floated in the waves, giving the water a teal hue. Under the powerful lamp, the lit and shaded parts of the model soon achieved a temperature differential. The water turned into vapor, rose and flowed, and coalesced into clouds. As the clouds grew more distinct, the astonished onlookers whispered to one another. After some time passed with the clouds drifting about, tiny dust particles in the air finally attracted enough vapor to form water drops. A gentle rain fell upon the sloping mountains, bathing the verdant patches. Everyone clapped in celebration.

As Gielle watched the rain fall on the trees and flowers she had planted, she was too moved even to speak.

———————

Gielle was so excited all day that she didn't have time to think about where she and Rudy were going the next day.

In fact, Rudy had invited her to go to the lab to see photo-electric membranes. She had been too thrilled at the time to hear him clearly. But if she had been paying attention, she would have realized that such membranes were made not in Rudy's lab but in Pierre's.

PIERRE

Gielle is my light, thought Pierre.

Every time he repeated the line to himself, Pierre felt a subtle sense of despair. He was the same age as Gielle, and they had gone to the same classes, partnered in science lab, even worked the same internships. He knew Gielle as well as he knew his flowers. She was the brightest beam of light, while he was content to remain in her shadows. She was joyous, full of life, his very opposite. She was always direct and courageous, and those qualities were what he liked the most in her. Lacking those traits himself, he loved to watch her, to see her laugh or be angry. If he could always remain in the background observing her, if he could once in a while make her laugh, if he could just listen to her clear and melodious voice... that would be bliss.

Pierre watched Gielle quietly. She and Rudy were walking ahead of him, chatting and laughing as they looked around. Pierre felt his heart tighten. He wasn't foolish. As soon as Rudy walked into his lab with Gielle, he knew what he was after. But he remained silent, refusing to say anything or to show his feelings. From the office to the workshop, he never made a peep. Throughout the visit, only Rudy and Gielle talked.

"Pierre has a lot of creations," Rudy said to Gielle, glancing back at the younger boy.

"That's right," said Gielle, laughing. "He's always been the top student in our class. I remember him solving in a few seconds math problems that stumped everyone else. Unbelievable."

Rudy nodded and said casually, "In our new plan, Pierre's reflective film plays a big part."

"What reflective film?"

"It's like a mirror, but very thin and light. It can be made very large and it's flexible, so it can be shaped into a curved surface. Circuits can be etched into it so that its position and shape can be adjusted remotely. If we suspend a piece of the film in space, it will reflect sunlight where we want it to go."

"Oh," said Gielle, though it wasn't clear whether she was following.

"Don't underestimate this material," said Rudy, glancing at Pierre again. His voice was patient and full of interest. "It's key. If it's deployed correctly, we can keep the lake warm. At night we can use the film to bring sunlight from the other side of the planet to ensure that the water doesn't freeze. During the day, on the other hand, we can use it to focus heat on particular regions to produce localized temperature differences."

"And then?" Gielle scrunched up her face attentively.

Rudy smiled at her. "And then we'll have flowing water, clouds, rain, and forests."

"Just like in the simulation!"

"Yes. And the city up in the mountains. Do you like that?"

Gielle nodded vigorously. "Definitely. I loved it when I saw it working yesterday."

Pierre said nothing but kept his eyes on Gielle.

She was her usual self, vivacious, energetic, every shred of emotion written on her face, laughing with her chin lifted like a little kid. He loved looking at her when she was like this, completely absorbed in whatever she was saying, unconscious of her surroundings, exclaiming whenever an interesting thought came to her, careless of how she sounded. As Pierre took note of the way she was looking at Rudy, the depressed feeling in his heart turned into a piercing pain. He thought he should be angry, but for some reason the despair held a special attraction for him, and he wallowed in it without wanting to act.

He wished he weren't like this. Sighing inside, he interrupted Rudy.

"I've tried, but I can't be sure. Like I told you the other day, the size of the film you're asking for is too big."

Rudy looked at him without changing his expression. "Don't worry, we have plenty of time. We can apply for funding first and, after it's approved, continue the trials."

Pierre turned to face the vacuum room. Inside, the robot arms hummed as they worked rapidly. The vacuum room was like a tiny castle with thick curved walls and small circular windows. They watched the operating arms floating inside the magnetic field stretch a smooth, clear membrane tight; a spray gun hovered nearby, its nozzle glowing with a flickering mist. Layers of molecules were being carefully laid down, resolving the contradiction between opacity and thinness.

Looking at him, Rudy asked, "This is on the surface of Mars. Would it help to move production into space?"

Gielle was peeking through one of the small windows curiously, her face pressed up against the glass, hands shading the sides of her eyes. She wore her hair in an updo today, though a few escaped curls hung down to her cheeks. She didn't notice Pierre looking at her. He was thinking how beautiful she looked, more so than usual. She would look even more beautiful if she didn't work so hard at appearing serious. There was no reason for her to suppress her laughter and her carefree nature. She didn't even know that she was a bright beam of light.

He turned to Rudy. "Gravity isn't the biggest problem. The problem... is that the size of the membrane you require is too large for the crystal lattice structure to be maintained. But... it's possible that we can make it work by adding in a support skeleton. I have to do more computation, though."

He tried to be objective in his assessment, without exaggerations or reservations. His feelings for his films were similar to his feelings for his family, and knew them as well as he knew his own body. He lived in their embrace, and they kindly accepted his care. If he said they could be grown larger, then they could. If he said they couldn't, then they couldn't. He was confident of his judgment, since there was no one on Mars who knew them as well as he did. As he continued to gaze at the sparkling surface in the vacuum room, a warmth arose in his heart. The warmth mixed with his feelings for Gielle, and the despair he felt grew stronger as well. He had a premonition that in the end he would get nothing: not his films and not Gielle. Anything he was devoted to would be taken away from him.

He knew Rudy's intent, but he didn't want to involve Gielle. He could tell that Gielle had no idea what was going on. That made him sad.

As the three of them exited the workshop, Pierre asked Gielle if she would be interested in checking out some new materials on exhibit in the gallery by herself. Always on the lookout for potential new fabrics, she went away happily. Pierre and Rudy were left in the corridor by themselves.

"You shouldn't have brought her," he said.

Rudy smiled at him. "I sincerely hope to have your support." Pierre stared at his relaxed expression, saying nothing.

"All right, maybe I shouldn't have done this," said Rudy. "But on the way here I discussed our plan with Gielle. She really likes the vision of the crater city. I'm not lying to you."

"I believe you."

"There are only three days left…"

"So you want me to be part of the defense for your plan."

"Gielle will be there among the audience. Imagine how she'll gaze at you, eyes full of hope."

"This has nothing to do with her," said Pierre. "Whether I support you or not *won't* have anything to do with her."

Rudy stared back at him, and his smile gradually disappeared.

"Fine. But I want you to think it over carefully. We really need you."

Pierre didn't respond. Gielle was back from her visit to the gallery, waving at them from the other end of the corridor. They broke off the discussion, and Rudy didn't mention it to Gielle either.

Saying nothing, Pierre walked the two out of the atelier. At the door, Gielle waved him goodbye and turned to go with Rudy. Pierre could see the way she looked up at Rudy as they walked away, and his heart was in agony. He had not realized how easy it was for him to be hurt.

———

A despondent Pierre cleaned up around the lab, left work, and got on the tube train to the hospital.

On the way, his thoughts returned to Gielle. Though he was eighteen, he had little experience with girls. He liked Gielle, but that was limited to watching her contented smile from a distance. He had never even tried to get close to her—except that one time when a group of them were out on a field trip and Gielle was in a light dress that showed off her curves so well; sweat beaded on her forehead, and as she lifted a hand to wipe it away, he had the urge to embrace her. That was it. And even then he had not acted on his impulse at all. He didn't dare to imagine that she would be his girlfriend, and was disgusted when other boys discussed tricks for picking up girls. She was his light, sacred. He hoped that his decision would be his own and not be because of her.

Every day after work, Pierre came to the hospital. His grandfather remained in a coma, on life support, and he would sit next to the bed to read. There was little he could do to help, but he had nowhere else to be. Grandpa was his only family, and without him home was just an empty set of rooms.

Pierre had few friends and joined few activities. Being at gatherings of people made him nervous. He liked the purity of math but found the vulgarity of people distasteful. Rather than going to a party, he far preferred working out proofs in Riemannian geometry at the hospital.

As he sat next to the bed, he glanced at the displays of the medical equipment around the bed. Everything seemed normal. The small screens formed a semicircle around the head of the bed, the blinking faces of the host of instruments.

He looked at his grandfather's face. *Grandpa*, he said in his head, *it's time to make a decision. All their plans for keeping the water warm have serious flaws, and only my idea offers any hope. The other ideas, such as banks of batteries or an artificial sun, involve too much expenditure of energy. They've thought of using solar reflectors, but only my material is thin and strong enough. Grandpa, if I say it's impossible, then the Waders will win, and we won't have to move. A white field of ice will surround our crystal city, reflection heaped upon reflection. Do you like that future?*

The old man didn't budge, but Pierre thought he detected

movement under his eyelids. He knew it was most likely an illusion, but he preferred to think it was real.

He talked to his grandfather every day, telling him things he couldn't say to anyone else. He found it odd that he spoke to his grandfather more now than he ever had when the old man was awake.

I think I've decided, Grandpa. Do you agree with my choice?

They won't understand it. I can already imagine the responses. But they don't understand anything. They use what has already been created as though it's the most natural thing in the world, without the need for thinking. Thinking is considered lazy, and only false conviction is deemed hard work. Our glass houses are our pride, everyone knows, but how many truly understand what that means? No one.

He pulled the blanket up, as though the old man were going to kick it off. In the back of his mind, his grandfather remained that severe man who was easily angered, who stood ramrod straight and kept himself busy, never relaxing for a moment.

Who understands the beauty of sand? Everyone knows only the crystal clarity, the smooth flowing curves, as though houses were built to be transparent and smooth. They don't understand the true beauty of the material, don't know that the walls are compound glass, that the solar panels are amorphous silicon, that the coating on the walls is metal and semiconductors of silicon oxide, that the oxygen in the houses is a by-product of silicate decomposition. Everything comes from the sand. Our houses are grown from the sand, like flowers blooming from the desert. Who understands this? Who understands that crystal clarity and gritty coarseness are just two sides of the same matter? Who really understands why our houses cannot be replaced?

He lowered his head and buried it between his hands. The

white bedsheet hung before his eyes, making him slightly dizzy. His bent back tightened. The face of his grandfather, in repose, seemed to calm his anxiety. Light-green text flickered on the screens; three undulating lines crossed and recrossed like the flow inside an hourglass, the caress of time.

At least I understand; at least I know the nature of things; at least I get what should be continued and passed on. Grandpa, you agree with my choice, don't you?

Three days later the defense of the two competing plans took place in the Boule Chamber.

Pierre sat by himself in the penultimate row of seats, not a part of any faction. Rudy had been very solicitous, arranging everything for him that morning, introducing him to the various legislators and praising him profusely. Once the defense commenced, Rudy would have to sit in the front row. Pierre had no desire to join him.

As he watched Rudy glad-handing the crowd, he felt unmoved. He understood that some were born to be the center of attention, while others found such attention oppressive. He and Rudy had always been different. Even as a toddler, Rudy was used to his every move being the focus of all those around him. Whatever he did, others paid attention. His research papers were naturally cited and discussed. To him, there was no greater embarrassment than to be ignored. Pierre knew, however, that most people were not like that. Most remained in the shadows, struggling to survive in obscurity.

Only attention could attract more attention; only opportunity brought more opportunities. It was always a positive-feedback loop, and there was no adjustment that could change that basic fact.

Legislators rushed about the chamber to finalize last-minute preparations. Whenever an elder passed by and greeted him, he responded with the fewest words possible. He had no talent nor interest in small talk. He was sitting as far as possible from the podium, and he looked around as the lights came on one by one, haloing the heads of the bronze statues arranged around the chamber.

A hand touched his shoulder. He turned around and saw it was Luoying.

"Hey," she said, "have you seen Rudy?"

Pierre pointed in the direction of the dais. "He was there just now."

"Maybe he just went out for a minute. I'll wait." She sat down next to Pierre. "Are you presenting today?" He nodded.

"You've decided, then?"

"Yes. Who told you?"

"My brother," she said. In a comforting voice she added, "Whatever you decide is fine. I'm sure you've thought it through."

"I don't know about that," he said. "I can't tell if I've thought it through."

She looked at him as though uncertain about what to say. Then she said, "Something this important, that changes the fate of the country, isn't going to be decided by a few words from kids like us.

Don't drive yourself crazy."

"Sure," he said. "Thanks."

After a pause Luoying asked, "How's your grandfather?"

"All right. There's been no change in his condition."

"Did the doctor say when he might come out of his coma?"

"No." After a beat he added, "Maybe he won't ever come out."

Luoying was about to say something when Rudy returned to the chamber from a side door. Pierre drew Luoying's attention to her brother. Luoying stood up, said goodbye to him, and walked up toward the dais.

As Pierre watched her descend the steps, a word that she had said echoed in his mind: *fate*. He seemed to see all of them standing at a fork in the road surrounded by mist. They couldn't see far in either direction. He didn't understand why he suddenly had this feeling of being at a cosmic crossroads.

Fate isn't real, he thought. *I have to hold on to that.* The word added to his anxiety. *There's nothing real except the perfection of mathematics. Fate is just an escapist explanation for reality's causes and effects that we don't understand, an irrational sigh of acceptance. That is all. There's nothing more beautiful than proofs and laws, the soul of mathematics. Math is the only thing in the cosmos that is pure and eternal. Compared to the absolutism of mathematical laws, all human laws are mere clumsy compromises. All compromises are temporary, and all temporary things are crude.*

He repeated his credo to himself until his heart calmed down. Reciting his speech silently, he felt comforted by the familiar technical data. *What is beautiful is the material,* he thought, *the eternal material that exists according to eternal laws. Compared to that, what are systems, customs, profits? Mere epiphenomena, all. Why do we devote so much of our energy to these? The perfect cosmos should be our home for eternity.* He glanced at the sample film he held: the thin membrane glowed with a perfect light.

The defense began.

Almost every seat in the Boule Chamber was filled, a rare occurrence. All the legislators were present, their dress formal and their faces serious. Despite the number of people in the room, it was very quiet. As Pierre sat silently in his seat, speaker after speaker came to the podium. Both the Waders and the Climbers had assembled powerful teams of experts. After the leaders of both groups presented the basic outlines of the plans, multiple technical experts elaborated on every aspect of the plans. The speeches were long and the exhibits impressive. Two visions of the future of Mars competed on the domed ceiling of the chamber, and the questions were sharp and insightful.

It was a long time before Pierre's turn came. He strode onto the dais and looked around at his expectant audience, but in his heart he felt he was no longer part of this reality.

"As for the technical feasibility of the solar reflectors, my final answer is: Yes, I can do it. I can design a reflecting film sufficiently large and strong to achieve the stated goals. It will be adjustable in space, both in shape and positioning; it will be possible to direct sunlight at all times to specific locations on the surface to provide the energy for maintaining water temperature and sustaining evaporation; it will support the development of the migration plan.

"I'll go over the details and the technical data now…"

The audience whispered excitedly. He pretended not to notice. He knew that his presentation would be controversial, and he didn't care. He had made his decision against pressure from all sides, not just for Gielle, but also for the resolve that had long been buried in his heart.

He glanced around the chamber and realized that Gielle was absent. His heart throbbed. He didn't like to feel this way; he had hoped that he would be able to remain aloof, uncaring. But the pain stabbed him in the chest again and again as he looked for Gielle and couldn't find her.

SORIN

Sorin had not anticipated so many showing up at the demonstration. He had planned things out at the site, but so many people were showing up that his plan was in tatters. A sense of foreboding troubled him.

Runge was still in the middle of his speech. Sorin watched his angular profile, wondering if he realized the situation had changed. Runge never worried about anything, but Sorin wasn't like that. He knew that a stage with too many actors was no longer under the control of the director; all kinds of unanticipated things happened when the crowd swelled beyond a certain size. He was thirsty, but he couldn't find any water— actually, he was in no mood to look for water. He continued to survey the plaza tensely.

"Luoying!"

He turned and saw a redheaded girl running over, excitedly greeting Luoying. Sorin thought she looked familiar.

"Gielle! What are you doing here?"

"Rudy asked us to come."

"My brother?" Luoying was even more surprised.

"He told us that your rally is really important and needs more supporters. He wanted all of us to come."

"When did he say this?"

"Yesterday afternoon."

Luoying frowned. "I don't know why he didn't say anything about it to me. I saw him just half an hour ago, and he told me nothing."

"Probably because he was too busy. You know how in demand he is."

Luoying looked troubled. Gielle looked about eagerly, peppering Luoying with questions. Soon her attention was seized by Runge. The dozens of other youths who had come with her had scattered and merged into the crowd. Most joined the audience around Runge, but some were asking other demonstrators whether they needed help.

Sorin did some mental math. There were less than twenty people here from the Mercury Group. Earlier, about thirty or forty passersby had stopped to listen. Now, with the addition of all these new people, the tiny plaza was holding more than a hundred people. It wouldn't have been an issue in a larger space, but they had chosen to conduct their protest at a regular tube train interchange park. Though the park was already very crowded, more people continued to emerge from the train station, looking at the hubbub curiously. They came up to ask the people already there what was going on, and stayed.

As the crowd continued to swell, the banners and animated posters were being pushed into a corner. Almost all the footpaths through the plaza had been blocked off. Sorin grew even more concerned. Any unanticipated disorder was bound to turn into trouble.

Runge continued his oration, his impassioned delivery unchanged by the growing audience.

"In our world, control and obedience have reached unprecedented proportions. In the past, those in power controlled their subjects in basically three ways: traditional authority, embodied in a patriarch; harsh laws enforced by the threat of force; and personal charisma. But our world is different. It has evolved into a massive, complex circuit in which every administrative department is a component and every individual an electron. All we can do is obey, obey the voltage differential, obey the planned design. There is no refusal and no escape, and all spontaneous actions are unacceptable.

"For an individual, to build a shelter is without a doubt one of the basic tenets of personal freedom, and all are born with such a natural right. But in our world the system has stripped us of this right and placed it under its strict control. To build a house, one must follow the system's regulations, apply for the system's approval, submit to the system's decision, and live wherever the system says to like a nail being pounded into place. No matter how kind or honest you are, no matter how many friends are willing to help you, you cannot change your fate. What kind of world is this? We do not want it! We don't want the system to decide our lives! We want to breathe the air of our own land in freedom!"

"Yes! Yes!" A couple of new arrivals who hadn't heard the rest of his speech applauded. More people joined them.

Listening to Runge's voice, strong, rational, clear, Sorin could feel its power. Runge didn't appeal to pathos, but his view came through clearly and persuasively. The audience listened intently, and some whispered to one another. It was clear that the whisperers weren't mocking him or bored but seriously discussing his points. That was the goal of the demonstration. The movement ought to be considered at least partially successful.

But Sorin didn't feel good. In part it was because his sense of foreboding was growing stronger by the minute. In part it was also because he could see that those at the demonstration were now starting to act on their own. The mood of the youths had been growing more and more agitated, like a pot starting to boil, with streams of bubbles rising to the surface. Some were gathering in a small circle; some were waving banners at the edge of the plaza; some were shouting slogans along with jokes at someone's expense. Sorin guessed that the barbs were aimed at their teacher, always a good target at a protest.

Sorin didn't want to see any of these things. He had been opposed to a public demonstration and, in the end, had agreed to organize it only because Chania insisted that the protest would be a venue for peaceful discussions, a salon to stimulate the people into reflecting on their system and the philosophy of governance. He had always played the role of the organizer in the group, and the others trusted him. He had tried to plan for everything, but he never anticipated the growing chaos. He had no idea if Chania knew this was going to happen, and that caused him even more anxiety. *Did she deliberately keep from me what she thought was going to happen?*

He couldn't tell what the effect of Rudy's participation was either. Watching Rudy and Chania discuss the demonstration on their own had made him a bit jealous; he had never seen Chania so influenced by someone else. Sorin knew that both Runge and Chania hoped for the protest to make a big splash, the bigger the better, but he didn't. In fact, he wasn't even sure he agreed with the theme of Runge's speech. He felt that the two matters—the freedom to build one's own house and the circuit-like operation of society—were two distinct matters, and he wasn't sure that twisting them together was the right thing to do. It might even confuse the issues. He was hoping for discussion, for more clarity, but it was obvious that the others didn't share these goals. Chania was absolutely convinced that a revolution was the only desirable outcome.

At that moment Chania seemed to be engaged in some

heated argument with Luoying. Sorin pushed his way through the crowd, hoping to talk with them. They didn't notice him as he approached from behind, and he caught the last few snatches of their conversation.

"Why didn't you tell me?" demanded Luoying.

"I figured you wouldn't agree," said Chania.

"But why? Why have you done this?"

"We need supporters, don't we?"

Sorin's heart clenched. It seemed that Chania did know. Rudy must have told her about his plan to send Gielle and the others, or maybe the two of them had planned it together. He was angry that he had been excluded from their scheme. In his shock, he missed the next few exchanges in the conversation.

"So you've decided to believe in it this time?" asked Luoying.

"You said you hoped I would believe at least once, right?" Chania's tone was awkward.

"But what caused such a sudden change?"

"Call it… a kind of passion."

Chania stopped, as though unwilling to discuss the matter anymore. She bent down and began to push a large video poster through the crowd toward Runge so that it would be closer to the heart of the audience. She put her back into it and kept her eyes on the ground, as though trying to escape the argument behind her. Sorin and Luoying watched her, a bit amazed at her strength and agility as she maneuvered the heavy cart.

Was she talking about Rudy? thought Sorin. *Did she really believe him because of "passion"? Chania had always been so stubborn and mistrusted everyone. Why did she believe Rudy? Was it because Rudy spoke in such an impassioned manner? Or because he had done what she thought was necessary?*

Sorin looked back at Luoying. She hadn't noticed him at all but kept her attention on Chania. Her hand was raised next to her mouth, making her look deep in thought. Luoying was dressed in a white chiton; the protesters had the idea of having someone dress in a manner to evoke the spirit of classical Greece for their rally. As she stood still in the midst of the agitated crowd, glowing white, she reminded Sorin of someone from the ancient past, not a part of the everyday surroundings.

Sorin was about to go up to talk to her when a disturbance drew everyone's attention.

He saw that a fight had broken out between a few youths who had stepped on one another's feet due to the crowding. The argument was loud but not serious. He sighed with relief.

But the fight didn't peter out as he had hoped. The accident seemed to uncap some pent-up energy among the attendees. More voices rose around the plaza, and other arguments began, like a spark spreading across a grassland plagued by drought. Someone shouted, and many cheered in response. More people pushed their way into the small plaza. A few youths argued with adults; perhaps their parents trying to get them to go home? The youths shook off the hands of the adults and shouted defiantly, their eyes aglow. The noise of the crowd made it impossible to hear any conversation clearly.

Sorin was now really worried. The rally was already too large, and seeing kids arguing with their parents made things worse. He had no idea how this was going to develop. He disliked any situation in which he lost control and couldn't predict the outcome.

One voice managed to make itself heard over the noise:

"Let's go to Capitol Square! There's lots more room there! The Boule is in session today. Let's get their attention!"

"Hooray!" the crowd cheered. The youths, their energy at the boiling point, now exploded into action like a raging flame. Shouting, laughing, exclaiming, they began to move. Soon, the young protesters had coalesced into a mighty river. With banners and posters above their heads, they pushed forward like a ragtag army, squeezed onto the street like a torrent pouring through a sluice in the dam.

Sorin was astounded. To go to the Boule was a naked provocation. He wanted to stop the situation from worsening, but he found himself caught in an excited mob, unable to do anything. He saw Luoying standing still in the throng like a marble column.

If anyone can influence the situation now, it's her.

"Luoying!" He pushed his way through the crowd to her. She glanced at him, looking nonplussed.

"Are you okay?" he asked.

"Tell me," she said, "if you think someone has done something very wrong but he's also your closest family, what would you do?" Sorin hesitated for a moment. "Are you talking about your brother?"

Luoying nodded. "I don't understand why he has done this."

"You mean the people who he sent to our rally?"

"That's not the only thing." Luoying looked worried. "I have a feeling that he's made many other arrangements. Even the boy who just now shouted we should all go to Capitol Square—I think my brother had him do that."

"What? Do you know the boy?"

"I think I saw him once at our house. I can't be sure; I can't be sure of anything. But I'm scared. I don't know why he's doing all this."

"Can you stop everyone?"

Luoying stared at him. "How can I?"

"Tell them you think this is a bad idea." Sorin tried to make his voice comforting but determined. "You have this power. Everyone knows you, and if you say it, they'll listen to you."

"But I don't know if I *should* stop them," said Luoying. "This has always troubled me. I don't know if a person *should* try to make something happen, to try to fix the world's flaws. Chania's devotion to her ideal is real. I don't like the way my brother has done this, but I can't stop him."

Luoying's doubt and hesitation were laid bare in her eyes. Sorin never knew that hesitation and doubt could be communicated so clearly. He saw what was troubling her, but, like her, he had no answers. As the protesters streamed out of the plaza, the two of them were left behind. Troubled by different thoughts, they tarried in the same manner, uncertain whether they should follow.

Sorin realized that he was no longer the director. From the moment the stage was ready and the actors made their entrance, the drama had escaped his control. He had been abandoned by his actors. They wanted fervor, not a conservative director full of anxiety. He looked at the lawn and footpaths, strewn with pieces of trash, and knew that it wasn't his play any longer. He bent down to pick up the pieces, and Luoying helped him.

"Let's go with them," she said.

Sorin nodded. Together they ran to join the laughing, running demonstrators.

LUOYING

The longer they stayed at Capitol Square, the more Luoying wavered, uncertain whether to advance or to retreat.

The square was filled with fervent youths shouting and jumping, generating a heat that had not been seen in years. Usually the square was quiet, dignified, and somber, but now it was noisy, chaotic, agitated. Banners flapped with song, and frenzied youths laughed even as they screamed in rage.

Luoying stood to the side. One moment she wanted to impulsively jump into the chanting swarm; a moment later she wanted to ask everyone to calm down and go home. They reminded her of the time when she had marched and sang and laughed with the Reversionists. She missed the sense of being alive.

But at this moment she couldn't lose herself in the frenzy. The protesters had been brought here by her brother's inspiring, passionate words, but now they danced and chanted and screamed as though it had been their own idea. Something about all this felt wrong. She couldn't articulate why, but it felt *wrong*.

She knew that excitement was infectious. There was no need to know the source of the excitement, only to feel the sensation. On the way here, more youths who had somehow heard about the demonstration had joined them, and now hundreds were in the square, covering a large area. They were fired up, as fired up as they would be for a dance party or the Creativity Fair. They surrounded Runge and Chania, waving giant posters.

"Re-form! Free-dom! Re-form! Free-dom!" they chanted.

Where was Rudy?

Luoying suddenly saw about a dozen people in uniform walk out of the side door of the Boule Building, heading for the demonstrating youths. As they approached, they separated to the sides of the square. She couldn't hear what they were saying to the youths in front, but she could see those around her pushing forward. She ran sideways to the edge of the crowd and tried to get ahead.

"What's happening?" she asked someone next to her.

No one answered her. It was just too noisy and chaotic. But as Luoying pushed forward, others made way for her. She guessed it was because of her chiton, which made her stand out like an outsider.

The conversation up front wasn't going well. The adults were stone-faced, while the youths were impassioned; the adults' voices were so low as to be inaudible, while the screams of the youths were too loud to be understood. Contrasting moods and emotions clashed like waves. Some were shoving, others were shouting, and new participants kept joining the fray. She grew more and more concerned. Someone yelled. The square was like a boiling pot. More jostling, more screams, more anger and rage.

Just as the chaos had reached a crescendo, the front doors of the Boule Building opened.

Every pair of eyes swung over. The doorway was empty, revealing the shut set of inner doors. The elaborate floor was devoid of people. The opened doors formed a cave mouth through which a cold wind blew. Everyone quieted.

Sometime later a figure appeared at the top of the steps. "Luoying, would you come here a moment?" It was Reini.

Luoying didn't expect to see him here, and she certainly wasn't expecting to be summoned from the crowd like this. She looked around, and everyone around her looked back at her. She looked at Reini, who regarded her expressionlessly. She nodded, held up her skirt, and climbed the steps. No one spoke. The demonstrators' gazes followed her silently until she was standing between the columns at the top. She turned around.

"Please wait for me," she said to the crowd.

Her voice, unexpectedly cool and gentle, echoed above the square. Without waiting for a reaction, she turned to follow Reini into the Boule Building. The front doors closed slowly behind them.

Reini walked ahead of her without speaking until he had led her into a small lounge.

He turned around, took one look at her, pushed open the door, and indicated that she should enter first. The lounge was sparsely furnished, with a row of glass display cases along the windowed side. There was a painting on one wall, and along the other wall was a table with two glass fiber chairs.

Reini gestured for her to sit, but Luoying remained standing. She had just emerged from a deafening clamor into a pool of silence, and as she took in the slanting sunlight, she felt her ears ring. Her body felt light, unreal.

"Dr. Reini, what are you doing here?"

"I'm an archivist. An important session of the Boule like this one requires access to all files."

Luoying was uncertain how to continue.

Reini poured a glass of water for her and set it down gently on the table.

"I'll be brief," he said. "They won't wait long out there." Luoying nodded.

"Do you know why I called you in here?" Luoying shook her head.

"To show you this."

Reini walked to the display cases and lifted the cover off one. Carefully he retrieved an object, held it in the palm of his hand, and returned to Luoying, presenting it to her.

Luoying saw that it was a brooch in the shape of an orchid woven from ordinary gold-plated wires. Two glass beads were set in the tip. It was well-made but not anything extraordinary. She examined it carefully but couldn't see what was special about it.

"Who did this belong to?"

"An old woman."

"Who was she?"

"Just an ordinary retired woman," Reini sighed. "But she died in special circumstances. It was almost ten years ago, and she died right here, as the result of an accident in Capitol Square. This brooch has been kept as a memorial to that event." He paused and then added, "It will be ten full years in another two months."

Luoying sensed something terrible in Reini's tone. Her mouth felt dry, and she almost wished Reini would stop. But another part of her wanted him to continue, to resolve all her questions and doubts. All terrifying secrets were also terrifyingly appealing. The faster her heart pumped, the more she wanted him to continue.

"How… did she die?"

"From an air leak. One of the valves over the square malfunctioned from being impacted, and the air began to leak out. Whenever such an accident occurred, the network safety

562

system would automatically deploy the isolation doors to seal off the affected area from the rest of the city. On the day of the accident, the owner of this brooch was walking past the square. She was caught in a passage between two isolation doors, right where the leak occurred. The air rushed out, and she died in the near vacuum."

Color drained from Luoying's face. "What happened on that day?"

"There was a demonstration on the square, an even bigger, more chaotic demonstration than yours. The organizers were more experienced, skilled, and resourceful. They brought a robot to construct a series of models of glass houses on the square. The robot was very tall, and two lights at the top glared like two monstrous eyes. The demonstrators were all adults, and they chanted their slogans far more effectively than you. Eventually the Security System's constables were summoned. Someone probably said something they would regret, and a fight broke out between the two sides. In the ensuing chaos, the robot was toppled, breaking the air valve. Other than the old woman I mentioned, two other young protesters died in the stampede."

Luoying listened without blinking her eyes.

"Who... started that demonstration?"

"Your parents."

Luoying let out a held breath. What she had feared most was true. She felt lost.

"And then?"

"Then they were punished. Not just them. All the leaders of the protest and the constables were punished, although your parents received the severest penalty of all."

"So it wasn't for giving Arthur the plans to the central archive?"

"No." Reini shook his head gravely. "To be exiled to the abandoned Deimos mines was a very harsh penalty, and it was reserved only for actions that led to the deaths of others. If no one had died, nothing, not opposing the atelier system or giving a Terran the plans to the central archive, would have led to such a punishment. The head constable that day and his staff are still on Deimos. They failed in their duty to prevent the escalation of violence. Arthur left after the demonstrations. Because your parents were punished, he decided to return to Earth. Your father took the plans with him as he left the optical-electrical atelier and gave them to Arthur."

In Luoying's mind, she saw the photographs of her parents. Their carefree young faces appeared before her eyes like translucent clouds. The brooch in Reini's hand glinted like a needle piercing through the mist of time. Her vision grew blurry.

"Was it my grandfather who imposed the penalty?"

"Yes, and also no. Their sentence was handed down by the three justices of the Security System and the Archon of the Security System. But your grandfather had to carry out the sentence. He was in trouble himself. He had been consul for only a month, and it was the first crisis of his administration. Since the consul's own son and daughter-in-law led the protest against the republic and he couldn't maintain order, which resulted in multiple deaths and civil disorder, many people thought your grandfather bore a large share of the blame. They wanted him to resign or face impeachment."

"Impeachment?"

"He was a new consul, and the Boule was still in the process of reorganization. He wasn't secure in his post at all."

"What happened after that?"

"The debate in the Boule to impeach was fierce, and the situation was on the verge of spinning out of control. Your grandfather was unable to stabilize the crisis. But then Juan stepped in."

"Uncle Juan?"

She remembered the old photos in her parents' study, and the full-fidelity recording they led to.

Reini nodded. "Juan was the new Archon of the Flight System. During the debates in the Boule, he declared that he would be loyal only to your grandfather. This was taken by many to be a threat to launch a military coup. At that time Juan's influence and prestige in the Flight System was unparalleled. Even though he had just been promoted to the post, he had received a nearly unanimous vote of confirmation, an unprecedented event in the history of the republic. Your grandfather had also risen through the aerospace force, and on the day of the impeachment vote, the Flight System launched fighters to circle above the city.

"The impeachment resolution failed to pass. You can view this event from multiple perspectives, but it was true that your grandfather held on to the post of consul because of what Juan did. For many years afterward, there was much resentment."

Luoying muttered. "I didn't know any of this."

She recalled the face of Hans Sloan in the holographic recording: his angular features torn between pain and resolve. She tried to imagine the scene. She didn't know what emotion had the upper hand in her grandfather's heart: the pain of being denounced by his child, the pain of punishing his child, the pain of being blamed and accused by others. Her heart clenched as she realized that it was her parents who had brought such pain to her grandfather, and the pain had then redounded onto them.

"Does my brother know all of this?"

"I believe so."

"Then... why did he support us?"

"I…" Reini hesitated, as though holding back. "Let's finish discussing the past first. Do you know the theme of your parents' movement?"

Luoying shook her head.

"They wanted every family to have a home," said Reini. "They wanted every married couple to have a house."

"What?"

"Yes, that's the system we have now. Your parents' protest was suppressed, but their proposal later became the policy that was enacted by the Boule. We now live under the system they dreamed of."

"But… then what was the system before?"

"Before then, housing was allocated based on one's research accomplishments and position." Reini sighed, as though seeing the distant past. "When the city was first founded, resources were so scarce that everyone lived in dormitories. Only the most accomplished researchers could build their own houses, and the sizes of the houses were determined by their research results. The policy was reasonable at first, but after thirty years it was deeply flawed. If someone was unlucky and didn't produce any research results that found practical applications, then they would die in a dormitory. As a result, everyone became dependent on their supervisors, trying to curry favor with them so that their own research would be included in some engineering project. Power corrupted, and the distribution of housing became the tail that wagged the dog of scientific research."

"But I remember that when I was little, every family had their own house!"

Reini smiled. "You lived in a district where the other families of the founders of the republic and system directors lived. That was why they had houses."

"Then my parents…"

"They did it for Arthur."

"Arthur? And Janet?"

"Yes. Since Arthur had no place in the system at all, they could never be given a house. Your parents found this unjust. After seeing so much abuse of power and the rejection of their friend by this system, they began to crave the fairness of absolute equal distribution."

"But we...," whispered Luoying, "... we are opposing this."

"You want to build your own, to exchange with others, to have freedom. You oppose the absolute equality of even distribution." Reini's voice was very composed. "That's not new, either, you know? That was how things were before the war. Back then, everyone built their own house or bartered for it. Back then, the different camps belonged to different companies, and every person or group had to buy their own tools or hire the services of a larger company. That system was just a continuation of the tradition on Earth. But Mars wasn't Earth. On Mars, resources were extremely scarce, and much of the raw material could not be used directly. Only a few companies who held the key smelting and casting technologies could provide building materials. The oligopoly companies controlled the market and raised the prices. Almost anyone with skill and brains at the time realized that under such conditions it was impossible to obtain a better life by merit and smarts alone. The unfair allocation of resources couldn't be bypassed. So they risked their lives to found a new republic where anyone was free to earn a better life not by possessing capital but by utilizing their talents."

Luoying was gradually coming to a realization. "My parents rebelled against my grandfather; we rebelled against my parents; and my grandfather rebelled against the vision we're now trying to make true?"

"That's one way to think about it," Reini continued in a calm tone. "*Freedom*, *merit*, and *equality*—any of these alluring words will always be pursued by a generation."

"And be opposed by another?"

Luoying looked down, feeling lost. She didn't know what next step to take. The movement was fruitless. The world was always flawed, impossible to perfect. Toppling and erecting repeated in an endless cycle. She had no idea what to do. Her family had given so much to this effort, but it was unclear if the world had been improved even a little. If it had been improved, in what direction? And if not, what should people do? She felt the world emptying out. She was standing at the edge of a hollow universe. There was no end in sight, and heaven was nowhere to be found.

"Dr. Reini," Luoying said, her voice anguished, "did you know that I wasn't certain about this movement at all? For a long time I debated with myself whether I should participate. In the end I decided to join because I didn't know what else I could do, where else I could find the feeling I wanted. I was looking for a sense of life, a surging sensation of releasing my self, a… meaning. I wanted to do something that felt worthy of devoting my whole self to. I just wanted that feeling. I wasn't thinking much about the goal or the movement itself. I never even really thought about whether the movement was right. Simply, I wanted my life to burn, to feel that burn."

"I think I understand," said Reini.

"Do you think me naïve?"

"Not at all. I think many harbor such a hope inside. Do you remember what you said about the disease of 'great accomplishments dementia'? It's not so unusual a condition for humanity."

"Because of the love of grandiosity?"

"Not just that, but an even greater yearning: to complete the self. You're searching for some meaning to lose yourself in, and many others are searching as well. They yearn for the self to become significant against such a distant vision. Without that yearning, no control or instigation can be effective. Without so many people wishing to meld into a circuit, it's impossible to build a circuit. People aren't all obsessed with doing great deeds, but great deeds do give the individual that sense of presence."

"You're saying it's in fact meaningless?"

"That depends on what you consider to be meaningful."

Luoying pondered this for a moment. "What should I do now?"

"That, you'll have to decide," said Reini. "I can only tell you stories, but the ultimate choice is always yours."

Reini walked to the entrance to the lounge and pulled open the gold-colored door. The door frame, patterned like marble, was decorated with an elaborate floral edging. In the door was a mirror.

Luoying saw herself in the mirror. The chiton draped to her ankle, and white flowers bloomed from the artificial laurel wreath on her head. Her long black hair draped to her waist. She saw that her face looked pale and lost, just the way she had looked two months earlier. She had hoped that she would become strong and clearheaded, but after having experienced so much, she found herself looking even more perplexed and wan. She walked toward the mirror, toward herself. At the door, she stopped to look at Reini, who nodded at her. She reached out to touch her image as though touching another space and time.

The walk down the short corridor felt like a whole century to her. The floor was painted with scenes from human history, and the tips of her feet could feel the cold of the glass and colored metal. Round stained glass windows along the corridor glowed with a pure and sacred light and cast geometric shadows on the floor. The door ahead of her remained shut, holding the noise outside at bay.

Just before she opened the door, Reini stopped her. "There's one more thing that I thought I should tell you. Do you remember the mental patient who leaped to his death?"

"Yes."

"His name was Jenkins. Do you remember the mining accident that led to my punishment?"

"Yes."

"My punishment happened ten years ago. Jenkins was the system archon at the time, a headstrong and power-hungry man. Instead of devoting himself to the details of administration, he surrounded himself with a group of yes-men who stroked his ego. Before the accident, the production line for the mining carts was already in disarray. No one was paying attention to the safety inspections, and an accident was only a matter of time. Since I was punished, the investigation report covered up his role, and the Boule managed to save him. But instead of learning his lesson, he continued to mismanage the system. A year later another major accident occurred, and this time they punished him by stripping him of all power and ensuring he would never be promoted again."

"So he was the one responsible for ruining your life."

"*Ruin* is too strong a word. I think it's more fair to say that he bore some responsibility."

Luoying regarded Reini, unsure how to feel. The man Reini hated had died in front of Luoying, but Luoying and her friends had launched a movement to honor him. The man's incompetence had led to Reini's ruin, but then he had gone mad and died, winning their sympathy as a victim, stirring up their sense of justice.

"How did he go mad?" she asked.

"He couldn't stand the fact that others no longer praised him."

He rested a comforting hand on Luoying's shoulder, his thick palm giving her a sense of strength, of determination. She looked up at him, eyes full of sadness, but he only nodded at her without speaking. He pressed the button next to the door, and the two heavy metal panels slowly swung open. Luoying looked out. The bright square was like a golden ocean that blinded her.

She gazed into the light, a shining emptiness. She could see nothing.

Eventually her vision returned. She saw that the youths were still gathered below the steps in small groups, sitting, standing, arguing, talking. When they saw her, the noise died down and all eyes were on her, waiting for her to speak. She took a few steps down until she was sure they could all hear her. She felt Reini's gaze on her back, far behind her.

She cleared her throat.

"Let's all go home."

Her voice wasn't loud, but it was clear and carried far over the quiet square. Everyone stared at her, and for a long time no one said anything.

"Let's all go home now," Luoying said. "I'll explain the reasons another time."

The crowd became agitated. People looked at one another; there were whispers. The voices of doubt grew.

"You've got to give us some explanation. A reason!" someone shouted.

"It's because…" Luoying didn't see who had asked the question. "Because of history."

"What do you mean?"

"I will explain another time."

She saw that they were still restless and uneasy. She climbed higher and raised her voice, pleading. "Please! Please listen to me! I promise I'll explain later. But, for now, we have to go home. *Please*, let's go home."

Her voice grew anguished at the end. She waited, her heart pierced with the pain of an interrupted play. The drama had reached its climax, and she, like an usher here to spoil everyone's fun, had suddenly turned on all the lights. The illusion was broken; the stage had turned from the setting of heroic action to mere painted backdrop; the mesmerizing emotions had been cut off in mid-sentence. Everyone resented her.

She could see the indignation on their faces, and she knew how unwilling they were to give up their stirred-up passions. But she had no other choice except to be true to her conscience. She couldn't lead them forward when she didn't believe in their cause, and so she had to disappoint them. She waited for their reaction, and they waited for their own reaction. The cheerless silence over the square was like the sea.

Still standing atop the steps, she lifted her hands and placed them together right below her lips. The chiton and the Roman columns next to her made her seem like a vestal priestess of old. She felt her self and her voice growing even further apart, her voice adrift like bubbles in the sun.

But her voice had an effect. Gradually she saw the youths begin to move. They picked up their belongings and scattered to the edges of the square, departing by ones and twos. Luoying remained on the steps, saying nothing, until the noise that had once inundated the square descended, along with the sun, into silence.

She was very tired and wanted to go home herself. Reini

asked her if she wished to go into the Boule Chamber to listen to the debate. She shook her head and told Chania and Sorin to go instead. She just wanted to lie down and press everything she had learned and experienced into a dream.

Once home, she checked her messages, as was her habit. She wasn't expecting anything. But there was a new blinking message that pushed all thoughts of sleep out of her mind.

It was a letter from Earth.

Luoying,

I'm delighted to hear from you. My project isn't going so well, and I was feeling low, when I got your letter, a ray of sunshine. How have you been?

I'm running into so many walls that I almost want to give up. The environment on Earth is just so different from Mars, and the weight of history makes it difficult to push for change. Unlike the time of the French Revolution, it's much harder now to have a successful revolution. The connectedness of all nations paradoxically makes it almost impossible to change the lifestyle of everyone by creating concentrated change in a single spot.

Every time I try to describe to other artists the idea of the public domain enabled by the central archive, they suspect me of being part of some conspiracy to control them. Governments won't take up my plan because it will reduce the GDP related to IP transactions by billions. Businesses are even less interested, since the plan eats into their profits.

I suppose I should have anticipated all this. But I

find it hard to believe that a plan that has the obvious potential to promote the arts and the free flow of ideas for humanity as a whole would be opposed by almost every individual.

Fortuitously, I just heard some news about the Reversionists. We've been back on Earth for about a month now. The day after we got back, Theon began the design of the new theme park. Instead of flooding the net with advertisements, however, he chose to take advantage of the interest generated by news coverage of the Terran delegation's visit to Mars by posting viral videos of Mars City. People loved the idea of Mars City as an oasis in the desert, and now all the radical environmentalists and Reversionists have found a new set of objects to worship: glass houses; lush, romantic gardens; humanity and the environment merged into one. They are discussing, praising, looking up information, posting articles... When they found out that the technology of Martian houses has been brought back to Earth, interest went through the roof. They're treating this sudden interest in Mars as a new movement, and they've already made plans to visit the new theme park in large groups before construction has even begun. They're calling for others to join them on the web, but so far they haven't looked into who's behind the theme park. Theon is extremely pleased with the reaction so far. He's thinking of making the new theme park follow the idea of naturalism to attract more visitors.

There are so many movements on Earth now that sometimes I have a hard time telling what the goal of each is. And then I realize that I'm just one more voice in that clamor. Maybe Mars is happier, because those who walk a simple and pure path are always happier.

Tell me more about what's going on on Mars.

Your friend,

Eko

Luoying read over the letter twice and then sat on the window ledge. Drawing up her knees, she wrapped her arms around them and gazed at the setting sun outside. There was a dust storm, and the horizon was a blur of gold and black. The sun was almost invisible, a somber sight through the sand-filled air.

She felt exhausted, tired of humanity's fervent running about. She didn't know if such running about had an endpoint or where the endpoint was. Was one group of people doomed to always end up where another group started from? She didn't want to go anywhere at all, hoping only to see clearly why or how everything was happening. It was as though she had been tossed about by the winds of fate, and now she wanted the winds to leave her alone so she could remain still and watch. She had lost the enthusiasm for being vagabond, wanting only to sit still until the end of the universe.

She recalled a particular exchange with Reini in the hospital; the words now held a special meaning for her.

So what does "happiness" mean to you?

Sobriety. After a moment of reflection, Reini added in a quiet voice, *And the freedom to be sober.*

As she gazed at the horizon, she missed Anka. Each time she felt lost and helpless, she missed him more. The endless swirling sand and the blur of the setting sun wrapped about her like a stage curtain, and she was the lone actor who sat in a vast theater with no audience. She wanted to see the darkness clearly, to hold the steady hand of another as they were both wrapped inside the turbulent curtain. She missed Anka very much.

It had been several days since she last saw Anka. He didn't come to their rally, and never made an appearance at Capitol Square either. She didn't know what he was doing. She jumped off the window ledge to call him, but no one picked up on the other end of the line.

REINI

Reini watched Luoying leave and then returned to the Boule Chamber with Chania and Sorin. The debate was still ongoing. He had been gone for about an hour, but little progress had been made.

As an assistant archivist, he took the two youths with him to the observers' seats. The automatic cameras, like strange predator fish of the deep, breathed and took in everything under the waves of language without anyone noticing. Chania and Sorin sat behind him, looking around, full of curiosity. He kept an eye on the two of them. Chania maintained a look of severe annoyance, as though she was still angry at everything but forcing herself to hold it in. Sorin, on the other hand, looked far more moderate but also worried, his gaze shifting between Chania and what was happening on the dais.

All the lights in the Boule Chamber were on. The podium on the dais was the focus of multiple lights, and the edges of the podium as well as the mic gleamed, drawing everyone's attention. Spotlights above the bronze statues put a halo around every larger-than-life figure. Laser holographic projectors installed around the chamber combined to create three-dimensional scenes as visual aids in the middle of the floor, and everything—objects, buildings, people—looked as vivid as real life. The small raised platform upon which the speakers stood was illuminated by four spotlights; the effect was to make it seem as though the speakers were surrounded by blinking stars. Sunlight fell through the tall domed ceiling but was completely overwhelmed by the glaring artificial lighting.

All the speakers sounded impassioned; it was impossible not to be roused to such fervency under the gaze of so many eyes and lights. The person speaking now was an old man, a Wader as well as a founder of the republic. He spoke from history, recounting for everyone in vivid detail how the city in the desert had saved the nation of Mars, how the life of ease they now led in the crystal city was a paradise compared to the hardships of the past. He offered that the tranquility and leisure enabled by the city was the spirit of Mars, the perfect environment in which to conduct the search for truth, the Platonic garden at the base of Olympus Mons. To give it up was to give up their soul in the pursuit of an environment that didn't belong to them, a display of hubris that would ultimately be punished by fate. Many of the elders and conservatives in the chamber interrupted his speech several times with wild applause. In fact, when he said "Platonic garden," there were tears in many eyes and the mood in the chamber felt transcendent.

The audience reacted to the speeches in various ways. Some were completely in sync with the mood of the speaker; some showed no expression at all; some continued to whisper in private conversations, ignoring the speeches altogether; some rushed about on the ring gallery above the seats, preparing for the next speaker. Most legislators had long since made up their minds, and there were only a few votes still in play. Reini knew that while the defense session was formally the process by which legislators decided their votes, in reality the actual result was determined by the invisible maneuvers taking place behind the scenes, outside this chamber. Every time he came to a formal session of the Boule, he had the sensation of observing a performance, of witnessing some prophecy of the gods being fulfilled onstage.

Chania was very attentive. She leaned forward, resting her hands on the back of the seat in front of her, her eyes locked on the podium. She looked thoughtful, and from time to time, when something she didn't understand was said, she whispered a question to Reini. Sorin, on the other hand, was not paying nearly as much attention. To be sure, he was also listening to the speeches. But rather than the content of the speeches, he was more interested in which parts excited Chania. Staring at her, his brows were furrowed with concern.

Rudy stepped up to the podium as the penultimate speaker for the Climbers. Based on his relative lack of experience and engineering achievements, he shouldn't have been assigned such an important position. But Reini knew that Rudy had climbed up the career ladder at an astonishing pace. He had heard that many influential Climber legislators supported Rudy, including Richardson and Franz, famous for being harsh to newcomers. Reini had no idea how Rudy had done it, but he knew that the young man was politically talented. Rudy was now no longer just in charge of his magnetic project but also responsible for the communication and coordination between the various labs supporting the migration plan.

Rudy nodded at everyone in the chamber and turned to the side as a prepared holographic video played. He looked extremely confident as he smiled, his blond hair combed neatly. The holographic video showed a conceptual vision of cave houses on the slopes and magnetic cars. The images were optimistic and full of hope.

The video came to an end. Rudy cleared his throat.

"Ladies and gentlemen, good afternoon. I'm so pleased to

be able to introduce the last two components of the migration plan: transportation and economic reform.

"As you've seen in the video, once we move to the crater, the freedom and convenience of the magnetic cars will be a key advantage of our new life. Magnetically controlled, the fast-moving vehicles will glide along rails built against the mountainside, solving the difficulties of vertical movement as well as providing everyone with a fun way to travel. The technology's principles of operation are simple, and it's well within our fabrication capabilities. Let me give a brief overview."

He started another holographic video. This time, the audience was shown a cutaway view of a semispherical magnetic car, along with the magnetic coils embedded in the bedrock that propelled it along. Rudy began to explain, his voice smooth and confident. The speech had been carefully prepared so that it was easy for anyone to digest.

Reini saw Chania's attitude change. Her fingers were interlaced tightly, and her eyes showed a combination of suspicion and sweet bashfulness. When the legislators clapped at some part of Rudy's speech, she looked proud and pleased. Rudy was indeed speaking well, his voice infused with conviction.

The technology explanation over, Rudy shifted topics. "I also want to discuss the biggest improvement brought about by our plan: economic reform. Technology forms the background for life, while economics affects our lifestyle far more intimately. In our current city, each house is an integral part of the whole city, and each person is also a part of the city, without the right to choose their own territory. The primary reason behind this is technology. Since each house is based on blown glass for the structure and must be connected to the rest of the city, it has to be planned and added by the city. A single person or group cannot build their own house and cannot create other styles of housing. This is an insurmountable barrier for individual autonomy.

"Under the migration plan, we've come up with a solution aimed specifically at this problem. As Ms. Loke explained earlier, the caves in our plan are refinements of natural caves. The exterior walls and interior furnishing allow a wide variety of choices and styles, which means the establishment of many ateliers related to home construction, giving everyone the opportunity to create the home of their dreams. And if they're unsatisfied with the location of the house, exchanges will be easy, achieving the goal of total housing autonomy."

Reini felt Chania's hand on his arm.

Her lips looked pale as she asked in a whisper, "Dr. Reini, what does he mean by that?"

Reini looked at her. "I believe he's talking about a housing market."

"To allow everyone to freely exchange houses?"

Reini nodded. "That's one of the key points of their reforms."

"Have they been planning this for a long time?"

"Not very long. I think this was added only recently."

On the dais, Rudy continued to sketch his stirring vision. "If anyone doubts the significance of such autonomy, let me show you some facts. Since the implementation of the housing equalization policy, there have been three hundred and fifteen reports of dissatisfaction in the central archive, averaging to thirty-one instances per annum. This number, of course, does not include the many more instances of dissatisfaction not logged in formal complaints to the central archive, an extraordinary measure to take. Each individual should have the right to construct their shelter and decide where they live. This is a fundamental aspect of liberty.

"Even teenagers understand this truth. Today a group of

passionate youths, motivated by a sense of social fairness, have congregated right outside this august chamber to rally for reforms to this policy. They reflect the voices of many. They cry out for systematic reform, and their ardor should motivate all of us to try to make our country better. Honored legislators, let's heed their voices and take the opportunity of this historical migration to courageously and determinedly press ahead with social reform! This is a grand task worthy of Mars, worthy of each one of us."

Chania whispered again. "Is he saying this to get more votes?"

Reini glanced at her anxious face. "I suppose he's just adding one more reason for legislators to support his side."

Chania's hands trembled as she sat up ramrod straight in her seat. He could see how much tension was in her body. She stared at Rudy as he continued to orate, making no noise or movement. Sorin looked at her with concern and tried to talk to her. She didn't respond.

She waited until his speech was over. Rudy came down off the dais and walked along the aisle between the seats. Abruptly, Chania got up and ran down until she was standing in front of him. Rearing back, she slapped him crisply across the face.

The loud snap elicited audible gasps from many in the room.

Saying nothing, Chania turned and ran out the door at the side of the Boule Chamber. A shocked Rudy stood where he was, a hand over his cheek. Sorin got up and ran out after Chania. Many of the legislators gazed curiously that way; others, however, continued with their whispered conversations or focused on their notepads. Reini sighed inside in sympathy. It had happened so quickly, and yet it also seemed preordained.

Reini could sense the reasons behind Chania's rage. From

the way she had been looking at Rudy, he could tell that the girl had treated everything between her and him as real. He had seen how devoted she was to their movement, and he understood the emotions coursing through her now. Reini had heard rumors about the Climbers' plan for housing reform, but he had not anticipated that the youths would take their demonstration so seriously or that they would have so little understanding of the nature of politics. He recalled Chania's expression as she ran out: disappointment, rage, the anguish of having been deceived leaving a scar on her always-proud face. He felt her pain.

Rudy remained in the aisle, his expression suspended halfway between humiliation and anger, as though wavering between chasing after Chania or staying in the Boule Chamber. His hand caressed his reddening cheek as he looked at the door through which Chania had run. He hadn't anticipated her being here, and it seemed that his plans had been thrown into disarray. He took a few steps toward the door, stopped, then took a few more steps. But in the end he didn't leave. Instead, he sat down in a corner of the chamber. He stared at the dais, but it seemed that his mind was elsewhere.

Reini gazed at him from afar. He could still see in Rudy's face traces of the lively little boy he remembered: the same blond hair, the same straight nose. But on this older Rudy, he could no longer find the curiosity and adventurous spirit that had suffused the little boy's every expression. Instead he saw restraint, control, a mask of elegance. Reini knew that he was trapped, although he didn't realize it yet. Rudy had wrapped his will in adaptability, bought ambition with liberty. A person living for ambition had only one choice, and thus had no freedom.

Reini sighed and pulled his gaze back to the dais. He

could not and would not interfere with the loves and hatreds of young people. The penultimate speaker for the Waders was about to wrap up his speech. Reini hadn't been paying attention to the speech earlier, so he caught only the bare outlines: the possibility that the glass-covered river would provide a controlled environment for experimental biological organisms. The plan was not bad, and it was definitely feasible, but the speaker was unskilled as an orator and couldn't stroke the imagination of the audience into sympathy with his vision. When he was done, the applause was perfunctory. After a whole day of speeches, everyone was tired.

Juan came on next as the last speaker for the Climbers. As soon as he approached the podium, everyone sat up as though a lightning bolt had flashed through the chamber.

Reini knew well that Juan possessed a forceful personality that commanded attention wherever he appeared. In contrast to Rudy's refined elegance, there was always a wildness about him, and his unrestrained will was like a roaring hearth whose heat filled the room. He wasn't tall or muscular, and his rotund figure brought to mind a chef who enjoyed his own cooking too much. But when he spoke, when he issued orders in his cold, hard-edged voice, he seemed like a rumbling jaguar about to pounce.

For ten years he had led the Flight System, and his powerful presence and personal charisma had compelled the obedience of many proud and intractable generals.

Juan was the trump card for the Climbers. The Flight System was the foundation of the Martian Republic. Without their constant exploration and harvesting, many crucial resources for the city would be quickly exhausted.

As everyone listened, holding their breath, Juan spoke.

"The choice facing us today isn't merely a choice about

how to live. Our choice will determine the future of our race and the future of all humankind.

"Yes, we've already become a distinct race, both biologically and spiritually. We are taller than Terrans, more vigorous, more suited to high leaps and flight. We can tolerate harsher changes in temperature. It would be no exaggeration to say that we represent a more perfect step in the ladder of evolution. We are a brand-new type of humanity.

"In spirituality and wisdom, we far surpass the Terrans as well. Our race has inherited the best of human civilization and art, and our gaze pierces to the very edge of space and the end of time. Even the youngest child among us has a grander view of the world than any adult on Earth. We live as a unified whole, while Terrans have broken into fragments in their self-division. Shortsighted, selfish, they no longer remember the high ideals and values that humanity ought to possess. We are the true heirs of humanity, worthy of the name 'the human race.' We are Martians, the purest strain of humanity.

"What should humans fear the most? Is it storms, falling rocks, extreme cold and heat? Is it to struggle against difficulties? No! What we should fear more than anything else is rot and decline, that humankind's powerful survival instincts devolve to weakness, cowardice, softness akin to the slime we crawled out of! But *that* is the direction Terrans are headed in. They have become a bunch of sickly, fat, wretched, timid weaklings, lost in their ever-expanding, never-satisfied gluttonous desires, their senses dulled with grease and drugs, devoid of any higher ideals. They treat mere cleverness as wisdom and shamelessly buy and sell what wisdom they stumble upon, not understanding that wisdom requires lasting exploration, not realizing that the greatest spirits crave sharing and giving. They've forgotten their planet as they luxuriate in artifice.

Their understanding of the qualities of their own home reaches not even one half the depth of understanding of an ordinary resident of our fair city. They are traitors to their own history. We are ashamed to admit that we descend from the same ancestors, that we share their bloodline. Only in us, and not in those devolved beings squatting upon the face of the Earth, can we recognize the courage and pride that belongs to true human beings!

"It is our sacred mission to carry on the destiny of humanity, a duty that we dare not shirk. We stand at the frontier of humanity's reach into the cosmos. We know what it means to explore the unknown; we've been strengthened by our harsh environment; we've built the Tower of Babel to call forth the storm of wisdom. In the foreseeable future, we'll enter the opening act of a great drama: the spreading of humanity's seed across the vastness of space in a new age of exploration. Humanity is fated to surpass itself, and must do so. We must learn to survive in new environments and must adapt new environments to suit us. All extreme environments are mere ferocious monsters of today—and our dear friends of tomorrow. Before we've learned to tame them, we may choose to compromise in measure, but we must never surrender!

"We must leave the comforts of home and step into the cold to maintain our edge. To stay in this city forever is to invite upon ourselves the fate of the Terrans: devolution, decline, rot. This is an inflection point in history, and the choice is in our hands. Whether you like it or not, the future is coming!"

Juan didn't use and didn't need any visual aids. His powerful, deep voice boomed like bass drumbeats, carrying the audience on waves of rousing emotion. He gestured very little, but there was tension in every inch of his body, like a balloon about to burst.

As he gazed at Juan, Reini felt a rising tide of fear in his heart. A premonition of danger grew stronger with each sentence. *It's coming*, he thought. *It's finally coming*.

Reini didn't know Juan well, but he knew the archon's history. Even as a child, Juan had shown an unusually strong personality. His parents died early, but he never seemed to be bothered by that fact. When his grandmother died as a result of Terran bombing, he had screamed and howled and cried his heart out, but that was the last time anyone could recall him shedding tears. He showed no signs of unsociability, self-pity, or even sadness; he never accepted anyone's help. Growing up in the barracks of the Flight System, he knew aircraft better than he knew land.

At the time the war ended, Juan was sixteen. He refused to live anywhere except at the airport. Having lived a life in tough environments where he was used to doing everything himself, he stayed away from the kindness of the war orphans aid office. He refused all offers of help and rarely helped anyone else—with one exception: Hans Sloan.

Hans was older than Juan by fourteen years, and Hans was the only man he trusted or relied on. No one knew how their friendship had come about, but there were rumors that Hans had been the one who rescued Juan after his grandmother was killed by the Terrans.

Juan was someone who loved and hated with equal passion. There was no betrayal or forgiveness in his dictionary. Those he loved, he would be loyal unto death; those he hated, he would never forgive in a million years. He remembered his debts and slights with total fidelity. He had never forgiven the Terrans; even though Martians had started the war, Terrans were the enemy.

Reini knew that this was the source of Hans's concerns.

Though he had long tired of exercising power, he couldn't retire. Hans feared that once he was no longer in charge, a cold flame that could not be repressed would erupt out of the tranquil sea to strike at another world with unforeseeable consequences. This was the biggest threat facing Mars. Hans saw clearer than anyone else that, compared to all the other flaws, the desire for conquest was the only true crisis. All the problems with the system could be improved: the feedback system in the central archive and the democratic institutions for policy making were relatively complete; all that was needed was patience. But the desire for conquest was different. It was the greatest threat for a nation that didn't believe in heaven, that didn't fear an afterlife, that possessed a concentrated dose of intelligence. A nation like this had strength and focus but had no imaginary hope; and thus it had no pride in itself but required conquest of the other to prove itself. Hans had been worried about this possibility for a long time. Martians devoted themselves to causes more easily than anyone else, and thus were most susceptible to the temptation of a sense of historical mission.

The day is finally here, thought Reini. *The day Hans has tried to delay so many years is finally here.*

Hans took the podium as the last speaker for the Waders. He and Juan passed each other, and Hans stood still in the center of the buffeting emotional waves left by Juan like a submarine slowly surfacing in tumultuous waters. He looked determined, at peace, and also very old. He swept his eyes across the room as though surveying the conclusion written long ago by fate. The chamber quieted.

Hans stood still a few moments longer and took the desert eagle badge from his shoulder. He held it up to show everyone before placing the two shining golden eagles on top of the lectern.

"Let me make something clear first. As consul, I'm not supposed to support either side in this debate. My role is to ensure the fairness of the process. But I want to speak at the defense session today to express my personal views. Therefore, I'm taking off the symbol of my office. In another month, the election for the new consul will be held. Since my term is almost over, I may as well resign now."

A low murmur of shock filled the chamber, but Hans seemed to not notice.

"I'm going to describe some aspects of my side's vision for the city, but I'm also going to present some objections to the migration plan. After comparing the two plans, we, the Waders, believe that humanity has not yet reached the technology level for living outside an enclosed environment.

"Under the continuation plan, city planning isn't limited to merely replicating the existing model. We hope to expand upon our foundation of mature technologies and develop an endless series of new models and forms. With the water from Ceres and a river that we can design and control, we can build a string of cities along the course of the river and no longer be confined to one city.

"In these new cities, we'll be able to experiment with different models. Although they'll still be based upon a glass shell, we can develop different variations, including trials at living directly off the land. In this future, the construction of houses won't be controlled by a single atelier and department of the government. We'll open up the technologies, which means more talented groups will learn and develop the technologies and receive funding support. Each of the new cities will have its own independent boule to determine the best way to allocate the city's resources and ensure its smooth functioning. Intercity transportation will be handled by ground effects vehicles—

a technology we've been using for many years and is absolutely reliable. The city will be the basic unit of future Mars. Along the glass-enclosed river will be a strand of prosperous cities, each developing its own unique qualities.

"More importantly, in these sealed cities scattered across the plain, we'll be able to run more scientific experiments to gradually adapt the human body to the environment, to lay a firmer foundation for the eventual day when we step out of the glass dome. Low-pressure environments, low-oxygen environments, high-radiation environments—all these can be simulated in the laboratory over years of trials until our bodies, or the bodies of our descendants, have changed significantly from today, so that we can walk out of the sealed enclosure and into nature. Evolution is a long and unpredictable process. The humanity of today will be surpassed, but not right away."

As Reini listened to the speech, he recalled the conversation between Hans and himself the previous afternoon.

Hans went to the Registry of Files to access some reference materials, and afterward, he went to Reini's lounge to have tea with him. Reini thought he looked worried.

"Reini, I don't know much about insects, but I've heard that it's impossible for insects to grow to be very big. Is that right?"

Sitting across from Reini, Hans spoke in a low and slow voice, like a quiet river. Reini could see the signs of aging on his face. Hans's face had always seemed to him as hard as an angular cliff face, and for thirty years he had looked the same. But he appeared to have aged quickly the last few days. Behind Hans, the clock's pendulum swung through the air, marking the passage of time.

"That is true," said Reini. "Insects breathe through their

bodies, and if they grow to be too large, they'll suffocate. Moreover, insects have exoskeletons, which can't support very massive bodies."

"So what would happen if an insect body were forced to expand and grow beyond its limit?"

"It would split apart," said Reini.

"For certain?"

"For certain."

Reini had often seen fantasy sketches of animals that were either much larger or smaller than in real life, as though the actual sizes in real life had been assigned by mere chance. But he knew that wasn't true. Evolution constrained an animal's size like the physics of music constrained the size of the violin. It wasn't that it was impossible to deviate from the sizes seen in life; rather, it was because expanding or shrinking an animal's body plan was certain to lead to less optimized results. Evolution was a bidirectional process that led to a compromise between the organism and the environment. A bird selected the site to build the nest, and the nest then selected the next generation of birds. At a certain point, the processes of selecting and being selected achieved a balance. This was a fact often ignored by people: the end of evolution wasn't some extreme but a compromise that balanced all the opposing pressures.

Hans rested his hand on the cup, thinking, and nodded only after some time had passed. Someone unfamiliar with his habits might have suspected that he hadn't heard. Reini refilled his cup, and they continued to sit and converse as the pale green curtain behind them drifted in the occasional gust of air.

"What do you think is the key to change?" asked Hans.

"To go slow," said Reini.

Reini knew what was bothering Hans, though he neither asked about it nor mentioned it. They spoke in koans, posing fate's riddles to each other.

———

The Hans on the dais now was more emotional than the day before. Instead of quietly pondering questions of destiny, he infused his arguments with his swelling emotions. Even his voice took on an air of lament, in contrast to his usual peaceful delivery. Perhaps he was treating this speech as the final monologue before the curtain fell on his forty-year political career. He put all of himself into it, and emotion broke through the cracks in his usual armor.

The choice facing Hans was difficult. He had thrown his support behind the continuation plan not only because of Galiman's glass house but also because he distrusted blindly jumping into a new living environment. When he was younger, his father warned him often: *An impulsive bout of courage is often mere recklessness.*

He could still recall the hunger and cold of his youth. Those were the early years of the war, when the rebels had to pay a heavy price for their gamble. They had lost the supplies from Earth and lacked the ability to make the wasteland bloom. The impulsive insurgents were on the verge of being wiped out, and only an indomitable spirit and occasional victories due to luck sustained them.

To leave the crater for the glass house was their turning point. From that point on, they could plant and grow inside a sealed environment, possess air and heat, and keep death at bay. The first years after the war were almost as difficult as the years during the war. They repelled not only the enemy but also the only source of goods required for survival: transport ships from

Earth. It was no longer possible to seize supplies; everything they needed had to be obtained from the desert, a practically impossible task. It took years of struggle before they managed to negotiate a peace with Earth and begin trading again. After having experienced all of these, having witnessed years of deaths and painful memories, he instinctively distrusted a rash departure. He couldn't put his faith in such a move. They lacked too many things to believe that a strong will was enough.

"Let me ask a final question of our Climber friends." Hans locked eyes with Juan, sitting among the audience. "Do you agree that humanity remains quite frail, so that, after years of trials in laboratory environments, our chances for successfully living in an open environment will be far greater?"

Juan stood up and faced Hans somberly.

"If we take that route, at that point in the future, we won't have the water supply that we possess now." Juan's voice was resolute and decisive. "If we divert the water from Ceres into the ancient riverbed, then it will be impossible in the future to gather up all of it to deposit into the crater. Maintaining a large body of water and pocket of air on the open plain will be many times harder than inside a crater, and we won't be able to capture another object with so much water then. If we don't take this chance, we'll never be able to build a truly open environment on Mars." Hans refused to back down.

"Then let me ask you: In your plan, where will we obtain all the necessary materials?"

"From mining. Our extraction and refining capabilities have improved by leaps and bounds in recent years. We can also exploit more asteroids."

"But you know as well as I do that we cannot obtain everything we need by mining."

"We can get most of it."

"No." Hans shook his head determinedly with a hint of anguish. "You know this. To maintain air pressure, we must have nitrogen. Can we get all the nitrogen we need from mining? To build the cave houses in your plans, we need light metals, which cannot all be obtained from Mars. Aluminum, magnesium, sodium, potassium—all of these are rare on Mars, but your design requires lightness and flexibility. The city we have is constructed from glass, the only material we possess in abundance, a material you propose to abandon. You also propose to lay massive amounts of underground cables. But I must ask: Where will you obtain the necessary insulators? Plastics, rubber, organic materials—you need all of these, but where can you get them? We have small amounts of rubber and can trade for more from Earth, but the mega-engineering project to modify a crater will require far more than can be supplied by these means."

Juan was silent for a moment. "These are mere details."

"No!" Hans shouted.

Juan answered him with more silence.

"Look at me," said Hans. "I think I know the real answer. You are thinking of obtaining these materials by force. Am I right?" Juan looked at him but made no answer. "Am. I. Right?"

Finally, Juan nodded.

"But that means war, don't you understand?"

"No, I don't understand." Juan spoke in a deliberately casual manner. "We only have to maintain a certain level of control and deterrence. The threat is enough to force them to comply."

"No, that isn't possible." Hans put every ounce of his strength into his aged voice. "Do you really not understand? It's impossible to have what you want without resistance and bloody clashes. We will have war dragging on for years without cease."

Juan remained resolute. "I don't view that as a problem."

"Have you not suffered enough?"

"We have!" said Juan. "That is why we must become powerful. We must go back and be victorious! We have the right to be strong. I see nothing wrong with that. Without us, the Terrans will kill themselves sooner or later with their self-destructive squabbles. We will eliminate the weak, save the soul of humankind from the frying pan of selfish profit. Earth should welcome us!"

"Utter nonsense!" Hans's voice cracked. "These are mere excuses. You have the right to be strong, but you do not have the right to rob, to steal, to take from others what isn't yours."

"Without fighting, there is no survival."

"No one is forcing you to choose that kind of life." Hans finally said the words he had kept buried in his heart. "I will not allow war. As long as I'm consul, I won't ever let you go to war."

Juan paused, then pointed at the desert eagle badge on the lectern. "But you've already resigned."

The chamber was absolutely silent.

Reini's heart spasmed with pain. He saw how, during the exchange, Hans had leaned forward, his fingers pressed against the podium, his body shaking with emotion. This was the first time Hans had ever exposed his feelings like this in public, and it would likely be the only time. His brows knotted as the muscles on his face twitched; his eyes glared from under his white eyebrows, burning with helpless pain and resolve. Watching from a distance, Reini also felt the pain of helplessness. He was watching Hans struggle against an inevitable fate. He had seen its approach from years away, but he had no choice but to step forth and confront it now.

Reini understood why Hans was so persistent. As a little

boy, Hans had seen his father, Richard, repent and regret in the middle of the night for his impulsive actions that precipitated the war. Richard was not a good war leader. The rebels made him their leader for symbolic reasons, but he hated it. In the grip of anger and grief, he murdered to avenge his wife, but he didn't plan for everything that happened later. Many times, he told Hans, still a little boy then, that he did not want this, that he wished there were another way. As he sobbed and repented, the five-year-old Hans wiped away his tears.

Hans was born in an airplane and grew up on fighters. He had no fear of death. But the cries of the dead haunted his nightmares. When Richard died in old age, his last wish for his son was to stop the war. Hans gave Mars his all to obtain independence in order to achieve this last wish. He approved the Ceres project and *Cerealia* because he wanted to avoid having to fight with Earth for water.

Juan knew all of this and waited patiently for his chance. He was not a man who craved power for his own sake; rather, he was devoted to his philosophy the same way he was devoted to Hans, who had saved him. Hans and Juan were the rare pair who truly understood each other, which also made them rare opponents. To understand that two people who respected each other were often also the fiercest opponents was to understand the friendship and rivalry between these two.

Grateful to Hans, Juan had obeyed him through the years. Also grateful to Juan for his display of loyalty during the greatest crisis of his life, Hans had allowed him the autonomy he desired. Juan had not given in, but he was waiting for the right opportunity. Hans wasn't fooled, but he understood that the root of the crisis lay in the spirit of the Martian nation, and if Juan didn't express it, someone else would. Hans understood that Juan craved conquest, but he harbored the hope that if they could overcome their difficulties and maintain a good, independent existence, the desire for conquest would slacken over time. But Hans had been wrong. It was human desire that created life, and not life that created human desire.

In the past, Reini had always been able to keep himself from being invested in the events he observed, but now he felt the agony of the bystander for the first time. The recording equipment before him continued to whirl and capture the scene in full fidelity. The equipment took no side, taking in everything objectively. The objectivity was intolerably painful to him.

The Boule Chamber's main door suddenly slammed open. A uniformed military captain strode into the chamber, located Juan, and walked right up to him. He leaned down to whisper in Juan's ear, and Juan's expression changed to shock before returning to normal. The captain didn't leave, as though waiting for instructions. Juan glanced hesitantly at Hans.

"What happened?" asked Hans.

"It's a matter within the jurisdiction of the Flight System."

"Tell me what happened."

"Nothing important."

"Tell me!" Hans roared. "Even if you no longer recognize me as the consul, I remain a permanent director of the Flight System. I have the right to know and advise about the internal affairs of the system."

After a beat, Juan answered in a quiet voice, "Two hydraulic engineering experts from Earth have escaped on a cargo shuttle."

"What?"

"They ran away."

"Why?"

"We're not sure."

"Then send people after them!"

"That's not necessary," said Juan, his voice cold and final. "I think that's not necessary at all."

ANKA

Anka glanced at the hazy sky outside the glass wall. The horizon was clear and sharp one minute and then a blur the next. *I guess the storm predicted in the weather forecast is coming*, he thought.

He tried to optimize his packing one more time. He pushed the headlamp, survival knife, and compressed dried food packets into the side pockets of his backpack. He wrapped the extra oxygen tanks inside the sleeping bag. Setting the backpack on the floor, he knelt on it to squeeze out as much air as possible and tightened the laces until the backpack was a neat and crisp rectangle. He was still unsatisfied, but he couldn't think of any other improvements. The provisions for this mission exceeded the standard allocation, and the backpack was clearly bigger than usual. He wasn't sure if it would fit inside the provision cubby, so he tried to measure it with his hand: three and a half palm widths, just at the limit.

Carefully opening the door to his dorm room, he peeked into the corridor. Empty. He stepped out, a book in hand, and gently pulled the door shut. He walked toward the coffee lounge.

The sky had grown even hazier. There were about two and a half hours left before the sun sank beneath the western horizon. As he walked, he gazed up at the glass dome, trying to determine the wind speed based on the drifting sand. The wind came in gusts, with periods of stillness in between. The storm wouldn't arrive for another few hours. The digital clock on the wall showed that three hours had passed since the escaped cargo shuttle had been forced to land. Based on the standard amount of oxygen and supplies on cargo shuttles, the passengers should be all right for another five to six hours.

The dark blue of the sky was hidden behind a layer of sand.

There were about four or five people in the coffee lounge. One of them was telling tall tales while a few of his friends listened. On the far side someone was reading an e-notepad. Captain Fitz was nowhere in sight.

Anka poured himself a cup of coffee and walked to a table on the far side. He put the book on the table and took out a notebook, pretending to be studying as he doodled. The man at the other table didn't look at him, and Anka didn't look at him either. Earlier, at noon, he had sat in the lounge and overheard the news. There were fewer people now, and he hoped he would hear more.

Captain Fitz had been gone for an hour already. If he was planning to come back to the coffee lounge, then this was about the time he should be returning. He would wait half an hour. After that he'd try something else.

Anka tried to read, but only fragments of sentences managed to make it into his turbulent mind.

Nos frères respirent sous le même ciel que nous...

What kind of news will Captain Fitz bring back? thought Anka.

He reread the bits of *L'Homme révolté* again. He liked the painful earth, the indefatigable navigator, the compressed nourishment, the harsh wind from the horizon, the ancient and fresh dusk. The words and phrases were as solid and simple as the Martian surface. He took a deep breath, and felt the chill in the air.

He had started reading this book last week. On the way here, he had grabbed it from the desk because it was easy to reach.

Though he was in no mood to read, the sentences he had read before jumped back into view on their own.

He calculated in his head. If he left the city right now, he should be back in less than two hours. Thirty minutes to get there, twenty minutes for changing vehicles, and another seventy minutes to get back with some margin for safety. Of course, this assumed everything went according to plan, a straight course with no complications. Only two and a half hours remained before dark, which meant that he had to decide whether to depart within the next thirty minutes. He disliked flying at night, which increased the chances of something going wrong. He preferred not to take such risks, especially on a day like this.

Once again, he reviewed the potential course he would take. The map showed that the site of the accident wasn't far: at the edge of the cliffs, before the craters. A straight flight path ought to do it. He could rely on the autopilot or take the stick himself. He was certain that he could find the site without trouble.

Captain Fitz still wasn't back, but Anka knew with growing certainty that he had to go on this trip.

The man who sat at the other table was familiar to Anka. His name was Berger, a lieutenant colonel and Captain Fitz's commanding officer, which meant Anka also belonged to his command. Earlier that day, when Anka had lunch here by himself, he happened to run into Fitz delivering a piece of urgent intel to Berger. Fitz belonged to Berger's inner circle, and their whole wing was commanded by officers Juan trusted and relied on. Intel that most had no access to would sometimes be spread via gossip in this coffee lounge.

When Fitz saw Anka, he hesitated for a moment. But Anka pretended to be absorbed by his book. In a low voice, Fitz then told Berger that the shuttle carrying the two escaped Terran hydraulic engineering experts had suffered a malfunction and was forced to land at a mountain pass on the edge of the cliffs. An SOS call had gone out.

Anka glanced at the clock. It was now past four. Three and a half hours had passed since then.

Fitz was back.

As soon as he saw Fitz at the entrance to the coffee lounge, Anka lowered his eyes to the book, straining to look like he had been there the whole afternoon.

Fitz strode quickly to Berger. Without sitting down, he said in a low voice, "The orders are to not rescue them."

Berger nodded, as though that was the answer he had expected all along. He asked Fitz what steps should be taken. Fitz didn't answer right away but cast a suspicious look Anka's way. Anka felt his gaze, closed his book, and stood up as though he had just remembered some appointment. As he walked out of the coffee lounge, he looked back. Fitz was sitting across from Berger, and the two were absorbed in conversation.

Anka rushed back to his dormitory. Time to carry out his plan.

He was no more surprised by this result than Berger. It was entirely foreseeable. From the moment he first heard the news about the escape, he had the feeling that the situation would develop this way.

Those two fools, thinking they could pilot a Martian space-craft, Anka thought. *Couldn't they sense a trap? And even if it hadn't been a trap, how could they imagine they could fly it? If an outsider can so easily steal a cargo shuttle and get away, then why does the Martian Flight System bother with years of training for their pilots? To fly from the surface all the way up to Maearth is a maneuver cadets who have been training for a few years already can't accomplish, let alone two Terrans who know nothing about these machines.*

The reason for their escape, on the other hand, is obvious. For the last couple of days, rumors that war is imminent have been rampant within the Flight System. Even people in other systems and ordinary engineers have heard them. The two Terrans must have thought their lives were in danger and sought to escape to Maearth by sneaking onto a cargo shuttle.

And then they crashed.

Juan isn't going to rescue them because they're the perfect sacrifices. He'll tell everyone that the two Terrans had stolen crucial intelligence against Mars and were trying to escape. The secret Terran conspiracy against Mars, thus exposed, will stir up popular anger against Earth, leading to easy passage of a declaration of war.

Even if that plan doesn't work out, the deaths of the two Terrans will enrage people on Earth, forcing their governments to launch a strike against Mars. Mars will then have to go to war to defend itself.

Juan has been looking for a casus belli for a long time, and these two Terrans have been working hard to deliver him one.

They don't respect flight. Anyone who doesn't give flight the respect it demands will pay a price. To fly is to gamble with your life.

Anka changed into his flight suit, put on his backpack, and stepped out into the corridor. He took one more look around his room: still reasonably neat, with two shirts draped on the back of his chair and the pillow and bedding arranged for bedtime. He thought about taking the model airplane, a gift from Luoying, but after hefting it, he decided it was too awkward to carry.

He wondered if he should send a message to Luoying first to let her know of his plans. But after glancing at his watch, he decided against it. He was already tight on time, and besides, he knew that Luoying was part of that rally today; she was probably too busy to check her messages.

I'll talk to her when I'm back tonight. Assuming I make it back.

He strode through the corridors, deliberately picking a round-about route that he normally didn't use to avoid bumping into any friends or acquaintances. There was no group training that day, so pilots were returning to the dorm by twos or threes. After the intense drills and missions of the last few days, most of the pilots just wanted to catch up on their rest. The corridors were deserted, with all the dorm rooms' white doors shut.

His own footsteps sounded like the regular beating of a cold heart. He was thinking about Luoying and the others from the Mercury Group, wondering what they were up to. Their rally had started hours ago. He wasn't a participant, but he was on the distribution list for their group messages and knew the plans. He never joined the discussions but observed from a distance.

He had no idea how to explain to Luoying his own feelings. She had asked him if he was going to participate, and he had answered ambivalently. It wasn't that he didn't care about what they were doing, but he didn't believe in that kind of movement.

What are they hoping to accomplish? To change the system? And then what? To change the way people live? What's the use? That won't solve the real problem. Any lifestyle or system is going to have flaws, unfairness, prejudices. The solution isn't to change the system. In the pursuit of perfection, humans have tried all kinds of systems, all of which have unfairness. The only difference is how those who benefit choose to sing their world's praises. The real problem is human nature. If a man oppresses others, he will do so no matter what kind of system is in place. What's the point of hoping for change? There is no hope.

The problems of human nature can be changed only through human nature, but there is no such solution. However, an individual's problems can be solved by helping that individual. When there is a specific injustice, then it's possible to confront that specific injustice. That is all we can do. Nothing else.

Even in the most perfect society, there will be children who die unjustly. All human effort can achieve is to reduce, like an arithmetic series, the infinite sufferings of the world.

Anka was walking quickly and calmly. He wasn't nervous at all, though he was concerned. Nervousness did no good. It was his habit to focus on specific details to keep the instinct to panic at bay. He was concerned about the color of the sky. The pink had darkened, meaning the wind was rising. The dust storm was approaching. It was still far away, but it could speed up at any moment. He had to complete his mission before the storm arrived.

There was no one at the airfield. No one would be so foolish as to fly in weather like this. He approached his own fighter and popped the canopy. Around him, the other parked fighters looked like a school of white sharks resting at sea. On the sides of every fighter, under the cockpit, flame decals evoked the toothy grin of a shark. In the quiet of the airfield, some consciousness seemed to be breathing in its sleep. After the tumult of the military parade and intensive training of the last few days, the ferocious beast was at rest for the moment.

Anka opened the supply cubby and pushed the backpack in; it barely fit. He had brought enough food and oxygen for two extra people in case they had to spend the night outside the city. The tiny fighter could seat only two, and the cargo bay intended for emergencies was filled with the giant folded wings and the motor. There was no extra space. Anka checked to be sure he had enough solid fuel. He checked the air intake, the valves, the spark plug. Everything seemed fine.

Having repaired this fighter himself, he was as familiar with it as with his own body.

He had taken part in the drills the day before. The fighter had performed well—at least, it had kept up with the others, which gave him some confidence. He had not known that he had the skills to be a mechanic, though he had done it only because he refused to submit to Fitz, and he didn't think open confrontation with Fitz was wise.

The drills had involved flying in tactical formations. Twenty-five fighters had flown in three different formations, attacking jet-propelled airships with laser cannons. The drills provided the commanders with valuable data on how well the fighters supported one another and how quickly they overcame their enemies. Anka enjoyed the drills. He had to admit that diving through the air, covering one's brothers-in-arms and being covered by them, striking the target, and then glancing back at the arc one had made through the sky—this was the most thrilling experience one could have in the world. Even if he hated war, he liked the sensation of living on that speeding edge.

Everyone around Anka was talking of war, some in favor, some opposed. The discussions were fervent, like the impassioned debates about the Ceres project. It was the one topic that dominated all other topics. He could understand their fervor, though he was against it. After decades of ordinary life in peace, there was nothing more stimulating than the prospect of a real war. The fighter pilots normally were miners, either excavating and blasting ore themselves or serving as cargo camels. They craved combat, craved a battle in which they lived on the border between life and death, and in which survival required the devotion of all their intellect and strength.

Anka understood Juan. His speeches to the pilots had always been powerful and moving. He was not a man who fought for shameless self-aggrandizement but because he truly believed in the ideals he fought for. A man like him was particularly dangerous, and particularly effective. For the sake of the vision of victory, he could hold himself back for years, building up strength and waiting. Juan wanted a grand future for the humans on Mars, to initiate a new epoch of cosmic history. Because he was strong, he wanted all Martians to be strong. Anka didn't despise Juan at all. Compared to some of the mindless bullies or yes-men who served under him, Juan was far better. Some said Juan was dictatorial, but based on Anka's experience in the Flight System, Juan was not the worst by that measure.

The real problem with Juan wasn't his dictatorial tendency but his dogmatism. Anka could almost agree with Juan's views on nobility and baseness, strength and weakness—if he hadn't been to Earth. He could have hated the evil Terrans as much as Juan did. But the fact was he had been to Earth and he had spent time among the Terrans. They were not the numb, worthless caricatures in Juan's speeches, just as Martians were not the numb and worthless caricatures in Terran speeches. He couldn't scorn all Terrans as a collective in the same way he didn't want the Terrans to scorn all Martians as a collective.

Anka could not think the way Juan did. There was no such thing as a base or worthless people, only craven and base individuals. One could only solve one concrete problem after another concrete problem, not attempt to resolve all problems through one abstract collective warring against another abstract collective. That never worked.

Anka climbed into the cockpit and strapped himself in. He adjusted the seat and checked all the systems. Seven mirrors showed him the view in every direction. The wind speed and pressure gauges were all still. He initiated power to the propulsion system. Electricity charged the rails beneath the runway. The fighter began to glide along the rails. An electromagnetic beam sent the departure signal to the hangar gate. The fighter was moving along smoothly, its alloy fuselage feeling solid around him, giving him the confidence to trust it to keep him alive.

The fighter reached the hangar gate. Anka sent along his fingerprint and personal code, waiting for the system to verify his identity. The hangar gate was the only exit from the city that didn't have human guards. The reason was simple: anyone who could pilot a plane out of here had to have the necessary permit. Technical skill was the best defense. Every pilot was allotted a certain number of opportunities to leave the city to practice on their own. Anka had been given five, and he had used up only two when he tried out his fighter after the repairs.

The hangar gate, an airlock, opened slowly. One set of doors, another set of doors, and a third. Anka took a deep breath, eyes on the empty, desolate land that appeared before his gaze. His fingers hovered over the instrument panel.

The fighter accelerated, at first propelled by the electrical current surging through the underground rails, and then its own engines took over. As the plane's speed reached the threshold for takeoff, it began to burn solid fuel. Jets of accelerated air blasted out of the nozzles and the fighter lifted off, shooting into the sky. In the rearview mirror Anka could see the airfield shrinking. The jettisoned air precipitated into a white column of mist.

The fighter felt smooth and steady. All the indicators were within normal ranges, and the fuel combustion was optimal. As he gazed at the wide-open sky and ground before him, Anka felt his spirit open up in response. The sense of ease was not the same as happiness but transcended it. It rose and fell without cease like the arcing course of the fighter, and therefore it had neither sharp peaks of joy nor acute valleys of sorrow. He experienced this sense of ease each time he took to the sky, and only felt it in the sky. He flew for this sensation, for the endless view of the dark sky and the gray-yellow land.

He kept his hand steady on the stick. The fighter was flying very fast, and he carefully guided it along the red line on the navigation screen. His fighter remained in contact with the ground control center, and the coordinates of the stranded cargo shuttle had been transmitted to his navigation system. The spot he was aiming for was easy to find: about two hundred meters before the cliffs.

Those two Terrans aren't complete fools. To manage to land their shuttle in such conditions is already quite an accomplishment. Sure, cargo shuttles generally have extremely stable landing systems, which were no doubt of great help to the two Terrans. If no one is injured, it'll be easy to get them back to the city. Just a straight flight back.

No matter what, leaving two people to die in the dust storm is wrong.

Sand roiled on the horizon like rising flames. The storm appeared to be even stronger than the forecast had predicted.

Though it was still unclear how fast the storm was moving, the swirling dust was like the sign of an ancient invasion from the horsemen of the steppes.

They'll die if they are left where they are. That must not be allowed. There's no justification for leaving two people out in the sand. Vengeance might be the one exception. But that's different, for in vengeance it is one person righting a wrong committed against him personally. What Juan is doing, on the other hand, is to sacrifice these two for a goal, a very suspect goal. The storm is coming, and they won't survive the night.

Luoying and the others talk about resistance. But this is the only kind of injustice that can be resisted. Look at the consequences of abstracting justice and injustice to collectives: it leads to confronting the Terrans as a whole. In order to overcome imagined evil, we are now committing evil first. That's wrong. It's shameful.

Glancing at the swirling sand on the horizon, his concern grew. The storm was coming faster and stronger than he expected. He accelerated, burning more fuel than planned in the hope of buying more time. Based on the progress of the storm, there was now a better-than-fifty-percent chance that he would be caught by the storm on the way back, far worse than he had anticipated.

What other choices did he have? One possibility was to land and try to survive inside the shuttle overnight. He had planned for this by bringing along extra supplies. But having seen the strength of the storm, that was unlikely to work. The storm was strong enough to bury them or to topple the shuttle, and larger rocks, which had in the past destroyed houses in the city, could be fatal. He estimated their chances of surviving the night inside the shuttle at less than twenty percent.

Another choice was to go to a cave inside one of the craters.

But that would work only with a survival suit. He had one with him, but the Terrans probably didn't have any on the cargo shuttle. Survival suits were precious resources and generally not part of the equipment of cargo shuttles. The last time they had been caught out, it was lucky that Runge had gotten them a mining ship. Mining crews often needed to perform extravehicular activities, which was why they had such suits. Without survival suits, the thin atmosphere would kill very quickly. To choose the cave was also to doom the Terrans, and his mission would be meaningless.

In the end, the best choice still seemed to be flying back tonight. The chances of success weren't great, but it was worth a shot.

He asked himself if he had been too reckless, had under-estimated the danger. But after pondering the matter a while, he came to the conclusion that he had foreseen the risks adequately. This surprised him. Before departing, he had thought he was going to be perfectly safe, but now, as he combed through his own thoughts, he realized he wasn't shocked by the crisis. In his subconscious, he had in fact known this was a possibility, but in order to harden his own resolve, he had deliberately avoided the implications. To fly was to bet one's life. He had always known this.

This is why I'm out here, right? In such weather, it's impossible for anyone to survive without help.

He glanced at the rising sand twisters off to the side, and a fighting spirit rose in his heart, along with a smile on his face. *Let's race, then. I may still win.*

The cargo shuttle came into view, exactly where the distress signal had been sent from. Apparently, the Terrans had stayed put after being forced to land. He guessed that the two were probably confident that Mars wouldn't let them die, and they were probably, right at this moment, rehearsing an explanation for why they had taken the cargo ship.

Anka slowed down and circled above the cargo shuttle. He reduced the jets so that, with each turn, the fighter lost more altitude. At the same time, he raised the cargo shuttle on the comms, asking them to get ready. As his fighter neared the ground, the jets turned vertical and slowly set the plane down right next to the shuttle.

Anka extended the evacuation tube from the fighter's tail and manipulated it until the other end locked onto the cargo shuttle's airlock. He unbuckled himself, put on the survival suit, took the wings, and popped open the canopy. He climbed out, stood on the fuselage, closed the canopy, and put on the wings. He attached the motor to his lower legs and then tied a length of cable between his waist and the fighter's tail.

He gestured at the two Terrans through the window of the cargo shuttle, explaining that they should open their airlock and crawl through the evacuation tube into the fighter. The two Terrans appeared to be overjoyed and followed his directions. Soon the two were seated under the fighter's canopy, one in the front, the other in the back.

Anka knelt down on the fuselage and gestured to the person sitting in the pilot's seat in front, teaching him how to press the buttons to initiate the takeoff sequence. It took multiple tries before he got it right. He looked perplexed, gesturing at Anka to ask him what to do next. Anka smiled at him, telling him to relax.

The fighter roared to life and lifted straight up into the air. The engines were at maximum burn. Vertical takeoff was the key to the agility and adaptability of the Martian fighter, but it was also the Achilles' heel of its design. To accommodate this capability, the fighter had to be made very light and small, which limited the crew to two and constrained the amount of supplies it could carry.

Excitement overcame Anka's anxiety. He crouched near the tail of the fighter like a sprinter at the starting line. As the fighter rose higher and began to accelerate forward, he could feel the wings on his back catch the wind, pulling him up. He tensed his muscles and waited as the force on his back built up. Then he pushed off with his arms and legs. After a brief moment of free fall, he felt the wings hold and lift him into the air.

The sensation was familiar. He was a banner flapping in the wind, a kite like the day he had flown with Luoying. Although he had set the fighter's speed to cruising—about half as fast as he had flown here—it was still far faster than Runge's mining ship. The fighter was on autopilot now, heading back to the airfield on its own. This was a capability shared by all Martian fighters so that in the event of the pilot's death, the machines, like the horses of knights of old, would bring the bodies of their fallen masters back home.

Anka felt a kinship with those ancient knights. The roiling dust storm was now almost upon him, like an approaching horde whose faces could finally be discerned through the dust. He tensed his shoulders and back, trying to adjust the angle of the wings to avoid meeting the storm head-on. The wings were strong but thin, and if they were torn by the storm, he would be in trouble.

The light dimmed. Only half an hour before sunset. At their current velocity, the last part of their journey would have to be concluded in the dark. Anka wasn't worried. They'd be safe enough if they got close to the city. He glanced at the horizon. The sun at dusk was no longer so bright, and the proud white glow had faded into a moody gold. The swirling sand sometimes covered everything so that the sun was no more than a hazy halo. The black sky and the golden land merged at the horizon, and the sand was like the tides, crashing again and again into the sea of the sky. The sand buffeted him, tossing him up and down. A few blows were so hard that he swung from one side of the fighter to the other, like a reed in the wind swaying between black and gold. The whole world tilted this way and that.

As he flew, a pride born of loneliness arose in his heart. There was nothing between the sky and the ground, and only he was warring with the sand. The loneliness felt solemn, and it gave him a sense of peace.

The sand slammed into him in waves, and instinctively he dodged and swerved, maintaining balance. He had to devote all his mental and physical strength to it. There was no choice but to trust himself. There was no support, no companions, no rescue—only himself. Without that faith, he would die. He was an army of one.

Pain chipped away at hope and faith, that was why pain was alone, devoid of explanation.

Anka believed in himself. He had told no one of this, but he thought he could trust himself. He disliked talk of salvation: saving a civilization, a planet, humanity. No, he didn't believe any of that. There was no such thing as the salvation of humanity, and it could never be justice to let some die in order to save all. Those who proclaimed such things were either trying to deceive others or had already deceived themselves. There was only the saving of an individual. That was all.

"If they cannot all be saved, what is the use of salvation for one?" Dostoevsky said so in The Brothers Karamazov. *But what was it that Camus said in response? "If a single individual cannot be saved, then what is the point of saving the collective?"*

Anka was beginning to tire. His body felt sluggish even as the wind grew stronger. The wings, laden with sand, sagged. He struggled against the storm with his whole body, gazing into the distance as the light went out. There was still no sign of the city. He had flown for a long time already, but there was still a long way to go. He opened his arms, embracing the emptiness the way he would embrace hope. In a flash he felt the razor-sharp sand against his face. Sobered, he pulled his arms back protectively over his chest.

He thought of Luoying. The last time he had flown like this was with her, but now he was alone. He regretted not bringing the model she had given him or sending her a message. Perhaps he had subconsciously feared just such an outcome, which was why he had refrained from contacting her. But now he regretted it. She was the only one on his mind, the only one he couldn't forget. She had asked him whether he believed in any love that lasted forever, and he had said no. He had thought Luoying would not, like other romantics, ask such questions. But she did ask, and she had been disappointed with his answer. It was true that he didn't believe in forever. He believed only in the here and now. She was unlike anyone else. How many people could you fly with, side by side, in a lifetime? She was the only one. She would always be in his heart.

Darkness and sand overwhelmed him from every direction. He closed his eyes, feeling adrift in the waterless tides. He screwed up the last bit of courage, tensed his body, and held on to hope in the roaring, fierce storm. He opened his eyes. The blue city was ahead.

HANS

Hans sat next to Galiman. The room was as silent as the desert at night. For a long time he sat as still as a statue, even more so than the old man in bed. With no light on, the darkness of the night hid everything. The tranquil moonlight spread over the two statues like a gauze veil, cold comfort for their silent anguish.

Galiman, could you have imagined such an outcome?

Hans buried his face in his hands, his elbows leaning against the edge of the bed. He didn't make any noise, no sobs or curses of rage. He was in such pain that he had to use every bit of strength to prevent himself from losing control. The old man lying on the bed looked wan and frail, his sparse hair straggly. Tubes from numerous machines stuck into his body.

A life is fated to be filled with regrets. Is that so, Galiman?

He put his hand on the old man's shoulder, the way he had often done forty years ago. The bones pressed against his fingers as though the hospital gown were wrapped around a skeletal frame. He kept his hand there, as though hoping to transfer his own heat and emotions to that other body, awakening him back to life. But the old man didn't react.

Quietly, Hans let go. He stood up and walked to the window, pushing the panes open. He leaned over the window ledge.

The clocks in the room seemed to have stopped. Where life ended, time appeared to stop as well.

———————

Hans didn't know how to recall the last twenty-four hours, the most important twenty-four hours of his life.

Twenty-four hours earlier, he was inside the Boule Chamber, watching in exhaustion as the debate came to an end and the support staff began to clean up. He was tired but not sad, worried but determined. He didn't know the future, but he believed he had done all he could.

He had just had his fight with Juan.

We should go after the Terrans, he said.

There's no need, Juan said.

Why? he said.

They didn't take any intel of importance, Juan said.

Hans refused to yield, and so did Juan.

Hans then ordered Juan to call an emergency session of all the directors of the Flight System. Reluctantly, Juan agreed while insisting that the act was unnecessary. At the time, Hans hadn't known that the cargo shuttle had been forced to land. It was only intuition that told him that leaving the Terrans to escape on their own was not the right thing to do.

He waited in the Boule Chamber for Juan and the other directors. The chamber appeared especially empty after the noise and clamor. A terrible premonition grew in him, though he tried to dismiss it as merely the side effect of exhaustion.

He didn't know how long he sat there. So many scenes from earlier in the day, from earlier in his life, went through his mind. He thought about old friends, about the four decades of conflict and friendship between Mars and Earth. The cleaning staff kept their distance, unwilling to disturb him. As Hans looked at them going about their routines, he felt like an outsider, an audience member watching the curtain fall on the stage.

He had been waiting for Juan and the other directors, but instead the terrible news came. He couldn't believe his ears, and his hands locked around the shoulders of the messenger like a pair of vises. He demanded more details, hoping that they would allow him to point out that the news was false. He so wanted it to be false.

———

When I saw that boy's body, Galiman—Hans whipped around at the window to face the man on the bed—*do you know how much I wished it was I who lay there instead of him?*

He slammed his fist against his chest, as though that were the only way to soothe his heart.

He saw that scene again, that terrifying but unavoidable memory. He couldn't forget it and would not allow himself to forget it. He forced himself to confront the terror of recollection.

The boy lay in the lone bed in the middle of the room. The walls were a dark blue, allowing only a little of the sun through.

The boy lay in shadow. Hans approached him, step by step. The white sheet draped over him made him look as though he had died in his sleep, but up close the twisted, broken body, the result of multiple impacts and heavy trauma, showed through the sheet. Hans lifted the sheet and forced himself to take in the reality. Then he gently put the sheet back down.

The body resembled a disassembled machine. The head and face were smashed beyond recognition. All the limbs had been fractured multiple times, and broken ribs poked out of the skin like unsheathed knives. A few long red scars on his body resembled the marks from a fight, but Hans knew them for what they were: the surgeons' desperate attempt to save the boy. But it was impossible to save a boy who had fallen from the sky, whose every bone had been broken. It was only because he had been dressed in a survival suit that the body was not torn to pieces, lost to the storm.

Hans extended a trembling hand, trying to caress the boy's forehead. But he couldn't touch him. He never sobbed aloud, but his whole body shook like a leaf in autumn.

This is my fault. Galiman, do you understand? It's my fault.

Hans pressed against the window ledge as though trying to push it into the ground.

The man who should have died is me. It's the fate that I imagined for myself in my youth, but because I've lost my courage, he died in my place, for my error. No, don't tell me that's not true. It is. It is my fault.

I deceived myself by reciting an empty aspiration, but I didn't do anything. I spoke about peace, about communication, but I allowed the desire for conquest to grow like weeds. I thought it was possible to stop the war with my orders, but when an army burns with the desire for war, how can I possibly stand in their way? This isn't Juan's fault; he's no more than the tip of the roaring flame, and I've been consumed by the fire.

When they told me that the Terrans had escaped, do you know what I thought at that moment? I wasn't thinking of their safety; I was only thinking of what effect they would have and what role they'd play in the negotiations with Earth. I saw them for their utility, not as human beings. Anka should not have died. If we had dispatched rescue ships right away, everyone would have been safe. What were we thinking? We were playing a game of chess.

Anka died in my place. He died for a weak, foolish old man's youthful self. I am beyond ashamed.

Hans tightened his fists, squeezed his eyes shut. He leaned outside the window and lifted his head as though trying to release the repressed air from his lungs with a long howl. But he didn't make any noise. In the moonlight, his arms and shoulders were tensed as hard as a sheet of iron.

After a long time, he relaxed, revealing even more exhaustion. He turned and sat back down next to Galiman, gazing with anguish at the peaceful face of his friend.

I didn't tell you, old friend, that my Luoying loved that boy. I don't know how to face her. I've hurt so many people I care about in my life. I've sinned so much.

———————

Hans stood by the window. By the time he sat down next to Galiman again, he seemed far calmer. The night was deep, and the lights in the other hospital rooms went off one by one.

Galiman, I've wronged so many in my life, including you.

I watched over the vote that decided to abandon your city. Are you angry at me? Are you unhappy that I didn't consult you? Are you going to, like before, argue with me until you've convinced me? Will you rage and shake your fists at me when you're awake? I hope you do. I really hope you do. Then I'll know that you're still you, and I'll feel better.

Hans lowered his head. So many things had happened all on the same day, as though to destroy his sanity. Luoying had rebelled just like Quentin, and then the simmering dispute with Juan exploded. And after that came the news about Anka, the nightlong search and desperate surgery, followed by seeing his corpse in the morning. Finally, on the verge of collapse, he nonetheless had to preside over the vote at the Boule.

Maybe this is the day both our lives will end.

There were two proposals up for a vote at the Boule this morning. One passed; one didn't. The proposal that passed was the Climbers' migration plan for the use of the water from Ceres. This was predictable. After living inside a sealed box for more than half a century, the idea of living in an open environment proved an irresistible temptation. The proposal that failed was Juan's plan to attack Earth. Juan had been building support for it in secret for months, and it seemed guaranteed to pass—until the news of Anka's death. It was impossible for the legislators to ignore his sacrifice. And the Terrans who had been rescued, out of gratitude, agreed to do all they could to help Mars in the upcoming negotiations with Earth.

There were multiple other small proposals. A vote like this happened once a year, and most proposals had been debated extensively in the central archive ahead of time. The vote at this point was a mere formality. Only the most important decisions would result in difficult differences of opinion.

From the dais, Hans carried out his last duty before his resignation became final. The sunlight, as peaceful as every other morning and unmoved by the grief or change below, scattered from the domed ceiling to illuminate everyone. Hans went through the familiar routines without any change in his usual demeanor. Despite a night of emotional turmoil, he acted as the perfect consul at the vote.

As Hans signed his name and added his seal to the passed resolution to implement the Climbers' plan, his hand hesitated for one second. He knew that as soon as the seal was pressed into the wax, the city that he and Galiman had fought for all their lives would become history.

His expression remained placid. He would wait until the abyss of the night to suffer the storm of his heart.

Normally, Hans resisted falling into reverie of the past, thereby avoiding the weakness and hesitation brought by memories. But once in a while he would slowly open the locked sluice gates of his heart, like a solemn rite, and let the flood of memories pour out. He would stand in the waterfall of memories, allowing the invisible water to strike his body.

As a child, he had lived in houses of stone and sand. In archive films, he had seen the half-buried shelters of old Mars, though he had never lived in them. His earliest memories involved cold caves and were permeated by the sounds and sights of war: preparing for war, scouting for war, fighting, observing, advancing, retreating. There was waiting, terror, more waiting, more terror. Deaths, so many deaths. Homes collapsing into rubble right in front of his eyes.

The earliest homes were in caves, with exterior metal sheathing. The metal sheaths, which had to be thin due to lack of resources, couldn't prevent radiation. In bombings, these caves were often buried, trapping those inside in tombs. The Martians struggled in such difficult circumstances for twenty years until Galiman, later in the war, made his breakthrough.

Glass was the most easily obtained resource on Mars. It was easy to mold and assemble and could quickly take shape with pressurized air. Destroyed glass structures were relatively easy to rebuild. Galiman's houses were not mere buildings but entire miniature enclosed ecosystems. The houses produced energy, regenerated air, circulated water, cultivated living organisms, and broke down waste. It was like an acrobat carefully keeping many spinning plates in balance. In the heat of war, the Martians burrowed into the ground, and on the ruins of the old they quickly blew up new homes like crystal bubbles.

Hans never witnessed the kind of slaughter described in ancient history. His war was fought in space, and even later, as a pilot, he never saw the faces of his enemies. In his childhood memories, war involved occasional explosions: without flames, without whining bombers, without clouds of billowing dust and smoke. A heavy metal bomb would simply fall and plunge into the ground and explode with a dull thud, causing half a mountainside to fall and bury the caves, whose inhabitants would be left in a permanent slumber. Such incidents only occurred once every few months, but the days between were filled with terror. The more rarely such attacks occurred, the more terrifying they became through anticipation. The Martians grew used to living in the darkness, without sight of the sky, until Galiman's houses allowed them to face the oncoming missiles with a steady gaze. The houses gave them the courage to face the sky, to expose their terror to the cosmos, as well as the tenderness in their hearts.

———

Galiman, back then you were so brave. You weren't even twenty yet, and yet you had no fear of slamming the table as you advocated your plan to the elders. Surprisingly, none of them got mad. Do you still remember that? You were a genius, a roaring lion.

Could you have imagined today? All of us were so young back then, still teenagers. Do you remember us drinking and boasting, imagining we would become pillars of the future republic? We were just joking then, but we managed to make those dreams come true. No one can take away what we've done. But are you satisfied? How much has this living republic deviated from the one in our idealized imaginations?

You've always been too proud. Your pride is why your

enemies despise you, and also why your friends admire you. You are too proud to even boast of your accomplishments, thinking it beneath you. You never mention your contributions, treating them, and allowing others to regard them, as mere details, nothing worth making a fuss about. But only I know how much you care about all that you've done. Why can't you put away your pride and admit it? You love your technology, your creations; you are so dedicated to them that you agonize over every aspect of them. Even the weekend before the disease finally brought you down, you were researching the heat properties of silicon-based materials in order to improve the glass houses. Why can't you let everyone know about that? There's no shame in caring about your creations. If you weren't so proud, perhaps those who didn't understand you wouldn't have viewed you as an old man hoarding his position based on past accomplishments—and would have been willing to help you to improve our future.

Galiman, in the end I had to sign the document that will result in the abandonment of your city—our city. Are you going to hate me? I've always hoped you'd awaken one of these days, but right now I hope you'll never wake up. Then you can always live in your idealized dream without facing the relentless reality and the ruins of this forsaken city. I don't know what's worse: a life of frustration and hardship, or to have all your accomplishments taken away right before death.

Old friend, I'm still here. Can you hear me?

Hans knew that Galiman couldn't hear anything he said, but he wanted to tell him everything. He knew that the person lying here was no longer the young man he knew, a lion in his prime, but a powerless old man asleep like a child. All the sharp claws of his disposition had been retracted, all his yesterdays put away.

_____

Of all the things that had happened in Hans's long life, the one that gratified him the most was that he and his friends had made important contributions to Mars. He became consul; Galiman devised the glass houses; Ronen crisscrossed the Solar System, caring for Ceres; Garcia captained *Maearth* for thirty years, established diplomatic relations with Earth, and negotiated for the student exchange program. They had fought side by side as comrades, and that fight had continued even after the war as they fought together for the republic, for a vision.

For five decades, there was no recrimination between them, no breakdown, no deception. This was the greatest joy and pride of Hans's life. He rued not being able to protect his friends and disappointing their hopes. He couldn't save Garcia from being pushed out of the bureaucratized system; couldn't protect the settlement on Ceres that Ronen loved; couldn't even save Mars City, for which they had all given so much. He had not been a good friend, but none of them had blamed him. Their friendship, Hans felt, was the greatest gift of his life.

Since Ronen and Garcia spent most of the later parts of their careers far from Mars, Hans's closest companion turned out to be Galiman. They had gone through the ups and downs of postwar Martian politics together, built the new city together, experienced the pain of losing children together. Galiman's son and daughter-in-law had died in an accident when their spaceship, returning from Phobos, exploded during descent. It was similar to Quentin and Adele's fate. The shared experience, though undesired, brought them closer. A companion who understood your pain was the best medicine for the bitter years.

Five years earlier Hans had switched Luoying with Galiman's grandson, Pierre, sending her instead of him to Earth. He hadn't been sure whether it was a good thing or not to go to Earth, and since Galiman's only family was this boy, Hans didn't want to put him in danger. Instead, he sent Luoying, because even then she seemed full of new ideas, waiting to be stimulated.

———

Galiman, Pierre is a good child. You must be happy to have such a grandson. He faced greater pressure this time than anyone else. After the debates, many of the elders shook their heads, saying that he had betrayed your final wish, betrayed what you worked all your life to build. But I know you wouldn't think that way, old friend. I listened to his speech, and he hasn't given up your dream; instead, he's changed it and brought it into the sky. Only Pierre understands what you've done, your technology. He inherited your curly hair and your intelligence but not your leonine ferocity. His name will be remembered by generations to come, of that you may be certain.

Pierre is better than Rudy. He knows what's most important to him. Your grandson supported my grandson, and I signed the order to give up your glass houses. We said we wanted to be as close as brothers, to fight side by side all our lives. Have we fulfilled our promise? What about them? Will they even want such a promise? The things that mattered so much to us... will they matter to them at all?

Perhaps it's time for us to hand the world on to our descendants. They don't think the way we do, and maybe their thinking is what's needed now. They don't understand the meaning of security and thus don't understand our lifelong pursuit. What they crave is a stage, only a stage. They envy us only because we once dominated the stage. Perhaps it's time to yield the stage to them.

Old friend, it's time for us to rest. Ronen is already dead, and Garcia is dying aboard Maearth. And you... well, the end of the road is close at hand for all of us. I know that if all of you were gone, I wouldn't want to keep on going either. Perhaps it's time for all of us to plan to reunite in another state of existence.

Hans held Galiman's hand for a long time before gently placing it under the blanket. The walls were still a deep azure, and the night was silent. Near the floor, behind the walls, a ring of lilies bloomed.

Galiman, everyone speaks of how much you've given of yourself to your career. But you and I both know that it's not the person who gives himself to his career but his career that gives itself to the person. What we've done and continue to do are parts of ourselves, and without them we'd be incomplete. The young are always impatient when they hear their elders recount their accomplishments, but that's because they don't understand that we just don't want to lose ourselves. Old friend, you should be satisfied. You've accompanied your life's work to the end of your own life, and it will end together with you. Few can be as fortunate.

Hans buried his face in his hands, his elbows on his knees.

What about me? I've spent all my life making decisions, but what kind of decisions have I made? One of my dearest friends I sent into space, and I decided to destroy the city another dear friend spent his life building. I sent my son to Deimos. And I punished Reini, the one person I admired the most among the new generation, so that he would never have a proper career. What kind of life's work is this? Has my life been a life of failure?

I'm not optimistic about the future. I can only say this to you, old friend, because you, like me, are no longer a player on the stage. The youths are always discussing the central archive, but they don't understand what makes our central archive function. Our population is only twenty million, not even as large as a medium-sized city on Earth. They speak with pride of how Mars's two million strong once managed to defeat Earth's twenty billion. But the small population is the foundation of our stability, our system. Our freedom of communication has an upper limit, and we've already grown so much that we're pressing up against it.

I fear that the migration into the crater will lead to fracture, to division. A pile of sand can grow only so high before it collapses, and a cell can grow only so large before it must split. A civilization's division does not need a reason, because societies are like insects, and their structure determines their scale. The republic will not last as one nation.

I've done all I can, Galiman. I remember what you said: we're born from the land, and we'll return to the land. We have always sworn our oath of loyalty to the land itself. As you put it: The sky is silent; let the land witness and weigh our soul.

Hans stood up and pulled the blanket tighter around Galiman. He poured a glass of water and left it on the nightstand. A crisply folded uniform sat at the foot of the bed. Hans knew it was Pierre's work. Pierre had pinned all of Galiman's medals neatly on the uniform. Hans knew that the boy also wished for his grandfather to awaken. He wanted to be like Pierre, to do everything to prepare for Galiman's awakening. That way, if he were to awaken, he wouldn't face the prospect of having been forgotten.

Hans checked the readings on the instruments one last time to be sure everything was normal. He stood up and saluted

Galiman as solemnly and forcefully as the first day the two of them had saluted the flag of Mars.

He turned and strode out of the room, as resolutely as the day he had strode into battle for the first time.

LUOYING

Luoying called Anka's name again and again. There was no response. She was the only one who could hear her cries. Her helmet rang with her own amplified voice, and the vibrations went into her head, buzzing around her brain. She lifted her face to the sky, trying to make her voice carry farther, to the ears of the boy who could no longer hear anything.

Luoying was standing in front of the cave where she and Anka had spent a night. Before her was the crater in which they had soared; behind her was the ground on which they had sat; on the cave floor were pieces of the wing that had kept them warm; in her eyes was the wondrous sight they had seen together in the morning; beneath her feet lay the slope they had tumbled down side by side. She could see every detail, each recollection stabbing into her like a cold, bone-piercing blast of air.

She opened her eyes and saw Anka crouching and modifying the wings, looking up at her with a smile. She closed her eyes and saw him tumble to the ground from midair, crashing to his death. She opened her eyes again and he was standing in front of her, fingers still busy, face still smiling, carefree. She held out her hands to that illusion, and he disappeared into the wind. She dared not open her eyes or close them. She was lost in visions that would not leave her alone.

The crater was completely still, without a hint of breeze. In

630

the bright sunlit air, she still seemed to see traces of their flight. She remembered how Anka and she had danced in the air. Then the wind had risen, and Anka had helped her land against the cliff face. Her heart had pounded from terror, and Anka had crouched over her, protecting her against falling stones with his arm. His body had been a shelter against the falling sand and rocks raining down around them.

Anka's eyes were a pure, clear blue. He had always looked a bit sleepy, and those eyes seemed to say so much. She recalled the time they left the Registry of Files, when he had his arm around her in the tube train, as she recalled her great-grandparents' night in the dust storm. She said she would probably meet with disaster, and he said no, she wouldn't. His look had put her at ease; his eyes were his smile.

And the night that she broke her leg, when she returned to the corridor leading to her room, seeing his figure leaning against the wall, illuminated by the single lamp, smiling with the pudding in his hand. She knew then that her courage had returned. His casual pose, apparently without a care in the world, and his eyes full of reassurance, were so comforting.

He stood face-to-face with her on the footpath in front of her house. She brushed a leaf off his nose; he grinned in response. He told her to get plenty of rest, not to put too much pressure on herself for her dance.

He grabbed her hand when she had fallen behind the rest of the Mercury Group. *Come with me*, he said, completely at ease. He led her through so many roads, so many years. When he looked back at her, his clear blue eyes always said *Come with me*. He appeared whenever she felt lost. He took her flying, showed her the most beautiful clouds at dusk and sunset. She would never see such beautiful clouds again—never. He was flying up, up, until he was part of the sunset, part of the clouds.

Luoying couldn't think anymore. Her heart was too full. For the last few days she had been numb, refusing to remember anything.

But now, as she sat on this special plot of land, everything came back to her. Intolerable.

She stood up and danced on the ledge. Because of the cramped space, she turned all the long leaps into spinning jumps. Trying to release the pain accumulated in her body through movement, she had never danced with such power. She hadn't practiced for many days, but she never felt so full of strength. She had to put all her energy into every movement to keep up with her emotions. She could feel the emotions spilling out of her, memories seeping out of the tips of her fingers and toes. She spun; she leaped straight up; she pressed against the ground, unleashing the pent-up energy. She had to maintain control lest she fall, or tumble over the edge of the ledge. For the first time in her life, she didn't pay attention to her movements but allowed her emotions to meld with her body. It was her most painful and strenuous release of the day.

As she thought of Anka, the props and backdrops of the world disappeared, leaving behind only him. There was no world, no revolution, no glory—only a person standing in the middle of the empty universe, angry and mournful, a proud look that would not be tamed. He was there. This was her true dance, and the only dance.

She had to stop, exhausted. She stood at the lip of the ledge and screamed with all her strength into the crater. Her heart pounded against her ribs painfully.

Anka!

Anka!

Anka!

For a second she experienced the desire to jump. The ledge

protruded from the cliff face like a perfect diving platform, and the slope beneath her was a broad, sheer avenue dropping to the bottom. The earthen-yellow mountains stood around her, magnificent, heaven-scraping, offering the only comforting and magnanimous embrace in the universe. The sunlight was like a lullaby, and the wind seemed to bring to her his voice.

Dazed, she fell.

An arm stretched out and held her up from behind. Gently, it supported her until she sat down. She looked up and saw Reini's sympathetic gaze. She was back in the present. And after swaying for a moment, she collapsed against his shoulder and sobbed.

She was finally crying. Tears flooded from her eyes, merging into torrents. She let all the pent-up tears go, unable to hold back any longer. She wept as if she were going to cry out her heart, her memories. Reini gently patted her back, saying nothing, letting her cry.

This was the first time she had cried since his death. The first time in three days.

A week later Luoying attended the funeral with Hans and Rudy.

It was a funeral for three people: Anka, Galiman, and Garcia. Galiman's organs had finally failed, with no possibility of resuscitation. Garcia had died in peace on *Maearth*, and his body had been brought down so that he could rest in his homeland. The deaths of the three had cast a pall over the whole city, and everyone could tell it signaled the end of an era.

Anka and the two elders would be buried in the special cemetery reserved for Heroes of the Martian Republic.

To be interred in this cemetery was a singular honor, as every tombstone was the equivalent of a statue for a decorated hero. Strictly speaking, Anka didn't qualify. Since he had died to rescue Terrans, not Martians, there was no formal honor for which he was eligible. Nonetheless, Hans asked that the young man be buried as a Hero of the Martian Republic. To create room for Anka, Hans yielded the plot that had been reserved for himself. Hans planned to be cremated upon death, with his ashes scattered in space. That way he would be free—free to fly forever.

At the funeral, Luoying sat next to Pierre. Gielle sat next to her mother, her eyes red and swollen. Though Garcia had not been on Mars in many, many years, Gielle still loved her grandfather deeply.

Her memories of him from when she was a little girl made her sob uncontrollably. Pierre, on the other hand, didn't cry. Instead, he simply gazed at a photograph of Galiman, oblivious to passersby.

"My condolences," whispered Luoying.

"Thank you," said Pierre, without any emotion.

Luoying looked at Pierre. He seemed to have become taller, more mature. He still talked to few people, but his eyes no longer looked shy. He was now a group leader for one of the engineering teams on the migration plan, the youngest group leader. His solar membrane would be mass-produced, and he would go on to invent more creations for the new Mars.

Luoying had found out about Hans switching her with Pierre. She didn't know if Pierre knew, but he certainly never brought it up. Sometimes she wondered how life for both of them would have been different if he, instead of she, had gone to Earth. But there was no point in indulging in such hypotheticals. Once life had gone down one branch of the fork, there was no way to ever rewind and try again.

Once again she asked herself just how Earth had influenced

her. She had asked this question more than a hundred times, and she was certain she would ask it a hundred times more. Earth had given her so much heartache but also so much joy. She didn't know which side should be trusted, but she had been given the ability and desire to understand both peoples. She vacillated between the two, empathizing with both. She had felt lost because of her vagabond heart, but now she experienced it as a condition to be borne with equanimity. It felt like fate.

What is fate, she thought, but to be changed by chance and then take the inevitable path that belongs to no one else?

She bid Pierre goodbye and walked to the front of the mourning hall, where Hans and Rudy were greeting mourners and directing them to their places. Rudy, charged with organizing and executing the event, was in constant motion, working efficiently and professionally, while Hans stood in the middle, bowing to everyone as they came up to leave flowers for the dead. Hans was no longer the consul, while Rudy was one of the directors of the new engineering project. The two contrasted sharply in their demeanors: the somber and quiet dusk against the fresh morning, full of potential.

Luoying walked up to Hans. "I've decided, Grandpa."

"Oh?"

"I'd like to go to *Maearth* with you."

"You're certain?"

"I am."

Luoying didn't know what kind of life she would lead as a result of this decision, but she felt this was the future she wanted to pursue at the moment. Hans had decided to take over for Garcia and spend the rest of his life aboard *Maearth*, and Luoying had chosen to go with him. She wanted to be his closest companion in his final years, but she also wanted to foster good relations between Mars and Earth. If they could understand each other better, perhaps some conflicts could be avoided, and Anka wouldn't have died in vain. Often, in order to forestall the final, disastrous moment, it was also necessary to turn away all the nameless moments that led up to it. She had already seen Babel. Perhaps all differences could be resolved in another tall tower, in which planet was no longer different from planet.

She was going to return to *Maearth*, to return to Charon. There, on the ferryboat above the river of the underworld, she would reside with the dead.

On Mars, everyone was looking forward to the construction of their new home. But Luoying didn't want to be a part of it. The mega-engineering project that would change heaven and earth had consumed everyone's attention, but Luoying cared far more about an individual's frail, simple fate. She wasn't choosing *Maearth* to accomplish great deeds but for herself. As she watched herself take one step after another into her destiny, for the first time in her life, she found peace and composure in the courage of accepting.

AN ENDING BUT ALSO A BEGINNING

The flood would be the turning point of history. The past would be washed away, the lingering gaze frozen into statues. The ark was laden with the power of rebirth.

As the source of floodwaters descended, every singing voice paused. The audience gazed at the projected image upon the domed ceiling from different angles, holding their breaths.

In space, a long-wandering dwarf planet had lost half of its mass. A giant block of ice mixed with mud, in orbit around Mars, was being accelerated by fusion reactors. Like a giant torch, it was glowing as it approached the atmosphere. It had bid farewell to the planet of its birth and was descending to a new land. Many orbits later it would land in the middle of a crater.

Simultaneously a thin and broad sail unfolded in space. It stretched and extended, precisely and delicately adjusting itself to face the sun. Like a giant eye, it gazed down at the many eyes below. It directed sunlight down in a glowing pillar of light that enveloped the watching audience. Powerful machines waited in neat array in ancient caves; houses, still uninhabited, honeycombed the slopes; turbines and waterwheels were ready to spin, and elevators hummed the music of silence.

As everyone paused in preparation for the momentous

occasion, Consul Laak delivered a speech from the Boule Chamber, his first major speech since he had taken the oath of office. In the empty chamber he looked ahead, letting his gaze penetrate the marble-patterned floor, the statues of the founders of the republic, the infinite distance outside the wide-open doors. He knew that his face was being broadcast to every room, projected on every window. He felt the importance of the moment, but he was also completely at peace.

"Today, let's begin by remembering four people who have given so much to Mars, and to today. Without them, we wouldn't be witnessing this historical moment.

"The first is Ronen. For decades he served as the connection between Mars and Ceres, and then accompanied the inhabitants of that planet as they headed away from the Solar System. He's no longer with us, but *Cerealia* continues its journey toward Proxima Centauri. We will honor them with the gratitude of our entire planet. Without their courage, our survival would be in jeopardy.

"The second is Garcia. He was the captain of *Maearth* and our ambassador to Earth. Through his unrelenting effort, he won us the negotiation opportunities and the necessary technologies, including the hydraulic engineering technology that is key to today's success. Though he won't be able to enjoy our new home, we will honor him with the gratitude of our entire planet. There was no one who pushed further the limits of our frontiers.

"The third is Galiman. He was responsible for the glass houses with which we built our old city and which we're about to abandon. He devoted his entire life to improving our living conditions and ecological systems. Seven days ago he lost his long battle against cancer. Even though we're about to leave behind his designs, we will honor him with the gratitude of our entire planet. We will never forget that our civilization began in his city.

"The last is Hans Sloan, someone we're all familiar with and love. He served as consul for the previous two terms and led Mars for a full decade. In his youth he was an active pilot who did much for the construction of early Mars. Later he presided skillfully over the contentious decision to capture Ceres for its water, and then to devote that water to the construction of a new home for all of us. Selfless, farsighted, honorable, he helped secure our prosperity and stability and propelled us onto the path toward this important historical change. Now he has taken over *Maearth* and continues to serve Mars as our ambassador. We will honor him with the gratitude of our entire planet. He has given all his life to Mars, and Mars will celebrate him with a new way of life."

Inside the control room for the descent of the water source, Rudy looked up at the face of Laak in the suspended screen. Gielle, standing next to him, held his hand. Gently he withdrew it from her grasp and returned to the flashing numbers on the instrument panel. Gielle, red-faced, seemed about to fly into a rage but in the end held herself back. Pierre, passing by the control room, paused for a moment and then continued on his way, his eyes betraying his agony.

Next to a fountain, Chania looked up, her fingers caressing the water plants in the pool while holographic projections made the fountain look like a broad, beautiful lake. Next to her, Sorin sat with an arm around her waist. As they listened to Laak's speech, they were also writing a letter to Luoying. From time to time Chania looked up at Sorin, happiness suffusing all her features.

Between the bookcases, Reini looked up at the image of Laak projected on the wall. Laak was gazing back into his eyes as well. A strain of music sounded; pages of books fluttered. He looked over at the door, where Janet smiled back at him. She waved, and he waved back. Neither said anything. The storm they had weathered together and the settling dust afterward had sealed their friendship.

At the training field of Fourth Base, Juan looked up, his face expressionless as he listened to Laak's speech. Laak was not someone who would support Juan; he knew that. He didn't like it, but there wasn't much he could do. Still, he didn't feel discouraged or demoralized. Instead, he continued to prepare for the military parade and inspection. Even with all the changes, no one could challenge the prominence and leadership of the Flight System. He was still strong and in charge. There would be plenty of opportunities in the future.

Laak paused. He looked around and seemed to see the shadows of many figures. The eight white pillars glowed with the pride of classical Greece, with the ancient dreams and worries of humanity. Laak had attended countless meetings and debates here, both as an audience member and as a speaker, including the debate that determined the fate of the Mercury Group. This was, however, the first time he spoke as consul, and he gazed around, making sure he remembered every detail of the chamber.

"We've evolved along with our planet. From the first day humankind set foot upon this land, it has been the foundation of our survival. We have grown our food here, lived in its extrusions, sculpted it with our machines, changed the atmosphere with our exhalations. From this day forward, our mutual dependence will deepen. We'll have to slow down the wind erosion, thicken the air, warm the ground, improve the soil quality. Our planet will give us life, give us the possibility of breathing in the open. From this day onward, we will no longer be a species in isolation but will evolve together with our planet.

"We can be lazy, but we cannot lie to our planet.

"Ex-consul Hans Sloan once told me something Galiman had said, which I will now repeat for all of you. No words seem more appropriate to this occasion: 'The sky is silent; let the land witness and weigh our soul.'"

The glowing torch of mud and ice now approached the surface of the planet, and the engines began to brake, to slow the descent. As everyone watched, a glowing wheel of light slowly approached the rim of the crater. It would collide with a plateau, melt in the subsequent explosion, and flow along the canyons into the bottom of the crater to form waterfalls, rivers, and, finally, a lake.

In various places on Earth, the same scene played out on various screens—though just a few clips lasting mere seconds, to fill in gaps in the financial news, a change of pace for exhausted nerves. Here and there, a few people glanced up from the noisy crowd, trying to imagine the fantastic myths being played out on another world. Stories of Mars would always be myths, even if they really happened.

Eko sat in his bedroom watching the computer screen, his mind ablaze. On the screen a fiery planet spun in space while a tiny rock, like a drop of water, circled it. Pride and a dreamlike sense of unreality came over him as he recalled that he had once set foot upon that world.

Maearth drifted in space, steady as always.

Hans and Luoying were both in the weightless gym at the

stern of the ship, so that they could face Mars. Luoying lay on her back in the air, floating in the middle of the cabin. Her dress and hair drifted with her, like ribbons in a dance.

She was finally back here, the locus of joy and movement, the repository of the group's best memories, the only stable place in the cosmos. She looked up at the curved ceiling, where Uncle Laak's face was superimposed over the red planet. At the edge of the cabin, near the handholds, Hans stood in full dress uniform, saluting the screen overhead. Luoying thought her grandfather had never looked so handsome: the wrinkles in his face seemed carved by a knife, his white hair drifting with the air currents.

Maearth was heading for Earth. The empty quarters would soon be filled with trade goods. The photographs on the walls had been changed. They were still clean and neat, but the hands dusting them now belonged to a different old man.

Laak was nearing the end of his speech. His voice felt heavy and his gaze was like fire burning underwater. He seemed to see everyone looking back at him. They were all speaking to him, and he was speaking to all of them.

"We exist as momentary gatherings of dust, brilliant flashes of fireworks. Yet each of us carries in our atoms the history of the entire cosmos. Each of our gestures reflects the culmination of the movements of the eternal sky and sea over the eons. Our actions today will be seen by the sky, while our spirit will be etched into the soil.

"The sky is silent; let the land witness and weigh our soul!" In the bright sun the floodwaters fell from the sky.

One story was over and another chapter of history began. No one knew what the future held. Everyone looked up into the sky, and over the broad, vast land, silence reigned.

Acknowledgments

I would like to acknowledge Mr. Liu Cixin for giving me a lot of encouragement for the first version of this book and Ken Liu for the excellent translation. I'd also like to thank all my colleagues at Fangjing Sci-Fi, my studio, for supporting me throughout. Finally I'd like to thank my husband and parents for their love and care all these years.

Translator's Acknowledgments

I wish to thank all the wonderful people at Simon & Schuster who made the publication of this book in English possible, especially but not limited to: Joe Monti (editor), Lauren Jackson (publicity), Alexandre Su and David Chesanow (copy-editing), Christopher Milea and Benjamin Holmes (proof-reading), Madison Penico (manuscript assistance). I also want to thank Nic Cheetham and his staff at Head of Zeus for bringing out the UK edition, Erwann Perchoc for a critical piece of translation assistance, and Russell Galen, my agent, for his ongoing support.

Finally, the greatest share of my gratitude goes to Hao Jingfang, who created this beautiful book and entrusted me with it.

About the Author

HÁO JINGFANG leads the new generation of Chinese science fiction writers. In 2016, she won the Hugo Award for Best Novelette for 'Folding Beijing' (also translated by Ken Liu) – the first Hugo awarded to a Chinese woman. With a Ph.D in economics, Hao works as a macroeconomics researcher at the China Development Research Foundation in Beijing.

About the Translator

KEN LIU as author and translator, has won the Nebula, Hugo, World Fantasy, Locus Sidewise, and Science Fiction & Fantasy Translation Awards. His translation of Cixin Liu's *The Three-Body Problem* was the first translated work to ever win the Hugo Award. He lives near Boston with his family.